BEHIND CLOSED DOORS

Kathryn Croft

First published 2013
Copyright © Kathryn Croft 2013

Kathryn Croft asserts the moral right to be identified as the author of this work in accordance with the Copyright, Designs and Patents Act 1988.

www.kathryncroft.com

ISBN-10: 1500120952
ISBN-13: 978-1500120955

For Paul

ACKNOWLEDGEMENTS

A huge thank you to my agent, Madeleine Milburn, for believing in my book and loving it as much as I do. Thanks also to the whole editorial team at the Madeleine Milburn Literary Agency for making the book even better. A great novel is the culmination of many people's time and effort so thank you to all involved.

Thanks also to my family and friends for always believing in me and knowing – when I wasn't even sure myself – that I could do this. Particular thanks to my husband, Paul Croft, for always supporting my dream, and parents, Grace Mckee, because I wouldn't have been able to do this without her, and Phillip Mckee for reading the first draft and giving me the confidence to think I might just pull it off!

AUTHOR BIOGRAPHY

Kathryn Croft has a BA Honours Degree in Media Arts with English Literature and after training as a teacher she spent six years teaching secondary school English; a job she believes was invaluable to her writing career. Kathryn is currently working on her third psychological suspense novel. www.kathryncroft.com

CHAPTER ONE

I have never told you about the day I left Carl. For eleven years we'd woken up together, made a life for ourselves and raised our daughter, only for it to perish in an instant, as if the foundation of our marriage was built on air. How foolish I was to believe that was the worst life could throw at me.

It is the beginning of autumn when I leave the only home I've ever felt secure in. The sun teases us with its excessive heat, fooling us into believing we're still in the caress of summer, so it is a surprise when Carl trudges downstairs wrapped in a thick, black roll-neck jumper. My mouth opens to ask him why he's wearing winter clothes on such a warm day but I quickly change my mind. It's no longer my business what he does.

Carl begs me to stay that morning, hurling his words at me as if they are weapons. "How can you do this to Ellie?" he shouts in desperation. "And why Putney? You don't have to run away to the other side of London, for Christ's sake. I'll never see her!"

I avoid looking at him and shrug off the fact he's using our daughter as a bargaining tool. Running on adrenalin and fear of caving in, I throw items I'm not sure belong to me into boxes, paying no attention to the room labels I have scribbled on each one. I don't want to think about how I'll unpack this mess. All I can focus on is getting out of here before I have second thoughts.

Carl continues with his desperate plea and in my rush I drop the wine glass I'm haphazardly blanketing in bubble wrap. The tiny fragments of glass glisten on the floor and I stare at them, wondering how something that's shattered into pieces can still be so beautiful. I clear the pieces away and my resolve to leave the home I've pictured us growing old in together strengthens. Just like the glass, our marriage cannot be put back together.

Ellie appears in the kitchen doorway. Her eyes are bloodshot and her cheeks coated with tears. Carl finally gives up his plea and rushes to comfort her while I finish packing. I cannot look at either of them and trudge back and forth to the car, weighed down by boxes that are ready to burst.

When he's managed to calm Ellie down, Carl helps me with the last box and when I shut the car boot I'm surprised by how little there seems to be. Most of it is clothing; I have left all the household items for Carl because I don't want reminders of my old life. This is a fresh start for Ellie and me.

Outside the front door, I say goodbye to Carl and try not to crumble when I have to pull Ellie off him. She clings to his waist and howls while Carl looks at me, helpless, his eyes begging me to change my mind. "Come on, Ellie," I say, gently easing her off Carl and towards the car. "We'll call Daddy as soon as we get there, I promise."

And then Ellie surprises us both. Wiping her eyes with her sleeve, she stops crying and nods. "Okay. Bye, Daddy," she says, handing Carl a folded piece of paper. It must have been clamped in her hand this whole time because I've put all her bags in the car and she's wearing a dress with no pockets. Before Carl unfolds the sheet I know what it is.

Even at nine years old Ellie is a gifted artist, surprising her teachers and us with her accuracy and eye for detail. Carls opens the sheet and I can tell he's fighting back tears. Ellie has drawn a caricature of the three of us; we're all holding hands and smiling, standing in front of the house. Carl grabs Ellie and hugs her tightly. "I love you," he says.

He is still standing at the door as we drive away and with Ellie's small face plastered to the car window, watching Carl as if he'll disappear forever if she dares to turn away, I nearly change my mind.

For the whole drive to Putney, I constantly check beside me to see if Ellie is okay. She doesn't say anything but snuggles into the passenger seat and closes her eyes. I am powerless to help her. Nothing will ease the pain of me dragging her away from her father and I begin to wonder if either of us will ever be okay again.

As we pull up to the Victorian terrace on Woodborough Road, my mind is numb, my body going through cold, robotic motions over which I have no control. It feels like another world here, a million miles away from the familiarity of Winchmore Hill. Even the houses seem strange, each one blending into its neighbour with barely a distinguishing feature, and I wonder if this can ever become home for us. Shaking off these thoughts, I remind myself why I'm doing this and why there is no way back and as I help Ellie out of the car, her face puffed up from crying, the only thing that matters is that I get my daughter through this.

I hand Ellie her purple rucksack. "I've packed some paper and colouring pencils in there," I tell her. "So as soon as we get in you can do some drawing while I unpack." She nods and her face brightens a fraction but she doesn't speak.

We arrive later than I'd arranged and the estate agent is already waiting for us by the front door. She is not the woman Ellie and I met the first time we looked at the flat and I am disappointed. It would have been nice to see someone familiar. She paces up and down the narrow garden path, a brown, misshapen envelope dangling from her fingertips. I stare at her wispy hair and deeply lined face; she can't be more than thirty yet she looks as if she's been crumpled like scrap paper.

"Welcome to your new home!" she says, handing me the envelope. "Here are your keys. I'm late for an appointment so have to rush off now but please call the office if you need anything else." She glances up at the top windows of the house. "I've just met your upstairs neighbour and he said if you need any help with anything or have any questions about the property you can just ask him. He seems nice. You'll have no problems with noise or any kind of disturbance."

I stare at the upstairs windows and hope this is true. Carl and I have never had trouble with either of our neighbours so it never occurred to me to check who Ellie and I will be sharing a property with. I turn back to the estate agent but she is already rushing off to her car, leaving Ellie and me alone.

Inside the communal hallway, which is now filled with our belongings, Ellie paces back and forth, in desperate need of the bathroom. I am amused by her bouncing around while I struggle to find the keys I've only just been handed but I don't say a word. I know she won't find anything funny at the moment.

"At last!" she cries, shoving her rucksack into my hand and barging past me as I finally get the front door open. Her footsteps pound on the floor before she throws doors open, trying to remember which one leads to the bathroom. With all the commotion, I don't hear the door next to ours open.

"Need some help?"

I spin around and you are standing before me. Your voice is deep and formal, completely at odds with the fraying jeans and scuffed trainers you are wearing. You look around my age but your voice belongs to someone much older. I can't form a concrete impression of you; you are just there. But whoever you are, I'm grateful for your offer of help.

As unsociable as I'm feeling, I make an effort at conversation as we lug boxes and suitcases from the hallway. I prepare myself to be asked whether I'm moving in alone but thankfully you steer clear of personal questions and instead fill me in on the local shops.

"Thanks so much for this," I say as you bring in the last box. You have piled them all neatly against the wall so they are barely in the way. All the room labels face outwards so if I'd only put things in the correct boxes unpacking would be a simple task. You have even sorted out all the boxes I've brought in because I certainly haven't arranged them with such care.

"I'd offer you a cup of tea but–"

"That's okay. I'm off out now." You hold out your hand. "I'm Michael, by the way."

"Olivia." Your hand feels warm and too soft. It is alien to me because it's the complete contrast of Carl's rough, calloused skin.

Ellie appears in the lounge, wiping her hands on her dress. "There are no towels," she says when she spots my frown.

"This is my daughter, Ellie," I say, beckoning her forward.

Ellie can't have noticed you because she halts in surprise and stares shyly at the floor when she realises we have company.

"This is our new neighbour, Michael," I tell her and she finally looks up, holding out her hand to you. And at that moment I burst with pride for her. You lean down to shake her hand and within a few minutes Ellie is showing you her sketches and you carefully look them over, asking questions about each one. I wait for you to glance at me and reveal you're just humouring her but you are so engrossed in her drawings you don't look anywhere else until you've seen them all. You only stay for a few more minutes but in that time I almost forget how Ellie and I have ended up here.

When you've gone, Ellie and I explore the flat. It's small but cosy and clean and most of the furniture looks brand new. The landlord has left a bottle of champagne on the kitchen table and Ellie scrunches up her face. "Yuk!' she says, and I promise to get her some coke.

The two bedrooms are the same size so I let Ellie choose which one she wants. For the first time since we've left the house she seems distracted from her sadness and I unpack all her toys and books while she sits on the bed, drawing a colony of penguins. I'm not worried about unpacking my own things, I just want Ellie to feel at home. Even though she seems better for now, I know she feels the gaping hole of Carl's absence and anything I say or do will only offer temporary relief.

I remind her she'll see Carl at the weekend and she asks where I think he'll take her. I wonder if it's a testament to the trust Ellie has in me that she has never questioned my decision to leave. Would I feel better or worse if she had? Perhaps I wouldn't have been able to do it at all if she had protested. Carl and I broke the news to her months ago so maybe us all still living together for a while softened the blow. But whatever the case, Ellie is strong. Stronger than I could ever have been at her age. When Ellie's room is finally unpacked and it looks as if she has lived here forever, I am choked by the panic I've managed to keep at bay until now.

"I'm hungry," Ellie says and I remember we haven't eaten since breakfast. I have no idea what the time is but it's dark outside so it must be after seven o'clock. There is no food in the flat so I tell Ellie I'll treat her to a McDonald's. It's not the dinner I wanted us to have on our first night in our new home but I don't have the energy for food shopping or cooking now.

"We'll have to walk to the high street, though," I warn her, but she is already pulling on her jacket.

After we have eaten, without anything to distract her, Ellie becomes subdued again as we walk home. She fixes her eyes on the pavement and isn't interested in any of the shops or scenery we pass. Normally she would be on the lookout for something to draw but tonight her sketches seem to be the furthest thing from her mind. My attempts at jubilant conversation only manage to extract grunts and mumbles from her so I give up and hold her hand tighter instead, trying to ignore the fact that my mouth is burning from the hot apple pie I've eaten.

We turn onto Woodborough Road and I begin to feel certain we will never feel at home here. How can we without Carl? We're not a family anymore; I don't know what we are now. Something split open and torn apart. Something that can never be whole. I've had to drag my body across London but anything I consist of other than skin and bone has been left behind in those four walls that now allow Carl more space than he'll ever need. But at least I made the choice to do this. Ellie did not.

Approaching the house, I look up to see if your lights are on. I'm not sure why; maybe it's just the comfort of knowing someone else is in the building. But there are no signs of life emanating from your flat and a flutter of disappointment stirs within me.

I give it no more thought as I put Ellie to bed and spend the rest of the evening cleaning and unpacking. But no matter how much I polish and scrub, something feels wrong. This is not our home.

Hours later when I finally sink into bed, tears dampen my pillow as I spend the rest of the night watching the glowing blue numbers on my clock flick towards dawn. When it gets to five o'clock, I can't bear lying here anymore, unable to sleep but in no state to do anything constructive either, so I cross the hall to Ellie's room. She has left her door wide open – something I have never known her to do – and her small reading light glows in the corner of the room. Concerned, I step over to the bed and study her face; it is crumpled and her legs are pulled up to her chin but she is lost to sleep. As I watch her, I picture scooping her up, running to the car and driving back to Winchmore Hill. It would be so easy, I wouldn't even care about the things we'd leave behind, as long as Ellie and I are back home. But then I picture Carl waiting for us at the door, pleasure on his face and his arms stretched out to welcome us back. And I remember. And then I know that we can never go back. No matter how hard it is to be here, this is where we must stay. It's just the two of us now.

CHAPTER TWO

During those first few weeks without Carl, keeping busy is the only thing that holds me together. It is easy at first because there is so much to do in the flat but eventually everything is unpacked, new furniture and accessories bought and arranged and all that's left is for Ellie and me to enjoy our new home. But neither of us can, even though on the surface we both try to be strong for each other, constantly persuading the other we are okay.

Although I love being at home with Ellie, I begin to look forward to her starting school again because at least then she will be busy with homework and new friends. I itch to get back to work, to distract myself from failure. I may not be able to keep my marriage together but at least work is somewhere I can succeed. I've always loved my job but now it is more important than ever. Writing reviews for an online magazine might not be the most exciting career choice, or the best-paid, but there is nothing else for me. Along with being a mother, it is who I am. Most of all my work allows me freedom to spend time with Ellie and to express myself with words.

After three weeks off work, the day finally arrives when I am due back. It's also Ellie's first day at her new school and because it's only a short distance from our flat, we walk there. I try to convince her she'll be okay and even though she nods I can see she is lost in her thoughts. At the school gates she hugs me goodbye and trots off without any complaint. I stare after her, marvelling at her strength and I stay rooted to the spot long after the other mothers have disappeared, full of guilt and wishing Carl was here too.

With spending too long at the school and the new journey to work, I am over an hour late by the time I arrive at the tiny building in Waterloo that masquerades as an office. It is clamped between a dry cleaner's and a florist's shop and with no sign alerting people to its whereabouts, it's easy to miss. The building is run down and cramped but it is a retreat for me because apart from Ellie, it is the only stable thing I now have.

Nothing has changed since I've been absent and I'm grateful for this. My desk is exactly as I left it except now it is coated in a thick layer of dust.

"I told the cleaners to leave it alone," Leon says, rushing over to me. "I didn't want them to disturb anything important."

I am touched by this and I stand before Leon, wondering whether to hug him. He might be my boss but he's been my friend for even longer. Perhaps he is thinking the same thing because he shifts forward awkwardly, unsure what to do with his arms. He looks around and sees Myrah and Sophie watching us so whatever he was planning, I only get a pat on the arm. "So glad you're back, Olivia. It's been...quiet without you. Just get settled and we'll talk later, okay?"

Thanking him, I sink into my chair. I watch him head back to his desk, his huge bear-like frame incongruous in this tiny office space. His work area is not far from mine, even though he could easily use the separate room by the kitchen, which is now a store room for junk. I wonder how many other bosses would choose to share cramped office space with their employees. Sophie and Myrah might have suspicions about why Leon sits with us but I know it's not to check up on us. That's not his nature. If he thought he couldn't trust any of us we wouldn't be working here in the first place.

Behind me, Sophie and Myrah are now engrossed in their computers; I'm sure they're trying to be tactful by not staring at me and I'm grateful for that. I haven't told them about separating from Carl but Leon will have told them why I've had three weeks off work. I'm glad they know. Now neither of them will bring up Carl's name.

Myrah brings me a mug of tea I haven't asked for and squeezes my arm but all I can manage in response is a weak smile. It's hard to define our relationship but we sit on the borderline between colleagues and friends. It is Myrah's openness that's brought us closer together. The way she talks about her family makes me feel as if I know them personally and every morning I look forward to hearing the Collins family news. In return I tell her snippets about my life. Or at least I did until now. I was never able to slot the words in between Myrah gushing about what a great husband David is.

Sophie doesn't say anything but drops her eyes whenever I turn my head to look at her. I'm surprised by this; she is divorced herself so is the one person in the office who should know how I'm feeling. I've never been her favourite person – most of the time my requests for administrative help are greeted by scowls and grumbles – but now I long for her to reach out to me, offer me some words of comfort. Anything to show me I'll be okay. But maybe the permanent frown on her face and snide tone of voice when she talks about other people to Myrah are a glimpse of my future. The bitter woman I will become. Sophie can't be far into her forties but she has already given up on herself, wearing clothes way beyond her years and scrunching her hair up into a permanent and messy bun at the back of her head. She has written herself off and maybe I will be powerless to prevent myself doing the same.

It takes me all morning to wade through three weeks' worth of emails and by the time I've finished I'm exhausted, even though I haven't moved from my desk. I must have read thousands of words but now I've closed my inbox I can't remember a single one. I thought work would be a distraction but everything is still overshadowed by emptiness. Nothing is the same; even being somewhere unrelated to Carl.

"I can't do this," I say to Leon when I find him in the kitchen. "I'm not ready."

"Nonsense," he says, spooning coffee into his mug. He pulls another one from the cupboard but I shake my head and rush from the kitchen. Ignoring the surprise on Myrah and Sophie's faces as I fling the office door open and escape outside, I take a deep lungful of thick smoggy air and try to control my breathing.

All around me people rush by, their strides purposeful and determined. I am invisible here. Part of the scenery nobody bothers to notice. But quickly the urge to escape the office – and probably my whole life – passes and I begin to feel foolish. I have been back at work for half a day and I can't even hack that. At least it will give Sophie something to gossip about.

Just as I am wondering what to do now I've made such a show of myself, Leon appears beside me and grabs my arm. "Come on. I think you need some lunch." He leads me past the cafe we all regularly crowd into for sandwiches and around the corner to a pub I've never been to before. "Just in case Sophie decides to go for a walk," he explains.

Inside, Leon ushers me to a booth in the corner and heads to the bar to order us food. He hasn't asked what I'd like and I feel like a helpless baby, needing to be looked after and incapable of making the smallest of decisions.

Even though the pub is fairly quiet for lunchtime, Leon is kept waiting so long that I have time to try and pull myself together. I haven't acted professionally today and even though I've known Leon since our university days he is my boss now and has to put his business before anything else. Even friendship. Showing any sign of favouritism towards me when he has two other employees to consider won't sit comfortably with him so he will have to tread carefully. Perhaps he will fire me and is still at the bar because he's finding the right words to tell me I'm out of a job. But even the thought of losing my job is nothing compared to what I have already lost.

Leon eventually joins me at the table with our drinks and places a glass of coke in front of me. Three ice cubes float around the top but there is no slice of lemon. "How did you know?" I ask.

He chuckles. "Olivia, you've been ordering the same drink every day at lunch time for four years. I've also ordered you a ham and cheese baguette, no tomato. That's right, isn't it?"

And now it is my turn to laugh. "Thanks. But when did I get so predictable?"

"Not predictable. You just know what you want. There's nothing wrong with that." He takes a sip of his drink and I stare out of the window, feeling far removed from someone who knows what she wants.

I apologise to Leon. There is little I can say to explain my behaviour so I hope it will be enough. His huge face beams at me from behind his glass. "Don't apologise. For anything. I'm just worried about you."

I should have known Leon would react with kindness and I dig deep to find something else to offer him. "Maybe I just haven't given myself enough time? This morning I thought I was okay but–"

Leon slams his glass down. "Work is the best thing for you. What else will you do except sit and stew at home?" His voice is stern but somehow still kind so I don't object. Leon has that way about him. He doesn't manipulate people but I am willing to bet he can get almost anyone to do anything he wants. We agree that I'll take the rest of the day off and come back tomorrow. I rattle the ice cubes in my drink and try not to dwell on how I'll get through tomorrow.

Leon's mobile phone rings and he smiles an apology before bellowing a greeting into it. I can tell it's a business call because he fishes out a notebook from his pocket and starts scribbling something illegible to anyone but him. I watch him talk and wonder how a man like Leon is still single. Although he is a huge man, he's not obese and his face is warm and kind. He's had several girlfriends since I've known him but I've never heard him rave about any of them. I've questioned him about this several times over the years – usually after a dose of alcohol – but Leon remains cagey about his personal life, brushing it off by saying his standards are probably far too high.

Our food still hasn't arrived by the time Leon finishes his call and he checks his watch and looks around the pub. "It's okay," I tell him. "You don't have to stay here with me. I know you've got a million things to do."

Leon's expression falls, as if I have offended him. Surely he should realise nothing I say or do at the moment should be taken seriously? "No, I'm just starving," he says. "I don't need to rush back yet. Besides, I'm worried about you. I don't want you to be on your own at the moment."

I reach for his hand and his cheeks flush red. "I have Ellie, don't I? Besides, you don't have to protect me, Leon. I'll be fine. I'll get through this." I'm sure I don't sound convincing, but then, how can I be when I don't believe my own words?

"Just don't forget to be kind to yourself," Leon says, squeezing my hand. "You're allowed to be upset...cry, shout, scream, whatever it takes. Just don't beat yourself up for not feeling like you anymore." He pulls his hand away and his face crumples into a grimace. "Bloody hell, just listen to me. I sound like a second-rate psychiatrist or something. Just ignore me, eh? What the hell do I know anyway? I've never even come close to getting married."

The food arrives, saving us both from an awkward conversation, and Leon devours his sandwich while I only take a few bites of mine. My attempts are futile; it will only be a matter of time before Leon questions me and I am once again made to feel like a baby.

Leon's phone rings again and this time it's Sophie. I can hear her on the other end asking where he is and reminding him he's got a meeting in ten minutes. For the first time since I've known her I notice her voice is loud and confident, completely at odds with her appearance. She sounds more like Leon's wife than his secretary and I wonder if they've ever slept together. Perhaps it is even more than that and they're having a relationship. I'd like to think Leon would be able to tell me if this is so, even if he knows Sophie and I aren't the closest of work colleagues.

"I have to get back," he says, standing up and slipping his phone into his pocket. "That was Sophie reminding me I have a meeting now. Sorry, Olivia. But I'll see you tomorrow? Unless...Oh, never mind."

I'm too exhausted by the effort of dragging myself up from my seat to ask Leon what he was about to say. "I'll be there. Ready for work, I promise. And there's a film preview tomorrow afternoon so I'll get stuck into that."

"Only if you're sure you're ready," Leon says, and although I nod enthusiastically, I know what it will take to sit through a film, making notes to put together into something people will want to read, while everything else in my life is unrecognisable. It's hard to believe it was only this morning I was excited about getting stuck back into work. And that for three weeks I've longed to be writing again. But now even that is crumbling away, despite what I'm fooling Leon into believing.

Leon insists on walking me to the station even though he is already running late. "Sophie will tell you off," I say, looking for any sign on his face that they are more than just colleagues. But Leon rolls his eyes so I don't push it further. It starts to dawn on me that in less than a minute I will be alone again, heading back to an empty afternoon until it's time to pick Ellie up. And even when she's back at home with me the flat will be too quiet and we will both feel the heavy weight of Carl's absence.

I say goodbye to Leon and search my bag for my Oyster card. It is buried deep within my handbag and takes me a while to fish it out.

"Carl's a fool," Leon says, but by the time I've realised he's spoken he is already across the road. I watch him head back to the office and as he fades from sight, his words fade along with him so by the time he's gone I wonder if he said them at all.

CHAPTER THREE

It takes several weeks but I slowly settle back into work and Ellie begins adapting to the change in our circumstances. There are moments of laughter – although rare – and I relish the times she can smile. She makes a couple of friends at school and her quiet, withdrawn episodes become less frequent. Part of what helps her manage is that Carl turns up, without fail, every Friday evening with a whole weekend of activities planned for them both. I haven't seen him since I moved out and although we only communicate through short, formal emails, we at least manage to be amicable.

Carl's routine on these Fridays is to wait in the car for Ellie, beeping the horn to let us know he's arrived. He refuses to come in, explaining that he doesn't want to see a home we've set up without him, and I don't push the issue. It is easier to let Carl deal with things his way and it doesn't seem to bother Ellie. So when the buzzer chimes one evening, just before Christmas, I am shocked to find Carl shivering on the doorstep. Against my better judgement I hold the door open and he steps inside, looking around before plonking himself down on the sofa with a prolonged sigh. He is early so I make us coffee while Ellie finishes packing for the weekend.

Carl cradles his mug and stares at me as I sit down next to him. He is still wrapped up in his thick winter coat and scarf and perches on the end of the sofa. "Come home, Olivia," he says eventually. It is only now I notice how dishevelled and thin he has become. Usually quite stocky, his jacket swamps him and his jeans hang loosely around his legs.

Carl's eyes plead with me; he is a different man than the one to whom I've always felt inferior. He's never done or said anything to cause this feeling; it's just his calmness and togetherness which intimidate me. To Carl, no problem is without a solution and his self-belief has served him well because until now he has made a success of everything he's done. Carl has fixed every problem I've ever had, but it's only now I can see that being with him made me a helpless child.

As I watch him now, shrunken and crushed, I am determined something good will come out of this; I have to be able to fix my own problems, to be the strong one for Ellie, just as Carl has been for me.

I don't know how to answer his demand so I ignore it. "What have you got planned for Ellie this weekend?"

Our game of avoidance continues as he pretends I haven't asked him anything. "It's not too late. We can sort it all out so you can move back. What can I do? Just tell me what to do to show you we can work things out." If I look any longer at the desperation in his eyes I know I will be in tears and in his arms within seconds, so instead I focus on the bubbles floating on the surface of my coffee. There is nothing he can say to convince me, no words that will give us back our life together. But it's pointless explaining this to Carl. To him nothing is impossible if you want it badly enough. I open my mouth to speak, not even sure what words will form, but thankfully Ellie chooses this moment to burst into the room.

"Daddyyyyy!" she cries and throws herself at Carl. His coffee cascades onto the carpet and I rush to the kitchen to grab a damp cloth. Rather than feeling annoyed at the inconvenience, I am relieved to escape from Carl's melancholy. Being in such close proximity to him and seeing the state he is in gnaws away at my resolve and I cannot let this happen.

Now that Ellie is in the room, Carl plants a smile on his face and changes the subject, asking her about school and nodding enthusiastically at her replies, even though he will only be half-listening. Determined not to mess Ellie up, we have both honed our acting skills so she never has to see the despair our separation has brought us. Our pain is silent, not to be discussed in her presence. We are just two parents who love her and while we know we can't wrap her in cotton wool, we do all we can to shield her from the truth.

"Come on, Pumpkin!" Carl says, standing up. "Grab your stuff – we've got a film to go and see!" He's said the magic words and Ellie races off to fetch her backpack and coat. Not for the first time, I marvel at her resilience and strength of character. The second Ellie has disappeared, Carl turns back to me. "Please can we at least talk about this?"

"Soon," I say. It's the best I can offer him.

Once Carl and Ellie have gone, I close the door and stand in the hallway, facing the emptiness of the flat. I've got used to this over the last few weekends and can normally fend off the loneliness that swamps me once the door closes by busying myself with housework. But tonight the gaping hole I am left with hits me like a bolt of lightning and I sink to the floor, burying my head in my knees.

When I eventually look up, my vision is distorted by a curtain of tears. This isn't how my life is supposed to be but

I feel powerless to change anything. Curling up even more, I make myself as small as I can, shrinking away from the reality I can't face. This time last year I had a family and a home. I had a future. Now there is only a void.

It's only after several minutes pass with me frozen in the foetal position that I notice a folded sheet of lined paper under the front door. Assuming it's from Carl, my heart lurches as I grab it and stare at my name. Everything is blurred so I have to wipe my eyes before I realise the handwriting is neat and slanted, definitely not Carl's. *Olivia, fancy a glass of wine this evening? Just knock. Michael.*

Despite the brevity of your note, I read it several times just to make sure I fully understand it. The words don't seem real. They are too confident to come from someone I've barely crossed paths with. My mind races and I force myself to slow down and take a deep breath. I wonder if it's more than just a casual invitation. But how can it be when you know nothing about my relationship status? I read it again. This time it's glaringly obvious it's just a friendly note from a neighbour; I would be a fool to read any more into it than that. I imagine accepting your invitation and knocking on your door. Will I feel uncomfortable? Perhaps I will have nothing to say and you will quickly realise you've made a mistake. But at least your invitation means I will be able to escape my loneliness and Carl's words for a couple of hours.

You don't mention a specific time in your note and it's only five o'clock now so I take my time and make a jacket potato and salad for dinner. It's not enough but I still struggle to eat it. I have no appetite; all my stomach wants now is wine.

I soak in the bath with the radio on far too loud. I don't recognise any of the music and the station is more suited to someone in their twenties but the beats are fast and catchy and lift my spirits.

The bubbles in the bath begin to diminish and the water turns lukewarm but I am lost in my thoughts. I am about to have a drink with a stranger. A man I know nothing about. I'm not used to being in male company, other than Carl's or Leon's, so the idea of having a drink alone with you seems daunting. But when I consider the alternative, I know immediately I will face whatever kind of evening awaits me upstairs rather than the suffocating emptiness of my flat without Ellie.

Once I've dried myself, I leave my towel draped over the bath and because Ellie isn't here I don't bother with my dressing gown and walk naked to my bedroom. I catch my reflection in the mirror; my solid body is not as thin as it was before I had Ellie but I'd rather have my daughter than a perfect body.

Shuffling through the clothes in my wardrobe, I am at a loss as to what to wear. I pick out a blue knee-length cowl dress but as soon as it's on I know it's wrong. It's too dressy and the last time I wore it was when Carl and I went for a meal to celebrate our eleventh and final wedding anniversary. I hastily strip it off and leave it crumpled on the floor, pulling on jeans and a fitted polo neck jumper instead. This is fine; we are neighbours having a friendly drink, not two people going on a first date.

This is the thought that stays with me as I turn off the lights and lock up my flat. Tonight will allow me to escape the mess I have become for just one evening. I have no other motive as I stand in our hallway, knocking on your door.

"Olivia." Opening your door, you seem surprised to see me and with horror I realise I must have made a mistake and somehow misread your note. But you hold the door open for me and usher me in so clearly I'm expected. "You

21

shouldn't have bothered dressing up for me," you say, staring at my jeans and Ugg boots. I search for a retort but your mouth quickly gathers into a smile. I giggle nervously and immediately feel stupid; I don't know what impression you're getting of me but it can't be a good one.

I follow you up a flight of beige carpeted stairs and notice you're also wearing jeans. The scent of your aftershave lingers behind you as you climb. It is different from anything Carl wore and I'm grateful for that.

At the top of the stairs, a wailing sound blares from your pocket. Fishing out your mobile phone you glance at the screen, a frown creasing your forehead. "Sorry," you say. "I have to answer this. The kitchen's through there, could you pour us some wine?" You point to one of the closed doors leading off the hall and then head in the other direction to another closed door.

"No problem," I say to your back as you disappear through the door to what I assume is your bedroom. I look around the hallway and feel like an intruder, violating your privacy with my presence. Your flat doesn't feel lived in; there is no artwork on the magnolia walls, nothing to offer a glimpse of your personality. It is just spotlessly clean and bare. The carpet beneath my feet looks brand new and I check the bottom of my shoes for mud, wondering if you expect guests to take off their shoes. The layout of your flat is similar to mine but it couldn't feel more different. Something is missing here. I decide when you reappear I will ask how long you've lived here because it's possible you've only just moved in and haven't had the time to make it a home yet.

Before opening the kitchen door, I peek into the room next door to it and find your lounge. I am not surprised to find the room is minimalist and immaculate with the same beige carpet following on from the hall. There isn't a speck of dust on any of the furniture and two huge black leather sofas face each other at each end of the room, both dust- and smudge-free.

It is the same in the kitchen; every surface sparkles and the inside of the kitchen cupboards is no exception. I can't even find the smallest of smudges on the wine glasses I eventually track down. In the corner a wooden wine-rack houses a wide variety of bottles, all with the labels facing outwards, and I wonder how it's possible I've never heard of any of the names on them. You've given me *carte blanche* to pour the wine so I pick a bottle of red at random from the middle of the rack. It only occurs to me as I'm pouring the second glass that maybe this is a ludicrously expensive bottle you've been saving for a special occasion.

"Good choice," you say, joining me in the kitchen. "Sorry about that. My little sister. She's a bit of a pain but I feel bad if I don't answer when she calls."

"No need to apologise," I tell you, handing you a glass.

We take our drinks to the lounge and I sit down on one of the sofas, amazed that it still looks immaculate this close up. You put two coasters on the coffee table and place your glass on it before opting to sit on the other sofa. There's an awkward silence as we contemplate each other and I wonder if you regret inviting me here.

"Let's put some music on," you say, jumping up. "I can't stand a silent room." While you sort out the stereo I notice all your CDs are in alphabetical order and it reminds me to ask when you moved here. "Eight years ago. Well, nearly nine now," you say. I try not to show my surprise and scan the room again, searching for personal objects. But apart from the CDs there is nothing to show who you are or that this is your home.

For over an hour we drink our wine to a backdrop of classical music. It's not something I've ever thought of listening to but somehow it feels right in your flat and the soft dulcet notes relax me. I quickly notice that you don't make small talk, as if you refuse to waste a single word or thought. It is clear to me you are an intelligent man, unlikely to fall short of topics to discuss. But you aren't intimidating or arrogant and when I admit I don't know much about politics you playfully scold me instead of rolling your eyes.

I am so wrapped up in our conversation that I don't immediately notice we are no longer talking about world affairs. You have somehow managed to turn the conversation onto me and before I have a chance to think about what I'm saying, I am telling you all about Carl and how Ellie and I ended up living downstairs. But while I talk you start to fidget with the buttons on the stereo remote control and barely look at me, only offering the occasional nod. I am close to tears by the time I finish but you don't seem to notice. To begin with I am grateful for your detachment. It makes me feel foolish for getting so emotional and I quickly snap out of my mood.

When you go to the bathroom I realise I have been unfair, lumbering a virtual stranger with my issues. I can't work out what possessed me to mention Carl when I had made up my mind to avoid this subject. Finishing my glass of wine, I decide when you come back I will encourage you to talk about yourself. After nearly two hours in your flat all I know about you is that we're the same age and you have a sister.

But when you return, another bottle of wine in your hand, you fire so many questions at me in such quick succession that I have no chance to direct any back at you. It is flattering that you show so much interest in me; I am always wary of people who talk only about themselves and show no interest in others, but as the evening progresses I wonder if this is just a diversion tactic and you are deliberately being cagey.

Eventually you exhaust all lines of questioning and mention that you're a maths teacher in the secondary school around the corner. This is not what I imagined you would do for a living and I try to picture you dressed in a shirt and tie rather than your standard casual uniform of jeans and a t-shirt.

By eight thirty we've already managed to finish two bottles of wine and I am trying hard to fight tipsiness. It feels wrong to be drunk around a stranger and I don't want to start talking about Carl again.

"I'm glad you've moved here," you say, out of the blue. I must look surprised because you quickly explain yourself. "I mean... it's just nice to have someone so close by to socialise with for a change. I only really have a couple of friends down here. And my sister, of course. I think I've got a bit too used to nights at home on my own." You say all this without a hint of self-pity and I warm to you a bit more.

I study your face. It's not what I would call a friendly face but the harshness in your blue eyes is not unattractive. Your hair flops across your forehead and I lose count of the times you flick it back. This must be a gesture you stopped being conscious of long ago.

Carl doesn't enter my thoughts for the rest of the evening and somehow your company has lifted the black cloud I've been under and planted a seed of hope that I may just be able to have a life again.

But when you jump up and tell me you're tired and should probably get to bed, I am right back under that cloud. It's still early and I don't know what I was expecting but it wasn't to be ushered out of your flat so suddenly. "Think you can make it home okay?" you say as I'm leaving and we both laugh. Only yours is genuine.

CHAPTER FOUR

I can't remember the last time I uttered a single word; if I heard my voice now would I recognise it? Talking is good, they say. It's what I need to do. But my thoughts are unspeakable so I remain mute while they become more frustrated by my stubbornness.

Most of the time I ignore them and they do likewise. This is an arrangement I'm happy with because it means all I have to do is lie here and focus on the constant question feeding on my brain. How can things fall apart before they have even begun? Just like with an old building, the cracks go unnoticed at first or get ignored. I missed them all because I thought I'd been through the worst already but now there's no avoiding or escaping them.

I try to make our first Christmas without Carl special for Ellie. Our decorations can probably fill Oxford Street and it is hard to spot the deep green branches in between the mass of gold, silver and blue tinsel draped on the tree. But it makes Ellie smile so I am happy too.

Carl suggests we all spend Christmas together at the house but I need to prove I can survive the day without him. Ellie is disappointed and even the promise of a new bike doesn't perk her up so eventually I cave in and compromise with Carl. We'll spend the day in the flat then visit Carl in the evening.

Cards arrive from family and friends and it occurs to me to write one to you. I haven't seen you for a few weeks – since the evening in your flat – but considering we've spent time together it seems like the right thing to do. But when I shuffle through the multi-pack of cards I've bought, they all seem wrong somehow; not good enough. I can't see you being impressed with the cuddly animals or smiling Santas adorning every card.

After an agonising search in a gift shop, the card I eventually post under your door is deliberately understated with a tranquil scene of woodland blanketed in piercing white snow. I struggle over the words to write inside but eventually settle on *Dear Michael, have a lovely Christmas, from Olivia and Ellie*. Once the envelope is sealed I start to regret not writing 'love' or at least putting a cross after our names. You probably won't care one way or the other but my neglect bothers me.

For days leading up to Christmas I check my mail in the hallway for a return card from you. Even on Christmas morning I still have a glimmer of hope that you've suddenly remembered me and rushed downstairs to pop a card under our door. But by Boxing Day the line of cards Ellie and I have hanging on a string stretched across our living room still doesn't include one from you.

I replay that Friday night in my mind, and try to recall if I might have said something to offend you. The only thing that could have bothered you is hearing details of my separation from Carl but you seemed more indifferent than annoyed. I try to be rational, tell myself it's just a Christmas card and doesn't mean anything but there is more than that. Nothing I think of can explain your rush to get me out of your flat.

You can't have been expecting something to happen between us because there was no point in the evening where you sat anywhere near me. I try to remember how I felt in your presence. You are an attractive man but it didn't feel as if there was anything physical between us. I don't know if that's on both our parts or just mine because it's hard for me to think of anyone in that way after Carl. Carl was meant to be the last man I'd ever sleep with so it's difficult to get my head around the fact that he won't be. So it shouldn't bother me that I haven't heard from you. It shouldn't but it does.

Weeks pass with no sign of you. I rarely see your lights on or hear you leave for work in the morning so I make up my mind to find out what's going on. I start by inspecting the communal hallway: there is no mail piling up and the spider plant that must be yours looks healthy and watered so I'm convinced you haven't gone away.

But I don't stop there. Every evening after putting Ellie to bed, I keep the television volume so low it is barely audible, just so I won't miss hearing you entering or leaving your flat. The urge to find out why you haven't been in contact eats away at me with a ferocious appetite I cannot fathom. Thoughts of you somehow push any of Carl and the wreck of my life to the side and even though I can't understand it – you are still virtually a stranger to me – I welcome the relief brought by dwelling on something else.

Each evening is the same; a battle between trying to occupy my mind and wondering what you're doing. On one of these occasions I settle on the sofa, determined to enjoy my own company. Ellie is asleep and I've just finished writing a review of a remake of *Jane Eyre*. I am pleased with what I've written; it's been a long time since I've felt I've produced anything good enough. Opening the new crime novel I've been holding, I try to lose myself in a fictional world I assume is even more messed up than my own. It's only when I get to page fourteen I realise I have no idea what's happening in the story and can't even name the main character.

Within five minutes I am knocking on your door, unsure of what I'm doing but desperate for you to answer. There is no light seeping underneath the door but I still wait for several minutes before admitting defeat. I retreat to bed, disappointment seeping through my body. Only when I wake up in the middle of the night do I realise it was for the best that you didn't answer. I had no idea – and still don't – what I would have said to you if you'd answered the door.

It's nearly three o'clock in the morning when Ellie appears at my bedroom door, squinting to try and make out my shape in the dark. Her hair is sticking up on one side and she rubs her half-closed eyes. I immediately panic. Usually nothing can drag Ellie out of bed; she'd sleep until dinner time if I'd let her, so I sit up and grope around for the lamp switch. Once light envelopes the room, Ellie runs over and sits on the bed.

"I'm really thirsty," she says, and I'm about to explain that she knows how to get a glass of water when plump, glistening tears begin rolling down her cheeks. "I've had a bad dream. And I really miss Daddy."

My stomach is in knots as I try to comfort and reassure her. "Let's call him," I say, knowing that nothing else will be enough to help her back to sleep.

Ellie's eyes widen but then narrow again as a frown appears on her forehead. "But it's the middle of the night, Mum! He'll be asleep."

I hug her tightly then look her directly in the eyes. "Listen to me, Pumpkin. There is no time, night or day, that your dad wouldn't want to speak to you. Do you understand that?" She looks uncertain but then nods in agreement. And

I am right. Carl, after a moment of panic at our late-night call, is more than happy to speak to his daughter.

While they are talking, I hear the front door of the building slam and before I know what I'm doing I am at my flat door, staring through the peep-hole at a blaze of light in the hallway. I hear whispered voices and giggling before I see you so immediately know you aren't alone. I look away; this is none of my business and spying on you feels like a violation. But seconds later, my willpower vanishes and I manage to glimpse a mane of curly blonde hair disappearing through your door.

Nausea sweeps through me as I digest what I've just witnessed and then I realise how stupid I've been. Your relationship status has never come up in any conversation we've had so I don't know why I assumed you're single. I shouldn't be so shocked to see you with a woman; I hardly know you and we are nothing more than neighbours. Shivering in just my thin cotton nightshirt, I turn away and lean back against the door, disappointment lurking in the pit of my stomach. I must put a stop to whatever I am feeling – no good can come of it. After the last year I can't even trust that I know what my feelings are so you being in a relationship has to be for the best.

I settle Ellie back into her bed then curl up in my duvet and try not to think about what you might be doing upstairs.

The next morning I make a full English breakfast, piling two plates with scrambled eggs, crispy bacon, sausages, hash browns and tomatoes. The persuasive aroma of toast fills the kitchen, mingling with the scent of bacon. I even make a pot of Earl Grey tea. Ellie squeals with delight as she walks in and notices her usual bowl of cornflakes has been replaced with a feast.

"Don't get too used to it," I warn her, and we both smile and tuck into our food. She doesn't need to know that the main reason I have prepared this feast is to keep my mind occupied so I don't think about you and what I saw last night.

As I eat, and Ellie chatters away about going to her friend Izzy's house this afternoon, I mentally prepare a list of all the things I need to do. Cleaning is not enough so I plan to call the landlord later and ask if I can paint the flat. I convince myself I'll feel more at home once the off-white walls have been replaced with a brighter colour and it is a task that should keep me going for the next few weekends. I don't particularly relish the prospect of painting, especially in the middle of winter when the windows can't be left open, but I need a project to focus on, because since last night I cannot stop myself thinking about you. The vision of the blonde woman following you into your flat leaves an indelible imprint in my head and it irks me that we spent an evening together and you didn't mention anything about her.

I try to consider this from a rational angle; we hardly know each other and nothing has happened between us so it's none of my business who enters your flat. But the underlying feeling I have somehow been wronged won't go away. After all, I bared my soul to you, told you every detail about my life with Carl, yet it didn't occur to you to mention that there is someone in your life. This, I decide, is what I'm really upset about and I comfort myself with the thought that it's nothing to do with romantic feelings. It is merely annoyance that you didn't open up to me that night.

Despite the fact it's clear now why I haven't heard anything from you, my routine of listening and watching out for you continues. Riddled with guilt for doing it and fully aware it's become an obsession, each night after putting Ellie to bed I mute the television and wait patiently for a sign of you. The images from the television flicker in front of me, but I don't notice them. Nor do I read the book that flops in my hand, still open at page fourteen. Every sound from outside has me rushing to my peep hole, my heart pausing as I wait to see if the blonde woman will make another appearance. But more often than not it's either not you at all or you are alone. Every time I spy on you I feel like I'm committing a crime but this doesn't stop me. And even though I haven't seen you again with the blonde woman, I continue my immoral stakeout.

Ellie catches me one evening, glued to the peep hole with the lights off and television muted, and asks me what I'm doing. I tell her I think I heard a noise and need to check it out. She turns her head to the side and looks at me as if I have gone insane. "But it's probably just the man upstairs, Mum," she says, before trotting off to the kitchen for a glass of water.

When Ellie's gone back to bed it occurs to me it would be simpler to ask you about the blonde woman and save myself a lot of time. It wouldn't be hard to manufacture an accidental meeting in the hallway as most mornings you leave for work only about ten minutes before I do. I could even invite you in for a drink, perhaps leave a note under your door just as you did, and mention I'm returning the favour after having devoured several bottles of your expensive wine. Either of these options would be perfectly natural but I shy away from both of them. Instead I remain silent, avoid an encounter with you and continue to listen and wait.

CHAPTER FIVE

Carl decides we should spend Valentine's Day together as a family. The minute he suggests it I know it is a terrible idea but he wears me down with his persistence. Christmas was one thing but how can we spend a day that's meant to be for lovers together when we're on the verge of divorce? He argues that if we don't spend the evening together we'll both be moping around trying to ignore something that may as well be a huge elephant in the room. But this is not what persuades me; he wins when he mentions how good it would be for Ellie, how it would show her that we are still a family even if we're not together all the time.

So I eventually agree and Carl sets about planning an extravagant meal to cook. My only condition is that we spend the evening at my flat because there is no way I'll be able to walk into that house. I know I can't avoid it forever because in the future there will undoubtedly be times when Ellie needs me to be there, but now is just too soon.

Valentine's Day falls on a Friday this year and I pray Carl won't use the excuse of it being the weekend to make it a late night. It's not that I don't want to spend time with him. Perhaps I just don't trust myself to stick to the commitment I have made to myself and managed to keep for months.

The day arrives and Carl calls in the morning to say he'll be round at five o'clock. But after school I have to take Ellie shopping as she's already outgrown the school shoes I bought her at the end of the summer. We rush around trying to make sure we get home in time but spend so long searching for a suitable pair of shoes that by the time we get home it's almost five. I know I don't have time to have a shower but I need to; sweat sticks to my skin and my clothes feel damp.

With scalding hot water pelting down onto my skin and steam wrapping me in a protective cloud, I wonder what plans you have tonight. I haven't seen you but a few days ago I spotted the blonde woman rushing out of the door early in the morning. I tried to get a good look at her face but she was gone in an instant, almost as if she'd never been there in the first place.

Ellie bangs on the door to let me know Carl is running late and I'm grateful for this. I'm nowhere near ready to step out from under the water. I try to focus on Carl and this evening, rather than dwell on you. I still have some reservations about this evening because I don't want to depend on Carl for anything, not even his company. But as I massage coconut-scented shampoo into my hair I can hear Ellie singing in her bedroom. I can't make out the song but her gentle, tuneful notes remind me what this evening should be about.

"It's bloody freezing out there!" Carl declares as he bounds into the flat, rubbing his hands together while two bulging Marks and Spencer bags swing from the crooks of his elbows. "You've painted in here," he says, looking at the deep burgundy walls. "It looks good." I am surprised he has noticed this since last time he was here he didn't seem in a state to take anything in, let alone something as irrelevant as the colour of my walls.

Carl looks better than he did last time; his face and body have filled out although he's not as stocky as he was. For the first time I notice a speckle of shiny silver grey in between his dark brown hairs but they suit him, not detracting at all from his attractiveness.

Ellie giggles. "Daddy swore!" she declares, throwing her arms around him. Letting the bags drop to the floor, Carl swings her around while they both howl with laughter. This vision of the two of them is bittersweet - in a couple of days' time Ellie will be missing her father all over again.

As Carl makes boeuf bourguignon with steamed potatoes and vegetables, it's almost as if nothing has happened and we are back in the house in Winchmore Hill. Ellie prances around the kitchen, singing a song with inappropriate lyrics which both Carl and I do our best to ignore, while I lay the table and pour us all drinks. Ellie watches me fill two wine glasses and a small tumbler for her then asks if she can have her Ribena in a wine glass. I frown, puzzled by her request.

"So I can be the same as you and Daddy," she explains. I grab another wine glass from the cupboard and transfer her drink into it. It's only a small gesture but I need Ellie to know we are still a family.

The dinner is delicious and because Ellie does most of the talking, the atmosphere is easy and comfortable. I'm grateful for her loquaciousness; it means there is no room for Carl to steer the conversation into awkward areas. While Ellie speaks, I am half-listening for any sounds from outside but everything is quiet. I can't even hear any creaking from your floors upstairs and the silence makes me believe you are out somewhere; probably in a restaurant having a romantic meal. The wonderful food Carl has cooked loses its appeal and I push my knife and fork together.

"I hope you're not full up," Carl says. "There's a chocolate cheesecake for dessert."

"Yippee!" Ellie yells, jumping up to fetch small plates from the cupboard, even though she hasn't finished her dinner.

"I just think it was a bit too much," I say to Carl, hoping he will buy my lie.

After dinner we sit in the living room drinking coffee while Ellie snuggles under Carl's arm with a hot chocolate. They will have to leave soon and I will once again be alone. I watch them both and know this will be a moment frozen in time. I smile because no matter what has happened, there will be more of these occasions when it's just the three of us and nobody else.

I feel content as I load the dishwasher and Carl helps Ellie pack for the weekend. This evening has been better than I imagined and I have not been haunted by yearnings for him. What worries me is what I've replaced them with.

Just as I consider this and once again wonder where you are tonight, I hear the communal door bang and my stomach begins its familiar churn. I need to see what you're doing and whether the blonde woman is with you. I assume she is as it's Valentine's Day. Carl and Ellie are still in her room so they don't see me rush to the peephole. My stomach flutters as you appear, alone. You struggle to get your flat door open as in one hand you're carrying a grease soaked take-away bag and in the other a precariously clasped bottle of red wine. I'm about to rush out and offer assistance but Carl's voice booming from Ellie's room reminds me I still have a guest in my home.

As your door slams shut I wonder where the blonde woman is. If you're in a relationship then tonight of all nights you should be together, not treating yourself to a solitary takeaway. And if something has happened and you're no longer together you don't look too upset or preoccupied by it.

"We're ready to go," Carl says, appearing next to me with Ellie's hand in his. Since your arrival home unaccompanied I don't feel as upset about being home on my own all weekend. I want to believe this is because the building doesn't seem as empty now that I know you're upstairs.

Standing outside, I watch the back lights of Carl's Ford Mondeo disappear around the corner, Ellie waving from the back seat. It's only nine o'clock but I decide to go to bed and give the novel I'm attempting to read another go.

The last thing I expect to see when I shut the front door and turn around is you standing at the door to my flat. A hot flush surges through me and I hope you don't notice my cheeks are burning bright red.

"Hi. I thought we could have some of this," you say, holding up the same bottle of wine I saw earlier. "But I know it's late so if you're busy–"

"No, no. Just shocked to see you there." I move closer to my door. "Actually, I was planning an early night but maybe I should live a little – I'm thirty-five not eighty-five!"

You smile and flick hair out of your eyes. "Well, it is Valentine's Day. I thought after what you told me you might like some company," you say, your eyes flickering to my closed flat door.

I'm relieved you didn't knock a few minutes earlier; even though I have nothing to hide or be ashamed of it would have been an awkward moment introducing Carl to you after everything I told you that evening.

"Come in," I say, feeling guilty as I shut the door. "I'll pour the wine," I add, grabbing the bottle from your hand and hurrying off. It's best not to think about what I've been doing. Before I reach the kitchen I turn back and see you making yourself comfortable on the sofa.

Only minutes ago it was Carl sitting on the sofa next to me, yet now you are here in his place and I have no clue why. I wonder if you know what I've been doing and you're here to confront me. Is it possible you can hear footsteps scuttling across my wooden floor every time you get home?

"So what have you been up to since we last spoke?" I ask. "Did you have a good Christmas?" It feels strange talking about Christmas in February but it still bothers me that you didn't give me a card. I am also desperate for any conversation that will stall you from confronting me about what I've been doing.

You flick your hair from your eyes. "I'm not a huge fan of Christmas. I know that sounds awful but it just gets in the way of things. But thanks for the card. For thinking of me. Anyway, I've just been busy planning lessons. Marking. More planning and then more marking. Just the usual. What about you?"

Before I even form an answer, I know I have nothing interesting to say. "Just working and spending time with Ellie. Nothing else really."

You regard me carefully. "But you're a writer. That must be exciting?" You don't wait for a reply but look sheepish. "Actually, I've got a confession to make. After we last spoke I checked out some of your reviews online. You're really good."

Before I have a chance to respond to your compliment you stand up. "I'll pour us some more wine," you say, already heading off to the kitchen. Neither of our glasses are empty.

While you're gone I sneak out to the hall and study myself in the mirror, suddenly conscious of my appearance. With the chaos of the divorce and house move I haven't even considered that I am long overdue for a haircut; it's too long and mousey and the ends are splitting but somehow it looks just about presentable. I've got large, grey bags under my eyes so I grab my concealer from my handbag on the floor and within seconds they've vanished. Quickly attacking my hair with a brush, I decide I'm not doing too badly considering everything I've been through lately. As I tiptoe back to the lounge, it occurs to me I didn't make even this tiny bit of effort for dinner with Carl.

As we start on our second glasses of wine, you move across to the armchair, leaving me alone in the middle of the huge sofa and when I try to ask you questions, just like last time, you shy away from revealing anything important. In fact, the only information you do share is that your sister lives with her husband in Chiswick and your parents live in Cambridge. But you're happy to let me talk about myself and while you watch me from across the room I have no idea what you're thinking.

At some point in the evening, fuelled by alcohol and frustration, I lose my inhibitions and finally feel brave enough to question you about your relationship status. You smile as if you know I've been waiting all evening to ask and pause to wipe away a trickle of wine that's sliding down your glass.

"I've been single for about two years now," you state, nonchalantly. I am fully prepared to finally learn who the blonde woman is so the news you have just delivered surprises me and I don't know how to respond. I wonder briefly if you're lying but nothing in your tone or expression suggests dishonesty. In that instant I know I am attracted to you and just the idea of it – being interested in another man – excites me. Right now the man I've loved for most of my adult life no longer exists. All I can think about is that I don't want you to leave yet.

I hardly listen as you explain how life is much simpler being single; instead I watch you talk and wonder how I'm so attracted to you when you're so unlike Carl. Besides that, I barely know you and what little I do know is shrouded in a haze of alcohol. But even though you say very little, the few words you utter intrigue me and I am desperate to be fed more. You have an interesting face; deep lines burrow into your forehead, making you look wise and sophisticated. But none of this explains why I'm attracted to you.

"Can I join you on the sofa?" you ask, and I nod, moving over to make more space for you. You sit close to me and as your leg brushes against mine, a surge of electricity tingles through me and I can barely focus. You say something about a Harold Pinter play you've seen recently and ask if I know it. I shake my head, ashamed at the visions intruding into my mind.

I giggle and you stare at me sternly, as if I'm a naughty student. I'm about to apologise when you pull me towards you and your lips press against mine, your tongue frantically exploring every part of my mouth. My whole body feels like it's on fire and I don't have time to consider what I'm doing. How crazy this is. All I can focus on is this feeling I've never felt before. Even with Carl it felt nothing like this. You pull me closer to you and I am desperate for you; our clothes feel like a river-wide barrier between us and you must think the same as you hastily rip apart my dress. Some of the buttons ping to the floor as first your hand and then your mouth finds my breasts beneath the bra I'm desperate for you to undo.

Within seconds I am naked underneath you. You pull your t-shirt over your head but have no patience to take off your jeans. Instead you wrestle with your belt and when you pull down your zip I can see you are as hard as a rock. Your hands touch every part of my body and I am drenched, screaming as you finally push inside me.

"Are you okay?" you whisper afterwards, collapsing on top of me and wiping the river of sweat from your forehead. I'm not sure I can form coherent words so I squeeze your hand tightly to reassure you.

Your belt digs into me so I slide from under you but turn so we're face-to-face. And for the first time we talk as if we aren't strangers. I don't even notice we haven't slept and daylight is making an appearance outside. It's only when I get cramp in my arm that I suggest we go to bed instead of lying on the sofa but you're already pulling on your t-shirt.

"I have to drive up to see my parents today and need to leave soon. But thanks for tonight. Or this morning. Or both." You squeeze my hand and grope around on the floor for your trainers. "Can I see you again?" you ask, avoiding looking at me.

I smile at you as I cover myself with the sofa throw. "Well, seeing as we live in the same building..." I begin, but when your hand reaches under the blanket I feel the same surge of electricity so nod and ask when you're free.

At the door you give me a quick kiss goodbye but even that is enough to make me want you all over again. Watching you open your door reminds me of the blonde woman and I finally ask who she is.

You chuckle as you head into your flat. "That's my sister! Why, who did you think she was?"

CHAPTER SIX

I am floating on a cloud, dizzy with exhilaration and bursting with hunger for you. My mind, and all the trouble that's been on it for so long, is frozen, usurped by my body which now controls all my actions. And painful with intense yearning, it doesn't allow me to think of Carl. There is only space for you.

For three months we ravish each other's bodies. There is no time for eating or sleeping and even talking seems a waste of valuable, limited time. I know there is no feeling that is unique to one human being but when you're inside me, ripping me apart, I can't believe anyone else has ever experienced what I do.

Ellie and my job keep me so busy that moments when you and I can be together are rare and much longed for. And just when I've started fully functioning at work, all I can do now is spend hours staring at a blank computer screen, daydreaming of what you will do to me next time we're alone. While I try to deal with the guilt I feel over limiting our time to weekends, you never complain about how little time we spend together. I try not to worry about why you are so laid back about this because when I'm naked before you, you are ravenous for me and your body reveals more than any words could.

Yet as our fourth month together begins, emptiness and uncertainty creep in. I need more than what you're giving me. I don't mean commitment or any other cliché; I just need more of *you*. It takes me a while to realise it but we know little more about each other than we did that first evening in your flat and we haven't even ventured out in public together.

I broach my concerns with you one morning when you're somewhere in that state between shallow sleep and full consciousness. But even as the words pour from my mouth I know this isn't the best time for an uncomfortable conversation.

Opening your eyes, you stare at me as if I've delivered your death sentence. I wait for you to say something but you pull yourself upright and close your eyes. I watch as frown lines begin to crease your brow and continue to wait but you offer no response. Sick with humiliation, I throw the duvet off me and climb out of bed, thankful I only have to travel downstairs.

"Wait." You grab my arm. "I'm sorry but I'm not going to be bullied into saying or doing anything that doesn't feel right. If you're not happy then you need to walk away." Your words are not spoken with spite. You deliver them calmly and rationally, making any argument futile.

I am a fish out of water; I only have my relationship with Carl to compare to ours and the two couldn't be more disparate. It was easy to talk through issues with Carl. We might not have always agreed on things but he was someone who tried to listen. When I don't respond to your admonishment, you slide back down and turn your back to me, pulling the duvet over you so only the top of your hair is visible. I make no move to get back into bed but nor do I get up. My clothes are strewn across the floor in a stark reminder of last night and with my legs dangling over the side of the bed, I close my eyes and wish I hadn't spoken this morning.

Before long you reach behind you and grab my hand, pulling me back to bed. But your gesture can't eradicate the rejection I feel. I wait until your eyes close and your breathing deepens before I slip from your bed and gather up my clothes. As I close your door with a quiet click, all the elation I've felt over the last few months dissipates and is replaced by a feeling I can't put into words. Something doesn't feel right. But despite the wall you've put up between us with your reluctance to open up, when I remember last night I am certain I cannot walk away from what we do have.

I should ignore the loud tap of your knuckles on my door, but instead I open it and let you enter. A waft of aftershave, which I now know is Fahrenheit, accompanies you as you step inside. The sweet aroma reminds me of all the nights we've spent together, dissolving the silent rage that I've been hoarding inside me for weeks. In this time I've tried to put you out of my mind as best I can. Sometimes I am successful in my endeavour, other times I fail and my mind replays the cold words you delivered to me that morning.

We stand together in the hallway and you pull me towards you, gripping me in an uncomfortably tight embrace. I let myself fall into you and ignore all the questions ready to erupt from my lips. The urgency to ask them is lost and everything falls away. I do want to know what has brought you to my door after five weeks of silence but as I breathe in the familiar scent of your skin it only matters that you are here now.

When you kiss me I only half allow myself to let it overpower me but even so I am shocked and indignant when, as if stung by a shock of electricity, you break off and back away from me.

"I hope you're not busy this evening," you say. "A few friends are coming over for drinks and I thought...you might like to come?" You look embarrassed; inviting me to a social occasion is clearly out of your comfort zone.

As it's Saturday, Ellie is with Carl and all I have planned is a night with my book. But something makes me hold back. It is a juvenile and asinine game but I am powerless not to play it.

"Can I let you know? I might just have to change a few things around."

The words sound false and I'm convinced you see right through me but you play the game well. "Okay." There is no hint of any emotion in your voice and when you leave me standing in my hallway, watching you disappear into your flat, I am the one who has lost.

I don't think you find it any surprise that a few hours later I'm at your door. The bottle of Châteauneuf-du-Pape I hand to you is my silent apology.

"I'm really glad you came. You look really nice," you say, and perhaps this is your apology.

Large gatherings make me uncomfortable and tonight is no exception. Your flat is almost unrecognisable; the serene and clinical atmosphere having been replaced with the bustle of several conversations blending into one sound. The floors are cluttered with empty glasses and bottles and I wonder how long it will be before you give in and clear them away.

Suddenly I need some air, or at least a quiet space that hasn't been invaded by strangers, so I head to the bathroom. I shut the door on the noise and splash cold water on my face. The black strapless dress I'm wearing rides up my thighs and I stretch it down over my knees. I almost wore jeans instead tonight but after your compliment at the door I know I made the right choice.

When I emerge from the bathroom I can't see you, so I push through the strangers gathered in every room, feeling their questioning eyes on me as I walk past. I must be the only person who has turned up alone, the only one who doesn't know a soul apart from you, so I don't blame them for their curiosity.

I finally spot you in the living room, a room I've already checked twice, and pause in the doorway to watch you. The man and woman you are speaking to lean into each other as they talk, their hands gesturing wildly with every phrase. The fact that they're both doing this and the way they're standing together make it appear as if they've morphed into one person. You seem firmly engrossed in the conversation, relaxed and at ease as you gently nod and smile at each of them.

Seeing you surrounded by people is bizarre. I've only ever known you as a solitary figure so it's as if I'm watching a stranger. As I observe you, I realise that true intimacy is not being naked with someone and giving your body to them. Seeing you now talking to your friends, without you realising I am looking at you, is as close to you as I have been before.

I watch you circulating, dividing your time between your guests, and my anxiety mixes with anticipation for the moment I can be alone with you. There are still unanswered questions between us; I don't even know if we're still seeing each other. You might have invited me here this evening but so far we haven't had a chance to speak.

I am envious of all the people here who have known you for years; you so easily offer them warm smiles while you laugh at their jokes and share anecdotes. I am not a part of this and still unsure what part I play in your life. But I wait patiently, smiling politely at strangers and trying to guess how you know each of them. Anything to speed up the painfully slow crawling of time.

"Hi, I'm Chloe."

The blonde woman I've only ever seen the back of thrusts a bottle of Becks into my hand. "You'll probably want this," she continues. "Everyone's way ahead of you in case you hadn't noticed."

Now I feel foolish. I've been at your party now for nearly an hour and haven't had a single drop to drink. I thank her and take a gulp, immediately feeling much better.

Your sister is not what I expected. Even brief glances of her back helped me form an opinion of her and the woman standing before me is a far cry from what my imagination conjured up. For a start, I didn't notice how tiny she is. Not just in height but her whole build. She's like a delicate china doll and looks as if she could break in half with only a slight shove. Her skinny jeans and strapless black top cling to her minuscule frame and I feel like a giant next to her. Her make-up is immaculate and short spiral curls spring from her head, bouncing as she talks. I hold out my hand to her, feeling a mixture of fear and excitement at meeting a member of your family.

"So how do you know my brother? Are you a teacher too?" And I come crashing back down to earth. You are always telling me how close you both are yet she knows nothing about me. Nothing about us.

"I'm just the neighbour," I explain. "The flat downstairs." Telling Chloe this is not a lie. It is closer to the truth than anything else I could say.

"Oh," she says, "how long have you lived there? I'm surprised we haven't met before now. I'm here quite a lot."

I take another sip of beer and don't mention that although she may not know me, I've seen her several times before tonight.

"Anyway, I'd better get Michael's cake ready. You won't believe how long it took me to arrange thirty-six candles! Mum warned me I should just buy numbered candles instead but where's the fun in that?" The news that it is your birthday renders me speechless and all I can do is nod. She continues, oblivious to the confusion I'm feeling. "Well, I at least hope he's grateful. He wasn't happy when he realised I'd invited so many people, but then, Michael's not the most sociable of people, is he?"

Even though I know it's rhetorical, I wish I could answer her question but I am no more qualified than the postman to analyse your character.

Chloe bounces off, her blonde curls floating behind her like small snakes. I watch her disappearing through the crowd, a little pixie in a land of giants, and notice she is wearing flat ballerina shoes. I must be at least four inches taller than her but I still don't feel comfortable without heels. While I admire her confidence, I resent her for not knowing I am sleeping with her brother.

Even though there doesn't seem much to stay for, I remain at your party, finally summoning up the courage to make small talk with the strangers surrounding me. But all the time I am smiling and nodding, I am only waiting for an opportunity to talk to you. That chance doesn't come but as time passes I decide to be more positive. Although you didn't tell me it was your birthday, we haven't spoken for weeks before today so I can hardly blame you for not rushing to mention it. And maybe your sister doesn't know about us but how often do brothers share intimate details about their sex lives with their sisters? I curse myself for being so negative; I was never this way with Carl and I hardly recognise myself anymore. I have become desperate without knowing what I'm desperate for. It's not that I hunger for a man in my life. I have Ellie and our life together is more than enough for me. My urge for you is about something else.

The music dies and someone rushes to put on another CD. *Don't You Want Me* by The Human League begins to blare from the stereo. The man sings desperately about the woman he wants and I cringe because he is speaking for me. I can't let myself be that person. I will enjoy myself at your party and not worry if I end up going home to my own bed when it's over.

At some point in the evening someone has cleared away all the discarded bottles and paper food plates because even though there are still over thirty people in the flat, it looks immaculate again. But it's not you giving in to your need for cleanliness. Instead of enjoying herself and mingling with the guests she has invited, your sister is rushing around clearing up spills and crumbs from the vast array of party snacks covering the dining table and darting to the kitchen with rubbish to throw away. She smiles every time she whizzes past me but doesn't bother starting another conversation.

It is when I escape to the kitchen, trying to dilute the cocktail of alcohol in my system with tap water, that I first meet Andrew. Thinking I am alone, I jump when I realise I have company.

"Sorry, didn't mean to scare you. I've just been having a cheeky fag," he says, closing the kitchen window.

I explain I needed a glass of water and he smiles, his hair flopping across his face. He fills a glass for me and lifts his own. "Well, cheers!" he says, clinking it against mine.

He introduces himself and asks how I know you. This evening I have become a master of concealing my frustration at repeatedly being asked a question I can only answer with half the truth. But it's not his fault so I smile and fill him in on some of the details while we perch on the granite worktop, taking it in turns to dip into a bowl of twiglets. As the bitter taste of each one lessens with each bite and becomes more palatable, I marvel at how it's possible to both love and hate something simultaneously.

"Disgusting, aren't they?" Andrew says, popping another twiglet into his mouth as if he's been thinking the same thought. "But I can't resist them. My wife can't stand them – she won't let me anywhere near her if I've had even one. I can brush my teeth three times and she still claims she can taste them! Personally I don't believe her for a second."

I nod. "My ex-husband was the same with Marmite. But I suppose now I'm free to enjoy it by the bucketful." I don't know whether I'm sad or happy about this but Andrew takes my comment for the latter and asks me about Carl. He smiles and pats my arm in all the right places as I speak and this is when I know without a doubt that Andrew is a decent man.

"There you are!" Chloe bursts into the kitchen with a tray full of empty glasses. Setting it on the table, she rushes over to Andrew and pulls him from the worktop. "Come on, you can help me light the candles but I'm warning you, it could take some time!"

"You should have listened to your mum," Andrew replies, fishing a cigarette lighter from his pocket. As the two of them set to work, laughing and playfully mocking each other, I feel like an intruder. Leaving them to it, I am disappointed at this wasted opportunity. If I'd known Andrew was your brother-in-law I would have grilled him for information about you.

It is gone midnight when a few people start to leave and someone turns the music down a notch. Still hopeful that more than a couple of words will pass between us tonight, I distract myself by joining groups of conversations wherever possible.

I am so busy listening to some of your teacher friends describe their worst moments in the classroom that I don't notice you creeping up beside me until you are pulling my arm, leading me away from the overcrowded sofa. I'm about to make an excuse to the group but nobody seems to notice me disappearing.

Minutes later you close the bedroom door and we are alone.

"Michael, I–"

"Shhhh!" You cover my mouth with your hand and push me back against the door. "I don't want to talk," you whisper, your warm breath tickling my ear. I'm about to protest but then your hands are fumbling under my dress. I want to stop you but can't. I want to be alone with you but not like this. Not right now. This doesn't feel right; we are only inches away from a room full of people who know nothing about us and through the chorus of voices outside I can hear Chloe. She's asking where you've got to and I panic. There is no lock on your bedroom door.

I'm sure you can hear her too because you freeze for a moment. When I begin to wriggle out of your grip you push my dress further up and fall to your knees, my thighs shaking as your tongue violently explores in between them. I protest again but seconds later you pull me to the floor. Each time you thrust into me my head slams against the bedroom door, shadows from people in the hallway dancing in the gap of light shining underneath the door. As I explode inside, I cannot respond when you whisper my name over and over. I enjoy the sound of it and grip you tightly, pulling you further into me. But then you lean into my ear, plaster your hand firmly across my mouth and tell me I'm a dirty whore over and over until you are spent.

Afterwards, we quickly gather our clothes and dress, neither of us mentioning the words you spoke. I remain silent when you explain our strategy for escaping the room unnoticed – you will leave the bedroom first then ten minutes later I will follow – but I don't believe it's possible to feel any cheaper than I do at this moment.

Once you have gone I have time to compose myself. I contemplate what has just happened and why I let it. But underneath all the disgust and shame I feel I am more excited than I ever remember feeling. Checking my clothes and smoothing down my hair, I have no idea what is meant to happen next with us, not just now but tomorrow and the day after that. I am scared. Not by the uncertainty but by the fact that I like this feeling.

Opening the door and scanning the hallway, I nearly jump out of my skin when Chloe emerges from the bathroom. There is no hiding where I have been and my brain quickly searches for a valid excuse to present to her. But I am spared further indignity when, rather than questioning me, she smiles and trots off to the living room.

Within seconds dread engulfs me. Chloe is probably looking for you to tell you I was in your bedroom. To her I am just your downstairs neighbour and have no right being there. No doubt you will blame me for not being careful enough. Prepared for the worst, I head back to the living room, the excitement of what we've just done long forgotten.

I try to find Chloe but she is nowhere to be seen and you are by the window taking it in turns to puff on a cigarette with Andrew. It surprises me that you're a social smoker but not that you're making him smoke it out of the window.

"Hi. Olivia, isn't it?" Chloe taps my shoulder. "Would you mind helping me in the kitchen? I've got to refill the snacks and it will be much quicker with two of us doing it." The serious expression etched on her face warns me this might be more than just a plea for help but I'm happy to explain what she saw so agree to help.

Alone in the kitchen, we fill snack bowls for several minutes before she speaks. "I'm a bit confused. What were you doing in my brother's bedroom?"

My chest constricts. I'm not expecting such a direct confrontation. I admire Chloe for being forthright but wish I wasn't the person it's directed at. There are only two ways I can respond to her question and neither of them is appealing. If I lie and say I was just snooping around then I will look like a complete freak. She will probably throw me out and I'll be humiliated when I've done nothing wrong. But if I tell the truth then you will despise me. Various scenarios flash through my head and I speak before I realise I've chosen an option.

"The thing is, Michael and I are more than just neighbours. We've been seeing each other for a few months."

Chloe stops pouring crisps onto a plate. "Oh, I see." She stares at me for a moment, a shadow of doubt flickering across her face. "He never said anything."

"Well, it's early days so we haven't told anyone yet. Actually, there's not much to tell really."

Chloe considers my words while she empties the rest of the crisps from her bag. "Sorry if I was a bit rude. I was just shocked to see someone coming out of my brother's bedroom. But now you've cleared everything up." She smiles at me and I want to believe it is genuine but lately my judgement has been way off-kilter.

Chloe whistles as we continue re-filling the snacks but she doesn't probe me further. And when I think about what you and I have just done, I am grateful for her tact. But as we leave the kitchen, Chloe turns back to me.

"I'm not sure why Michael's being so secretive. Just be careful."

She leaves me no time to respond. All I can do is watch as she floats off, skilfully balancing too many snack bowls on her arms.

CHAPTER SEVEN

"We're going to Brighton. This Friday. It's all booked."

I sit up straight, not sure I've heard correctly. My alarm clock flickers to five minutes past one and I rub sleep from my eyes, puzzled more by your statement than the time you're calling. I ask you to repeat what you've just said and you oblige but sigh impatiently.

"So, what do you think? I thought it would be a nice surprise."

Ellie has been ill and didn't stay with Carl last weekend so I haven't seen you since the party. What you are suggesting is a bolt out of the blue because I'm not sure we're even together. But I don't want to seem ungrateful by hesitating for too long so I tell you Brighton sounds like a great idea. Not only will we finally be somewhere together other than your flat but I've never been to Brighton. People are always full of praise for the town so I've always wanted to see for myself what all the fuss is about.

"It will be fun," you say. "Being away somewhere together." I'm still half-asleep but hearing your positivity about us perks me up. You start listing all the things we can do and I smile while I listen. This is what I've needed.

A draft of cold air rattles the window and I pull open the curtains to see I've left the window too far open. This is a bad habit I need to address, especially living in a ground floor flat in London.

"Listen, there's just one thing, though," you say. "This weekend is not going to be about sex. In fact, it's strictly off the menu. I want to prove to you...after the other night, I mean...that I'm not using you for sex."

"So what time shall I be ready on Friday?" I ask, already planning what to pack.

The minute we arrive in Brighton, I am in love with this seaside town. Here, a city buzz co-exists in harmony with the serenity of the sea and unlike in London, people don't rush around with a heavy and selfish urgency. Even on this damp day the air is fresh and I inhale deeply, finally able to draw something clean into my lungs. Being here makes me wonder why I still live in London. Ellie would love it here, a new place to explore. It saddens me that Carl and I haven't shown her more of the country.

We've arrived too early to check into our hotel so, leaving our luggage in the car, we head out towards the pier. It's not very warm for May and a light drizzle trickles from dull clouds. But nothing can spoil my excitement as we wander along the pier, the wooden planks creaking under our shoes. We buy tasteless coffee and sip it from polystyrene cups while we lean over the railing, mesmerized by the rolling grey sea.

"I love it here," you tell me, and there is a shine in your eyes I've never seen before. "What do *you* think of it?" Your eyes focus intently on me, showing me how important my opinion is. This is when I realise how much Brighton means to you.

"It's definitely something special," I say. "I know I've never been here before but somehow I feel really at home. Sort of...comfortable."

You smile and stroke my arm, nodding your approval.

"Careful!" I warn you, nudging your arm away. "We're behaving ourselves this weekend, remember?"

You break out in a chuckle and I realise this is the first time I've seen you relaxed other than when we're in your bedroom. Is it because we're away from London or just that I've never been out of your flat with you? But I brush all my analysis aside when you explain that as a child many of your family holidays were spent here. This place holds fond memories for you and as we leave the pier, the rain heavier now, I hope one day I will be able to say the same.

The hotel you've booked for us lies along the seafront and I'm surprised to find it's a Hilton hotel. As we check in, I offer to pay half but you shake your head. "No, this is my treat," you explain, forcing your credit card into the receptionist's hand before I can protest.

We are allocated a sea-view room on the third floor and this overrides the disappointment I feel when I step into the bland, soulless room. Its brown and cream colour scheme doesn't fit the character of Brighton but I can see why you've chosen this hotel. It's not so different from your flat. I wonder if eventually this is what the whole world will look like: colourless and lacking individuality. But one look out of the window at the endless ocean and the inside of the room becomes insignificant.

There is a chocolate brown fabric sofa by the window and I wonder if you'll sleep on that tonight rather than the king size bed that dominates the rest of the room. I can only assume you will stick to your rule for this weekend as you've managed to keep your distance so far. I'm pleased at the theory behind your plan and try to brush away the idea that's been nagging me since we arrived. Surely your attraction for me can't have died in the few days since your party?

"We should unpack our suitcases now," you suggest. "That way we don't have to worry about it later."

I agree with your idea and imagine in a few minutes we will be out of this room and exploring Brighton. I can't wait to walk up and down The Lanes and explore the quaint shops I've heard about. But you have other ideas. Unlike me, you carefully unfold all your t-shirts and hang them up neatly in the wardrobe. You space the hangers out evenly and if I hadn't seen you hang them up I'd assume you'd used a ruler to check the distances are all the same. Your underwear is still folded neatly and you keep it that way as you place it in the dresser draw. I don't say anything but keep looking at my watch. The shops are due to close soon so there's not much chance of heading out now.

Finally you put your suitcase at the back of the wardrobe, making sure it is lined up and facing forward. "Would it bother you if something wasn't placed neatly?" I ask, no longer able to keep silent while I watch your rituals.

You stare at me and your face drops but it doesn't take long to recover. You don't answer my question but suggest we go for a cocktail in the bar downstairs. It's not what I hoped to be doing but I need to get out of the room. It feels too small and watching you obsess over how your clothes are put away is making me uncomfortable.

"Remember my friends, Finn and Stephen, are meeting us after dinner?" you say, as we make our way downstairs. "They both live down here now so couldn't make it to my party but they're great people, my closest friends really." I keep quiet but this is no reminder. It's the first time you've ever mentioned their names to me.

Instantly I'm thrown headfirst into a panic. What if your friends dislike me? Undoubtedly they will judge me and try to discern whether or not I'm good enough for you. They'll probably compare me to all the ex-girlfriends you've had, deciding at once whether or not I match up to them, and I'm not confident under scrutiny. They've also known you for half of your life while I've been in it for a matter of months so how can I possibly compete with that?

And then I do the very thing I've been fighting since the break-up of my marriage; like an addict unable to shed old habits, I begin questioning my worth. Common sense tells me it doesn't matter what Finn and Stephen think of me; you have chosen to be here with me. But instead of enjoying my passion fruit mojito, when we're finally served at the bar, all I can do is over-stir it with the black plastic straw I've been given, and dread their imminent arrival. I'm starving but not even the thought of dinner in the restaurant next door comforts me. You must notice the state I'm in because you grab my hand from across the table and squeeze it gently.

As soon as Stephen and Finn walk through the door, I know with certainty that all my fears are groundless. You stand up and the three of you embrace, patting each other on the back. Once free from the tangle of limbs you have all become, Finn pulls me from my bar stool and wrestles me into a tight hug. Stephen's hug is more modest but he kisses my cheek and I am so grateful to both of them; their affability instantly lifts my mood.

I offer to buy the first round of drinks but my motives are not strictly altruistic. I reason that if there's anything any of you want to say about me without me hearing then you can get it out of the way at the beginning of the evening. That way we can all focus on enjoying our drinks and each other's company. But while the bartender pours whisky for the three of you and a white wine spritzer for me, I look back and you're all admiring Finn's new iPhone. Admonishing myself for making assumptions, I ask the bartender to make all your drinks doubles instead.

Finn and Stephen are full of appreciation when I bring the drinks back to the table and both fire friendly questions at me, enquiring about my job and Ellie. They have put me at ease and I open up about my life. When I begin to wonder if I'm talking too much I look over at you but you wink at me and sit back, relaxed again. I ask how you all met and it's not long before the three of you are immersed in hedonistic tales of your student days.

I watch you, engrossed in your conversation, once again taking pleasure from seeing you so at ease. The smile I saw earlier on the pier adorns your face and at this moment I wonder why I have doubted us.

By the time the bartender politely suggests we finish our drinks and ushers us out, we're all a bit tipsy. He locks up the double glass door the second we're out of the bar and standing in the hotel foyer.

"Let's go for a walk on the beach," Finn suggests, and we all shrug in agreement, none of us able to think of any reason not to.

The rough sea breeze swarms around us as we step outside and I mumble something about wishing I had my coat. Then I make my first mistake of the weekend. Finn rushes to my side and drapes his arm around me. "I'll keep you warm," he says and in our drunken state we stumble along, laughing at everything and nothing. Stephen laughs too and rolls his eyes to the sky. He must be used to Finn's antics when they've had a few drinks. I turn to you and your eyes burn into me but you say nothing, increasing your pace until you're in front of us, your hands tightly crammed into the pockets of your jeans. While Stephen runs to catch up with you, Finn and I lag behind, the weight of his arm slowing my pace.

Finn's gesture seems like the most natural thing in the world and as it's not sexual in any way it never occurs to me that you might be bothered by it. He is your friend so I assume you are comfortable for him to mess around in this way but as we crunch along the beach, our feet sinking into the glistening pebbles, it becomes clear you're unhappy. You don't say a word to me but to Finn you remain affable and warm, laughing at his jokes and patting him on the back whenever you get a chance. I begin to think maybe I've got things wrong but the more I listen to the two of you talk, the more your laughter seems forced. And then I know what you are doing. This is my punishment and it probably won't end here on the beach.

Somewhere along the walk back to the hotel Stephen and Finn vanish. I question you about their whereabouts and with your head down you shrug, mumbling that they must have gone home. Despite my earlier reservations about meeting up with them, I feel disappointed they've gone because now the night is silent, bringing with it a stinging loneliness even though you're right next to me. And although we've been out for a couple of hours, it is only now the air feels dark and heavy, even amongst the lights of all the hotels which stare at us as we walk back to the Hilton.

You stride ahead of me and I give up trying to bridge the gap and fall back to my usual pace. Why should I cater to your unreasonable mood? As I stare at your back, amazed someone our age can act this way, I formulate a plan. As soon as we get back to the hotel I will ask at reception for train times back to London. I'll skip breakfast in the morning and get the earliest train so I don't have to spend another minute with you. I even consider asking for a separate room for tonight but the money Leon owes me for my last review won't be in my account until next week so I just can't afford it. I'll wait until you're asleep before I pack; that way I can defer any awkward confrontation. But of course planning all this is the easy part. Breaking the news to you tomorrow won't be so straightforward, even if I'm fuelled by anger at the way you're behaving.

Our room is cold when we get back so I pull on my denim jacket and hunt for the thermostat. Instantly, a warm draft kicks in but I don't remove my jacket; I cannot relax here now.

When you disappear into the bathroom I feel a sense of relief; now at least I will get a few moments alone. It was never like this with Carl. I never had to question my role in his life or watch what I did when other people were around. This relationship is hard work, a job I'm not sure I'm able to do any longer. But when I remember how it feels to be touched by you I know whatever I do will be a struggle. If I leave in the morning I will only be haunted by your absence and each time your front door opens or closes will be a harsh reminder that I no longer share your bed. And a day will come when you come home with company, someone who isn't your sister.

I fill the kettle and pour two cups of coffee. You haven't asked for one but it's there if you want it. Perhaps I am making a peace offering, giving you one last chance to unwittingly change my mind about leaving tomorrow. But when you emerge from the bathroom, you glance at the steaming cup I've placed on the small table and head straight to the bed, clicking the bedside light off without a word.

Although I'm partly expecting this, nausea sweeps over me like a tidal wave and my resolve to leave tomorrow morning cements itself. Even though it's not huge, I'm grateful there's a sofa and, still fully dressed, I lie down, hoping sleep will come quickly.

But it is hours before tiredness overcomes me and even when it does, sleep taunts me, showing its face and then disappearing as quickly as it arrived. My arms and legs are folded awkwardly beneath my body and pins and needles make any movement painful. There is no clock visible to me and it's too dark to make out the hands on my watch but through the window, blackness keeps dawn at bay. Time seems to freeze and it feels as if morning will never surface.

Then I make my second mistake. Over on the bed your somnolent body forms an unnaturally still hump and for a moment I wonder if you're still breathing. I unfold myself from the sofa, ignoring the tingling pain in my limbs, and lie down beside you, close enough that I can feel your warm breath. What is it I've done to you? I want to shake you awake to demand an answer but know that would be futile; you will not be forced into saying or doing anything and that is as much as I know about you.

I am still fully clothed as I lay watching the sporadic rise and fall of your chest. At least the bed is comfortable; I might just manage to sleep now, however lightly. Whenever insomnia gets the better of me I try to imagine a pleasant situation I could be in and like an actor on stage I perform the chosen scenario until it blends into a dream. It's not often this fails so I try it now, picturing Valentine's evening with Carl and Ellie. Only this time I change the script. Carl doesn't leave and we end up talking. It is not small talk that passes between us but a life-changing dialogue. This time, as never before, I am able to accept his words of remorse and I hold him tightly against me, breathing in the sweet scent that has long been a comfort to me. There are only three characters in this play; you don't get to make an appearance.

Warm hands stroke my skin, starting at my neck and working their way down to my stomach. My body pulsates and tingles beneath the firm, cold touch. Massaged by a wet, smooth tongue, my nipples harden and I let out a soft moan. Then my eyes snap open.

Fully awake now, I am instantly aware of your weight pressing into me. Fumbling with the zip of my jeans, you yank them down and huff with the effort it takes to get them over my feet. I push your head and try to wriggle sideways but I make little progress; my arms are pinned to the bed. This is all wrong, cold and emotionless and I don't want you like this. I want to scream but nothing comes out. You let go of my hands but before I can push you away my mouth is smothered, my neck clasped in your tight grip. Your sweat-drenched body crushes me as you ram into me. You say something but I'm in too much pain to make out the words. Your hand slips from my mouth but the scream that is has stifled dies in my throat as I give in to you, burying my face in your shoulder and biting into your skin as together we become a frenzied animal.

Later, as the aroma of coffee and toast drifts into my nostrils, I stretch awake. A breakfast feast, which you're already tucking into, is spread out before me on the bed.

"I'm sorry," you say, placing your forkful of omelette back on your plate. I want to ask which part of yesterday you're sorry about but forcing you into a corner will only cause harm. And at least you are saying this much. "It's just such a disaster," you continue. "The whole weekend, I mean. I wanted to bring you here to prove to you that, you know, we can have something more than just..."

"It's okay," I assure you, stroking your arm. I don't need you to finish the sentence. In the cold, harsh light of day there is no way to express what we do, what we have. Besides this, you will never admit what's really bothering you about yesterday, so I let you lock it away and we carry on eating our breakfast as if nothing is wrong between us.

"Thanks," you say afterwards, pulling me into the crook of your arm. A large question mark hovers over whatever it is you're thanking me for but I choose to believe it's gratitude for not pushing you to tell the truth.

CHAPTER EIGHT

Over the next few months I try my best to make things work for us. I have already given up on my marriage so I'm determined to make this work. I trust my instincts and I know in your own way you're trying too. But as much as I wish for it and endeavour to make it happen, I still can't transform us into an even remotely normal couple. Your friends and sister know all about us but we still don't go out in public and you are oblivious to my protests. I give in and cling to the moments we are alone in your bedroom. These are the times when I no longer care whether we are normal.

It is as if I am gliding along on a bike, passing too quickly through time to notice anything around me, ignoring the rough bumps and holes that threaten to fling me to the ground. Occasionally I do fall but jump straight back on the saddle, covering my cuts with plasters that will too easily peel off. But still I cling to the times I can sail along, the scenery on either side of me just an irrelevant blur.

Ellie, as always, is the joy of my life and in my frequent moments of sadness my soul is lifted when I think how lucky I am to have her. Anything else can be taken from me or denied me, but nothing matters when I see my daughter's sparkling smile or hear her garbled screeching about the latest boy band she's in love with.

Just before the end of term, the secretary at Ellie's school calls and asks if I can meet with Ellie's teacher. She assures me there is nothing wrong but I'm thrown headfirst into a panic and once again can't focus at work. What if I have been too wrapped up in my own issues to notice that my daughter isn't coping at school? I know Ellie's mood has lifted significantly since Christmas but have I been too blind to see that she's not her normal self? The divorce and change of school is bound to have affected her and there's nobody to blame for that but me. Carl didn't want this, after all, and I could have chosen a different option. To make things worse, all my energy is being spent on worrying about us, instead of where it should be. But whatever is said today, I will accept it and deal with any problems.

When I arrive at the school, most of the children have already been picked up so it's quiet and almost a different place to what I'm used to when I drop Ellie off each morning. The urgency and bustle have faded away and even the twins running around the playground are quiet. Ellie has her art club today so I can't see her before I meet with her teacher.

A receptionist directs me to Ellie's classroom and I peer through the smudged glass window of the door. Ellie's teacher sits at her desk, her head buried in a pile of papers. I've only seen Miss Jackson a few times but she seems nice enough so I try to ignore the dread building in the pit of my stomach. She is probably in her mid-forties but still seems to have the passion of a new teacher and Ellie is always singing her praises.

She looks up and, noticing I'm at the door staring at her, waves me into the room.

"Mrs Taylor?" she asks, pushing her chair back to stand up. I cross to her and shake her hand. Her grasp is vigorous and confident and I don't know if this makes me feel better or worse. Her brief smile warms her stern face and she motions for me to take a seat in front of her desk.

"Sorry about the mess," she says, eyeing all the papers scattered across her desk. I don't say anything but offer a perfunctory smile. I am anxious to know why I've been called here and can't deal with small talk at the moment.

"Ellie is a wonderful girl," Miss Jackson says, her poker-straight, long, black hair swinging from side to side as she nods her head. "She's settled in really well and made a few friends, which is hard when you start a new school. I'm particularly impressed with her art work."

I should be happy hearing these words but my instinct tells me this meeting is more than just a report on how well my daughter has settled in. "It's not been easy for her since..." Somehow I can't manage to utter the words and my eyes flick to the floor. There are large clumps of dust underneath Miss Jackson's desk and I have a strong urge to blow them away.

"Yes, I understand," she says. "When we spoke at the beginning of the year I said I'd keep you updated but I've not been concerned at all until now." She hesitates. "The thing is, at lunchtime yesterday Ellie came to me in tears saying she's being bullied by a boy in the class."

My face drops and Miss Jackson rushes to reassure me. "Now, please don't panic, I've spoken to Charlie and he did admit he might have said a few nasty things to Ellie but he seemed very apologetic and assured me it won't happen again and he'll stay away from her in future. I've given him a detention and spoken to his parents so I think it's best to just draw a line under it now. I will, of course, be keeping an eye on both of them." She pauses for a moment, allowing me time to digest this information.

I don't quite know what I have been expecting but it isn't this. "I had no idea," I say, feeling like the worst kind of mother. "Ellie didn't say a word to me."

"You see that's why I've asked to see you," she says, shuffling forward in her chair. "When I told Ellie she must tell you what's happened she shook her head and burst into even more tears. It was hard to get much sense out of her but I gathered from what she said that she was too worried to tell you because she didn't want to upset you."

I need to get out of this room and find Ellie but Miss Jackson drones on, something about being concerned when children don't want to tell their parents things. I assure her I will talk to Ellie this evening and leave as quickly as I can.

"I'm sorry, Mum," Ellie says as I prepare her dinner. This evening I can only manage to throw some fish fingers in the oven and mash some potatoes but at least it's one of her favourites. She sits at the table drawing a picture of a lion, her yellow pencil flicking upwards with gentle strokes as she colours in its huge, fluffy mane.

I didn't mention what Miss Jackson told me until we got home because I couldn't bring myself to see the smile on her face, after having so much fun at art club, disappear. I am not angry with Ellie. I only blame myself for being so wrapped up in you that I failed to notice when my daughter needed my help. But worse than that is the fact my nine-year-old daughter felt the need to protect her mother. It should never be this way. I am the one who is meant to be the protector but instead I've been focusing on a man I've known for just a few months while Ellie has been dealing with her problems by herself. It is not enough that I feed and clothe her or that I'm here with her every day after school. It's not even enough that I play games with her, read with her or take her out when I can. Nothing I do is enough when I cannot even see when she really needs me.

I pull the tray of fish fingers out of the oven, a fierce wave of heat burning my face. "Ellie, you don't need to be sorry. I just want you to know that you can tell me anything, any time." I ruffle her hair and she smiles up at me before focusing once again on her lion.

Over dinner we talk and laugh so much I almost forget what's happened today. Afterwards, when I wash up, Ellie squirts Fairy liquid soap bubbles at me and I decide not to worry about the mess I'll have to clear up later. I'm still smiling when my mobile phone vibrates on the table. And I am dealt a crushing blow.

"Can you look after Ellie for me?"

"What?" You look as if I've asked you to give me your life savings.

"Please, Michael. Just for a few hours. She can come up to your flat if that's easier but please. I wouldn't ask if it wasn't important." I'm aware that I'm begging but this is no time for pride.

I immediately know you are searching for an excuse not to help me. "Erm... but my sister's popping round soon and we're going for a drink at The Boathouse. Anyway, I don't know if Ellie would feel comfortable here with us. What's happened, Olivia?"

"Forget it," I say, turning back to my open door, not surprised or hurt by your reaction. I am too numb to react in any way at all.

"Wait!" You call after me. "Bring her in. We'll look after her."

Back in my flat, Ellie doesn't make the slightest fuss when I hurriedly inform her you'll be looking after her for a few hours. All she's concerned about is whether or not you'll let her use your computer and if you might have some plain paper for her to draw on. She has filled up her latest sketch book and even the printer paper I've given her to use until I can go out and buy more has run out. "I'm sure that's fine," I assure her. "Just ask nicely."

"I promise!" she cries, skipping off to pack her rucksack. She doesn't know what's happened and I don't like keeping things from her but now isn't the time to explain. I will have to deal with that later.

The drive to Muswell Hill is interminable, my mind unable to grasp the news Carl has delivered. The North Circular is almost at a standstill when I finally edge onto it but I am grateful for this; it allows me time to think about what I will say when I get there. There is nothing I nor anyone else can do at this moment so I make the most of the time I have before I hear the words I already know.

Barbara Taylor lives in a beautiful, well-maintained Victorian terrace. Despite her age she can regularly be seen in the front or back gardens, digging up weeds or planting flowers. The only thing she trusts to delegate to someone else is mowing the immense front and back lawns and even this is done under her supervision. Although this isn't Carl's childhood home, she's lived here as long as I've known her and it's been a second home not only to Carl but to me as well. For the whole of our marriage I visited Barbara at least once a fortnight and I'm furious with myself for not making the effort to see her since Ellie and I moved out.

Opening the door, she hugs me with a ferocious strength. "It's been too long, Olivia," she admonishes, finally pulling away and fixing me with a hard stare. A stare I learnt long ago is a sign that she cares. The scent of lavender wafts over me as she ushers me into the house and I wonder if she realises how overpowering it is.

"I'm so sorry, Barbara. Carl just told me." I have so many questions for her I hardly know which one to begin with.

"We'll talk about that soon, Olivia. First, we'll have some tea."

"Okay, but I'm making it." I try to make my voice firm, expecting a protest.

She chuckles. "Fine with me. I like it strong, remember?"

I follow Barbara into the kitchen. She looks so healthy I think there must be some mistake; doctors are only human, after all, and nobody is infallible. As I wait for the kettle to boil I can't stop staring at her. Even though she's sixty-five, her dyed hair and virtually wrinkle-free skin make her look at least fifteen years younger. And as my eyes are fixed on her, my brain secretly trying to fathom how this happened, I notice she's doing exactly the same to me.

"I know what you're thinking," she says, as I join her at the kitchen table. "It doesn't matter how healthy you look or actually are, cancer can get any one of us." She taps the coaster in front of her, a reminder not to put the cups directly on the glass table.

Staring into my cup, I focus on a tiny black speck that's found its way into my tea, afraid I'll burst into tears if I look up and get caught in Barbara's stare. Crying is something I know will make Barbara uncomfortable.

When I do finally look up, she's not looking at me at all but is staring through the French doors to the garden. A wave of sadness washes over me to see her doing this. Barbara doesn't waste a second of her time and thinks daydreaming is a sin so to see her this way is devastating.

"Oh Barbara, I'm so sorry," I say, forcing her attention back to me. "How did you find out? How long have you known? Carl only just told me this evening."

She takes a delicate sip of tea and gently places her cup down. "Oh dear, I know it sounds awful but I found the lump months ago. I've just been too busy to—"

"Barbara!"

"I know, I know. But I've been doing so many things since I retired, there just hasn't been any time to see the doctor." She shifts her body so she's sideways to me and can more easily see into the beautifully landscaped garden. Her continuous avoidance of eye contact makes me realise what she's really afraid of. It's not so much the fact she's got breast cancer and everything that involves. It's more that she doesn't want to be helpless. Barbara is so used to being a strong matriarch that she abhors the thought of being looked after. That's what is making this even worse for her.

Reaching across the table to take her hands, I notice they are covered in prominent blue veins and translucent wrinkled skin, betraying her face by revealing her true age.

"So what happens next?" I ask.

"They'll operate and give me chemotherapy but they're worried it might have spread. I've got a scan on Tuesday so we'll see what that shows up." She looks at me. "Don't worry, Olivia, I'll be fine." She speaks as if this is nothing more than a flu bug we're talking about and I want to shake her, make her face this reality and tell her I'm here to help her through it. But I hold my frustration back.

"Are you scared?" I ask. I'm still clutching her hand but I'm the one who needs the comfort more than she does.

"I've had a good life, dear. I've accomplished many things. What's there to be scared of? And since William..." She leaves that thought unfinished. It's been over two years since Carl's father died and even though Barbara presents a show of strength to the world, I know how much she misses him.

Once we've finished our tea, Barbara takes me out to the garden to show me some roses she's recently planted. The brief window for talking about her illness has passed and now it's only a matter of time before she mentions the divorce. I try to distract her by enquiring about the plethora of plants and trees surrounding us but my knowledge of gardening and nature is limited so I quickly run out of questions.

"Carl brings Ellie over most Sundays, you know." Barbara sits down on the wooden bench at the end of her garden and waits for my response.

"I know, I'm sorry I haven't been over. It's just been difficult. Actually, I wasn't sure you'd want to see me." Now it's my turn to avoid eye contact and I stare at my shoes.

"Ridiculous!" She folds her arms and sighs, a deep frown creasing her forehead. "You're a daughter to me, Olivia, and you know it."

I remain standing and although I'm not looking at her I can feel Barbara's eyes boring into me. "I just assumed...because I left Carl—"

"With good reason."

I'm surprised by her words. They are not what I am expecting to hear. "I thought you'd hate me."

"My dear, Carl is my son, my only child and I love him more than the world but that doesn't mean I condone what he did. Nor do I blame you for not being able to forgive him. I'm sure it wasn't a decision you made lightly." She smiles up at me and once again I convince myself the doctors have got it all wrong.

I sit down next to her and rest my head on her hard shoulder. "I tried, Barbara, I really did. For Ellie's sake more than anything. But no matter what we did or where we went I just couldn't get that image out of my head." I choose my words carefully. As close as I am to Barbara, she's still Carl's mother so won't want to hear sordid details.

"I'd have supported you no matter what choice you made."

I wrap an arm around her solid frame. "Thank you."

We sit for a while longer, neither of us moving or speaking. But as we finally get up to head back into the house, Barbara says, "Thank *you*, Olivia."

It's only on the drive home, as I crawl back along the North Circular, replaying my conversation with Barbara, that I understand what she is thanking me for. Today in the end I was the helpless one and that meant she didn't have to be. For now, at least.

By the time I make it home it's past nine o'clock. Tapping on your door, I listen out for you but there is nothing but stark silence. I try again, this time louder, and eventually there is a pounding of feet flying down the stairs before your door springs open.

"Ellie's asleep in the spare room. Are you okay?" you ask, as we head upstairs. I explain what's happened and you put your arm around me and kiss the top of my head. "I'm sorry," is all you say, but it's enough and more than I have dared to expect.

In the lounge, Chloe is sprawled on the sofa reading a copy of *Cosmopolitan*. Her feet are stuffed into fluffy boot slippers and she wiggles them about as she reads. "I hope everything's okay, Olivia," she says, without looking up from her magazine. There is an empty bottle of wine on the coffee table in front of her and two glasses, both containing remnants of wine. "It's been great having Ellie here," she continues. "I think she tired herself out so we thought she could do with a nap. And we weren't sure what time you'd be back."

"Thanks," I reply, not even sure I mean it. When I first met Chloe at your birthday party she gave me the strong impression I'm not her favourite person and even on the few occasions I've met her since she treats me with disdain, injecting snide comments into our conversations at every opportunity. I can't think of any reason for her to dislike me so intensely other than the fact that I'm seeing you. Perhaps she thinks I'm not good enough for you or maybe she's friends with one of your exes. But whatever it is, I wish she would just give me a chance. You don't seem to notice; either that or you're ignoring what is right in front of you.

You offer me a coffee but all I want to do is get Ellie home and tell her what's happening to her grandmother. They're so close I know she'll be devastated so for the second time today I will have to choose my words with care.

Ellie is drowsy as I pack up her rucksack and take her downstairs. I tell her I'll make her a hot chocolate before bed as a special treat and she just shrugs her shoulders, plonking herself down on the sofa. I'm surprised she's not asking where I've been.

It takes me a while to hunt down the packet of tiny marshmallow pieces Ellie loves to have in her hot chocolate, but when I eventually bring in our steaming mugs, she's still sitting in the same position on the sofa, her arms folded on her lap.

"Are you okay, Pumpkin?" I ask as she takes her drink.

"Yeah. Just really tired."

I look at her and, remembering the bullying incident, want to ask if she's sure. But there are dark shadows under her eyes and I don't want to push her so have to believe she's okay.

"Did you have a nice time with Michael and Chloe?" I ask instead.

She shrugs. "It was okay," she says, offering nothing further.

"What did you do?"

Ellie shrugs again. "Computer games. Drawing." She sips some of her drink and shuts down completely, looking even more tired than she did a few seconds ago. Because of this I make up my mind not to tell Ellie about Barbara tonight. Instead I offer a vague explanation of having to help her dad with something. I don't know what I will say if she asks what but she's so overcome with fatigue that all she does is nod. I tell myself she'll be fine in the morning and ready to face the news with her usual strength of character.

But as I put Ellie to bed and finally make it into my own, I cannot help but worry about her silence.

CHAPTER NINE

For the next few weeks, I am fuelled with panic and anxiety. I worry about Barbara's cancer, about Ellie and about how Carl is coping. Ellie copes well with the news but perhaps this is due more to childhood naivety than anything else. Every weekend Carl takes her to see Barbara and these visits seem to help all three of them. While they confront Barbara's illness head-on, I bury my head in the sand and hope it will go away. Barbara helps me do this because when I call her every week she refuses to mention anything to do with cancer. But even through the most trying of times there is usually a sliver of light to cling to and surprisingly you bring this light to me.

You don't speak much about what's happening to Barbara but squeeze my hand whenever I go quiet. And out of the blue you announce that every Friday night should be date night for us. At first I am sceptical; I've always considered the idea of a couple setting aside a specific time to do something nice together to be solely for unsatisfied married couples or those needing to spice up their sex lives. We fit into neither of these categories and we implement it solely so that for at least a few hours we are not alone in private together, confined to the bedroom.

You devise a plan that every Friday evening we will go for a meal at a different restaurant and no matter how much we like a particular place we can't revisit it until we've at least attempted to eat in every decent restaurant within commutable distance from us. We alternate who chooses the restaurant each week and have to keep it a surprise until the last moment. This means that after only a few weeks we've covered the whole of Putney so have to venture further afield.

When it's my turn one Friday, I earnestly search Google, poring through restaurant reviews of Tapas bars before settling on Lola Rojo. I pick it for its name more than anything else. It sounds more like the name of a glamorous 1950s actress than a restaurant but it is enough to convince me this should be our destination tonight.

London is vibrant this evening; it's about that time when tired rush hour commuters gradually morph into carefree revellers trying their hardest to leave the office behind. Although I will always prefer a night at home to an evening in a bar or pub, tonight I am glad to be out and part of the buzz of the city.

Even catching the bus to Fulham isn't the chore that journeys on London transport usually are. There are no seats free so we stand against the window and I lean backwards into your chest for support. Wrapping your arms around me, you breathe in the coconut scent of my hair and exhale slowly.

Three teenage boys sitting near us hurl insults at each other, each one getting more heated as the venomous words shoot back and forth from their snarling mouths. Scowls cross their faces but quickly disappear as the boys erupt into cackles, all invectives forgotten as they debate whether to get a Burger King or a kebab.

A tall middle-aged man in a pin-striped suit peers over his *Metro* at us and I wonder what assumptions he is making. Does he think we are a couple in a loving relationship? Married perhaps? We are both at that age where strangers probably assume we are married or at least on a second chance at love. From his position there is no way he can tell your hand is sliding down my denim skirt or that you have grown hard against me. And nobody on the bus would ever guess the words you're whispering in my ear. They are far from 'sweet nothings'.

There are only a few tables occupied at Lola Roja when we arrive and after scanning the vast red room you ask the waitress for a seat in the corner. It's disconcertingly close to the toilets but you don't seem bothered. It's the table that will give us the most privacy. In heavily accented English, the waitress recommends we try a jug of Sangria and you nod enthusiastically, not even checking with me first. As she dashes off to the bar, you scan the menu for a moment before closing it and telling me to choose dishes for both of us.

"Tapas should be shared," you say, when I give you a quizzical look. "And I think you should choose for us." You fix a hard stare on me.

"But I don't know what you want," I protest. "Why don't we choose them together?" I sound like a whining child and you scowl at me, as if I am ruining something important.

"Because it's your night, remember? You chose the restaurant this time so you should pick the food. Is it that much of a big deal?" You raise your eyebrows, challenging me to argue.

Although I think your suggestion is pointless, it's not worth fighting about. "Fine. But don't blame me if you don't like it."

A smug smile spreads across your face; once again you are aware that you are the one in control. And not for the first time this all feels like too much hard work and I wonder what I'm doing. Even though you've been making an effort lately it's all too easy for us to slip back into our roles.

When the food arrives, you tuck in, clearly pleased with my selection. "It's delicious," you say through mouthfuls of chorizo. "Well done, good choice!" I wonder if you'll offer me a gold star next. But you're right, all the dishes are lovely and your mood has elevated since we first arrived. As I watch you eat I feel sad that I felt so negative earlier. Perhaps I'm being too quick to walk away without giving things a chance. Maybe I can learn to accept we have a complicated relationship. It's nothing like my marriage to Carl but how can I use that as a yard stick when we're on the brink of divorce?

The waitress returns to gather up our plates and even though our stomachs are bursting, we order key lime cheesecake and wash it down with the remaining sangria. Through mouthfuls of dessert you tell me about the hectic day you've had at school and admit you might be ready to pack it all in. "But what would you do instead?" I ask, surprised you feel this way but happy you're finally opening up about it.

"I don't know. Work in a shop? Anything not to have to listen to anymore whining or arguing from hormonal kids."

"You'd miss it," I say, only half believing my own words.

You look thoughtful for a moment and wipe condensation from your glass. "No, I really don't think I would."

Just as I'm trying to think of some comforting words, you lean forward and whisper, "Go to the toilets. And take off your underwear."

With such an abrupt change of topic, I'm not sure I've heard you correctly. "What?"

"You heard me. Go to the toilets and take off your underwear. Then come back."

I quickly scan the restaurant; it's a lot busier than when we arrived and even in our corner we're still highly visible to both staff and customers.

"Now? But why?"

You shrug. "I just like the thought of it. What's the matter? Nobody will know what we're doing. And just the thought of it's really turning me on. See." You lean further forward and pull my arm under the table, guiding it to the front of your jeans, as if showing me evidence will convince me to do what you're asking.

Logic and reason fight with desire in my brain and nearly win control. I'm not a prude but neither am I confident or adventurous enough to do what you're asking. I look at you and I'm more afraid of not granting your wish. It's not that I think you'll be angry, I just don't know what there will be for us if I don't comply. So without a word I head off to the ladies' toilets, my cheeks heating up as I pass a waiter who's rushing to someone's table with a credit card terminal. There is no way he can know what I'm up to but I feel self-conscious nonetheless. Before I push through the door I turn back to look at the other diners. Quite a few of them are couples and I wonder how many of them would do something like this. How many would need to?

This evening is one of those rare occasions when I've opted to wear a skirt in place of my usual jeans and perhaps that's what has given you this idea in the first place. I will be more open to exposure in a skirt. I look down at my legs; at least my skirt reaches to my knees so maybe it won't be that bad. But then I notice the buttons leading all the way from the waist to the hem; they can pop apart as easily as tissue tearing.

I don't formulate a decision about what I do next; it's as if my hands begin to move without waiting for permission. With a nervous chuckle, I pull down my pink lace knickers and whip them off, shoving them into the bottom of my bag. I feel exhilarated, as if I am bursting free from something, breaking out of restraints that have held me captive for far too long. A quick glance in the smudged mirror confirms that my cheeks have returned to their usual milky complexion and I leave the toilets, eager to see how excited you are that I've done what you wanted.

But when I reach our table you are sitting sideways, facing away from me and speaking in hushed tones on your mobile phone. Deep lines crease your forehead as you press it further against your ear. You're not saying a lot, just listening and drawing invisible circles on the table with your finger. You don't even look up as I sit down so I know whatever you're being told is not good news.

The waitress brings over a small leather wallet with our bill tucked inside and after a quick glance at you, she slides it in front of me with a smirk on her face. I glance at the bill and dig in my purse for my credit card. "I'll be back with the machine," she says, and wanders off, getting side-tracked by another customer on her way to the till.

"We have to leave," you say, as you finally cut off the phone call.

"What's happened?

"I'll explain on the way home but we have to go now." You stand up and wrestle with the sleeves of your jacket. "Come on!"

I remind you we haven't paid the bill yet but you're too flustered to register what I'm saying.

"I'll wait for you outside," you say, when the waitress returns. "Hurry, okay?"

Outside the sun is only just beginning its descent so the air is still pleasantly warm. People are overflowing from pubs, drinks in their hands and full of animated conversation. There are rare moments in London, when surrounded by bars and restaurants and engulfed by warm summer air, it's almost possible to forget you're in a polluted concrete jungle. Laughter mingles with booming voices, filling the atmosphere with anticipation and excitement and I have trouble digesting the unusual situation we now seem to be in.

Pacing back and forth as we wait for the bus, you still don't explain what's happened, even though I've tried several times to prompt you for information.

"For fuck's sake," you say every time a large vehicle that isn't our bus rounds the corner. We've been waiting for at least fifteen minutes and even I'm beginning to lose my patience now.

You ponder whether it might be better to walk and I'm about to agree with you, because at least then we will be doing something, when finally the seventy-four bus turns the corner and crawls towards us.

Once we're seated I ask you again what's happened.

"My sister's gone missing." You whip your phone from your pocket and begin typing a text message.

"What? How? What's happened?" I don't know what I've been expecting to hear but it definitely isn't this.

And then comes another surprise. "Stupid bitch. She does this all the time," you say, still focused on the message you're writing. "She's just doing it for attention. I don't even know why I'm bothering with it. D'you know what she did last year?" You look up from your phone. "She told Andrew she was taking their dog for a walk one evening and she disappeared for three days! Eventually someone found her wandering around Hammersmith, drunk out of her skull. We still don't know where she'd been or what she was doing."

"Was she okay? What about the poor dog?" I ask.

"She didn't even bloody take him! Andrew was in the shower when she left so he didn't realise the dog was still there. My sister was fine, it's Andrew I feel sorry for."

I slide closer to you and place my hand on your arm. "I thought you two were really close?"

"We are. She just does these stupid, selfish things sometimes without a thought for anyone else. I know she's my sister but fuck knows why Andrew married her." You finish typing your message and stare at your phone.

"So what happened tonight?" I ask.

With your eyes still glued to your mobile, you tell me Chloe went out after work yesterday with some friends. She didn't let Andrew know her plans so when she didn't come home from work he started to panic. Eventually he managed to track down a friend of hers who, rather embarrassed, explained that Chloe was with her in Leicester Square and they were in the Cheers bar. Andrew didn't bother to ask to speak to Chloe. He thought he'd save the lecture for when she got home but then Chloe didn't turn up for work and nobody has seen or heard from her since.

It's not with anxiety that you recount the details of your sister's disappearance. You are more annoyed than anything else. "Aren't you worried?" I ask.

"I'm just so fed up with her doing things like this. She causes my parents so much grief. She'll be fine, just hiding out somewhere and then suddenly she'll waltz through the door as if nothing's happened."

"But what if you're wrong? Shouldn't we do something?" As soon as I've said this I know it's not what you want to hear.

Your face hardens and your eyes become slits. "D'you know what? It's not really anything to do with you, it's private family business. I shouldn't have told you all this. Just forget it."

Your words sting me like a slap in the face and I pull my arm away, turning to the window so you can't see the river of tears building in my eyes. But even worse than what you've said is the fact I'm now sickened and humiliated that I'm sitting here with no underwear on. To distract my tears from leaking out, I formulate a plan of what I'll do when I get home: I'll make myself a hot chocolate, curl up on the sofa in my dressing gown and watch a film that doesn't have a happy ending. I'm starting to believe these are the only endings that exist.

An eternity of uncomfortable silence passes before we reach our stop. You leap off the bus, striding ahead of me until you become a tiny dot and then disappear altogether. So I make my way home alone, noticing how quickly the atmosphere in London can change. It's now eerily quiet; a far cry from earlier in Fulham.

At home I can't bear to think of all that's happened this evening so I stare at the television, not even aware of what programme is on, and shut out all thoughts of you. When the phone rings I assume it's you and ignore it, counting the pairs of beeps in my head. By the time I've reached nine, I've had enough of the monotonous chime and grab the phone, snarling a surly greeting into the mouthpiece.

But it is Carl's voice that drifts into my ear, not yours. I soften as he explains he's calling because Ellie misses me and adds sheepishly that he does too. I don't remember the last time I've been so pleased to hear from Carl and we talk until past midnight, like two old friends who've been distant for a while but are now just catching up on each other's lives. I marvel at the ease with which we can still communicate. It's the opposite of how you and I respond to each other, showing me how ludicrous it is to persist in trying to make a go of things with you. Even though I've lost Carl, or given him up as he prefers to think of it, surely I am worth more than this?

As is all too often the case since I let you into my life, I have ridden a rollercoaster today and as I head to bed, switching the lights off and closing my bedroom door on an evening I want to forget, I am torn between love and hatred.

Thinking this reminds me of eating Twiglets with Andrew on the night of your party and I wonder how he is. He must be going out of his mind worrying about Chloe and when I consider this it starts to make sense why you're so angry with her. Somehow I manage to sleep, although it is fitful and the oppressive silence of my empty flat makes me anxious for morning to arrive.

A loud pounding against my front door wakens me and I'm frozen, unable to move as I listen out for more thuds. A few seconds of silence pass so I relax a bit and try to remember exactly what I might have been dreaming about that involves all this noise. But I can't recall even having a dream. Then the thud comes again, louder this time. Living in a ground floor flat in London, the threat of a break-in is never far from my mind but still I'm not prepared for this situation. There is nothing in my bedroom I can use to fend off an attacker; I am completely vulnerable.

I reach for the phone, not quite sure who to call when I hear your voice accompany another bang on my door. "Livia!" you shout and pound again.

Grabbing my dressing gown, it occurs to me I'd probably be better off if it was an intruder making all this commotion. "What the hell?" I say, opening the door just enough to check it's actually you.

"Lemme in," you slur, leaning against my door. If I open it any further you will topple to the floor.

Even though I'm on the other side of my door I can smell the alcohol streaming from your pores. "You're drunk, Michael. Just go to bed."

"No! Lemme in!" Those seem to be the only words in your vocabulary at the moment and it's too late to stand arguing at the door so I foolishly open it wider and step aside. You stagger in, looking around as if you're expecting to find someone else here.

Strong coffee seems like a good idea so while you collapse onto the sofa I boil the kettle, furious with you for doing this. Furious with you for everything you do.

"I'm really sorry," you say as I pass you a mug. Somehow you've managed to pull yourself together in the few minutes it's taken me to make the coffee. You crack your mug down on the table and oblivious to you, coffee sloshes over the top of it.

I sit on the floor across from you, pulling my knees up to my chin. "What exactly are you doing here, Michael? It's nearly three in the morning."

"Sorry," you say again, as if the word has the power to erase all your actions.

"What exactly is it you're sorry about? What do you want from me?"

There seems to be nothing you can say to this, clearly you don't even know the answer yourself. After a while you join me on the floor, leaving your coffee untouched. "It's all just a big mess and I'm really sorry, Livia."

I want to explain that empty apologies don't mean anything but one look at your vacant expression tells me any attempt at conversation is futile at the moment.

"Less juss put this awful day behind us, eh?" Your clammy hand reaches for me and is halfway up my leg before

I slap it away. Then your face lunges towards mine, close enough that I can smell the sour mix of gin and whisky on your breath.

Despite the state you're in, electricity still surges through me when your lips eventually find mine and this feeling is no less powerful than any other time you've touched me. My mind is repulsed by the stale mixture of alcohol I can taste on your mouth but every other part of me is desperate to have you again, even in this state. Not even the sweat pouring from your body can stem the urgency with which I need you.

"The bedroom," you say, wrenching me up as if time is running out. And I eagerly follow because I know what awaits me.

Surprisingly, only seconds after we've climbed into bed you turn onto your side and are asleep before I can offer a word of protest. Anger and frustration well up inside me but it's not directed at you. I'm the one who has let you back into my bed. Carl says I always try to see the good in people and that's what I do now. This could be a positive thing. Spending the night together with no sex. So with this thought in mind, I snuggle into your back and wait for sleep to catch me.

My bedroom curtains are dark and thick, blocking out the glow from the streetlight behind my garden, so when I'm abruptly woken up by rustling paper it takes me several seconds to make out any shapes in the room and work out the source of the noise.

Instead of lying next to me in bed, you are sitting on the leather chair in the corner of the room. The glow from your mobile phone lights up the pages of the newspaper you're reading. It isn't even morning yet but I don't bother asking what you're doing up so early.

"Come over here," you whisper and, hypnotised, I follow your command and climb out of bed. A few hours' sleep seems to have sobered you up and you seem alert and focused, watching me intently. I'm only wearing a black t-shirt that barely covers me and goose bumps pop up on my arms and legs as I pad over to you.

When I reach the chair, I stand still in front of you for a few seconds, wondering and waiting. It is not long before your cold hands slide down my body. Although this is what I longed for last night, it irks me that everything we do is done according to your schedule, never mine. I consider feigning tiredness and slipping back into bed but all my willpower evaporates when you pull me closer and lift my t-shirt over my head.

"Come with me," you say, and before I have a chance to question you, you are pulling me through the flat. Somewhere along the way you discard your boxer shorts so by the time we're in the kitchen we are both naked. I don't feel conscious though; partly because it's so dark but mainly because excitement and anticipation seep through me and overshadow everything else.

"Where's the key?" you whisper, nodding towards the patio doors. There is something about the still of the night that urges people to whisper even when there's nobody around to hear them.

"Why?" I ask, even though I'm already lifting the key from its hook by the fridge.

"I want you outside," you reply, unlocking the door and sliding it open.

"No, Michael," I begin, but my whispered plea goes unheard as you pull me out into the darkness and drizzle.

Then I am flat against the side of the house, you ramming into me while rain spits down on us. "Someone might see us," I say, but you don't reply. Instead you smile and force yourself further into me.

The next morning while I'm still lying in bed, not yet ready to face the day, you bring me a mug of strong, sweet coffee. You climb back into bed and cuddle up to me, wrapping yourself around me so tightly I don't know where my body ends and yours begins. "This feels nice, doesn't it?" you say. "I wish we could stay in this moment."

I look at the clock and see it's only half past eight. "Well, we can, can't we? At least for a bit longer."

You sigh heavily and explain your car is booked in for a service in an hour's time. I'm disappointed we can't spend more of the morning together and there are things we need to talk about but I won't push you. Today you are the man I love being around.

After you've gone I lie in for a couple of hours, neither sleeping nor fully awake. It's only when I get up to search for my t-shirt that I notice the newspaper you've left on the chair. It is one of the free weekly local ones but something about its presence here is odd. I never bother to read these papers when they're shoved through my door and I put them straight in the recycling bin. You couldn't have got it from there, though, because they are emptied on a Friday morning. So it must be yours, even though I don't remember you having it when you pounded on my door.

Then like a punch to my gut, horror hits me when I pick it up and focus on the page you were reading. It is the classified ads and you have circled three of them in red pen. And the words of these faceless women offering their services taunt and mock me while I stand here, numb and foolish.

CHAPTER TEN

It is the middle of summer when I start to feel cleansed, as if I've stood under a waterfall and had all traces of you vigorously washed away. In the aftermath of my separation from Carl I have learnt to put the past behind me and wipe the slate clean, no matter how painful it is, even if the past I'm escaping from is recent. I cling to small mercies like the fact I never told Ellie or Carl about us. After all, what was there that was appropriate to tell?

I don't answer the phone anymore without checking to see who is calling. It's nearly always you so I let it ring, hoping each time will be the last time you bother trying. We are still neighbours but I've become skilled at evading you and every morning I wait until I hear you leave before venturing out. When I come home from work I walk on the opposite pavement, scanning the street so I can carry on past our building if I have to. All of this is only a slight inconvenience and nothing compared to what I will have to deal with if we cross paths. There is every chance it will happen eventually but this doesn't stop me trying my best to prevent it. Thankfully you don't knock on my door. Perhaps it is shame that keeps you away.

Because Ellie has finished school for the summer, Leon is kind enough to let me work from home as much as possible. But when going into the office or attending a screening is essential, Carl gladly takes Ellie. It means several days spent at his office but she insists she enjoys it. As long as she can sit and draw she is happy.

One morning at work I catch Myrah staring at me, a lopsided smile on her face. "Olivia," she says. "You've been single for a while now. I think it's time you met someone nice." My face crumples. This is the last thing I am expecting to hear her say. Seeing my anxiety, she attempts a softer approach. "I just mean you're still young and you're beautiful. You shouldn't be alone."

Looking at Myrah's grave expression, I can see she has given this a lot of thought. She's thirty-eight and has been married for eighteen years so to her being without a partner is unfathomable. "I'm not actually alone, though, Myrah," I tell her. "I have Ellie."

Heading to the kitchen to make us both a cup of tea, I hope that when I come back she'll have forgotten what we were talking about. Apart from Myrah and me, the office is empty today. Leon is out meeting with prospective advertisers and Sophie is at home with a migraine so there's little to distract Myrah from grilling me.

But I couldn't be more wrong because when I return with our drinks, Myrah informs me she has found someone perfect for me. He is a dentist called Jonathan, who works with her husband, and after inviting him for dinner last night it dawned on her what a good match he and I would make. She insists she doesn't normally try and set people up but she has a strong gut feeling about this. I consider telling her about you and how I'm quite happy to be out of a relationship at the moment but after spending so many weeks shutting you out, I refuse to let you creep back in. And Myrah will want details I'm not able to share. So I keep quiet and listen to her gushing about the dentist and how as it is Friday we should meet for a drink tonight. Put on the spot like this, I can't construct a valid excuse not to meet up with him so I reluctantly agree. At least then for the rest of the day Myrah will keep quiet so I can get some work done before Leon returns. I don't want him thinking I'm slacking. I've already let him down by bringing my personal issues to the office so I have to prove I take my work – his business – seriously.

By six o'clock the rain is hammering down at an odd sideways angle so, despite the fact I'm clutching a large umbrella, by the time I make it to The Anchor and Hope pub on The Cut I look as if I've been swimming in the Thames. No part of me wants to be here but the alternative is listening to Myrah moan about my lack of a love life for the next few weeks. Meeting her dentist friend is the lesser of two evils so I huddle in the doorway and wait.

It didn't occur to me to ask Myrah what Jonathan looks like so he could be any one of the smartly dressed men heading in this direction. I wonder if he's waiting inside even though it's been arranged we'll meet outside the pub. But I can't bring myself to walk in there alone; especially when I don't even know the person I'm meeting. I decide to give him five more minutes before I give up and head to Waterloo station. It doesn't bode well for a first meeting that I don't want to wait more than ten minutes.

Across the street another man is waiting to cross the road. He is tall and slim, almost swamped in his navy blue suit and wears glasses that even from this distance I can see are speckled with rain drops. There is not much to distinguish him from any of the other men I've seen striding along since I've been standing here but somehow I know this is Jonathan. His hair is short and neat, almost the same chestnut colour as my own.

I don't know what I'm supposed to feel as he draws closer, a nervous smile appearing on his face. He is neither attractive nor unattractive; he is just a man making his way towards me. Should I be nervous? Excited? I feel neither of these emotions. Instead I struggle to shut out thoughts of you and how strange it feels to be meeting another man for a drink.

Jonathan holds out his hand to me as if I'm a business acquaintance. Clearly he's as new to this as I am so at least we have that in common. His hand is ice-cold and wet and he rushes to hold the door open for me. Following him inside, I wonder what I can possibly talk to a dentist about. We must live in different worlds.

"So...Myrah forced you to come this evening, didn't she?" Jonathan asks this question without any hint of annoyance so I admit the truth. We sit by the window with gin and tonics in front of us and I try not to get distracted by the rain slamming against the glass behind Jonathan's head.

"But that doesn't mean I want to leave," I add, and this is also true. I'm not interested in starting any sort of relationship with him but I feel at ease sitting here and home seems a long way away. There is something comforting about being safely cocooned here in the pub while the rain pounds down outside.

After a short time I almost forget that Jonathan and I have only just met and I sit happily listening to him talk about his work and his life. While he talks he removes his glasses and wipes smudges from them with a small cloth he pulls from his pocket. It's refreshing to hear someone speaking so openly. Having a detailed and personal conversation is such a rare opportunity these days. Even when my phone beeps three times in a row, I ignore it and carry on sipping my gin and tonic while Jonathan regales me with anecdotes about his patients.

"I think I should get something out of the way before you start to fall for me," he says, with a grin. "I don't know exactly what Myrah's told you but I'm divorced. And I have three children I never see because my ex has moved to Scotland. I do try to get up there when I can but it's...you know...difficult." He sips his drink. "But there's more. Even though I might look thirty, I'm actually forty-two."

We both laugh but in this moment I feel sorry for Jonathan. Although he's made light of his circumstances it must have taken a lot for him to tell me this so soon. He searches my face, probably looking for any signs I've been put off by what he's said, but his words have no effect on me. He could have told me that he has three wives all living under the same roof and it wouldn't make any difference because he's not you.

Only then do I see the unfairness of being here, talking, drinking and laughing with this seemingly decent man when I have no intention of taking anything further. But I can't insult him by walking out now. Besides, he's Myrah's friend so I need to be kind to him. To assuage my guilt I offer to buy Jonathan another drink even though neither one of us has emptied our glass. It only occurs to me when he accepts my offer with an eager smile that my gesture is probably raising his expectations even more.

While I'm being served at the bar I remember the text messages I haven't yet checked and dig around in my bag for my phone. A hot flush comes over me when I see your name on the screen. Underneath it are just three words. *I miss you.* The other two texts say more or less the same thing. Throwing my phone back in my bag, I quickly grab the drinks and head back to Jonathan.

"Are you okay?" he asks, small frown lines appearing across his forehead. He finally stops wiping his glasses and puts the cloth back in his pocket. I wonder if this is something he does to ease his nerves.

I'm about to tell him I'm fine but the simple warmth of his question is an invitation and without planning to, or even knowing why I'm doing it, I tell Jonathan everything that has led me to be sitting in the pub with him this evening. It's easy to open up to someone when there is no fear of being judged. I barely pause for breath and the whole time I speak he listens intently, leaning forward, sympathy etched onto his face.

But when I finish explaining what happened the last time I saw you, doubts creep in about why I am disclosing something so private. Hearing my own words spoken out loud brings it all back to life and despite many weeks having passed since I saw you, it's as raw as it was that morning I found the newspaper. Jonathan grabs my hand but says nothing. He doesn't have to; I can tell what he is thinking from the look on his face.

Closing time arrives and we follow the last few stragglers out into the damp night. In the last few hours I've learnt more about Jonathan than I will ever know about you and as he waves down a taxi for me I thank him and hug him tightly, wishing I could feel something more for him. "You will always have a friend," he says, as he hands a twenty-pound note to the driver.

"No, I'm paying," I say, but it's too late. The taxi rumbles off, leaving Jonathan standing by the kerb, watching. Only as we disappear from view do I stop to consider how he is getting home himself.

Several times in the taxi my mobile phone beeps and each time I check it the same message glares back at me. *I miss you.* More than once I want to reply but instead I bury my phone in the bottom of my bag. You are a man I don't know and can't trust. I'm not even sure what it is I can't trust but there may as well be a label carved into your flesh because I won't be able to look at you without my stomach sinking.

Habit forces me to look up at your lounge window as the taxi pulls up to our building and the open curtains tell me straight away you're not home. If it's disappointment I feel, I quickly push it aside. I remind myself that it's not meant to be this hard. Carl wasn't and I don't think Jonathan would be either. But neither of them are you.

I don't bother to flick the hall light switch so it's only when a passing car briefly illuminates the hallway that I notice the white envelope taped to my flat door, my name scrawled across it in red pen. Ripping it open before I've even put my key in the lock, I quickly decipher the spidery writing. And once I have, something changes.

Sweat coats my palm as I clasp the phone in my hand, the dial tone perforating my ear drum as I listen and wait. Your mobile rings for only a few seconds but it feels more like hours as I stand here, too nervous to sit and half wondering if I should hang up before it's too late. Each passing moment you don't answer offers me an escape route, but I remain motionless, listening, my heart ready to pause if you answer. I give it more time; surely by now you should have heard your phone ringing? I picture you staring at my name on the screen, a smug smile on your face because you know what it's taken for me to make this call. But perhaps I am being unfair and misjudging you again; your mobile could just as easily be in your pocket, the ring tone drowned out by whatever noise surrounds you. Either way, I know I have given it enough time so I finally hang up, once again deflated by the conflicting messages you send me.

I don't want to think the worst of you, that you are deliberately avoiding my call to torture me, but in the short time I've known you nothing you've said or done outside the bedroom encourages me to be more positive.

As soon as I replace the phone back in its charging stand it rings and relief floods through me as I rush to answer it. But it is Myrah, screeching down the phone at me, excitement in her voice as she urges me to tell her how the evening went.

"Well?" she asks, finally pausing for breath when she realises I haven't spoken yet.

"Myrah, he's really nice. I just –"

She cuts me off. "Not attracted to him? I understand. Still, it's a shame. You know, attraction can grow, Olivia. Love at first sight is just a myth."

I want to explain the idea of attraction didn't even surface this evening and that I could find no fault with Jonathan. I want to tell her he seems a decent, caring and emotionally intelligent man. But if I say all this then she will never understand.

"Well, it's a shame we can't control who we are or aren't attracted to," I say to Myrah, ignoring her last comment even though I agree with it. This leads Myrah to deliver a monologue describing how when she met her husband there was no attraction at all and she could hardly bear to look at him. Although she means well, I grow impatient, anxious for the conversation to end because maybe you are trying to call me back at this moment. I know you could try my mobile as well, but I can't take the chance that you'll give up at the first hurdle.

"Someone's at the door, Myrah, I better go," I say, cutting her off mid-sentence. "It might be Ellie's dad bringing her back early for some reason." I don't like dishonesty but keeping the line free is more important than a small white lie.

I've always thought of water as being able to cleanse away more than just physical dirt so I run a steaming hot bath and watch as the bubbles froth and expand, floating out to cover the whole surface of the bath tub. As I sink into the scalding water, I imagine it is ridding me of all the emotions I've felt today. All the emotions I've felt over the last year. And finally I begin to relax.

Leon told me once how classical music helps him wind down after a stressful day at work so I decide to turn on the old rusty radio that is a permanent feature in the bathroom. It was here when we moved in and is probably on its last legs but laziness has stopped me throwing it out, something I'm grateful for now. It takes me a while to find Classic FM and although I cannot name any of the music, the smooth tones soothe and comfort me as I close my eyes and drift further under my blanket of bubbles.

My eyes snap open when a shrill sound pierces the calmness of whatever piece is playing and it takes me several moments to register what it is. Across the hallway my home phone is ringing and I panic, cursing myself for not bringing it with me to the bathroom as I'd planned. There is no time to dry myself so I grab a towel and ignore the trail of water that's left in my wake as I greedily grab for the phone.

"Olivia, it's me," you say, your words enveloped in sadness.

I don't know what to say. All night I've been waiting for you to call but now you have my lips are frozen.

"I'm outside your door," you continue, and I'm glad you cannot see my smile.

Something has changed and I feel it as soon as you walk in. Your hunched shoulders scream out that you're sorry and your eyes are swollen and red. I don't say anything but grab you and wrap your arms around me. At first your body is tense but then you soften and I pull you into the kitchen to make us both a hot chocolate. I don't even know if you like it but that doesn't seem important. All I can think of is your letter. It doesn't even matter if you don't mention it; you have already told me all I needed to hear.

We take our hot mugs to bed and enjoy the silence of companions, the comfort of two people who know that nothing needs to be said. And when you reach for me this time it is with a different passion, slower and thoughtful. There is no pain and several times you gently whisper my name. It is me you are with now.

"Is it all the truth?" I ask afterwards.

"What?"

"The letter. Was everything you said honest?" I wait for a huge sigh but it doesn't come; all you do is grab my hand and squeeze it.

"I just wanted the chance to explain myself. You know, why I've been such a bastard. I'm not making any excuses for my behaviour but I hope it helps you see that I'm the one with the issue and you've done nothing wrong. Nothing at all."

"But did you really think I'd be happy about that ad? That I'd want us to do something like that? How could I stand there and watch you fuck someone else?" My words are direct and I can tell you are startled by this. Never before have I had the confidence to speak my mind this way to you.

"I know that now. It just makes me realise how much you care. That I was wrong about what I wanted from you." You trail off and look at me, sadness still haunting your eyes.

I consider your words and want to believe them. I convince myself I am not one of those desperate women who will believe any lie she is told by a man. Sometimes forgiveness is as simple as the right words being said. No more, no less.

"And Sarah?" I ask tentatively.

"It was three years ago. I need to just get over it."

"Sometimes it's not that simple, though, is it?" I say, thinking of Carl and the painful effort it has taken me to move on.

You move closer to me and pull the duvet further over us but let go of my hand. "I know this sounds melodramatic but she crushed me. I couldn't get out of bed for weeks. I didn't care about anything, not my job, home, health. Nothing mattered. I just drank myself into oblivion."

Although it's probably of little comfort, I stroke your arm and brush my lips against your shoulder. "I do understand. You could have talked to me, though. I've just been through it myself, remember?"

"That's different," you say, a familiar sternness creeping back into your voice. "You walked away from Carl, he didn't leave you. You had a choice, Olivia, I didn't." There is no hint of nastiness in your voice but I still feel affronted by your words.

I try to keep myself from erupting. We are both treading on fragile ground. "But, Michael, he still hurt me," I say. "Anyway, it's not a competition to see who's suffered the most, is it?"

You reach for my hand again. "I know, I'm sorry. But can we please not talk about this again? Either of them."

To start with this seems like a sensible agreement, but as you drift off to sleep with the radio playing soft jazz beside us, I realise how much I need to know all the details of what happened with Sarah. I am intrigued by the fact you had such strong feelings for someone and I try hard to picture you in a loving relationship, doing simple things like food-shopping or watching TV together. Even though things might get better for us now, it bothers me that I haven't seen the side of you that's capable of expressing such strong emotions. It was easy to forgive your frostiness when I believed that was just in your nature. But now I know differently.

You have no trouble drifting off but sleep eludes me so all I can do is watch the clock flashing forward, while my mind torments me with scenarios of you and Sarah, a faceless woman. I see you doing things together: sitting cuddled together in a cinema or tucking into a meal at a restaurant. I even picture you walking in the park, your arms wrapped around each other as you bury your heads together and whisper private words that nobody else can ever know. This is bad enough but my stomach twists in knots when I see you both stretched out on the rug in your lounge, lying naked together. And even though I don't know what Sarah looks like, in my visions she is flawless.

With the arrival of morning, my rationality returns and I am disgusted with myself. I will never get back the hours I have wasted on destructive, poisonous thoughts. So I cuddle into your back and tell myself I have nothing to worry about. We will be all right now. You reach behind you to grab my hand and I am comforted by the familiar squeeze. Maybe one day you will grow to feel the same way about me that you did about Sarah. Myrah mentioned love being able to grow, so maybe it's possible that is what will happen with us.

The alarm clock finally summons us, a deafening bleating, and at first I can't recall whether I've actually slept or not. But then it all comes flooding back. A fragmented dream of two people. I am not one of them.

CHAPTER ELEVEN

Over and over again I am told all the right things, meaningless mantras straight from a self-help book. Phrases that are supposed to save me from myself. *There was nothing you could have done. It wasn't your fault. How could you possibly have known?* But these words mean nothing. How can they be any comfort to me when they cannot change anything? And life doesn't follow any rules. At least not rules that can be captured and made sense of.

Now I wonder how you kept things going over the next year. How externally you put on such a brave front of normality while inside you were being ripped apart. At least that's what I assume it must have felt like for you; but I will never want to know if I'm correct. But thinking of the torture each day must have brought you is no comfort to me, not when you still have your life to live. What I wonder more than how you functioned, though, is how I remained so oblivious.

"It seems silly us living in separate flats. Maybe we should think about moving in together."

We are seated at your kitchen table, halfway through a late breakfast, and my toast almost lodges in my throat when you utter these words. Butter oozes down my chin and I quickly wipe it away before I speak. You stifle a laugh but cannot hide your amusement.

"What, here you mean?"

You nod and I search your face for any hint that this is some sort of joke but your expression is serious. Things have improved between us lately but I am not expecting you to suggest us taking this step. It is a huge move and one I need to be sure of. While I think it would be good for the two of us – living together is bound to bring us closer together – I need to think of Ellie before myself.

Before I have a chance to give you an answer, you smile and take my hand. "We don't have to decide anything now. You've still got a few months left on your lease so there's no rush, is there? We can talk about it nearer the time but I definitely think it's a good idea. And it will give Chloe more than enough time to sort herself out. She can't stay with me forever."

I have to think carefully about how I respond to this. Chloe left Andrew weeks ago, shortly after her disappearing act, and has taken up residence in your flat, making spending time with you awkward. She doesn't go out much but fritters away her time listening to music and reading magazines. Whenever I am there she suddenly appears in the lounge, making sure she joins us for dinner or to watch TV. I wonder if she still has a job to go to but I know better than to ask you for details.

When you are around she smiles pleasantly and makes an effort to start conversations with me but the moment you are out of the room she is stony and silent, regarding me with disdain. I don't want to imagine what judgements she makes about me and remind myself it is only your opinion that counts.

Andrew is the one I feel sorry for. I wish the two of them could sort things out, not just so Chloe will go home but because he's a decent man and I can't bear to think about what their separation is doing to him. But she is your sister and I have to support you however I can. So I keep my mouth shut and tread carefully whenever her name is mentioned.

"Do you think they'll sort out their problems?" I ask, although I have no idea exactly what their problems are. And as far as I know you are just as oblivious.

"Not according to Chloe," you say, spooning scrambled egg into your mouth. "But I'm staying out of it and letting her make her own decisions. She's a grown woman, she can take care of herself."

I'm taken aback by your nonchalance. Andrew has always been a good friend to you yet you're doing nothing to help them work things out. It can only be a matter of time before my questioning causes you to explode but I decide to see how far I can push this.

"It's just such a shame," I say, taking a sip of my lukewarm tea. "Andrew's a good person."

"I know. But Chloe's my sister and I have to put her first, don't I?"

As if she's been summoned by our discussing her, Chloe appears in the kitchen doorway. Although it's nearly midday, she's wrapped in a short pink dressing gown that gapes at her chest. Suddenly conscious of my own heavy chest I turn my attention back to my toast.

"Who's putting the kettle on?" she asks, bouncing to the table. The question may be aimed at both of us but it's me she turns to, her face a picture of innocence.

"Michael is," I say. "And I'll have another one, please." Since she arrived Chloe has been treating me like her personal servant and this morning seems like a good time to fight back. After all, you are in the room so surely she won't expose her contempt for me?

"Well, do as you're told, Michael," she laughs, ruffling your hair. You shake her off and as I lower my head to read the newspaper, I feel her eyes boring into me.

With our tea in front of us, Chloe announces she's taking me out for a drink tonight. "Your daughter's with her dad, isn't she, Olivia? So I think we should spend the evening getting to know each other a bit better. After all, you're seeing my brother so I have to vet you carefully!"

You raise your eyebrows and scowl at Chloe but make no protest about her whisking me off for the evening. You don't defend me either so I take it upon myself to stand up to your sister again.

"Well, it's a bit late for that, Chloe. Michael and I have just been discussing moving in together as soon as my lease is up." I don't know what I'm expecting to happen after I make this announcement but the air becomes thick with tension. Nobody speaks and I can't look at you. I know you will think I've done the wrong thing. Instead I keep focused on my newspaper and repeatedly read the same line, waiting for someone to speak.

After a moment Chloe jumps up from her chair, the loud creak it makes on the tiled floor cutting into the heavy silence. "Nice of you to tell me," she says and I can't tell who she's talking to. By the time I realise what's just happened she's already fled the kitchen and is slamming the bathroom door shut behind her.

Turning to you, I prepare to face your wrath. "Sorry, Michael. I didn't mean to tell her like that. I just didn't like what she said."

"She wants to know every bloody thing. She'll get over it," you say, your eyes flickering towards the kitchen door.

"Yes, it might take a few years, though," I say, and we both smile. Neither of us can deny Chloe is hard work.

As evening arrives I'm still at your flat, relaxing on the sofa, safe in the knowledge that Chloe will be too angry with me to want to go for a drink now. Ellie calls my mobile and gushes about what a great time she's had at Grandma Barbara's. After I hang up I feel sad that I can't spend time with the two most important people in my life together. I still haven't told Ellie about us but maybe now it's time, especially if moving in together is just around the corner. I should be more excited about our plans but Chloe's tantrum earlier has dampened my enthusiasm. What if there is a chance you will have second thoughts because of her?

You're in the kitchen cooking dinner and the pleasant aroma of charcoaled steak hits my nostrils as I pick up one of Chloe's magazines to flick through. It is full of airbrushed celebrities and gossip about people I've never heard of so I throw it aside, clueless as to what she finds so fascinating.

"Hurry up, we're wasting valuable drinking time," Chloe says, flouncing into the living room. She's wearing a short strapless dress and the highest heels I've ever seen.

"Oh, I thought—"

"Forget what I said earlier. I didn't mean what I said about vetting you. Come on, get changed and we can go."

"I'll just wear this," I say, and when Chloe eyes my jeans and casual fitted t-shirt I start preparing my defence. She opens her mouth to speak but quickly closes it again. Perhaps things can get better between us after all.

We're already outside the house when Chloe realises she's left her purse inside. "Wait here, I'll be two secs," she says. "I'm sure you don't want to be paying for all the drinks!"

After ten minutes, Chloe still hasn't appeared and my patience wears thin. I'm considering going back inside and telling her I'm too tired to go out when your front door slams and she finally rushes outside, somehow managing to stay balanced in her shoes. She doesn't apologise or look the slightest bit sorry. "I couldn't find it. Michael had to help me hunt," she says.

We head to the high street and my stomach sinks at the thought of a whole evening alone with her. We haven't even left yet and I'm already fed up. It's difficult, but I remind myself I'm doing this for you.

The bar is too loud and I seem to be the oldest person in here but at least we're not far away from home. Watching Chloe tottering on her heels as she heads to an empty table, I suddenly want to give her a chance. I want to be able to like her because she's your sister but I can't shake off a sense of foreboding about this evening. It's impossible to work out why Chloe's asked me here but if this will make you happy then I will keep smiling and try to ignore my misgivings.

"I'll get the drinks in," Chloe says, dashing to the bar before I've even told her what I'd like. She comes back smiling and plonks a gin and tonic in front of me before taking a greedy gulp of her wine.

"How did you know?" I ask her, as I take a sip, trying not to imagine my drink is tainted because it's been bought by someone I know doesn't like me.

"Oh, Olivia! I do actually pay attention to people." She pulls a compact mirror from her handbag. A large crack snakes across the middle of the glass so I'm surprised she can see clearly enough to smother on another thick layer of red lip gloss. When she's finished she stares at me, her bright, shiny mouth making her look clownish. She's trying too hard and I wonder why; doesn't she realise she's beautiful? If I haven't noticed that before it's because her domineering persona tarnishes her appearance with ugliness. But tonight I will look past that. For your sake.

For at least an hour Chloe and I make polite small talk, both knowing that certain topics are landmines to be carefully avoided. So it is a surprise when, bolstered by her third glass of wine, she is suddenly asking me about you.

"Do you love Michael?" Asked this by anyone else, it is a harmless enough question but delivered by Chloe it is a ticking time bomb. As his sister, she should want me to say yes but her cold, glassy eyes challenge me to answer with something she doesn't want to hear.

"We've not really discussed it," I say, and this is no lie. Even after over a year, neither one of us has uttered those words of commitment.

"Typical!" she says, raising her eyes to the ceiling. "And that doesn't bother you at all?"

I sigh and prepare to respond to her question. I should have known this evening would turn into an interrogation.

"Love is just a word, Chloe. Aren't actions more important? Why do people feel the need to hear someone saying 'I love you' when it should be enough that they're there for you every day." I try to make my words convincing but I'm not sure she's buying it. After all, if I'm not convinced myself about what I'm saying how can I hope to persuade your sister?

Chloe is silent for a moment and it's hard for me to read her. I hope she'll let this go but it's doubtful. "So are you saying Michael's there for you every day, then?" Her tone is scornful and I feel as if I'm her quarry, hunted down and forced into a dark corner. She knows you much better than I do and this knowledge of you is her weapon. I wonder what she knows about the difficult beginning we had.

"Chloe, I really don't feel comfortable talking about this. Michael and I are together and that's enough for me."

"For now," she says, once again pulling out her mirror to examine herself. "And what about trust, Olivia? Isn't that important too?"

Ignoring her comment, and with no desire to find out exactly what she means, I decide to question her about Andrew.

"I can't go back to him, Olivia. Surely you can understand that? I mean, you left your husband, didn't you? And you've got a child together. All Andrew and I have is the dog. And believe me, that's just not enough to make a marriage work." For once, Chloe seems genuinely sad and once again I soften towards her.

"But what did he do? It was different for me, you know what Carl did, but Andrew has done nothing except love you."

She nods her head slowly, swishing her glass around but not drinking any of the contents. "I know, I know. But what can I do when I just can't love him back?" Chloe's sentence is final. Once a truth like that lies on the table there's nothing more to be said. She scrapes her chair back and announces we need more drinks. Mine is nowhere near finished but I don't try to stop her. Chloe is as stubborn as you are.

While she's at the bar, I text you to let you know how the evening is going. There's no point admitting it's been awkward, especially when – with the help of alcohol – the atmosphere seems to have thawed a little. So I explain we're having a lovely time and leave it at that. I place my phone on the table and stare at it, quite sure you won't reply because you rarely text anyone.

After a few minutes I slip my phone back in my bag and turn to the bar to see how Chloe is getting on. She's still waiting to be served but doesn't seem in any hurry to get the bartender's attention. A man leans over her, dressed as if he's come straight from the office. His purple tie hangs loosely around his neck as he whispers something in her ear. She flicks her head back and laughs, whipping his face with her mane of hair. I assume it must be someone she knows as they seem too familiar with each other to have only just met. He looks a lot younger than Chloe, barely into his twenties, but perhaps they work together.

I fumble in my bag for my phone but there's still no reply from you. Finishing my drink, I turn back to watch Chloe again. Somehow she has found an empty barstool and is perched on the edge. The young man is leaning down to her, still whispering in her ear, and I smile because from this angle it seems as if he's kissing it. My eyes drop down and then I realise what she's doing. Chloe and this man are not just having a conversation while they wait to get served. His hand is in between her legs.

Without thinking, I grab my phone and text you again. I don't provide all the details but I let you know what Chloe is doing. This time my phone bleeps with an immediate reply. *Bitch.*

Chloe still hasn't been served so I head off to the toilets, more to have a break from her than anything else. Once I'm in the quiet back corridor, I call Carl to check everything is okay with Ellie. Barbara is staying with him at the moment and they've taken her out for pizza. Hearing what a good time they're having, a wave of nostalgia washes over me and I wish I was with them. I'd rather be anywhere than here.

When I return to our table, Chloe still isn't back. Our glasses remain where we've left them, Chloe's empty and covered in a smear of lip gloss. I scan the bar area but she's no longer there. Her friend has also disappeared. I look around the crowded room to see if he's anywhere in sight but I don't think I'd recognise him if he came and sat right next to me. One suited man blurs into another here and panic rises in me. Chloe's in a vulnerable state at the moment and despite your angry words, you would never forgive me if anything happened to her.

I try to be rational and calmly consider the options. She could have gone to the toilets but if that's the case we would have passed each other. I decide to sit down and wait for a while, just in case she comes back, but after twenty minutes of sitting alone it is obvious Chloe has left without me.

As I head outside I realise this was probably her plan all along; to leave me here alone looking like a fool. She's probably already back at your flat telling you what a great trick she's played on me.

With this thought in my head, I am unprepared for what I see when I walk out into the cool evening air: Chloe is sitting on a low wall by the side of the building, slumped over and staring into an empty wine glass. Her feet are bare and her shoes lie strewn underneath her. Her hair flops in her face and her lips have lost their shine. Her already-too-short dress is hitched even further up her thighs.

I join her on the wall and stretch her dress to her knees before putting my arm around her. She nestles her head into my shoulder but doesn't utter a word. We stay in this position like statues for some time as people and time pass us by, oblivious to why two strange women are sitting silently on a wall outside a bar. I, too, have no idea.

"You'll be okay, Chloe," I finally say. "You'll sort things out with Andrew, one way or the other. And believe me, it does get easier."

Although I don't know if this is what's upsetting her, it's obvious she needs some words of comfort. There are tears in her eyes so I find a tissue in my pocket and hand it to her. When she's finished wiping her eyes she hands the tissue back to me, caked in thick black smudges of mascara.

There is no malice in her tone or expression when Chloe finally turns to me and speaks; just resignation. "You have no idea, Olivia."

You're asleep on the sofa when I get back to your flat, even though it's not that late. We agreed this morning that I would stay the night but here you are, comatose with an empty bottle of whisky lying on its side on the floor. Chloe has gone to her house in a cab to pick up some more clothes while Andrew is out for the night, so we are on our own for the first time in weeks. Yet you've decided to waste this opportunity and knock yourself into oblivion. But when I look down at your face, calm and beautiful in your relaxed state, it's hard to be angry with you so instead I hunt down a blanket to place over you. An uncomfortable breeze glides through the wide-open window and I pull it closed. Even though it's mid-summer, this year the temperatures have been dropping considerably once the sun disappears.

I turn off the television and head to your bed alone, the image of Chloe and the man from the bar firmly ingrained in my mind. But rather than judge her for what she did, I pity her because tonight I have seen her more human side. She is vulnerable, just like everyone else, and this evening I saw through her act. No amount of make-up, tarty clothes or high heels can permanently hide her pain and insecurity. And even if Chloe doesn't love Andrew anymore, I know their breakup is torturing her.

Although I'm frustrated that you aren't in bed with me, I'm thankful I've made some progress with Chloe tonight. I'm still puzzled as to why she seems to have taken a dislike to me right from the start but I remain hopeful that our relationship won't be as strained from now on. Bathed in darkness and spread out across the whole bed, sleep comes easily to me, aided by the positive thoughts helping me feel at peace.

I hear the thunder of voices. One is male and the other female but the sounds are too muffled to discern any words. It takes several seconds to realise I'm awake, alone in your bed, and the voices belong to you and Chloe. I force my eyes open but squint against the bright red glare from your alarm clock. It's three forty-four a.m. The argument gets louder and your voice reverberates through me but I still can't hear the words being spoken. Then there is silence before a door slams, sending an echo through the flat. More silence follows before the thud of heavy footsteps and another door crashing shut. In the next room, where Chloe sleeps, I hear muffled crying, soft and slow, but it's not long before it turns into agonising wails. I contemplate going to check on her but decide it's best to stay out of it. This is between you and Chloe and I can understand you being upset with her. After all, Andrew is a good friend to you.

CHAPTER TWELVE

While I pretend to sleep, I hear them whispering. I know exactly what they think of me but I don't care that I'm the latest topic of their debates. Some of them blame me. Oh yes, they cannot fathom how I didn't know anything. *It's impossible. She must have known. Right before her very eyes.* They believe my involvement is not as a victim but at the very least a spectator. And they tut and huff and sigh at the shame of it all. But can I blame them for their mistrust?

Andrew and Chloe's flat in Chiswick is on the second floor of a new, purpose-built block close to the Tube. As I look up at the four-storey structure, I wonder how they manage to keep a dog in there. I stand in front of the entry panel and press the buzzer of flat twelve. It chimes and there is no going back now. I wait to hear Andrew's voice and prepare an explanation of why I'm here but there is no static from the intercom. Instead the huge glass double door clinks open so I push through it, my whole body heaving against the weight of it.

Guilt has accompanied me here. I am interfering in someone else's business and have no right. Neither of them are close friends of mine and Chloe has made it clear she doesn't love Andrew, at least not in the right way. But I'm convinced if he knows how she feels there might be something he can do or say. I, of all people, know that sometimes all it takes is someone to say the right words at the right moment.

I haven't told you what I'm doing today because all weekend you made it clear you don't think Chloe deserves Andrew. You've barely spoken a word to her since your argument and the atmosphere at your place is like the North Pole. Above all else, I am standing at Andrew's door now because it's all my fault. I'm the one who told you about what Chloe did that night so now it's up to me to put things right. I find flat twelve and rap my knuckles on the wooden door, burying my fear of you finding out I'm here.

When Andrew opens the door I am half-expecting to find a broken man; a face thick with stubble, unwashed hair and dirty clothes. But Andrew is far from this cliché: his t-shirt is crisp and clean and his skin smooth and recently shaved. He looks shocked to see me but holds the door open. The flat is tidy, the citrus scent of furniture polish lingering in the air.

"This is a surprise," Andrew says, leading me through to the kitchen. "Did Chloe send you? Or Michael? Because—"

"No, no," I assure him. "They don't know I've come. Michael would kill me if he knew."

He pauses and looks me up and down, maybe wondering whether I am trustworthy. "Well, I'm glad you're here. And I won't say anything."

Andrew flicks the kettle on and leans against the worktop. In the corner, Kipper yawns and stretches before settling back into his huge padded basket. "You know the worst part of all this?" he says. "Losing friends. Especially ones I've only just made." I smile and pull him into a hug, burying my face in his jumper so he can't see my eyes filling with tears.

While he makes us tea, I stare out of the low bay window at people strolling around the park opposite. I'm about to suggest we go outside for a walk but quickly reconsider. Andrew and Chloe must have spent a lot of time in this park, walking Kipper, wrapped around each other as if nobody else existed. I can't make him relive these memories. I'm about to offer some words of comfort to him but suddenly he is whistling, the tuneful sound blending into the whir of the kettle.

Sipping our tea at the small kitchen table, I ask Andrew how he is doing. His answer is one I have suspected since I arrived here.

"I'm good, Olivia. Really good."

"I'm glad to hear that but–"

"I know, it's strange, isn't it? I thought I'd be moping around for months but actually I feel great. Kind of free."

I don't know how to respond to this. I've come here to offer support and comfort to Andrew, maybe even to help him repair his marriage, so now I'm at a loss for words.

"But don't you love Chloe?" Even as I say it I know it can't be as simple as this.

Andrew takes a sip of tea and contemplates my question for a moment. "Love is only simple when you're a teenager," he says. "The minute it's real it starts to get complicated. But yes, I do."

"Then–"

"No, Olivia." His voice is firm, a warning not to push things. He takes a long swig of his tea and jumps up from the table. "Come on. You've never been here before so it's time for a tour."

The flat is modern and small and as I'm shown each room I notice there is a heavy masculine feel to the place and no sign at all that Chloe ever lived here. I know she's taken a lot of clothes to your flat but there is no way all her belongings can fit into your spare room.

When we reach the bedroom I feel as if I'm in a show home, admiring the furnishings and decor. I notice one of the bedside tables is completely empty; there isn't even a lamp on it.

"Where are all Chloe's things?" I ask, bracing myself for an attack before I remember that Andrew isn't you and I don't have to walk on eggshells around him.

He flicks a minuscule speck of dust from the bedroom windowsill and sighs. "I threw away anything she didn't take with her." He searches my face for any sign of admonishment but I avert my eyes to the glass wardrobes. "Does that make me a terrible person?" he asks.

I want to tell him how unfair he's been to Chloe but I have to choose my words carefully. After all, I am the one who's just turned up at his flat when he was minding his own business and getting on with things.

"No, I don't," I reply. "I think Chloe's just Chloe. But I don't think throwing her stuff away was right. Did she really deserve that?"

I'm defending Chloe but it feels as if someone else is speaking the words. I shouldn't care what Andrew's done with her things but once again I find myself pitying her. "I know she left you but—"

"Is that what she's been telling everyone? That she left me?" His face burns deep red. "That's just typical of Chloe. Not that it matters either way. Our marriage is over and how or why is irrelevant."

I am left stunned as Andrew walks out of the bedroom but I hastily follow, not wanting to be left alone in there. When I get to the kitchen, he's already lighting a cigarette and leaning out of the kitchen window, plumes of smoke floating towards the park.

I lay my hand on his shoulder and stare at the pale white mark circling my wedding finger. "I'm sorry, Andrew. I got the completely wrong idea. I came here thinking I could help you two sort things out but I can see now that's not what you want."

"What I want is to forget I ever met her," Andrew says, not with spite, anger or even sadness. Just acceptance.

"But what did she do that was so bad? She didn't cheat on you, did she?" There is no way Andrew can know about the man in the bar and even if he did, it happened weeks after Chloe moved out.

"I wish it was something as simple as that, Olivia. A simple case of cheating could be more easily forgiven." Andrew pulls the window shut and grabs Kipper's lead from the table. "I've got to take him for a walk now but thanks for coming." There is no clearer way of telling me I've outstayed my welcome but I'm not annoyed with Andrew. Despite his insistence that he's fine and over Chloe, this can't be easy for him.

Walking me to the door, with Kipper yelping by his side, Andrew hugs me tightly. "You're a good friend," he says, but I don't feel it at all. I've done nothing to help him and I've not been honest about everything I know. All I feel now is a fraud.

"You're too good for him, Olivia," Andrew says before the door clicks shut behind me and I walk away to the sound of Kipper scratching to get out.

As I head back to the station, my mind replays my conversation with Andrew. None of it makes any sense and trying to piece things together is like attempting a jigsaw puzzle with no idea of the picture being formed. All I can say for sure is that neither Chloe nor Andrew has been honest about why their marriage has fallen apart. I can't even share my concerns with you because you'll tell me to stay out of it; that it's none of my business.

Sandwiched between two people on a stifling and crowded Piccadilly line tube, Andrew's parting words come back to me but I quickly dismiss them. He's down on relationships at the moment and probably doesn't think anyone's has a chance of working.

It's nearly lunchtime when I get to Hammersmith and with a bus journey still to go I turn my anxiety to Ellie. I hadn't planned on my trip to Chiswick taking so long and she's been stuck with Chloe all morning. You made an excuse about needing to be at school today as soon as Chloe offered to babysit.

"I'm starving!" Ellie declares, the second Chloe lets me in.

Chloe huffs. "Ellie insisted on waiting until you got home so you could eat together. I did offer to make her a sandwich but she refused it."

Ellie clings on to me. "Mum, you've been *ages*. Please can we go home now?"

I mouth a quick 'sorry' to Chloe before Ellie drags me downstairs to our flat. Ellie hasn't said thank you or even goodbye to Chloe and it's not like her to be so rude. I decide to question her about it later. She's probably irritable from having to wait so long for lunch so I need to feed her before we discuss anything.

Watching Ellie chomping on her peanut butter sandwich, I ask her about her morning, ready to investigate why she was so rude to Chloe.

"It was okay," she says, dropping her eyes to the table. "But why were you so long? I don't like it there, Mum." She stops eating and decides to play with her food instead, mashing up her sandwich until it's an unappetising blob of brown and white.

I stop chewing and pause with my half eaten sandwich in the air. Ellie would never say something like this lightly. "Why? Has something happened? I thought you liked Chloe. She's looked after you before and you've never complained."

She begins kneading the mashed up bread. "I just didn't want to make a fuss. But they were fighting, Mum, and it was horrible."

I slap my sandwich back on the plate as it occurs to me Chloe must have invited a man back to the flat. Anger flares up from the pit of my stomach but I try to remain calm for Ellie's sake. "Who was fighting, Pumpkin? Did Chloe have a friend there?"

Ellie shakes her head and her hair flies from side to side. "No, it was Michael."

"Oh," I say, almost to myself. "He must have decided to stay at home." Picking up my sandwich again, I relax a bit. "Don't worry about it, Pumpkin. Brothers and sisters often have disagreements. It doesn't mean they don't care about each other."

Ellie nods and shovels the remains of her sandwich into her mouth. "I suppose so," she says, unconvinced.

We load the dishwasher together and I tell Ellie she can have some computer time. She thanks me but doesn't seem as excited as she normally is to take a trip into cyberspace. While she waits for my laptop to load up she shakes her head. "I'm glad I don't have a brother, Mum. They're yucky."

Later that evening, when Ellie is asleep, I call you at your flat but there's no answer. Your mobile is switched off and even Chloe's phone rings for an eternity before going to voicemail. I need to know why you said you were going to the school this morning. It doesn't matter to me whether you were or weren't at home; it's the lying that's the issue. In a stark reminder of the obsessive behaviour I displayed when I first met you, I keep trying both your numbers at half-hourly intervals. Andrew's words ring in my head each time I put the phone to my ear and then I recall Chloe's warning to be careful. If your own sister is warning me about you, then there must be something in it. At first I put it down to her not liking me or thinking I'm not good enough for you, but after what Andrew said surely there's more to this?

Then I remember something I've tried to push from my mind and for the first time since I read your apology I allow myself to think about it, to picture you with another woman, smiling because you know I'm there. My insides burn when I think of what you wanted us to do. What can possibly come after that?

Like a tightly coiled spring, I wind myself into a panic, my breathing fast and shallow as the phone slips from my hand and crashes to the floor. I can't go through this again, not after Carl. Carl, who I believe loved me but still managed to be unfaithful. So what hope is there with a man to whom the word love is abhorrent?

It is only when Ellie's sleep-filled voice calls me that I snap out of my panic and pull myself together. I switch my mobile off to avoid temptation and check on Ellie before dragging myself to my own bed. I know sleep will not come easily. I have too many unanswered questions and above all else, a terrible feeling I can't explain.

CHAPTER THIRTEEN

Over the next few days, all my instincts scream at me to question you, to mistrust you, to watch your every move. But I fight hard against my gut feelings and instead focus on becoming the perfect girlfriend. Giving myself this label makes me shudder. After all, I am used to being a wife and never thought I would once again be a *girlfriend*. Being in my thirties, it somehow seems inappropriate that I should have this youthful title, but nevertheless, that is what I am so I do my best to be a good one.

I keep silent about my fears, surprise you with home-cooked dinners, help clean your flat and do your food shopping while I'm getting mine and Ellie's. I even go out of my way to entertain Chloe when she's in one of her frequent melancholic moods, just to give you a break. I'm not doing all of this out of weakness or denial, nor is it a twisted way of proving you don't need anyone else. I'm doing it because I don't know what else to do. I have no evidence to confront you with so I all I can do is bide my time and wait. If you are seeing someone else then it can only be a matter of time before you slip up.

"I'm meeting up with Stephen and Finn in Edinburgh this weekend. For Finn's birthday."

We are in your kitchen making breakfast together and your announcement takes me by surprise. I try to recall whether you've already told me this news but can't remember you mentioning anything. What I do remember is the three of you always celebrate each other's birthdays with a weekend away together.

Piling our plates with fried eggs, sausages and bacon, you kiss the top of my head and carry the food to the table. My stomach churns but I tell you it sounds like fun.

"You don't mind, do you?" You slice your eggs open with your knife and I watch the yellow yolk invading the white of your plate.

I join you at the table with my cup of coffee. "Of course not." It's the only reply I can give and we both know this.

"I'm a bit worried about Chloe, though, she's a bit depressed at the moment. Would you mind checking on her over the weekend? I'll leave you my keys."

A plan begins to form in my mind. "Of course," I say, hiding my deceit behind my coffee mug. You haven't noticed that you're the only one eating.

I don't know whether it is guilt or frustration but the urge to be touched by you suddenly overwhelms me. Although I stayed over last night I went to bed early and can't remember you joining me. When I woke up you were already in the kitchen, reading a newspaper with a cold cup of coffee in front of you, so it's no wonder I feel the need to be held.

I get up and stand behind your chair, wrapping my arms around you and kissing the back of your neck. You barely move and when my hand ventures down the front of your boxer shorts you gently push my arm away. "I just want to have a shower," you say. You have never been a morning person.

Once I'm alone in the kitchen, the first opportunity for me to carry out my plan arises sooner than expected. Clearing away the breakfast dishes, I notice your mobile phone staring up at me from the table, unlocked and easy to navigate. I can hear the shower running next door and Chloe won't be up for hours so I have plenty of time. I hesitate, torn between morality and desperation. How can I invade your privacy like this? I would never have done this to Carl. Then I remember where that got me. Without further thought, I grab the phone and scroll through the menu. Your inbox is full of text messages and I carefully check each name. They are all from Stephen, Finn or male work colleagues I've heard you talk about. Next I check your contacts list but there are no names listed that I don't recognise. The call log tells me the same story so I scroll back to the menu screen and place your phone back on the table, careful to put it in exactly the same position as you left it. Feeling a mixture of relief and shame, I begin washing some plates and mugs that can't fit in the dishwasher, hoping this small act will pardon my sin. But I know now I have stepped over the line I will not be able to stop myself doing it again.

After your shower you join me back in the kitchen but I don't turn around from the sink. Wrapped in guilt, all I can do is stare at my reflection in the sparkling chrome. You come up behind me and whisper thanks in my ear but when I turn around to pull you against me you're already heading back to the table and slipping your mobile in your pocket.

"What are your plans for today?" you ask. "After you've finished cleaning my flat, that is."

I spin around and hurl the damp cloth I'm holding at your head. It narrowly misses and lands with a wet smack on the floor by your feet.

"Well, now you're just making more mess to clean up," you say, laughing at my futile attempt at revenge.

"Ellie's with Carl this week so I thought I'd cook you dinner again tonight. Maybe at my place? What do you think?" At least at my place we will have some privacy. Your rejection this morning stung me so I need us to be alone. I need to know it was a one-off. Today is already Wednesday and you leave for Edinburgh after work on Friday.

You hesitate for a moment, grab your phone out of your pocket and start pressing buttons that can't possibly be doing anything so I know tonight won't be happening.

"I'd like to. It's just that I told Andrew I'd meet up with him for a drink tonight and it will probably be a late one. He said he really needs to talk. Don't tell Chloe, though."

I can't be annoyed with you for this. You're doing a good thing by being there for Andrew, even if he's not as heartbroken as I assumed he'd be. I mask my disappointment and smother the words I want to say. "Okay, but we do need to spend some time alone together."

"I know," you say. "When I get back I promise we'll do something. Maybe a restaurant? You've got that work party on Thursday, haven't you? Otherwise we could have done it then." You search my face and for a moment it seems as if you're smirking, daring me to cancel my plans. But it's Leon's birthday and I won't miss that. You finish playing with your phone and slip it back in your pocket.

"Okay," I say again, retrieving the cloth from the floor and turning back to the sink. "Just make sure you bring me something back from Edinburgh."

Saturday night arrives and like a thief I wait until it's dark and sneak into your house. Having a key doesn't do anything to make what I'm doing more forgivable but I have to know. Chloe is out somewhere, probably drinking herself senseless so I doubt she'll find her way home tonight. I should be more worried than I am, especially as you've asked me to look after her, but she's thirty years old and doesn't need me checking up on her like a mother.

Stepping inside, I bolt the front door shut, just in case. There is a completely different atmosphere in your flat tonight, or rather, *I* feel different being here tonight. I have never been here alone so maybe that's it but whatever the problem is, I am out of place here. The staircase is a cave of darkness looming in front of me and I almost change my mind. But then I remember Chloe and Andrew's words. I have to know.

Your computer seems the obvious place to start so, leaving all the lights off and letting only the street lamps filtering in from outside guide me, I hunt for your laptop. As organised as you are, it's the one item you own that never seems to have a permanent home so it could be anywhere. When I eventually find it, it's in your bedside table drawer, neatly wedged against the back panel of the cabinet. My stomach sinks as I wonder why you've hidden it here. Pulling it out, I sit on the bed and wait for it to load up, wondering what I'll do if it's password-protected. If this was Carl's computer I would have a much greater chance of cracking the password because this is what comes with knowing and understanding someone inside and out. With you, though, I hardly know where to begin.

Luckily, you have been either lazy or naive and before long I am greeted by an image of palm trees stretching out across a dark sea, the sun setting in the distance. This is not what I would expect you to have on your home screen. It is another stark reminder that I don't know the man I'm sleeping with.

I scan the icons on the desktop and after a few clicks I am taken straight to your Yahoo inbox without needing to enter a password for that either. Nausea rises in my stomach as I wait for your emails to load and for a moment I close my eyes; I don't know what I will find and my head swirls as memories of Carl's betrayal taunt me. It's not too late. I can shut down the computer and end this now. But even as I think this I know there is no way back.

Slowly opening my eyes, I face what's in front of me. The first email is a receipt from the Travelodge in Edinburgh. I open it, just to check, but everything is as it should be. It's confirmation of three single rooms for this weekend. Below that sit nothing but junk emails advertising Viagra and other sex enhancements. I smile to myself; you don't need any of it.

I check the *sent* and *deleted* items but find nothing from any women. I want to feel relieved but all I can manage is shame at snooping through your personal things and invading your privacy. This is much worse than checking your phone. If you knew what I was doing our relationship would come crushing down on me; trust is one of the few fragile ties that bind it together. I snap the laptop shut. I feel stifled, the air a vicious quicksand pulling me under, eager to suffocate me. I shove your laptop back in the bedside table drawer, not even bothering to place it as it was or check I've switched it off properly. It takes an eternity to flee from your flat. I stumble in the darkness and scrape my elbow against something in my desperation to escape. I ignore the pain and finally reach the safety of my own flat. It is only later I notice the blood. It eases my guilt because I deserve it.

Sleep is fitful for me and even though I've found no evidence of you doing anything wrong, nothing at all feels right. Unable to focus on reading, I decide the television might be better company so I drag my duvet into the lounge and nestle it into the sofa. I make a cup of green tea and cradle it in my lap while I listen to the sounds outside. Even at this early hour there are plenty of cars passing by but it's not an annoyance, more a comfort for me. Evidence that other people exist in the world. I miss Ellie and would call her if it wasn't three o'clock in the morning. I wonder if Carl is awake but what would I say to him?

Three times I flick through all the channels but there is nothing to distract me. I eventually settle on a home improvement programme that only serves to depress me further as it's a reminder that I no longer own my own home. But it's the most interesting programme on so I stare at the screen, not liking any of the so-called improvements that are being made to a young family's home.

When the adverts come on I mute the television and decide to make another cup of tea, but when I pull myself out of the duvet I notice the sound of an engine whirring outside. Turning the television off so I can't be seen, I poke my head around the curtain and am surprised to see Chloe stumbling out of a car. There is a man in the driver's seat but I can't make out his features to see whether I know him. All I can tell is that the car is definitely not Andrew's.

Chloe fumbles around in her bag and hands something to the driver so it must be a cab. At least she has got home safely. I continue to watch her, just to make sure she's got her keys as it's clear she's been drinking excessively. Loose bits of hair have slipped out of her ponytail and her make-up is smudged under her eyes. She hunts in her bag but instead of pulling out her keys she drags her mobile from her bag and calls someone. Assuming she's forgotten her keys, I'm about to go out and let her in when she screeches into her phone.

"Don't hang up on me, don't you dare hang up on me!" she screams. The top small window in my front room is open so her words are clear but even with it closed I'd be able to hear her from the kitchen. "Fuck, fuck, fuck!" She pulls off her shoe and starts slamming it against the front door with a thrust I wouldn't have thought possible coming from such a tiny creature. "I need you," she says and crumples in a heap on the door step, tears rolling down her cheeks. "Please. I haven't done anything." Her head rolls back and smashes against the door but she is anaesthetised from the alcohol and doesn't flinch. After a few seconds she stands up, evidently calmed down by whoever she's talking to, and finds her keys.

Even though we have a difficult relationship, I know I have to see if she's okay. Her phone call is proof she hasn't given up on her marriage and it will do her no good to be alone tonight.

"Are you okay?" I ask her, as I open my door.

She looks up, shocked to have company so late at night, and doesn't seem pleased to see me. "I'm fine. Just, you know, had a little drink. I'll be fine, just got to get to bed." She lunges towards your door and jiggles her keys.

"Why don't you stay at mine tonight, Chloe?" I say, gently. "I'll make you some coffee. Or tea?"

"Oh. No. I just need to get to bed." She rams the key into the door, nowhere near where the keyhole is.

I want to tell her I've heard her phone conversation and that I'm here for her if she needs me but the words won't form. I don't know whether it's because of how she treats me or that I expect she'll reject my kindness but either way nothing is forthcoming.

"Well, okay. Michael will be home tomorrow evening," I say instead, hoping this will at least be of some comfort to her.

"Yes. That's good," she says, finally managing to unlock your door. Without another word or even a glance behind her, she closes the door and I am left standing in the hallway, wondering what's just happened.

Today I heard a kind voice. A gentle, soothing voice that reminded me of someone I couldn't place and still can't hours later. It was an ageless voice, just as likely to belong to an eighty-year-old as a child. The voice spoke clearly but all I could hear were sounds. Beautiful, commanding and comforting. But perhaps the voice didn't belong to someone I know at all and it's just another trick, another way for them to get to me. Because that's their ultimate goal and they aim to achieve it any way they can; I've already been dealt a horrific deck of cards so what does it matter what else is done to me if it gets all the boxes ticked? Done and dusted.

But now, trick or not, I long to hear that voice again. And this time I will listen. *I promise!* I scream inside my head. *I promise!*

CHAPTER FOURTEEN

"He's still in bed," Chloe grunts, when she opens the door. "As I was."

I smile at her, determined to be pleasant and avoid stooping to her level. She turns without another word and runs back up the stairs. I watch her disappearing and wonder how it's possible for anyone to be so tiny and not break in half. The pyjamas she wears are more likely to be yours and hang off her spindly legs and in a white vest top and barefooted, she looks as innocent as a child. It's hard to believe this is the same woman who a few nights ago was a crumpled mess. I follow her up the stairs, feeling like an elephant as my boots clump up each step. I could have worn more feminine footwear but it wouldn't stop me feeling colossal next to delicate Chloe.

At your bedroom door I pause for a moment and smooth my hair down. I haven't seen you since you came home from Edinburgh and I'm nervous. What if you know I was snooping around your flat? I knock loudly but don't wait for a reply. You're still half-asleep when I enter and close the door behind me. More to shut out Chloe than anything else.

Your room is warm and clammy with the thick smell of night sweat and even though the sun is making an appearance outside, the thick curtains block out all the light so it could easily be night.

"What time is it?" you ask, your voice cracked and croaky.

I sit down on the bed and pull my boots off. "I know it's early but I haven't seen you for ages." I don't admit it's not even eight o'clock yet and try to obscure your view of the alarm clock by moving closer to you. It's stupid to think you won't notice the huge glowing digits but I drape my arms around you in a futile attempt at distraction. Underneath the sheets you lie rigid, as motionless as a statue on your back, with your eyes closed. Despite your body feeling warm and sticky I want to touch your skin but you are immune to my touch, flinching and pulling away from me.

I ask how your weekend in Edinburgh was and while you mumble something vague I slip off my jeans and climb under the covers, pulling them over me in spite of the intense heat. We lie quietly for a while, side by side but barely touching. At one time it would have been impossible for us to be in the same room without ripping each other's clothes off. Remembering how you feel gives me the determination to have that again so I slide my hand along your leg and stroke you until you're growing harder in my grip. Feeling confident now, I take my top off but you make no move to touch me and your eyes are still closed.

"Sorry, Olivia, I'm just really tired. Let's just rest for a while."

I once again pull the duvet over me and lie still, suddenly cold all over even though the room is like an oven. I drift in and out of sleep, but it is not a restful sleep; my mind is plagued by your rejection.

I'm awoken by a clang from the kitchen. As Chloe crashes around, opening cupboard doors and letting them slam shut, she hums to herself so she must be in a better mood than when she let me in earlier. She is a different woman from the other night.

You stir beside me and look peaceful and younger than you are. But I am furious with you for being so relaxed when I'm in turmoil. Remembering Chloe's desperate phone call to Andrew, I gently nudge you with my leg until you open your eyes.

"It's great news that Chloe is trying to work things out with Andrew," I say.

Your eyes fix on me. "What? There's no way they'll get back together," you say, pulling yourself up. "He wouldn't."

"Why not? How do you know?" You are too angry to notice I'm being argumentative. I knew you would be.

"I've had enough of this," you say, bolting up and groping around on the floor for your jeans.

In the kitchen, Chloe has made us all scrambled eggs on toast and she's still humming as she piles food onto our plates and hands us each a mug of coffee. Full of energy, she bounces around and every time she passes me I catch a whiff of her lemon shampoo.

"What's all this about Andrew?" you say sharply once Chloe sits down. "I hope you're not messing him around."

Chloe stops humming. "What are you talking about?"

"Just leave him alone, Chloe."

Chloe looks hurt. "But I *am!* Where is this coming from, Michael?"

You glance at me but don't say anything and the room falls uncomfortably silent.

After a while Chloe shovels a forkful of egg into her mouth and breaks the silence. "Actually, I've met someone else."

We both stare at her; this is the last thing I expect Chloe to say and I'm sure it is as much of a shock to you.

"And I was going to ask you both if you'd have dinner with us tonight. Here. I'm going to cook something."

A deep frown appears on your face. Perhaps you are trying to work out if this is another one of Chloe's manipulations but you say nothing.

"Will you just give him a chance, please, Michael?" she says. "I'm doing what you wanted and leaving Andrew alone. Just let me live my life. Can't you just be happy for me?"

Taking a sip of coffee, I feel like an intruder, as if I have no business eavesdropping on personal family matters. I like Andrew but it's up to Chloe what she does and he's made it clear he wants to move on. You can't know the truth about how their relationship ended because you're placing all the blame on Chloe. This seems strange considering you met up with Andrew recently, but then, maybe you're not as close as you assume. But even though I feel sorry for Chloe, I can't tell you what I know because I am also tangled in this web of lies.

"So who is he?" you ask, getting up from the table with your plate. It's still piled with untouched food but you walk over to the bin and hurl it in before slamming the plate on the worktop.

Chloe looks horrified. "What the hell, Michael?" she screams. "I cooked that for you, you ungrateful bastard. Go to fucking hell!" She jumps up from the table, her chair flying out from under her as she flees from the kitchen, her face swollen and red.

"Don't expect me to be here tonight," you shout after her. I shake my head and gather up the breakfast dishes. I'm sure neither of you will mind the food being thrown away. I look at you and you must sense I have questions because you say, "I just think she's being a bitch. They've only just separated so how's she suddenly met someone new?"

"Why don't we just give him a chance?" I say, stroking your arm. You stare at me for a while but then you smile and help me load the dishwasher. Even though you seem to have calmed down a bit, we clear away in silence and through the clink of crockery I'm sure we are both thinking the same thought. You won't be at home this evening.

I sit on the sofa, watching Chloe plaster on her make-up. She is wearing the same dress she had on the night we went for a drink so it's doubtful it's the same man coming here tonight.

"Thanks for staying for dinner, Olivia. It means a lot to me," she says, peering at me over her compact mirror. I wonder why tonight is so important to her when she's only just met this man. For a fleeting moment I am overwhelmed with sympathy for her. She's just trying to prove she is over Andrew. I can't think of any other reason why she was so insistent we both be here tonight.

I don't blame you for leaving. Chloe barely knows this man and has said nothing about who he is or how they met. "But won't it be a bit weird, just the three of us?" I ask.

"Oh, don't worry, Michael will be here. He's too nosy to stay out for too long. You'll see. By the way, you look nice." She turns to me and nods approvingly. I look down at my white flared skirt and espadrilles and wonder if she really means it; either way, it's the first compliment she's ever paid me.

Because she spends so long getting ready, Chloe abandons her plan to cook dinner. Instead we order an Indian takeaway to arrive just before her guest turns up. Unsure what her new boyfriend likes, we order a large selection of dishes that we can share between us.

"Everyone likes Indian food, don't they?" she asks me, and for the first time, I sense her nervousness. Since she finished applying her make-up she's been on her feet, tidying things that are already in order, and pacing up and down. When the buzzer finally chimes she freezes and looks at me, her eyes pleading for something I can't work out.

Alex Butler is not the man from the bar and not who I would expect Chloe to be attracted to. He is the complete opposite of Andrew; slight and wiry with smooth skin that looks as if it's never been shaved. I wonder how old he is but it's impossible to tell; he could be anything from twenty to forty.

While Alex sits next to Chloe on the sofa, shovelling broken pieces of poppadom into his mouth, I pretend to be engrossed in my food and watch him surreptitiously. I make assumptions about what has attracted Chloe to him. She barely knows him, so it's got to be physical. His face is pleasant to look at, kind and genuine. But more than this, he talks animatedly, as if he's excited just to be sitting near her and he takes every opportunity to clutch her hand or pat her knee. When Chloe speaks, Alex fixes his eyes on her, engrossed in every word that leaves her mouth. This man is the complete opposite of you.

Alex is polite enough to remember I'm in the room and takes the time to ask me about my life. While I launch into the details of how I know Chloe, his hand firmly squeezes hers but he fails to notice her eyes constantly flicking to her watch. Even if he did happen to notice he would only jump to conclusions and probably assume she's bored of his company. Only I know the real reason she's checking the time. It must be upsetting for her that you haven't bothered to come home.

Giving in to pity, I clear away the empty food cartons and plates and while I'm in the kitchen I send you a text. All I bother to say is *where are you?* Now even I am starting to think you're being cruel to your sister.

When I get back to the living room, Chloe and Alex have started on a second bottle of wine. Alex fills my glass and I realise I quite like him. He's intelligent but also has a sense of humour and a way of putting people at ease. Despite this, I start to feel I should give him and Chloe some time alone so when I reach the bottom of my glass I feign a yawn.

"You're not going to bed," Chloe insists, seeing through my act. Once again her eyes plead with me and once again I give in to her. I stay sunk into the sofa while she tops up my empty glass. The chilled liquid flows through me, relaxing every part of my body. I can't remember how many glasses I've had but this one is like an anaesthetic and I feel myself drifting off.

My eyes snap open but it's pitch-black. Disorientated, for several seconds I wonder where I am before I notice the familiar cold feel of your leather sofa against my legs. Out of the silence, soft giggling erupts from the corner of the room so I lie still and listen, dazed and fuddled by alcohol. I am lying on my side and gradually shapes merge into identifiable objects. It is then I make out Chloe on the other sofa with Alex. She is naked and hunched over him, even smaller now that she's shed her clothing. Underneath her, Alex nibbles her small breast while she slides up and down on top of him, flicking her head back and grabbing his legs for balance.

I freeze, momentarily too shocked to look away. If I move even a fraction they will hear me and then what would I do? All I can do is pretend to sleep, close my eyes tightly and pray for them to hurry up. But it doesn't end quickly and I am forced to focus on their heavy breathing and moaning; a torturous reminder of what I'm not doing with you. I never thought I would be but at this moment I am jealous of Chloe.

Finally the groaning dies down and silence fills the room again. I don't know what they're doing, my eyes are still fixed tightly shut, and somehow this silence is worse than what came before.

After a while, there are whispers and rustling. I dare to open my eyes and see Alex, now fully dressed, walk out. Chloe hasn't bothered to put her clothes back on but follows him downstairs and after more whispers the front door clicks shut.

I stay still until I am certain Chloe has shut her bedroom door then I curl up in a ball, my tears forming a small pool on the arm of the sofa. I want you to come home so I can show you I need you to do to me what Alex has just done to Chloe.

I feel along the sofa for my mobile but I have no idea where it is. I can't remember if I brought it back from the kitchen after texting you and this fills me with despair because I don't have the energy to search for it. I try one last thing and dangle my arm from the sofa, sliding my palm across the carpet. Within seconds my fingers are pushing into the glass of my phone and I scoop it up, relief flooding through me. But there are no messages.

I open my eyes and you are standing over me, a puzzled expression spread across your face. Light is streaming into the room and at first I think it must be morning, but then the automatic hall light sensor clicks off and we are shrouded in darkness. I pull you down towards me but you shrug me off and sit on the floor by the sofa, facing away from me.

"Are we okay?" I ask, fearing the reply you will give me.

You turn your face to me and I can smell whisky. "Why wouldn't we be?"

Now I am angry. "You never touch me anymore. What's the point of us being together?" I stare at your back, grateful your eyes can't bore into me because I don't want you to see the shame plastered all over my face. I am a spoilt child, in my words and actions, and I despise who I have become.

"I can't win with you, can I?" you say calmly. "First you're not happy because our relationship is all about sex and now it's not you're still complaining. I'm just not in the mood. Why can't you accept that?"

Even delivered softly, your words are like a bullet tearing my flesh apart and I want to hurt you as much as you're hurting me. Blinded by rage, I tell you about what Chloe has done tonight on your sofa. And as I deliver my monologue time slows down. You turn towards me but say nothing, letting me talk and spill details that no brother should ever have to hear. And after I finish, your face is tight with tension and I realise, too late, I have done something awful.

I wait for you to speak but you don't say a word. Your silence chastises me and I want to take back what I've said because I know I've crossed a line. I want you to shout at me, tell me to get out, anything that will make things all right again but you do none of these. Instead you pull me to my feet and rip my skirt from around me. I should push you away, tell you it can't be like this, but I am fighting a losing battle. Even if I were to protest would you listen? Excitement boils within me as I watch the crumpled material fall to the floor and I have soon forgotten what I've done tonight.

"This is what you wanted!" you say, yanking your jeans off. "To be treated like a dirty whore." You grab my neck with one hand and squeeze it, ramming yourself into me. Your other hand covers my mouth, even though there are no sounds of protest to stifle. And just when I think I have no breath left in me, you lift yourself off me and collapse in a heap.

We both lie there for some time, the silence of the flat deafening. Only I seem to hear the click of a door.

CHAPTER FIFTEEN

Not for a second do I consider myself to be an abused woman. Yes, there are deep red lines etched across my neck, but I am not a victim. How can I be when I enjoyed what you did? In the harsh light of day, it's easy to shudder when I admit this to myself, but at night all I'm left with is yearning. For the unspeakable. And I play it over and over in my mind, relishing it and sickened by it at the same time. After all, you were right when you said this is what I wanted and now I am torn, stripped of my dignity and maybe my morality. I am two different people now: a mother when I'm with Ellie and the rest of the time someone I can't even begin to describe.

We pretend nothing has happened and keep our distance from each other for days that drag into weeks. Our communication is brief; phone calls filled with small talk and irrelevant details about nothing punctuated with heavy silence. Perhaps, like me, you are not willing to analyse what's happened, not willing to open your eyes and see who we really are. Or perhaps it is something that can never be understood, even under a microscope of intense scrutiny. One thing I know is that no amount of thinking can add meaning to that night. It is what it is.

With only two weeks left of the school summer holidays, Ellie begins to grow restless and subdued. And I am frantic, consumed with fear that I've been neglecting her. Common sense tells me she's just desperate to be back at school with her friends – six weeks is an interminably long time for a child – but my guilt screams that Ellie's lethargy is my fault. Even though I'm always physically present in her life, lately my obsession with our relationship has left little emotional space in my head for my daughter. I can't even remember the last time I took an interest in one of her drawings. In fact, it's possible she hasn't even picked up a pencil in the last few weeks. How would I know when all I can think about is you?

I try to think of ways I can help Ellie perk up but my brain is addled, unable to process more than its own self-perpetuating cycle of torture. So I turn to Carl, just as I always have when I feel alone and helpless.

"It's simple," he says, as if I've asked him the answer to two plus two. "All you need to do is plan some exciting trips for Ellie. There are a million things to do in London, just get some ideas from the internet and I'm sure she'll cheer up. She has been stuck in a lot lately." I'm about to defend myself but he quickly adds, "With both of us, I mean."

Acting on Carl's advice, I frantically cram as many trips as possible into two weeks and take Ellie to Thorpe Park, Legoland, London Zoo and, on the last Friday before school starts, Madame Tussaud's. Carl is right and these excursions quickly lift Ellie's spirits. I am full of gratitude towards him as I watch her capturing memories of her days out with her pencil and sketchpad.

Madame Tussaud's is her favourite of all the places we visit, even though she doesn't recognise a lot of the models. On the crowded and stuffy tube home, she informs me that one day there'll be a model of her in there for being the greatest artist ever known. Or doctor. Or archaeologist. I can't help but smile at her innocence. As adults we lose the belief that anything is possible. Maybe I could be a lot happier if I allowed myself to believe our relationship will work out. Or even just that it has some meaning.

When Ellie and I arrive home, both of us tired and hungry, I am surprised to find you sitting on the front doorstep, three scrunched up coke cans lying dotted by your feet.

"Chloe's finally gone," you say, without looking up.

"Gone?" I fumble around in my bag for my keys, confused as to what you are trying to tell me and dreading to hear about the trouble she must have caused now.

"Moved out. Finally." Your words aren't spoken with the relief I would expect at finally having your flat to yourself again and I wonder if you parted on bad terms. I haven't seen you since the night Chloe invited Alex over and there could have been any number of rows taking place upstairs without my knowledge.

I tell you I need to make Ellie a sandwich and ask if you want to come in but you shake your head. "I'm fine here. But come back out when you've finished so we can talk. Please?"

Inside I make cheese and Marmite sandwiches and Ellie and I greedily tuck into them. Even though we had a huge slice of pizza in town, walking around all day has given us a healthy appetite and we both devour the bread until there's barely a crumb left on our plates.

When we've finished I let Ellie watch television and head outside to talk to you. The short walk through the communal hallway seems to take forever and I feel as though I'm walking the plank, in slow motion. It's not often you tell me we should talk. It can only mean you've made a decision about us that I'm not going to like, so as I head towards you I prepare myself for the worst.

Wiping dust off the step, I perch next to you. The doorstep is narrow but I make sure there is a gap between us so our legs don't touch. I don't know why I do this but somehow it feels appropriate.

It's cool out here now and too quiet. The distant hum of diminishing rush hour traffic quickly fades into oblivion and we are left alone. I cannot bear the silence; I need to hear something, anything that will signal there is life beyond our doorstep. Something to prove to me my life will carry on after this. But there is nothing but my own breathing, heavy as each breath escapes from my body. My anxiety drowns out everything else.

"So where's Chloe gone?" I ask, desperate to stall you from saying something that will change things forever.

Shaking your head, you explain. "Apparently she's staying with that Alex until she can find somewhere to rent. Good luck to him."

"Oh." Nothing Chloe does surprises me yet it is still strange she's made this huge decision so lightly.

"Well, at least it gets her out of my hair." You shuffle up closer to me. "And now you can move in, can't you? We spoke about it a while ago, remember?"

Your words render me speechless and there is something needy, almost desperate, in your voice that is incongruous coming from your mouth. This is not what I was expecting you to say this evening.

My mind replays that night a few weeks ago and I have trouble associating what happened with the idea you are now presenting to me. Surely what we did and your plan to move in together are so far removed that they can't possibly co-exist? I want to discuss this with you but how do I even bring it up? And now, with the benefit of time, I can't be sure I'm accurately recalling what happened. So once again it sits between us like a dormant volcano, easy to ignore and push aside. Until it threatens to erupt.

And this is not all I have to worry about. How can I walk inside and announce to Ellie that we're moving upstairs when she doesn't even know about our relationship? She's had so much disruption over the last year and this will only make things worse for her. It's only now she's starting to accept that Carl and I are separated so it would be cruel and unfair of me to drop this bombshell on her as well.

But I don't share any of these thoughts with you. Instead I am mute, nodding and snuggling into you because you are waiting for me to say something. You must take my silence for happiness because the expectant look on your face morphs into a smile. I cannot bear to look at you so I bury my head in your shoulder and once again focus on the silence around us.

When your hand reaches up my skirt all my doubts evaporate and I can only think of this. Of how I am burning up inside just from the touch of your fingers.

"I want you now," you whisper, pulling me inside our hallway. And then there is no more left to say because you are inside me again, filling me up with everything I need so that I forget where we are.

Later that night I flop down at my kitchen table and bury my head in my hands. Every possible consequence that can result from us moving in together plays out in my head and I analyse how it will affect Ellie. I am trapped because I want to be with you every day and have the chance of a normal relationship. Living together will surely mean things have to change between us for the better. It will mean we are a family: you, me and Ellie. You will have responsibility for my daughter. And Ellie does like you. I know she's not keen on Chloe but now Chloe's sorting herself out that shouldn't be a problem.

When I can't put it off any longer, I make two hot chocolates and take them to Ellie's room. She's tucked up in bed reading a book about pirates and looks like an angel with her long blonde hair fanned out on the pillow. I sit on the bed and we both sip our drinks. I feel sick to the pit of my stomach about what I'm about to tell her. No amount of hot chocolate will be able to comfort Ellie once she knows her life is about to change again. And this time, surely, is worse? Now it won't be just the two of us, safe in our own comfortable world.

I've barely broken the news when Ellie's face crumples in a way I've never seen before, not even when Carl and I told her we were separating, and within seconds she's in floods of tears and howling like an animal. I pull her close to me and grip her tightly as her tears soak my t-shirt.

"I hate him, I hate him," she wails. "What about Dad?"

I stroke her hair and whisper I'm sorry but my words die in the air because they are just not enough. Eventually, when Ellie's tears subside slightly, I tuck her back into bed and leave her to try and get some sleep. I tell her things will be different in the morning because nothing ever seems as bad in the daylight but she ignores me and turns over, burying her head in her pillow.

In the kitchen I dose myself with coffee and wonder just how I'm going to break the news to Carl. In some ways it will be harder than telling Ellie because at least she's not losing me. Carl, however, will know now I have gone for good and even though we've lived apart for over a year I know it will be a blow to him. He will know my place is with someone else. His mind will picture me with another man and it will torment him to the core, because no matter how much he tries to block it out, it will always resurface like an armband in a swimming pool. Then there will be the comparisons, the wondering if sex is better with someone else. I know this because it's exactly what I went through with him. But even though his betrayal crippled me, I want to spare Carl what I had to bear.

While I'm contemplating all this, Ellie stomps out of her room and rushes into the kitchen, thrusting something into my hand. I stare at the heavy object for several seconds before I realise it's the phone. "Dad wants to talk to you," she says sadly.

Steeling myself, I place the phone to my ear and listen to Carl's outpouring of anger. "Not now," I say to him when there is a brief pause in his torrent.

He sighs deeply and growls into the phone. "Bring Ellie to Hyde Park tomorrow. We need to talk properly. She's devastated, Olivia, and quite frankly, so am I."

I'm about to remind him he was planning on taking Ellie to Barbara's tomorrow but now isn't the time to argue.

It's the first day of September and leaves are already dropping from the trees, whisked around by the brisk breeze before carpeting the ground. Ellie and I crunch through them on our way to meet Carl in Hyde Park. We're both wearing summer tops and jeans, not quite ready to accept that autumn is here once again, encroaching into our lives.

Ellie has been silent all the way here even though she gratefully accepted the can of Fanta and packet of Skittles I bought her when we got to Waterloo station. Now, though, her pace increases and she gets a surge of energy as we approach the cafe in Hyde Park where we've arranged to meet Carl. My heart sinks as she spots him sitting at a table and runs to him, throwing herself into his outstretched arms. Tears sting my eyes as I watch them. We used to be a family and even though Carl is the one who first tore us apart, now it is me who is shredding us into tiny pieces.

Carl helps Ellie into a seat but doesn't look in my direction so I head to the counter to get us all some drinks. I don't need to ask either of them what they want; I know them both as well as I know myself. A spotty teenage boy takes my order and searches my face before dropping his eyes to the till. I hastily grab a napkin from the counter and pretend to blow my nose; I know my eyes are streaming so have to do something to mask the real cause of it. I even add a couple of coughs for authenticity but the spotty boy has his back to me now, engrossed in making our drinks.

Neither Carl nor Ellie thank me for the drinks and it's suddenly silent when I join them at their table. I stir sugar and milk into my tea and pretend this is a normal family day out we're having.

"I've brought Ellie's roller skates," I say, pointing to Ellie's rucksack, which is on my back. "I thought it would be nice if she could have a skate around the park while we talk."

Ellie's face briefly lights up; she loves skating and didn't know I'd planned this.

"Okay, but not too far. Stay in sight of us, Ellie," Carl says, still not looking at me.

We finish our drinks and while Ellie puts her skates, on my mobile vibrates in my pocket. Seeing it's you, I head outside the cafe to answer it. Carl scowls but doesn't say anything and I'm grateful Ellie's here to help diffuse the bad atmosphere.

It's strange talking to you while Carl is in my line of sight. Almost as if I am committing a betrayal. The person being wronged cannot be determined, though; perhaps it is all of us in some way. You ask me where I am and I lie without hesitation. You won't even try to understand the truth so I don't bother explaining. It's bad enough having one man angry with me; the last thing I need is to have an argument with you as well. I tell you I'm working and you offer to cook me dinner this evening. Normally this would put a smile on my face but all I can think about is salvaging what I can of my broken family, or whatever it's called now. I tell you I'll stop by later, just as Ellie whizzes past me and Carl appears next to me, an accusation spread across his face.

"So was that him?" he snarls.

"Carl, you're hardly in a position to be angry. Do I need to remind you what you did?" I set off after Ellie, watching her closely as she glides along, weaving in and out of people and dogs. Carl follows, his hands buried in his pockets in an act of defiance.

"This is not about me, Olivia," he says. "I'm not the one taking our daughter to live with some stranger."

"He's not a stranger. I've known him for over a year. He's a teacher–"

"Yes I know all that. Ellie's told me everything. So why keep it a secret for so long?"

"I don't have to put up with being interrogated by you. It's none of your business, is it?" Now it is my turn to be too angry for eye contact and I stare at the ground, feeling Carl's eyes burning into me.

"It *is* my damn business who my daughter lives with," Carl shouts, and an elderly couple in front of us turn around to stare. Knowing he is right, I don't reply but walk faster to try and overtake the nosy couple ahead.

"For fuck's sake, Olivia. You already live in the same building as him. Why do you have to give up your flat?"

It is only now I realise why Carl is so upset. This isn't just about him losing me to someone else; perhaps that's not the issue at all. It's about Ellie living with someone else. Someone who one day she might think of as a father. As soon as this dawns on me I know what I must do. So I lie. I deliver a speech to Carl that is worthy of a Nobel Prize. I tell him what a great man you are and how much you adore Ellie. I argue that you're loving and caring, a man incapable of hurting anyone and someone who always puts me first. I explain how hard you work and how you were there for you sister when she needed you even though it was difficult living with her. I emphasise to Carl that nobody will *ever* replace him as Ellie's dad and by the time I've finished my monologue, Carl's shoulders have relaxed and the frown lines on his face have blended away.

"I just ask one thing," he says as Ellie circles around us. "I want to meet him before you move in there. That's only fair. After all, this man will be sharing a home with my daughter."

I nod, already knowing and dreading what you will say when I tell you Carl wants to vet you before he'll allow Ellie to live in your flat.

"Do you realise Ellie doesn't want to move? She said she hates this Chloe woman and if you move in she'll have to see her all the time. What's that all about?"

I think about this for a moment. Although I've picked up on some negativity from Ellie towards Chloe, I've never fully explored what the problem is. I've always assumed it's the same reason I'm not enraptured with Chloe: she's a very hard person to like. I tell Carl this but he remains concerned.

"Chloe's moved out now, Carl. It's not a problem." As I say these words, a bit like during my speech earlier, I'm not sure who I'm trying to convince more.

"Well, I'll be talking more to Ellie about it all this weekend," Carl says. "Let's just hope she comes round to the idea. But I'm still not happy about this, Olivia. I know I've been an idiot so I've only got myself to blame but I can't bear the thought of Ellie being hurt more than she already has been."

"Neither of us want to cause Ellie pain. I've just had to move on," I say, linking my arm through Carl's, glad he's being more reasonable now.

Ellie rolls towards us, tired out by her exertions and back to being quiet and withdrawn. She reaches for Carl and he helps her replace her skates with her trainers. As he ties her laces, Carl glances up at me and winks.

"Don't worry," he says, and I wonder how someone with such a big heart could have done what he did.

Together we walk to the Hyde Park Corner exit, Ellie clinging on to Carl's hand and me lugging her weekend bag and rucksack. *What am I doing?* plays like a mantra in my head but I am powerless to do anything. I feel like I'm on a train that's quickly gathering speed and not stopping at any station. All I can do is stay on it and see where I end up. But what sort of way is that to bring up my daughter?

At the gates Carl hugs me goodbye and reluctantly Ellie does the same. Carl has driven today while I'll be heading back home on the tube. He's taking Ellie to Barbara's and they're putting on a barbecue for some of Barbara's friends.

"I love you," I tell Ellie, and kiss the top of her head. "See you tomorrow."

"Bye, Mum," she says as she trots off with Carl, her pace increasing once again and her head bobbing from side to side as she talks animatedly about the barbecue.

The journey home is a blur for me and I negotiate escalators, platforms and sliding doors like a pre-programmed robot. Normally I'm happy for Ellie to be with Carl but today I just want her by my side, happy and smiling. If Ellie is miserable then nothing in my world is right.

I knock on your door and plaster a smile onto my face. I can't let you see something is wrong, and you especially can't know it's because of you. You answer the door and I keep my clownish smile in place. I don't notice anything, not what you're wearing or what you're saying. I force myself to eat the dinner you've gone to a lot of trouble to make and I wash it down with far too much wine which feels as thick as blood.

"Can you stay the night?" you ask me later when we're lying next to each other on the sofa. Canned laughter from a comedy programme blares from the television but you are the only one interested in it.

Fuelled by alcohol, I burst into giggles and climb on top of you, my mouth eagerly searching for yours. I know you're enjoying watching TV but I'm confident I can distract you from it. Still giggling, I clumsily strip off my clothes and press your hands to my breasts. You groan beneath me and grow hard between my legs. And now I know for sure everything will be all right.

CHAPTER SIXTEEN

Slivers of sunlight race towards me, forcing me to open my eyes. Today the slats of the blinds are too far open and the sun stares innocently, unaware of its violation. Closing my eyes again does no good. The rays have burnt an orange tint onto my eyelids and now sleep and escape are both impossible.

I need to empty my bladder and as usual my legs shake when I attempt to stand, even though the shrunken frame they support is barely more than a skeleton. But first I shuffle over to the blinds and twist the cord to freeze out the sun. Now I am safely bathed in darkness.

Closing the bathroom door, I lean against it, my back almost as straight as the wood supporting it, and listen. There is no lock on the door and they have promised nobody will ever open it without my permission but I wait a few minutes, just to make sure.

When I've finished, I throw the door open and am shocked to see sunlight has found its way back in. Before I've even had a chance to wonder how this has happened, a thick arm pushes through mine and leads me over to the chair in the corner. Since I've been here the bed is the only place I've sat but I move without protesting because that's what must be done here. And then the voice speaks to me; a comforting lullaby, it is what I've needed to hear.

"Sit down, lovey. There'll be no more lying around today."

I am guided onto the chair, the thick arm still clinging to mine. I want to look at this woman, to put a face to the kind voice, but fear prevents me from turning my head. It is strange seeing my room from a different angle; everything is out of place, including me.

"Oh, that's right," the voice continues. "You don't like to look at people, do you? Well, that's okay. For now, at least. But sooner or later you'll need to look at me. It's important to try that, okay?"

I shake my head slowly, a barely noticeable gesture, and turn towards the wall, convinced this is another of their tricks.

"Okay, that's fine," she says, patting my arm. "I'll just tidy up in here. Freshen the place up a bit. You sit tight."

Her clothes rustle as she walks away, her shoes click-clacking on the tiles. From the sounds she makes, I can tell exactly what she is doing in my room. It's funny how I've come to call it *my* room, as if taking ownership can offer me comfort, because nothing belongs to me anymore, either in here or outside. At least not anything that matters. The woman pulls dirty sheets from my bed and replaces them with clean ones. I know without looking that they will be paper thin and as uncomfortable as cardboard, but they have a pleasant lemony scent which I can smell from over here.

In the bathroom, she releases gushes of water from the taps and the mirror squeaks as she rubs it down. I want to shout out that cleaning the mirror is pointless. I will never need to know how my hair looks or whether I could do with some make-up. She hums as she cleans – an upbeat tune I've never heard before – and suddenly I emit a scream, summoning all the air in my lungs to make the loudest possible noise because, despite her lovely voice, I need her to leave me alone.

Sometimes, on rare occasions, life will present a nice surprise and contrary to my expectations, living with you is one of these times. Although you seem to have a rule for everything, particularly where to put things and how to clean up, I quickly grow accustomed to your quirks and learn how to do things your way. It's not as easy teaching Ellie new routines but she has always been fairly tidy and you are patient with her if she forgets to do something.

Another surprise for me in those first few months is how quickly Ellie gets used to our new living arrangement, and in no time at all turns your spare room into her own sanctuary. You agree I can paint the walls for her even though I know it breaks your heart to see the magnolia paint morphing into pastel pink. Within no time, it is hard to believe this room was ever just a bland space, sometimes occupied by Chloe and her clutter of clothes and magazines.

Inexplicably, Carl stops moaning and accepts our living arrangement. He still hasn't met you, despite his initial insistence, but every time I bring it up he has an excuse for why he doesn't have time at the moment.

Carl never calls the house phone, in case you answer, but buys Ellie her own pay-as-you-go mobile so they can contact each other any time.

"It's ridiculous," you say, once Ellie's out of ear-shot. "A ten-year-old kid shouldn't have a mobile phone."

I partly agree but given the circumstances don't see a choice. "Would you prefer having to answer the phone to Carl every day?" I ask, already knowing what your answer will be. Your frown and accompanying silence tell me I'm right.

It is a chilly Sunday in January when Ellie bursts though the door, full of excitement about her weekend with Carl. I stand at the bottom of the stairs and watch the trail of white powder footprints she leaves behind. With no clue how to get rid of snow before it forms a soggy wet patch, I grab the vacuum cleaner from under the stairs and suck up all traces of the mess she's unwittingly made, praying you won't choose this moment to arrive home.

"Shoes off!" I shout after her but she has already disappeared into her bedroom.

After checking every room is tidy, I start to prepare dinner. We have got into the routine of having a late Sunday roast when Ellie gets back from Carl's, but she's usually too full to eat it so today I decide to cook something different.

"How does spaghetti and meatballs sound?" I ask Ellie, as she plonks herself at the kitchen table with her sketch pad.

"Mmmmm, good! Where's Michael?"

"It's just us this evening, Pumpkin. He's visiting his parents."

"Good," Ellie responds, burying her head in her sketchbook. I turn to her and she must feel the heavy weight of my stare. "Sorry, Mum. I just mean it's nice for us to be alone for a change."

Ellie is right; moments when it's just the two of us are rare these days so should be cherished. "Yes, it's lovely. I've even got cheesecake for dessert."

"Yum!" she shouts, before turning her attention back to her drawing.

We are halfway through our meal when I notice Ellie's sketchbook is still on the table next to her, closed. "What are you drawing?" I ask.

For a moment she looks sheepish then fixes her eyes on her plate. "Oh, nothing. It's not very good."

"Let's see," I say, making a grab for the book.

"No!" Ellie snatches it away before my fingers reach the paper.

I remain calm and try not to show I'm hurt. Perhaps she is embarrassed her latest sketch is not up to her usual standards. Respecting Ellie's wishes, I tuck into my food again and motion for her to do the same.

"Eat up. We've got cheesecake, remember?" I try to think rationally about what's just happened; perhaps her need for some privacy is just a sign of her growing up. It can't be fair for me to demand to know everything she does, thinks or says. I tuck into my cheesecake and put the matter from my mind.

I have almost forgotten the incident until Ellie thrusts her sketchbook into my hand while I'm tucking her into bed. She smiles and shrugs her shoulders in what I assume is an apology. Flicking through the pages, I smile as I revisit drawings I've seen before, struggling to believe they have been produced by a child. My child. I reach the last page and it takes me a moment to digest the image. Carl's face stares back at me, a wide smile spread across it. Attached to his cheek is another face. One I don't recognise. It is female and her long, flowing hair is wrapped around Carl's neck like a scarf.

"Who is this with Dad, Ellie?" I ask, my stomach sinking.

"Oh, that's just Keira."

"And who's Keira?"

"Oh, I think maybe Dad's new girlfriend."

Somewhere in my heart or head – every part of my body – I must have been expecting this would happen eventually. Carl and I have been separated for over a year, more than enough time for him to move on, so I shouldn't feel as if my insides are being ripped out. But that is exactly how I feel. So many questions race through my head, none of which I can burden Ellie with. She has to see I'm okay with this, just as Carl is respectful of my relationship with you. So I say nothing and offer up the hugest smile I can muster as I pull the duvet up to her chin and smooth it out around her.

Showing wisdom far greater than her age, Ellie says, "It's okay, Mum, you can ask me about her."

So I do. Carl has finally got around to redecorating the house but, being pushed for time, hired an interior decorator. Keira. She's a bit younger than him, not even thirty, but they've been spending so much time together that the age gap can't be a problem for either of them. I shouldn't feel jealous as Ellie fills in the gaps about this woman, but in some ways it feels worse than when I found out about Lisa. At least I knew he regretted that immediately, that it was just one night of insanity which probably repulses him now. But this is different. Carl doesn't give his time to just anyone.

"Why did you keep it a secret, Pumpkin?" I ask, smothering my feelings. "Did Dad ask you to?"

"No. I just didn't want to upset you." Half of Ellie's face is hidden and her eyes shine brightly in the dim light of her lamp.

"But why would I be upset? I'm with Michael now, aren't I?"

Ellie shrugs her shoulders beneath the covers. "You're just always sad, that's all."

Her sentence sends a shooting pain through my gut, fiercer than the one I experienced a few moments ago. How have I been so oblivious to my daughter's thoughts and feelings? This idea crushes me more than the notion she could be right. I lean down to hug her and assure her she's wrong.

It's nearly midnight when you arrive home and find me slouched on the sofa, attempting to read. A half-finished mug of hot chocolate sits on the floor in front of me and, seeing your eyes fix on it, I quickly grab it and rush to the kitchen, hoping you won't notice the thick stains caked onto the sides of the mug.

When I come back you're wiping up something near the sofa and I prepare myself for a lecture. "Sorry, did I make a mess? I think I fell asleep."

"Don't worry. It's sorted."

A waterfall of tears cascades from my eyes and I am powerless to stop it. I don't want you to see me like this because then I will owe you an explanation, something I cannot even offer myself. I try my best to destroy the evidence but my eyes cannot recover quickly and you notice within seconds.

"Olivia, what's wrong?"

You pull me into you and your jumper soaks up my tears. I can't answer you and thankfully you don't try to force me to speak. Instead you stroke my hair, letting it slip through your fingers. For some reason your kindness sets me off further so I no longer know what I'm crying about. Surely I should be happy sharing a moment like this with you? I assure you I'm okay and you don't question me further.

"Come to bed," you say eventually and I follow you through the hallway, my bare feet sinking into the carpet, knowing only one thing can make me feel better now. And then we are no longer ourselves but two characters, well-rehearsed in the parts being played out. I am not a mother but someone who will let you do anything; unspeakable acts that return to haunt me in the harsh light of day.

Afterwards, as is usual, we don't speak about what we've done. It's not shame that keeps us from mentioning it, just acceptance that for us this is normality.

"Are you okay?" you whisper, and I smile to show you I am. I lie still, knowing if I try to move in any direction the pain, which only moments ago excited me to my core, will cripple me.

"Chloe's left that Alex bloke," you tell me the next morning. I'm still lying in the same position I fell asleep in, but risk turning over to face you. You're sitting up against your pillow reading *The Independent*, the page folded in half even though it's a tabloid-sized version. "She told me yesterday. I can't say I'm upset about it."

I sit up slowly, pleased the ache I feel is minimal, and rub my eyes until I'm fully awake. "But Alex was okay. You never even met him!"

"I know, but he's not Andrew, is he?" You return to your paper and I get up to wake Ellie for school, grateful the bathroom separates her bedroom from ours.

"Let's be civilised about this," Carl says when I finish ranting at him. I'm sure he must be holding the phone away from his ear because even to me my voice is uncomfortably loud. Yet there isn't a single note of anger in his words.

"You're a hypocrite!" I yell at him. "When I first told you about moving in with Michael you insisted on meeting him because he'd be spending time with Ellie, yet you let some random woman into her life without me even knowing she exists! What the hell, Carl?" My blood boils and Carl's calmness only increases my body temperature.

"Calm down, will you? I didn't bother meeting him in the end, did I? Because I trust you. Anyway, Keira's a lovely person and Ellie likes her. I wasn't going to mention it until I knew it was serious. Besides, Ellie meeting her was an accident. The other week we bumped into Keira and her sister at the cinema and I couldn't just pretend I didn't know her."

I am amazed at Carl's excuse. There are a million explanations he could have offered Ellie so he must have wanted her to know who Keira was. I grow even angrier when I think how I kept the truth about us from Ellie until recently, in the hopes of protecting her feelings. I explain this to Carl but as usual he has a convincing response.

"I don't think we should lie to Ellie. Ever. Yes, the truth hurts sometimes but at least we're being honest with our daughter."

Even though I know Carl's right I don't want him to win this argument. "Don't you think Ellie's had enough to deal with?"

"Yeah, from you!" Carl says, raising his voice for the first time. "I'm not the one who moved in with a stranger."

I have no choice but to let this comment go because Carl is right. The stubborn part of me wants to remind him that he was the one who destroyed our marriage in the first place but I'm too worn out for this battle.

"Just stop," I tell him, trying hard to keep my voice under control. "Ellie's all that matters so we need to stop this right now."

"I agree." He pauses for a moment and I am shocked by what he says next. "Look, I know I haven't met this Michael yet and you need to meet Keira, so why don't we all get together this week? It might seem a crazy idea but we'd be doing it for Ellie."

Once I'm over the initial shock of Carl's suggestion, I try to picture how an evening with the four of us would play out. It would be awkward for everyone and I can't see what good would come of it. You and Carl will never be friends and I'm not sure I'll be able to welcome Keira into my life. At least at the moment she is only a name and a description. I don't want her to be real. "I don't know, Carl–"

"Come on. There'll be less pressure on anyone if all four of us are there. Besides, have you got any better ideas?"

Once again, Carl's reasoning wins me over and for the next few hours I clean the flat and wonder how I will broach the subject with you. As I dust, mop and vacuum, it's impossible to tell which surfaces I've already wiped over as they were all smudge-free to begin with, but I have to be especially careful today; I need you in a good mood when I mention Carl's plan.

But I am wasting my time getting the already-clean flat in order because your mood is set before you even get inside. You slam the front door and thunder up the stairs, passing me in the hallway without a word. In the bedroom I hear you cursing through the closed door so I don't go in. I know better than to try and snap you out of whatever this mood is.

I make you a cup of tea and shout out that it's ready but it's barely even lukewarm by the time you sit cradling it at the kitchen table. Without preamble you begin speaking.

"Andrew called me today. He said Chloe turned up at the flat to try and take the dog and she had some guy with her. He's furious. She's just rubbing his face in it now."

"Was it Alex? I thought they'd split up."

"That's what makes it even worse. It wasn't Alex, just some random guy she's picked up fuck knows where."

I only half understand your agitation and reply without thinking. "I know Chloe seems to be on a path to self-destruction but she's a grown woman. Nobody can tell her how to live her life." I cringe as I say this, shocked that I have allowed myself to speak out loud in your presence any thoughts about Chloe.

But to my surprise, you don't shoot me down. Instead you hunch your shoulders and take a long sip of cold tea, making me stew before you finally reply. "I know. I just can't tolerate the way she treats Andrew." You lift your cup to your mouth but remember it's cold and screw up your face. "Anyway, fuck her, what shall I cook for dinner tonight?"

So for the time being the matter of Chloe is forgotten and all I have to worry about is how to mention meeting up with Carl and his new girlfriend. I plan to wait until we're in bed and you're a bit more relaxed so there's at least a minuscule chance you'll consider it. I know the odds are highly stacked against this; Carl's name may as well be forbidden in your flat unless mentioned by Ellie. And even when she brings up his name I can see your face tighten. You are happy to pretend he doesn't exist.

But once again fate, in the form of Ellie, takes matters out of my hands when she blurts the news out over dinner. "It's great you're meeting up with Dad and Keira. Now you can all be friends!" she declares, a gigantic clown smile spread across her face as she shovels fries into her mouth.

I haven't mentioned anything about this to Ellie yet so Carl must have told her. She's only had her mobile phone for a short time yet it's already begun causing problems.

"What's this?" you ask, midway through chewing a chunk of steak. You look at me, rather than Ellie, so I offer the simplest explanation I can. Perhaps it is better it's come out now rather than when we're alone in bed; at least with Ellie here you remain calm, nod and smile at her and pretend it's a great idea.

It is only later you reveal your true feelings. Once our bedroom door is closed and Ellie is too heavily asleep to be disturbed.

"I'm mystified. It's a ridiculous idea. What were you thinking of, agreeing to this? I don't want to meet your bloody husband!"

"Ex-husband," I remind you.

"Not yet, remember? You haven't signed anything or have you forgotten?"

Your words bring me crashing back down to earth and I am flooded with guilt. For most of our relationship I have believed your reluctance to get close to me was causing the wide gulf between us, so I have never stopped to consider my part in it. Not being divorced yet, when legally Carl and I could have done it months ago, must send out a huge sign to you that I haven't acknowledged before. But the reason for your bitterness this evening and aversion to us all meeting up is now apparent.

"Carl's with someone else now," I say. "And I'm fine with that. We all just need to be adults about this. For Ellie's sake." Saying this always works with Carl and I hope it has some effect on you too, even though she's not your daughter.

"Ellie's a strong kid, she'll be fine. Sorry, but I just can't go."

I lie awake for far too long, listening to your deep breaths, furious that you are able to dismiss so easily something that's important to my daughter. At some point in the night rain hammers against the window pane, reminding me of the night you took me outside and neither of us cared that we were soaked to the bone. Instinctively I reach under the duvet, take you in my cold hands and stroke you so that in no time at all it is your turn to be powerless.

In the middle of the week, Carl phones to tell me he's booked a table for Friday night at a pizza restaurant in the Strand. Just in case I try to come up with an excuse, Carl explains he chose this location so that it's convenient for all of us to get there and home again. He has arranged for Barbara to look after Ellie and assures me she's healthy enough to cope for a few hours. I'm sceptical at first but when I picture Barbara I remember she's made of titanium. Nothing can knock her down, not even this hideous disease that's inside her. I don't tell Carl you're refusing to come, still hoping I'll be able to convince you in the next few days that it's not such a terrible idea.

"Keira's really looking forward to meeting you," Carl says, and I wonder how this can be true. I am the woman with whom he shared over ten years of his life, the mother of his only child, so how can she be looking forward to seeing me face-to-face? I do want to believe someone can be a naturally decent person, good to the core, but surely excitement in this type of circumstance is beyond the limits of human nature? The only alternative is that Carl has made her feel so secure with him that I am no threat to her. I decide to reserve judgement until I meet this woman but I am already developing an intense dislike of her. I am not a good person. I am not Keira.

As Friday approaches you show no signs of giving in, despite the fact that I resort to enduring an uncomfortable couple of nights on the sofa. When I look in on you in the middle of the night, you are sleeping like a baby and show no sign of missing me being by your side. We don't speak about our sleeping arrangements and every morning you act as if nothing is wrong, making breakfast and joking around with Ellie. But as long as Ellie is happy, oblivious to the moods of the adults around her, I won't complain.

Before now I have never dwelled on what clothes to wear for an evening out but by five thirty on Friday I have already spent over an hour searching through my wardrobe, the simple task of picking one thing to wear seemingly beyond me. The bedroom carpet is barely visible through the pile of discarded garments. You walk into the room to get your laptop and scowl at me, undoubtedly reading too much into my inability to get dressed.

After several more futile minutes, I've had enough and throw on my skinny jeans and a sparkly camisole I've never worn before. It's not that I can't be bothered anymore; I have a point to prove to you. But I do choose the highest pair of heels I own because, knowing Carl, Keira will be tall.

In the living room, you are sunk into the sofa, your laptop open on your knees and a glass of wine in your hand. "You off, then?" you say without looking up from the screen.

I pull my hairbrush from my bag and use the mirror above the fireplace to help me see what I'm doing. I have already done my hair but I need something to do while I'm talking to you, something to prevent me from having to look at you when you can't be bothered to return the favour.

"Your jeans are creased," you say. My tactic has worked and at some point my nonchalance has confused you, making you pull your eyes away from your laptop. It is a minor victory for me and I can't help but feel pleased with myself because these moments are rare.

I carry on brushing my hair. "Well, I'm not trying to impress anyone, am I?"

You grunt something I can't be bothered to decipher and I am glad you're not coming. I don't want Carl to see this side of you and worry about what type of man I've dragged my daughter to live with.

There is still plenty of time to get to the restaurant but I decide to go now. I can take my time and browse one of the nearby bookshops; it will help me mentally prepare myself for this meeting. As I bend down to kiss you goodbye, the doorbell chimes and you jump up, almost knocking your laptop to the floor. Even before you've reached the stairs the doorbell once again shrieks. I am intrigued; whoever is out there is showing no patience so it must be something urgent. I hear you opening the door just as there is a furious knocking against it. And then I hear a loud drunken laugh that can only belong to Chloe.

I quickly throw my coat on but it's too late. Before I know what's happening, Chloe stands in front of me, wrapping her spindly arms around me and forcing me into a hug. She smells as if she's thrown a whole bottle of Chanel Number Five over her and it makes me gag.

"Olivia!" she shrieks. "Where are you going?"

You urge her to keep her voice down and pull her into the living room, even though it's not late enough for her to be disturbing the neighbours.

"I'm just being friendly," Chloe protests. "What's your problem, Michael?"

You have destroyed her blissful mood and she stares at you as if you've cut her arm off. You clearly haven't got over your anger at her for leaving Andrew but I start to feel sorry for Chloe again. To diffuse the situation I tell her where I'm going and despite being filled with alcohol, she listens attentively.

"Well, if Michael won't go then I'll keep you company instead," she declares. "I think you'll need the moral support." She looks at you and smiles.

Your face drops. "That's ridiculous. It's none of your business, Chloe, why would you even want to go?"

"To support Olivia, of course. Your *girlfriend*."

You glare at each other and it is up to me to end your battle of wills. "Well, I have to leave now, so..."

Suddenly you jump up. "D'you know what? I think I will come after all." You close your laptop and unplug the wire, wrapping it neatly around your hand before putting it in its box on the bookshelf. "Sorry if I was an arsehole about it before, Olivia. Just give me a second to get changed."

I turn to Chloe and she smiles triumphantly. I don't know what fight she thinks she has just won but it doesn't matter because at least now you are coming and I won't have to make up pathetic excuses to Carl.

It is with a heavy heart I walk into the restaurant. You and Chloe are in the middle of an argument some distance behind me and as I'm greeted by a gush of warm air from above me, I pause and wonder how I can face meeting a woman who one day could be Ellie's stepmother. A woman who will share in my daughter's progression to her teenage years and beyond and offer snippets of wisdom passed on from a family which has nothing to do with me.

It doesn't help that Chloe has tagged along and you are both too engrossed in your battle to realise how important this evening is. I don't know how I'm going to explain what Chloe is doing here. Offering an excuse for your absence would surely be easier than this.

Once you and Chloe have joined me inside, the waiter leads us to the only empty table in the room. It is too bright in here and I feel as if I'm under a spotlight, all attention focused on me. I am relieved that Carl is running late; it gives me time to prepare myself and hopefully once we start drinking you and Chloe will stop arguing. We order gin and tonics and a bottle of red wine and I watch Chloe, who has chosen to sit next to you despite the tension floating between you. Perhaps the brisk air outside has sobered her up slightly because she falls quiet, checking herself in her compact mirror and applying another heavy coat of black cherry-coloured lipstick.

There's still no sign of Carl when the drinks arrive and I cling to my glass until my hands are soaked with condensation and I'm forced to put it down before it slips from my grip.

"So, you must feel a bit strange," Chloe says, her smile daring me to challenge her. I look at you but as usual you are oblivious to the malicious undertone of her statement. Even when you are on bad terms with her you don't notice the game she plays with me.

You look up from your menu. "It's ridiculous," you say, before I can answer for myself. "I can't believe I'm here." Turning to Chloe, you bark at her. "This is your fault."

Chloe throws her head back and laughs. "Don't be silly. We would have been fine without you, wouldn't we, Olivia?" The two of you have regressed to children but I am not going to parent you.

Now I want to run. From you, from Chloe and most of all from a woman I've never met before. All around me I'm surrounded by couples, friends and families and not one of their faces shows anything other than enjoyment of the food they're tucking into. We don't belong here with our fighting and dysfunction.

I stand up, not sure what I'll do or where I can go, but before I can move my exit is blocked by Carl, who, with no awkwardness, wraps me in a hug. I quickly shrug him off, aware of too many eyes fixed on me. A short, slightly plump lady stands behind him, offering her hand to me. Surprised that she's not towering above me, I extend my arm and she grabs my hand, her grip warm and genuine. A kind smile lights up her plain face and I immediately see why Carl has chosen her. "I'm so glad to meet you," she says, her voice as comforting as everything else about her.

I make introductions and, to my surprise, everyone is civil, greeting each other as if we're about to have a business meeting. You shake hands with Carl as if you are pleased to meet him and even Chloe tones down her abrasiveness and pulls out a chair for Keira.

But Chloe can never sustain politeness and we've hardly finished our starters before she turns to Keira and begins firing questions at her. Keira shows no sign of objecting and responds graciously to Chloe's interrogation, even managing to ask Chloe a few of her own questions. I tune out and instead listen to the conversation between you and Carl, which to my surprise is amicable, both of you speaking animatedly about the latest football results. Everyone has the sense to stick to small talk, a mercy in all of this.

Even though nobody seems to notice, I am the only person with nothing to say and my second glass of gin and tonic does nothing to anaesthetise me and cancel out the discomfort I'm drowning in. The cacophony of laughter and chatter gets louder, making it impossible now to hear any individual conversation, but I am grateful for this. I no longer care what anyone is saying, I just want to get out of here and breathe again.

Things quieten down once the pizza arrives and everyone tucks in. Someone has ordered another bottle of wine and Keira tries to pour me a glass but I stop her and fill it with tap water instead. I need it to wash away the bitter taste of gin lingering in my mouth.

"Ellie's a wonderful girl," Keira says across the table, and I wonder if I have once again missed part of a conversation.

I want to shout at her. *Stay away from my daughter.* Maybe I even want to tell her to stay away from Carl but then I feel your hand reach for mine and reality hits me. This must be even harder for Carl because Ellie lives with you and not him. I think about how friendly he's been to you this evening and a river of shame floods through me. So I muster a smile and thank her. And in the conversation that follows I learn a lot about Keira and even more about myself. I have wasted days fretting about this woman when I couldn't have got her more wrong. All week my instincts have been screaming at me that she shouldn't be part of my daughter's life but now I know Carl is right to want her in his life.

After talking to Keira, I start to enjoy myself, finally feeling like any other person in the restaurant. Chloe suggests we order desserts and I let you pour me the glass of the wine I've so far resisted. I sit back and let my shoulders relax, once again only half-listening to the conversation at the table.

"So Keira's doing the interior design of my house," Carl says to no one in particular. "It was a real stroke of luck finding her."

Chloe laughs. "Just make sure he still pays you, Keira," she says, refilling both their glasses. I have never seen this side of Chloe before, a softer side, a person able to relate to another woman. But before I have a chance to work out how I feel about this, your hand – which has been clinging on to mine underneath the table – slips inside my jeans. I gasp but nobody at the table seems to notice so you delve further until your fingers are deep inside me and my face turns crimson.

I squirm and try to wriggle discreetly, hoping you'll take the hint that I don't want this. Not here and not now. But you push further in, showing me you are the one in control. I don't dare to look at you but take a sip of wine and try to push your hand away. "Just go with it," you whisper before sticking your tongue in my ear. And then my shame is overpowered by ecstasy and I am no longer at a dinner table with the man I used to love, his new girlfriend and your sister.

Just as suddenly as it began, you pull your hand away and reach for your glass. It takes me a moment to realise Chloe is standing behind you. She leans down to say something to you before heading off to the toilets and I can't help but giggle. Keira looks at me and laughs too. She must think I've just had too much to drink.

When I open my eyes the next morning, I remember very little of the night before. I can't recall saying goodbye to Carl and Keira or how we made it home. But what I do remember is what you did to me at the table and, now that we're in the privacy of our bedroom, I want you more than it should be possible to want someone. Smiling to myself, I turn over to wake you but your side of the bed is empty, the duvet smooth and flat. Puzzled, I climb out of bed and pull on my dressing gown, assuming you must be making us coffee.

You're not in the kitchen but I find you asleep on the sofa, your t-shirt and jeans scattered on the floor around you. An empty bottle of whisky lies half hidden beneath the sofa and I chuckle, picturing the hangover you will have when you wake up, and feeling glad I didn't carry on drinking once we got home.

"Good morning."

I spin around and Chloe stands in the doorway, wearing only a bright orange t-shirt which barely reaches her thighs. Her hair is scraped back from her face but a few curls have escaped and dangle over her forehead.

"Oh, sorry. Did I scare you? Michael said I could sleep in Ellie's room." She flicks hair from her eyes and stretches her face into a wide grin. "You don't mind, do you?"

I shake my head, too surprised to speak. It occurs to me that Chloe must have noticed what we did last night at the restaurant because she was sitting right next to you. A vague vision of her saying something to you straight afterwards floods back to me and I turn away from her, not wanting to see understanding on her face. On the sofa you begin gently snoring.

"Coffee?" Chloe pads off to the kitchen and I reluctantly follow her, annoyed that she has interrupted a morning we should be spending alone. But more than that, I am ashamed.

"Keira's nice, isn't she?" Chloe says while we wait for the kettle to boil. She turns to me with a gloating smile.

"Yeah." I busy myself by fetching mugs from the cupboard. Anything to avoid eye contact.

"She'll make a great stepmum for Ellie, don't you think?" Chloe spoons sugar into both our cups and stirs vigorously. I have lost count of the times I've told her I don't take sugar in coffee.

"Yes, she will," I agree. I will not rise to Chloe's bait today.

I thank her for my coffee then take it back to our bedroom. As I pass the lounge I stop and watch you for a moment. I glance at your hand, hanging down to the floor, and am haunted by what it was doing to me last night. While my ex-husband and his new girlfriend sat next to us. And I wonder how it's possible to feel both ashamed and excited at the same time.

CHAPTER SEVENTEEN

Leon strides into the office and stops short when he sees me at my desk. He has given everyone the day off today for working a bank holiday and I'm not supposed to be here. He frowns at me then reaches forward to pinch my arm.

"Oh, you are actually here, then. I thought for a moment I was imagining things. They do say these old buildings are haunted, you know."

"Don't ghosts have to be dead?" I ask, rubbing the pink bruise forming on my skin. "And that bloody hurt, by the way."

"Never mind that. What's the story?"

Somehow Leon always knows when something is not quite right with me, often before I know myself. I try to assure him I just want to catch up with some work, but he plonks himself on a chair and wheels himself as close as possible without being too invasive. "Come on. Tell me what's going on."

So I do. I tell him I'm living with someone and when I explain how long our relationship has been going on, he raises his eyebrows but says nothing. No doubt he is hurt that I haven't shared this information with him; not so long ago I would have told him everything. I try to make up for my lack of communication by explaining all the doubts I have, your coldness and the emptiness I feel even though we're meant to be sharing our lives together. I mention Keira and how perfect she seems. How I want to hate her but can't. It is a momentous relief to unburden myself but I still hold back. There is no way I can speak of the perverse acts you and I carry out together, let alone the fact that I enjoy them. Need them. So I play it down and only hint that there is a strong sexual chemistry between us.

Leon lets me finish then nods his head slowly. "I have to say I'm surprised, Olivia. I thought you'd be able to tell me that you've met someone. Are you sure it's not a rebound thing?" Suddenly I feel uncomfortable even though this is Leon I'm talking to. A man I've known for most of my adult life.

"Leon, I separated from Carl over a year ago. How can you ask me that?"

Leon looks apologetic. "Okay, you're right. I'm sorry. I suppose there's only one thing you need to ask yourself, then. Do you love him?"

Of all the things I'm expecting Leon to say this is not one of them. Something blunt and honest, yes, but not this. And then I surprise myself because after Carl it's not something I have wanted to think about.

"Yes," I say, looking directly at Leon. "Despite our problems, I really do. I believe in us."

Leon's face is unreadable. "Why do you think you're telling me about him now? You've been together a while so why have you chosen today?"

I have to think about Leon's question because it's not as straightforward as it sounds. Something about seeing Carl with Keira is making me question our relationship all over again. On the surface things have been going well since I moved in but it's what lies beneath which bothers me. And it burns me up to know that Carl and Keira would never do what we did in that pizza restaurant.

Leon watches me as I contemplate his question then shakes his head. "You don't have to tell me but just think about it. It's probably important."

I want to ask Leon what he thinks it means but I already know and fear the answer. I am on the rebound from Carl. Clutching onto something as fragile as a cobweb. But Leon spares me the humiliation of saying this. What he can't hide, though, is the look of pity in his eyes.

"I'll make us some coffee," he says eventually.

When he returns and hands me a mug, my hand is shaking and tears run down my cheeks. "The thing is, when I think about Carl, how kind and loving he was, it just makes a mockery of the whole idea of love. That you can be like that with someone and still betray them. The difference with Michael is I know where I am with him. He doesn't pretend to be someone he isn't just to spare my feelings. He is who he is."

Leon pats my arm. "Then just give it a chance, Olivia. It's early days, really, and you're still finding out about each other. He has taken a lot on as well. You know, with your divorce and Ellie..."

"I know," I lie. This is the first time I've considered this.

Leon leaves me to carry on with my work but I'm too distracted to do anything but worry I've taken you for granted. Every few minutes Leon looks over at me and each time I nod or smile at him to assure him I'm okay. I know he must feel good that I've opened up to him, even if it's long overdue.

The words on my computer screen are meant to be a review but instead they blur into dots as my mind, drenched in guilt, drifts to you. The only way I can think of compensating for my thoughtlessness is to cook you a special dinner tonight. I can arrange for Ellie to stay the night at the friend's house she's going to after school so we'll be alone. Chloe was still at the flat this morning and if she hasn't already left then I will try to persuade her to give us a night alone. Perhaps I will even tell you what I told Leon, what I haven't been able to say to you before but know I feel. It doesn't matter what we do under the sheets; we still share our lives together and have come a long way from the time when we didn't venture out in public.

My desk is so cluttered that it takes me a while to realise my mobile isn't hidden beneath the piles of paper and unopened mail. I need to call you to explain my idea for tonight but don't want to use the work line to make a personal call. Especially with Leon watching me like a hawk. I check my bag and coat pockets but my phone isn't there either. I can't remember the last time I used it so speculating about where it could be is pointless.

I settle back down to work, trying to force the black dots to form words again, but the minute Leon leaves to get some food I pick up the office phone and call you, vowing to myself I'll pay him back for the cost of the call. I wait five seconds, then ten, but the ring tone remains uninterrupted. Puzzled, I try your mobile, in case you've popped out to the shop. Your voice immediately clicks in, telling me to leave a message so I hang up. I am not worried or concerned because this is not unusual; you are not the kind of person whose mobile is another limb.

"Is it okay if I go now?" I ask Leon the minute he walks back in, munching a Big Mac. The smell of it reminds me I'm hungry and desperate to be back home cooking dinner for you. I even begin to feel relieved you're not home as now the dinner can be a surprise.

"Well, seeing as you're not even supposed to be here, I would say yes, that's fine." Leon puts his burger down and kisses me on the cheek, but ends up with a mouthful of hair because I'm already half way through the door.

Rushing into the damp evening, I am unprepared after the warmth of the office for the bitterness of this air. My thick wool coat is an insufficient barrier and I make a note to wear my gloves and scarf from now on. It is rush hour and I have no patience this evening for the swarm of people cramming their way onto the packed escalator at Waterloo station. Everyone seems as desperate as I am to get home and it is not the first time in my life when I fantasise that I can click my fingers and be home in seconds.

With a delayed train and being squashed by a herd of sweaty bodies, the journey home doesn't get any easier. It is a strange feeling to be without my mobile, as if I have lost my link to the world and I am alone. But I brush this aside, hating the fact I have come to rely on it so much. I don't even have the excuse of being a generation that grew up with mobile phones; I lived for long enough without one.

I am still thinking about this, wondering if I should experiment with not having a mobile, when I finally open the door to our flat and chaos explodes around me.

"Where have you been?" you shout, peering down the stairs. "Keep your coat on, you need to get to the hospital. Now!"

"What?" I cry. "What's happened? Ellie?" My stomach lurches.

"Ellie's fine. It's Carl's mum."

I sit on the stairs, clutching the banister, while you explain that Barbara has been rushed to hospital. "Apparently it's not good. Carl's been trying to get hold of you all day but says you didn't answer. I told him Ellie's going to her friend's after school and he said not to tell her yet. Why didn't you answer your phone?"

I can hardly digest what you are telling me. "I...my phone." And then, even with the mixture of emotions I feel, I remember something. I told Chloe this morning I was going to work so why didn't she call me there or tell Carl to?

As if she has been summoned, Chloe appears at the top of the stairs. "Olivia, you get to the hospital and we'll pick Ellie up from her friend's. Finchley Memorial. Don't worry about anything. Carl said it's best she doesn't go to the hospital." Chloe doesn't have to explain why. And suddenly it's not important to question Chloe; I just need to get to Barbara.

"Thanks," I say to her, and in reply she offers the first genuine smile I've seen her give me.

You hand me my car keys and kiss the top of my head.

"Wait!" Chloe shouts, as I open the door. I turn to see her waving something at me. "Your mobile. You left it here." She runs down and hands it to me. "Call us when you get there." And right at this moment she is the Chloe I have wanted her to be since I met her.

It takes over an hour to get to the hospital and I am on autopilot for the whole journey. The car radiator blasts stifling heat at me but I notice nothing, either inside or outside the car. I can only think of Barbara, a woman who is a mother to me, lying helpless in an uncomfortable hospital bed, away from everything she cherishes. Being away from her home must be the worst thing for her.

I circle the hospital car park several times before someone finally leaves and I can slot into their space. I don't know if I've got enough change but I throw all my coins into the parking machine, not knowing how long I will need, and run towards the unknown. Despite the car park being full, it is eerily quiet for a hospital and the desperate slap of my shoes against the concrete echoes around me.

Everything inside the hospital is too shiny and too white and I imagine this is what hell is like. Even being in one of these places for a happy event like Ellie's birth has done nothing to assuage my fear of them. Almost the minute she was born I was begging Carl to take us home, despite having been ripped open and stitched back together.

Instead of closing in on me, the corridors seem to widen with each step I take towards Barbara's ward, and the whole fifth floor is a maze with nothing to distinguish one corridor from another. I feel as if I am walking in circles and getting no closer to finding her, but then Carl appears before me and I run into him and squeeze him hard, as much for my sake as his.

"Thank God you're here. I've been trying to call you. She's been asking for you." He pulls apart from me and I notice his eyes are bloodshot but completely dry. This has to be a good sign.

"I'm sorry," I say. Now isn't the time for long explanations. "How is she?"

Carl shakes his head and his eyes fill with water. He glances towards a door behind us that has no name and only a small glass window. "Not good. She was much worse than she let on, Liv. It won't be long…" His voice trails off and I grab him again and cling to him even harder. And for a moment we are not in the present but the past, exactly as we are now, gripping each other in the same way, with the heaviness of grief shrouded over us. Only this time it is my mother we are losing and Carl is the one who must be the rock.

"Hi, Olivia." Keira's gentle voice breaks the spell, forcing us back to the present. "We're so glad you're here," she says, handing Carl a plastic cup of coffee. "Sorry, I would have got you one but didn't know when you'd get here. The cafe's just by the entrance, though, so I could go and get you one." She smoothes the front of her skirt.

I try my best to smile and back away from Carl, even though she is not showing any sign of minding. "No, thanks...I'm fine. I just want to see Barbara."

"Go through," Keira continues. "She really wants to see you."

I turn to Carl and he nods. "It's only a small room so I'll wait here. But Olivia, be prepared. She doesn't look herself."

I walk towards the room and hesitate outside the half-open door. Perhaps I am not quite ready to go in yet but something makes me turn back. Keira's arms are wrapped around you as you cry into her shoulder. And then I see it. I see things clearly. Even in the short time you've known her she has become your rock.

I drag myself forwards but stop before I reach the door. I don't want to see a different Barbara, someone far removed from the strong, dignified person she is. I tell myself it's all a mistake, that she's not as bad as everyone is making out and she'll soon be walking out of here. Perhaps we will have a cup of tea together, even if it is foul-tasting, powdery water. Convinced this is the case, I push through the door, my heart sinking as I see the unrecognisable hump under the sheet.

The room is swathed in darkness, the only light coming from the heart-rate monitor, so at first I don't notice how bad Barbara is. But as I draw closer I see that she is half the size she was, her skin hanging from her bones as if it's been thrown over them like paint. She fixes her eyes on me; they are huge in her shrunken head and light up as I bend down to kiss her forehead. The smell of urine hangs heavily in the air, mixed with a much more terrible, unrecognisable smell but I ignore it and try to breathe only through my mouth. I ignore the fear inside me and plaster a smile on my face.

"You came," she says, her voice quiet and strained. She tries to shuffle up in the bed so she isn't lying flat but slips back down again. "I don't think I'll be able to talk much—"

"It's fine, don't worry about that," I say, rearranging the pillow behind her so she is more upright. I whisper because even though this room is just for Barbara and there's nobody to disturb, it seems wrong to speak out loud.

"Ellie?" she asks.

"I promise I'll bring her next time." I immediately regret not going to pick Ellie up before I came here.

Barbara raises her eyes to the ceiling. "Yes, next time."

We sit in silence for over an hour and I hold her soft, clammy hand through the side bars of the bed. They don't need to be there; all they do is make her bed a prison. Barbara drifts in and out of sleep, her eyes searching for me every time they pop open. I squeeze her hand to show her I'm still here and she squeezes mine back. I don't doubt I am the one who needs this reassurance the most.

"Carl's found a good one," she says suddenly, her voice suddenly loud. "I just hope yours is too."

"He is, Barbara." I squeeze her hand again, just so she's sure. Just so I am sure. And then we are silent again, Barbara's shallow, strained breaths the only sounds in the room.

When evening arrives I am still sitting with Barbara, watching her sleep and trying to remember the woman she was instead of the one perishing in a hospital bed. At some point I must fall asleep myself because from nowhere Carl gently shakes me awake. He apologises profusely for being away so long but I understand his urge to have a break from this stifling prison cell. Barbara twitches and groans and we turn to her, powerless to do anything but watch helplessly, praying for the end, whenever it is, to be easy. Carl replaces me at Barbara's bedside and Keira hovers around, silently tidying things up in the room and rearranging a vase of flowers on the bedside table. She pours a glass of water and sinks a straw into it. Then, without disturbing Barbara, she straightens up the wrinkled bed sheets before lifting a chair from the corner of the room and joining Carl by the bed. She is a rock.

Watching the two of them with their chairs pulled as closely together as they can get them, I feel out of place, as if I no longer belong in this family unit. I know I will always be part of Carl's family because I'm Ellie's mother, but without Ellie here, Keira trumps any claim I might have to be the woman by Barbara's side. I whisper goodbye to them and give Barbara a kiss on the cheek. Somehow, as I walk back through the maze of gleaming white and try to remember where I've parked my car, it occurs to me I may never see Barbara again. I walk slowly to make this moment last longer because it is a moment when, even though she is ill, Barbara still exists in this world.

On the way home I get stuck in road works but once again I'm on autopilot, my tears blurring everything into only a vague impression of what I'm looking at. When I finally make it home I trudge through the door, hoping that at least Ellie will be asleep by now and not waiting to ask questions I'm not ready to answer.

The flat is dark and quiet, with just a soft murmur and brief flashes of light coming from the television. I check on Ellie first and she's curled up like a foetus on top of her duvet, fully clothed. Finding a blanket in her wardrobe, I place it over her and kiss her goodnight.

In the living room, Chloe is also asleep, curled up on one of the sofas. She's facing the wall so I can't see her face but she doesn't stir when I tiptoe in. You're sitting cross-legged on the other sofa and you point at Chloe and mime gulping a drink. Ironic, really, when there's a wine glass in your hand and two bottles on the coffee table. You hand me your glass and I down the rest of its contents in one go, ignoring the heaviness as the liquid slips down my throat. This is not a time to worry about etiquette.

You put your arm around me and ask how Barbara is. Retelling the details of the night is like reliving it over again and I can't face that at the moment so I give you a brief version, sticking only to facts. We share more wine from the same glass and soon my head is spinning, throwing around images of Barbara lying in her bed, slowly dying while Carl and Keira sit together at her side.

I'm so consumed with these images that it takes me a while to realise you have undone the buttons on my dress. I lean forward and push your arm away.

"Chloe's over there, stop it." I say this more loudly than I intend and Chloe murmurs on the other sofa. We both freeze for a second but then you push me back and pull my dress further apart so my breasts are exposed. I want to shout at you to stop and throw your hands off me but can't take the chance of Chloe waking up.

I wiggle and squirm, desperate to be out of your grip because this is all wrong but you shake me, as if trying to knock sense into me. "Relax, she's pissed out of her skull and fast asleep, there's no way she'll wake up."

And then I realise I don't have a choice. If I make too much noise then Chloe is bound to wake up. Maybe it will disturb Ellie and I can't have that.

"Please, let's go to the bedroom," I beg. It is a desperate plea that falls on deaf ears because you don't want to hear me. You kiss my neck and I stop squirming and let you, all the time keeping one eye out for movement across the room. When your hand roughly clamps over my mouth I jolt in shock but that is nothing compared to the searing explosion of pain when you bite into my nipple.

"Shhhhh!" you warn me, glancing over at Chloe. "You want this, you dirty whore. You always want this."

With your hand still smothering me, you force yourself into me; I am not a person to you at this moment, not anything. And now my tears come, hard, fast and silent. But somehow you manage not to notice.

CHAPTER EIGHTEEN

"Come with me. Just trust me, that's all I'm asking. Will you do that?"

Even though she is just a large shadow in my line of vision, I immediately know it's her. She has not given up on me, then.

I don't reply but close my eyes and wait for her to admit defeat. I can play this game better than any of them. I have nothing to get back to; this is my life. She, on the other hand, will have a husband at home and probably a couple of children too. Therefore, I will win. I can play the waiting game while they all, sooner or later, admit defeat.

But she doesn't move. Instead she plonks herself on the bed and with her weight pushing the mattress down I roll a few inches towards her.

"Hmmmm," she says. "Not very comfortable, are they? I'd ask for my money back if I were you." She snorts, as if she is being serious and we are not in this ghastly place. But still I play the game; keep my eyes shut and the muscles in my face tight.

For nearly two hours we sit like this; the only sound in the room her rich, melodic humming. It mesmerizes me, but of course I will never let this be known. Unlike last time, I don't scream for her to stop but sit and listen. If there is any chance they are trying to make me lose control again I have to toughen up and put up with her bringing her happiness into my room. So I let the sound transport me to another place and am surprised to find it is a better place simply because it isn't here. But then she stops abruptly and I am back in the room with the silence deafening me. Even though she has stopped humming, she shows no sign of moving. Perhaps with this one I have met my match. She knows how to play the game.

"Go away!" I croak at her. "Why are you still here?"

She snorts again. "Oh, lovey! I'm not going anywhere until you come with me. And I know what you're thinking. That I've got work to do so sooner or later I'll have to leave, but oh no. You see, today is my day off."

My eyes are shut – I've learnt this is the best defence against them – so I can't study her face to check for evidence of lies. "Then what are you doing here?" I say, keeping my eyes closed because opening them now will only invite her further in.

"I've come to see you, of course. Nothing else. I'm just here for you."   And then I do open my eyes and look at her for the first time. Her skin is smooth and black without a single crease lining it, even though her smile is as wide as the Grand Canyon. Her face is kind and ageless. Sending her to me is all part of their trick. In their desperation, they have commissioned her to attempt something in which they have all failed.

"Now, then," she sings. "Are you coming with me or not?"

And then it is too late for me to close my eyes against her.

For days I barely speak to you, unable to forget what happened the night I visited Barbara in hospital. This time it was different – incongruous after where I'd been that day – and only one of us enjoyed it. But worse than that is your obliviousness. You try to ignore the tension between us and even attempt to make up for it in your own way. But no matter how many cups of tea you make or dinners you cook for Ellie and me, I cannot forget so easily.

Although I have been expecting it since she was rushed to hospital, Barbara's death still comes as a shock. Carl can barely get the words out and I have to fill in the gaps for him.

"I can't believe she couldn't fight it," he says. "She fought everything." And he is right; Barbara never gave in to anything until now. But she could never have stood a chance against the cancer that had ravaged her body long before she suspected anything was wrong.

Ellie withdraws into herself, only communicating with nods when she needs something, and nothing I do seems to help. I don't want to burden Carl when he's stricken with grief but Ellie still needs both of us. I approach the topic carefully and ask him how she is when he sees her at weekends. To my surprise, he tells me she's dealing with Barbara's death better than he'd expected. Although she asks a lot of questions about her grandmother, it seems to bring her pleasure to hear stories about Barbara and what she was like as a young woman. She asked Carl for a photo of Barbara so she could sketch her but didn't seem upset doing it. Carl informs me that, given the circumstances, Ellie is doing okay. She still chatters away to Keira and never gives them any trouble. Puzzled by this, I come to the conclusion that either Carl isn't very observant or Keira is an expert at cheering up my daughter.

Carl arranges for Barbara's funeral to take place on Valentine's Day, insisting she would have liked this idea. And when I remember all the advice she issued over the years, I have to agree with him; she definitely was a strong advocate of love.

Even though you never met Barbara, you offer to come with us to the service. Carl has given his blessing for you to be there but I can hardly look at you, never mind let you stand beside me in the church. Barbara wouldn't mind – after all, she did mention you at the hospital – but *I* mind. I know I am punishing you but I try to ignore the satisfaction I feel in telling you I don't want you at the funeral. We have minutes to leave and you are already dressed and arranging your tie.

"Okay," you say, after barely taking a second to digest my words. There is no questioning or sulking to follow but I am sure I catch a glimmer of relief on your face as you unravel your tie and loop it over the open wardrobe door. But as you change back into your jeans, I begin to doubt what I have seen and start to feel guilty. I could still change my mind. It would be easy to tell you I'm sorry and that I'm all over the place at the moment and don't know what I'm doing. But instead I keep quiet and bury the guilt.

As I kiss you goodbye, you remind me you're cooking us a Valentine's dinner tonight. I want to tell you not to bother, that I'll hardly be in the mood for it, but I feel badly enough already so I keep quiet.

After the funeral, Ellie surprises everyone by throwing a tantrum. She refuses to get in the car when it's time to leave and screams when I grab her hand. A crowd of mourners I don't recognise turn to us with smiles of sympathy on their faces for the small girl who has lost her grandmother. At least they aren't judging me, thinking I'm a bad mother who can't control her child.

But still my face flushes with embarrassment as I continue trying to coax Ellie into the car. She won't stop howling and I am at a loss as to what to do, so I look around to see if Carl is anywhere nearby. The last time I saw him he was talking to the vicar with Keira by his side, their hands clamped together. I don't want to bother him – today is harder for him than for anyone else – but there is nothing else I can do.

Finally I spot him walking out of the church with Keira still attached to him, and I frantically wave him over, not even sure he can see me from this distance. I turn back to Ellie and attempt to reason with her. "Ellie, you need to calm down. Now. This is not a day for tantrums. Grandma would be so upset to see you like this, wouldn't she? Just take a deep breath and tell me what's wrong. Why don't you want to come home?"

Ellie continues sobbing, her small body shaking violently. But something I have said must get through to her because after a few moments her crying fades to intermittent sniffles and she finally speaks. "I just...want to...be with Dad."

My stomach lurches and I feel as if I need to lean on something. "But you know it's Sunday. You always come home on Sundays and you've got school tomorrow."

"So?" She shrugs her shoulders. "I just want to be with Dad," she repeats like a mantra. And then, seeing him approach, she runs towards him and buries herself in his chest.

Carl frowns at me and when I tell him what's happened he is just as surprised by Ellie's behaviour as I am. "She must just be upset about Mum, Liv. And she's never been to a funeral before, has she? Don't worry, she'll be okay."

I am not convinced but now's not the time for a prolonged discussion about it because Ellie is still burrowed into Carl. "You're probably right."

Keira – who is still gripping Carl's hand – suggests they take Ellie for the night. "She probably just wants to feel closer to Barbara by being with Carl," she offers.

I know she means well but how can she believe things are so black and white? After today, though, I am too worn out to protest, so I thank them both and help settle Ellie into the car before I set off home alone.

The only thing that consoles me about Ellie not coming home with me is that I can focus on you tonight and try to make up for earlier. We've hardly spoken since the incident after the hospital and it can only have added to the ever-widening gulf between us. I should be furious with you; what you did could have had serious consequences. It's bad enough that Chloe might have woken up, but it makes me sick to the pit of my stomach to think what would have happened if Ellie had chosen that moment to wander out of her bedroom. And when I remember that night, it's hard for me to be sure what really happened. The line between your violation and me wanting you is blurred beyond recognition.

I open the door of the flat and step into blackness. Fumbling around for the light, I dismiss the idea that you have forgotten about cooking for us and gone out without mentioning it. Perhaps you've just fallen asleep on the sofa.

But there are no lights on upstairs either, not even a glare from the television, and a quick search of all the rooms confirms my suspicion. I check my mobile, just in case I've missed a message from you, but the only notification is an email from Myrah. I quickly dial your number and wait for the phone to connect, nausea spreading through my stomach even though I haven't eaten since breakfast. There was no wake after the funeral because Barbara insisted she didn't want one, though she gave no hint of a reason why.

When the beeps finally start in my ear, it takes me a moment to realise there are two sets chiming out and your phone is ringing inside the flat. I follow the sound to the bedroom before I hang up and check it is your phone nestled into the duvet.

I start to panic because you would never leave the flat without your mobile. Then I remember the other day when I accidentally left mine here and went to work. I've never done that before so it is possible you could have forgotten yours. Especially if it was on the bed. Even though this is plausible, it still doesn't seem to fit. There is only one explanation for disappearing like this without leaving a message. You are trying to punish me.

The more I think about this, the more convinced I become. And the best way for me to react to your punishment is to do nothing. It is a cruel act to carry out on this day of all days, but I can't dwell on that now. I am exhausted and desperately need food. I decide I will make cheese on toast; worrying about you can wait until I've lined my stomach. I change into my jeans, happy to be more comfortable, but peeling my black dress off feels like saying goodbye to Barbara all over again and I sit on the bed and cry the river of tears that couldn't flow in the church. It has always been a nightmare of mine, to be at a funeral unable to shed a tear while all around you people are crying for their loved one, but as I sit here on the bed, I finally know that I am normal. I don't know how long I stay here, saying goodbye to Barbara in my own private way, but my stomach begins to growl and hurt as if my insides are being eaten away.

On the way to the kitchen I hear a light bang. I pause at the top of the stairs, rigid with fear. Something feels wrong. Seconds pass and the flat is silent once again but just as I begin to relax it happens again. This time continuous and coming from downstairs. I grip my mobile as if it is a weapon that can protect me, even though I have no idea what I might need protecting from. The noise continues but rather than making me more fearful it starts to become less sinister. It's hard to believe an intruder would make that much noise and draw attention to themselves, so the only other explanation is it must be the pipes or boiler.

Remembering that the boiler is in the large cupboard under the stairs, I become even more confident that this is the case and slowly head downstairs, still grasping my phone.

The banging continues as I reach the bottom of the stairs and I pray that nothing is wrong with the boiler. You are not here to sort out any problem and I have never even seen it, so I won't have the first idea about how to stop the noise.

I swing the cupboard door towards me and my heart nearly stops when I look down at the floor. You are sitting in the corner, your knees pulled up to your chin, smacking your head rhythmically against the wall. I'm about to laugh and pull you out, assuming you've had too much to drink, but when I lean in closer I see your eyes are blood-red and your cheeks wet and glistening.

"Michael? What's wrong?"

You turn your head to me and then the tears come hard and fast. I join you on the floor and you bury your head in my chest, your sobs causing your whole body to shake.

"I'm sorry, I'm sorry," you say, over and over, your voice muffled by my jumper. I hold you tighter and we stay like this for minutes, paused in time, lost in our own thoughts.

You repeat your apology but I don't know what you are sorry about. I hope it is for the other night, maybe for all the nights, but you are not fully to blame. I have played my part. But speculation is futile. I need to know why you are sorry because I need to know if you will ever be my rock, and I yours, just as Carl and Keira are each other's.

"Are we okay?" You stop crying and look up at me, your eyes shining and hopeful.

"We always have been," I say. "I wish you knew that."

You lean back and gently rest your head against the wall. You still hold my hand and we are at peace with each other once more. Comfortable.

"Things will be different now. I promise, Olivia." And then you kiss me. Not with the usual desperate urgency but slowly and carefully, as if you are finally seeing *me*.

When we eventually haul ourselves up to bed, I have almost forgotten Ellie's tantrum and the whole day seems to belong to a far-off time, sadness incongruous in the new place we have created for ourselves.

CHAPTER NINETEEN

I am not surprised that when things are going well between us everything else starts to fall apart. I have learnt life can be no other way. For weeks we are able to put the past behind us and forget who we were. And there is no more shame because I am not that person. Weekend mornings no longer start with you rushing to get out of bed, but instead we lie together, sometimes only holding hands, while time hurtles towards midday. Neither of us care; losing precious time is a sacrifice worth making now.

Even though you still keep the flat immaculate and I can see the tension in your face when Ellie leaves toys lying around, you have started to relax a bit more. Occasionally dishes pile up on the worktop but you are happy to sit at the table and read the paper before rushing to shove them in the dishwasher. So I finally let myself believe we are just like any other couple. We are normal.

But Ellie is not doing well. As hard as I try, I still can't extract from her a reason for her outburst after the funeral. She barely speaks and I bide my time, hoping it is just grief consuming her and she'll soon bounce back. After all, she has surprised me many times before with her resilience so it's easy to convince myself this is just one more obstacle she must overcome. As long as I am by her side she will be fine.

"I can't go to school," Ellie says, appearing in the kitchen as I pop bread in the toaster. It is Friday morning and there are only minutes before we have to leave, but she is still dressed in her pink pyjamas. She holds onto the doorframe, leaning into it as if it's the only thing keeping her upright. My eyes flick to the clock above the sink. There are twenty minutes before school starts. I turn back to her, trying not to appear annoyed but unable to stop my face wrinkling in frustration. There are a million things I have to do at work today and I can't get my brain in gear to start prioritising them. Ellie being ill is the last thing I need. I study her and although she looks a bit pale it doesn't mean she can't go to school.

"What's wrong? You need to get dressed quickly. We have to leave in ten minutes, Ellie."

She looks at me as if I've punished her. "I said I can't go, Mum."

I beckon her over and she finally peels herself away from the door frame and pads towards me, lost and forlorn, her small body moving in slow motion. When she finally reaches me I check her forehead. It's slightly clammy but no warmer than usual. "You feel okay," I tell her. "What exactly is wrong?"

"I feel sick," she insists.

"Have you actually been sick?"

"No." She avoids looking at me.

"Then you're going to school. Come on, go and get ready."

Then the tears come and although she doesn't say anything, her eyes plead with me to let her stay. I think of the deadline Leon has given me to finish a review of a French film that's due for release on DVD. I need to be sure Ellie is really ill before I risk taking the day off. I am about to suggest going to the doctor, convinced that if she is lying this is the last thing she'll want, but her whole body begins to shake and she crumples to the floor. I drop down beside her and wrap myself around her, cocooning her in a protective shell. She continues crying but grips me as tightly as her tiny hands can manage.

As we sit on the cold floor, I gently rock her and wait for her tears to dry up. The minutes tick away and I no longer care about the work piling up at the office. It is my fault Ellie is in this state; I have done this to my daughter. When she finally stops crying long enough to untangle herself from me, I order her to bed and promise to bring her some hot chocolate once I've called Leon. Telling him I've got a family emergency is a flimsy excuse but at this time I have no other information to give him.

The curtains are still drawn in Ellie's room when I take her a small mug of hot chocolate and some toast. Normally she is not allowed to eat in her room but today I make an exception. Finding out what's going on with my daughter is more important than a few crumbs being spilt on the carpet.

I open the curtains a fraction and Ellie squints as her eyes adjust to the light. She thanks me for the toast and drink but doesn't say much else so I sit at the end of her bed and wait, watching her rip the soft inner part of the bread away from its crust. She eats slowly and I wonder if it's because she's not hungry or whether she is delaying the inevitable.

When Ellie begins tucking into the crusts I know she hates, I whisk her plate away and deliver the speech I have already prepared in my head about death and grieving. She picks up her mug instead but nods and agrees with everything I say, assuring me she's okay about it.

"I know Grandma's in a better place now, and not in pain," she explains, as if she is the one dispensing advice to me. I am startled by her maturity and relieved until I realise that if she's okay about Barbara then something horrific must be wrong.

"Is there something else you're sad about?" I risk asking.

Biting her lip, she places her mug on the bedside table and studies my face for a moment. "Mum, please don't get upset, but would it be okay if I go and live with Dad? Just for a while...not forever...I promise I'll come back."

And with those words my world crumbles and I feel as if I've been flattened by a steam roller, all the air and life sucked out of me. I want to scream at her until she admits this is a cruel joke or pretend I haven't heard or just run from the room. But I don't do any of these. I reach for her hand and compose myself so my voice doesn't betray my fear.

"Ellie, I think you need to tell me what's going on."

For too long I stand at the edge of the driveway, staring at the house that used to be my home. My safe place. Nothing much has changed on the outside, yet everything feels different. Somehow older and worn out, no longer mine. The gravel path leading up to the front door needs to be replaced and even the grass on either side of it, with its straw-coloured patches, screams with neglect. I try to remember if the front garden was in this state when I lived here but I can't be sure. Any life I had here has fizzled away, replaced in my memory by the life I now have with you. But even though my memories have faded, I know that nothing is the same.

I need to move quickly because curtains twitch around here. Nothing is private on this street and I don't want to be the subject of scrutiny and gossip. So with my head down I rush to the door, push the bell and turn my back to it, searching out any sign of movement in the houses opposite.

I don't have long to wait until there is shuffling from inside and the door creaks open.

"Olivia! Hi!" Keira beams a thousand-watt smile at me. With her hair scraped back from her plump face she looks even younger. Her long skirt and fitted jumper skim her slightly overweight body, revealing its nice proportions. She must take everything in her stride because she doesn't look surprised to see me, even though I am the last person who should be here.

"Hi. Sorry, is Carl here? I just need to talk to him about something. It won't take long." I pray she doesn't ask what I need to talk about because what will I say? Our ten-year-old daughter wants to leave me and live with her father instead. There is no way I can or will explain myself to Keira, no matter how kind and welcoming her smile.

"Oh no, sorry, Olivia. He'll be late home tonight, he had to do a delivery up north." She pulls the door open wider and her smile stretches even further across her face. "But please, come in. I'll put the kettle on."

I am about to decline her offer but haven't had a drink since breakfast and it's a long journey home. I insist I can only stay for a quick cup of tea and present a list of reasons why I have to get home quickly. But as I follow her into my old house, I wonder why I'm bothering to do this. Perhaps setting a time limit is my way of gaining control because whenever I am around this woman I feel devoid of it.

The outside of the house might need fixing up but inside is a different story. Keira has redecorated the downstairs so it's unrecognisable. She leads me around, talking through every detail of the changes she's made and I think of the house programmes on television where a wreck is transformed into a show home. But Keira is not boasting and nearly every sentence she speaks has Carl's name in it. She has done this for him. In every room the furniture has been rearranged to maximise space and the whole place feels twice as large. I compliment her, and mean every word I say, but my insides are churning. She has done what I never managed to and I wonder if it's the same in their whole relationship.

"But don't look upstairs," Keira says, snapping me out of my negative thoughts. "I haven't even started up there yet. Also, Carl will have to get someone in to sort out the front and back gardens. That's not really my area of expertise." She chuckles to herself and I wonder how she can be only twenty-nine. She seems to have the understanding and mindset of a much older woman, or at least someone who is a mother.

Even Keira's tea is perfect and I sip it gratefully while we sit at my old kitchen table, which is shinier and cleaner than I've ever seen it. We make small talk and I start to admire the woman who sits before me. Exactly like the first time I met her, there is no hint of insecurity, jealousy or any other unhealthy emotion emanating from her, even though I am Carl's ex-wife and the mother of his child. She must know that Ellie will always come first, and by extension that means I do too. But she chats away as if we are just work colleagues or neighbours. How can it be that I am the one feeling uncomfortable while she treats me with kindness and friendship?

"Does it feel strange being here?" she asks, pouring me another cup of tea. I want to stop her and tell her I must leave but something prevents me. "I mean, you did live here for ten years, so it must be a bit weird."

I am taken aback by Keira's sudden change in conversation from small talk to whatever this is. "I'm not sure," I tell her, and I begin to grow more uncomfortable. With her, discussing anything not about interior design or the weather seems wrong. "Er, I suppose it is a bit odd, but you've completely changed everything so it doesn't really feel like the same house." My answer will have to satisfy her because I'm not prepared to offer any more.

She nods and smiles before taking another sip of tea. Perhaps she can sense my discomfort at the direction our chat has taken because just as suddenly as she changed the course of our conversation, she swings it back to a safer topic. No more personal questions follow and I am grateful for her tact.

I finish my tea and offer to wash the mugs but she insists she'll do it later. "Do you want to wait for Carl?" she says, as I stand up. "I could throw together some food for us. I'm sure he'll be back by the time we've eaten."

As lovely as Keira is, I can't think of anything much worse than having a meal alone with her. Sooner or later we would run out of small talk and be forced to discuss things I am desperate to avoid. I thank her and remind her I've left Ellie with her friend, Izzy, for a couple of hours and need to collect her.

"Oh, how is lovely Ellie?" she asks. "We're taking her to London Zoo on Saturday. I know it's a bit cold but she loves drawing the animals, doesn't she?"

And then it all comes flooding back to me: Ellie's request and the reason I came here this evening, hoping to see Carl and get his advice. Before I know what's happening, I am failing to force back tears and Keira is handing me a tissue and holding her arms out for a hug.

Unexpectedly, I pour my heart out to the woman who is now sleeping with my ex-husband, and tell her things I probably wouldn't even have told Carl if he'd been home. She listens with patience, never interrupting or frowning in judgement, and in return for my opening up to her, she offers me what I need most of all: honesty.

By the time I have talked myself dry, Keira has made us a tomato omelette and chips. "I think the problem is Michael," she says, piling the food onto two plates. My heart races as various horrific scenarios flash in front of me. She must notice my jaw drop because she is quick to reassure me. "No, no, it's nothing bad. But maybe Ellie is having trouble bonding with him. I mean, from what I can gather, he's not really a child-friendly person—"

"He's a teacher!" I protest.

"Yes, yes, sorry, I know that. I just think it's a bit different isn't it? When you raise children rather than just teaching them for a few hours a day. I don't know if he really *bothers* with her."

Keira explains that Ellie often insists Michael doesn't like her and probably wishes she wasn't there. She always has to worry about making the tiniest mess and it's hard for her to remember all his rules. Even though I know it's not her fault, and that this has come from Ellie, I want to argue with Keira. My instinct is to defend you and throw a hundred examples at her of when you and Ellie have had fun together, but when I try to find just one my mind is a blank page. The truth is you are a loner and barely have time for me, let alone my daughter. It's funny how this has never occurred to me until now. And I also can't argue about your expectations of tidiness in the flat. If I, as an adult, find it frustrating then of course any child would struggle with it.

Keira looks guilty when she finishes talking. "Sorry, Olivia. I know it's not my place to say any of this—"

I shake my head. "No, it's fine. Better to know, I suppose."

"Well, now you know you can do something about it, can't you?"

"Any suggestions?" I am half joking when I ask this but Keira chews thoughtfully, as if she is planning a political campaign.

"There's only one thing you can do. Talk to Michael and make him take his role seriously. It's both of you who are raising Ellie now."

Ellie's visit to her friend's house seems to have cheered her up because when I open her bedroom door to say goodnight, she smiles at me from under the duvet and tells me about having fish and chips for dinner.

"Did Izzy's mum wonder why you weren't at school?" I ask. She hadn't mentioned it when I dropped Ellie off earlier but I could tell she was curious.

Ellie shakes her head. "No. I just told her I was upset about Grandma and she let us have a bar of chocolate. She's really nice, Mum."

I know Ellie's not making a comparison but I can't help feeling affronted. As usual, I bury my feelings and tell Ellie I'm glad she had a nice time. She doesn't mention anything more about living with Carl, so neither do I. Perhaps I panicked unnecessarily, too quick to overreact because I'm still hoarding guilt at taking Ellie away from Carl in the first place. But I still need to address the issue with you and have already planned what I will say. The hard part will be finding the right moment.

Once Ellie is settled for the night, we are both too tired to cook so we order a Chinese takeaway and eat it on the sofa. I'm too worried about soy sauce oozing between the prongs on my fork to enjoy what I'm eating and wish we'd ordered pizza instead.

You finish your sweet and sour chicken and wash it down with green tea before I'm even half way through mine.

But when the phone rings, cutting through the silence, you don't move or even look up.

"Just let it ring," you say. "I'm sure it's not important." I don't protest because I'm trapped under the tray of food on my knees and have just shovelled special fried rice into my mouth. But whoever is on the other end is persistent and it rings for over half a minute before the answer machine saves us from the monotonous tone.

And then Chloe's voice, loud and brash, invades our evening as she demands you pick up the phone. "I know someone's there. Come on, Michael just pick up the phone. I *really* need to talk to you...I'm waiting....Comeon, comeon, comeon..." Each word slurs into the next, highlighting her state of inebriation.

I stop chewing and wait for you to say something but you stare straight ahead at the silent television. Even when the phone rings again and Chloe leaves another pleading message, you stay rooted to the sofa.

"Why aren't you answering?" I ask, after she leaves a third message. I have never known you to avoid a call from your sister; even when the two of you have your worst arguments you are always there for her, albeit reluctantly. This doesn't make sense. "Michael? What's going on?"

"Nothing," you insist. "I just don't feel like dealing with her tonight." You pretend to watch the muted television, a cookery programme I know you aren't interested in, while the phone rings again and Chloe curses us from wherever she is.

Finally I have had enough and, balancing my tray on the palm of my hand, I carefully head to the phone table in the hall. I can't risk dropping the remains of my greasy food so by the time I finally make it to the phone, it stops ringing and there is silence once again.

You glare at me when I go back into the lounge. "I told you to leave it. Just stay out of it. She's not your fucking sister, is she?"

This is clearly not the right time to discuss Ellie so I clear away the plates and takeaway cartons. I am hurt by your anger but know it is pointless trying to talk to you when you're in this mood. I take my book to bed and try to switch off.

At some point in the night I wake up, relieved to find you next to me. But I'm not sure what woke me so suddenly when you aren't stirring. I sit up, wondering if Ellie called out for me. It is past one thirty in the morning and I listen for incongruous sounds, but there is nothing more sinister than the rain pounding against the ground outside and trees rustling in the fierce wind. Deciding it's best to check on Ellie anyway, I grab my dressing gown and wrap it around me even though the thick towelling material does little to stop me shivering.

Before I've reached the bedroom door, heavy pounding on the front door breaks out, and I jump and gasp out loud.

"What the hell?" you say from the bed, pulling yourself up. You grab your jeans from the chair next to you but don't waste time with a t-shirt. "Stay here," you tell me, but I have no intention of doing that when Ellie is on her own.

The pounding starts again and simultaneously the phone rings, jolting me once again.

"Fucking Chloe," you say, slipping your trainers on. "It has to be." And then I calm down. Of course it is Chloe because nobody else would do this. You head downstairs and I'm glad it's not me on the other side of the door.

No longer in a panic, I head to Ellie's bedroom. If she is awake she will be terrified by this commotion. But her door opens before I reach it and she peers out from behind it, her arms wrapped around the cuddly lion Barbara gave her a few years ago. "What's happening, Mum?" she asks, venturing towards me. I put my arm around her and we both peer over the banister, listening silently as you address someone downstairs.

"How the hell did you get in the building?" you say. I am convinced now it is Chloe because there is no other person you would speak to this way.

"I've still got my key. See? But this fucking door was locked so I had to knock." Chloe's voice is unmistakable and my heart sinks. An intruder would be easier to get rid of.

"It's the middle of the night," you bellow. "You can't do this, Chloe. Just go home, all right?"

Beside me, Ellie clings to my arm when you begin to shout and I pull her with me to the top of the stairs so we can see you and Chloe more clearly.

Chloe snickers. "Oh you'd love that, wouldn't you? But I'm not going anywhere. Not until you talk to me. Just lemme in, Michael. Don't make me —"

You yank her arm and drag her towards the front door but she wriggles out from your grip and despite being unsteady, does her best to stay rooted to the spot. You grab her again and pull her towards the main door. "You're fucking drunk, stop making a fool of yourself and just go home. Now."

And then Chloe screams. A deafening sound as loud as a smoke alarm. "Get off me!" she yells, kicking against the door as you struggle to keep hold of her. When she fires profanities at you I grab Ellie's hand and lead her back to her room. She has already heard and seen more than she should have, but at least in here the sound is too muffled to decipher specific words. It's only when I tuck her into bed that I notice she is crying, silent tears that pool in her eyes but don't trickle down her cheeks.

"Oh, Ellie, don't worry about Chloe. She's just a bit upset, that's all. By tomorrow she'll—"

"I hate Chloe and I hate Michael!" Ellie shouts, leaving me stunned into silence. This is the second outburst she has had in the last few weeks, when for ten years before she hadn't even come close to a tantrum. I watch her as she buries herself in her duvet and turns her back to me, and I wish Carl was here to help me deal with this. It's two in the morning and I can still hear your muffled shouts downstairs. Now isn't the time to discuss Ellie's behaviour with her. I tell her we'll talk about it after school tomorrow and close the door on her grunts.

I don't know how you finally get rid of Chloe but it's another half hour before you are back in bed, both of us staring at the ceiling, wondering what's happened tonight.

"Is Chloe okay?" I ask, to break the silence.

"I don't know what she's playing at. I think that guy's left her and she just wants everyone else to be as miserable as she is."

I ask you for more details but you tell me you're too tired to care. And while you drift off to sleep with relative ease, I lie awake and worry. About Chloe. About Ellie. About everything. Only when light breaks through the curtains and it's time for me to wake Ellie for school do I begin to feel tired.

CHAPTER TWENTY

I can't remember the last time I felt daylight on my skin or smelt the sweetness of grass and for a moment I am dizzy, my head unused to anything but darkness and stagnant, recycled air. The bench we sit on is rickety and damp and I shift around, attempting to get comfortable. But no matter what position I try, the wood cuts into my bones. The woman sits next to me but doesn't seem to have the same problem and she leans back, stretching her legs out in front of her, as if she is lying on a sun bed. For the first time I notice that she's not dressed in a uniform but wears jeans and an ill-fitting t-shirt. Her huge breasts force her top to rise up so that a strip of skin above her jeans is exposed. It is as smooth as the skin on her face.

"I'm Henny," she says. "Just in case you were wondering."

I immediately like her name; to me it suggests strength and motherhood. It is the name of someone who cares, someone who can help me. But I don't tell her this. I have learnt that my thoughts must remain in my head. And I am content – now that she has forced me outside – just to listen to the angelic sound of her voice.

I don't know what month it is but warm air surrounds us and we both stare up at the sky and watch the cotton-wool clouds suspended above us. It is peaceful out here – something I never feel in my room – and I am grateful she has brought me here. But I will not tell her this and I won't thank her either. This could still be part of their plan.

There are several people walking through this gigantic garden, the narrow crisscross of paths leading nowhere and everywhere at the same time. Some of them are staff, carbon copies of each other in their sterile white clothing; a few are visitors and the rest are like me. I don't know what they call us here but whatever it is, names don't matter. Having a label doesn't change anything for me. It is a strange feeling to be this close to so many other people. It doesn't quite feel real because apart from the times when they infiltrate my world, I am solitary. Alone. Nobody else exists or matters.

I sit at my desk, staring at my blank computer screen and thinking about Chloe instead of work. All around me the office buzzes with activity. Sophie is on the phone arranging meetings for Leon, her voice warm and friendly while her expression is stony and full of contempt. She has been here since Leon started the business and I wonder how she's survived for so long; having to be nice to people is her worst nightmare. In the middle of the office, Myrah sits on the floor, surrounded by samples of brightly coloured bottles, all claiming to make women look younger or more attractive. She studies labels and takes tops off bottles to sniff each one, most of the time wrinkling her nose in disgust. At least Myrah will be honest in her reviews, much to the annoyance of Leon. "Unless you start writing more favourably, companies won't bother sending us samples," he insists, almost every week. But Myrah will not compromise her integrity, not even for Leon.

Leon flies around the office like a tornado, tidying up and making sure our cramped space looks as large and welcoming as possible. None of us need to ask him why he's doing this when the cleaner has already spent an hour here this morning. He will be entertaining potential advertisers today and only Leon can get the office to a high enough standard to impress them. Nobody seems to notice I'm not doing anything but to ease my guilt I begin opening the huge pile of mail I've been avoiding.

Even though I go through the motions of opening envelopes and pulling out useless pieces of paper, my mind keeps drifting back to Chloe. We haven't heard anything from her since she hammered at the door the other night and I worry about the state she was in. Something must have happened for her to be so desperate – drunk or not – and although I am furious she upset Ellie, what kind of people are we if we don't at least find out how she is? Even though she is your sister, asking you to contact her is pointless after the way you treated her so I will have to do it myself. I check my watch and it's not even eleven o'clock. There are at least two hours until I can hide out in the kitchen and call Chloe without being overheard.

I am still looking through letters, none of them containing anything interesting, when Myrah shouts across that I have a call. She transfers it to my phone and when I pick up, a voice I don't recognise, bright and chirpy and with no introduction, starts firing questions at me.

"Olivia, hi! How are you? What have you been up to? It's been a while, hasn't it?"

The vaguely familiar voice is hard to place and my mind comes up blank but if it is an important contact then admitting I am stumped is not an option. "Great...good, thanks," I lie. The only way out of this is to try and keep the conversation going long enough for me to work out who I'm speaking to. "How are you?" I ask, wincing behind the receiver.

"To be honest, I've been thinking about you a lot."

I sit up straight and press the phone closer to my ear, convinced now this is not a work call. It is only when I look over at Myrah and notice her watching me with a school girl's grin on her face that I realise who I'm speaking to. I haven't heard from Jonathan since we had a drink last summer, and all I remember is the disappointment etched on his face as I pulled away in the taxi he paid for.

"Oh?" I ask, my stomach sinking because I don't really want to know what he means. Even though nothing physical happened, it feels wrong to have this type of conversation with him. I check my watch; there are at least forty minutes before I can call Chloe so I relax a bit and decide to give him a break. After all, he was kind to me that evening, even when I told him all about you.

"I called you a couple of months ago. On your mobile. A woman answered and said she didn't know where you were." He chuckles. "I might have thought it was you pretending to be someone else but her voice was nothing like yours."

Now I remember the day I came to work without my mobile. Chloe must have answered it and not bothered giving me Jonathan's message. It was the night Barbara was rushed to hospital and Carl had been trying to get hold of me. When I remember this, anger I thought was buried deep within me begins to resurface.

"Anyway," Jonathan continues. "I didn't try calling again because I wanted to give you space to...you know...sort things out."

I immediately feel awkward and regret telling him what I did. How can I now explain to him that I am living with you? I can't find the words, any words that won't make me seem pathetic and desperate. My only option is to keep my mouth shut and listen while Jonathan makes polite small talk and Myrah smiles smugly, both of them unaware of my secret.

"So, d'you fancy meeting up?" Jonathan asks, blurting it out in the middle of discussing his chaotic day at work.

"I, er, I can't...Sorry."

There is a short pause and I wonder if he's hung up.

"Okay, no problem," he says finally. "I better go now. Patients waiting. But I'll call you soon, okay?" He cuts me off before I can say any more and I am left feeling uneasy about my dishonesty. I can only hope he realises nothing is going to happen.

I glance over at Myrah and she quickly turns away and sinks her nose into a bottle of moisturiser. She is my only link to Jonathan so I head over to her and perch on her desk.

"Well? Anything to report?" Her eyes grow huge, expectant, and I feel as if I am about to let her down again.

"Nothing's changed, Myrah. I'm just not ready for anything," I say, hoping she can't see through me. I know it would be easier just to tell her I'm with you now and that we live together, but the moment for that passed long ago. She would never understand why I haven't told her before. So I continue to weave my web of lies. I tell her I don't understand why Jonathan's called and her expression turns cold.

"I did tell Jonathan you weren't interested after you went for a drink, so I really think he's just being friendly, Olivia. He's a good man so just be straight with him if he calls again." Myrah finally smiles and I begin to feel reassured. After all, he is a good friend of hers.

For the first time today, I busy myself with work and focus on what I'm doing. When lunch time comes I stay at my desk sorting through all the folders on my computer desktop. I don't bother calling Chloe.

I long for the cold journey home to pass quickly so I can curl up on the sofa with my thick wool blanket and do nothing but read. Ellie is with Carl and you have a parents' evening at school tonight so I will have the flat to myself. I am starving but don't think I have the energy to cook; dinner will have to be a frozen pizza and glass of wine.

But I should know better than to plan anything because the minute I step through the door, I know something is wrong. The hall light is on even though neither you nor Ellie should be home, and the smell of burnt toast wafts up my nostrils, making me even hungrier.

"Hello?" I call, pulling my boots off.

You appear at the top of the stairs. "Oh good, you're home. You better hurry up." Your voice is almost a whisper so I know we have company.

Before I reach the top of the stairs, I spot Chloe in the lounge, huddled into a corner of the sofa. Even though my mind has been churning over what to do about her, she is the last person I expect to see here this evening. I'm so stunned that even when I'm less than a metre from her, I don't immediately notice her face is black and purple and her arms are tattooed with blood-red bruises. But when I do realise what I'm staring at, my mouth hangs open.

"Chloe? What the hell's happened?" I rush to her and grab her hand. Her fingers are like wire and she grimaces as she squeezes my hand.

"She can't really talk a lot, it hurts too much," you explain, perching on the arm of the sofa. None of this makes sense and for a brief flash I look at you, calm and authoritative, and wonder what your part is in all this. As if reading my mind, you quickly explain this is the parting gift Chloe's boyfriend gave her when she told him their relationship was over.

214

I stare at Chloe's ghostly, shrunken figure; somehow none of what I'm seeing or hearing seems real. Yet her hand tightly clasps mine and her nails dig into my skin, showing me my mind hasn't conjured this up. I offer to make her a cup of tea but she shakes her head and whimpers.

"Well, I'll have one," you say, offering me an excuse to escape to the kitchen.

I put the kettle on and, still starving, shovel a couple of biscuits into my mouth before you appear in the kitchen. You are too calm, as if this is a normal thing to happen on a Friday evening, and it unnerves me. Chloe is your sister so shouldn't you be raging about what this man has done to her?

"We should call the police," I say.

"I've tried, but she won't let me. She says she just wants to forget it happened."

"But what if he comes after her again?"

You shake your head. "That won't happen. Chloe said after he'd battered her he suddenly looked terrified and ran out of his flat."

"So what will she do now?" My stomach rumbles but suddenly food is the last thing I want.

"That's the thing. She'll have to stay here with us tonight until she sorts something out. Is that okay?"

I don't hesitate to agree; no matter what Chloe has done, she doesn't deserve this.

"Thanks." You hug me while we wait for the kettle to boil. "Could you make Chloe one, too? She just didn't want to put you out but I think she needs it."

Back in the lounge, Chloe has shrunk even further into the sofa and I've never seen her look so vulnerable. Her hand shakes as she grips her mug and for the first time since I've known her, her eyes are not heavily pencilled and her lips are pale and bare. But without her mask, she somehow looks even more beautiful.

"Can you call Mum and Dad?" Chloe asks you when she's finished her tea. "I need them to pick me up before it's too late."

"What for? You're staying here tonight."

"No, Michael, not this time. I'm not putting you and Olivia out anymore. Just call them for me, please?" I listen in disbelief. This is the first time I've ever heard Chloe put someone else first.

I feel like an intruder as you and Chloe discuss what to tell your parents, recounting past incidents in which you both agree they have overreacted. Neither of you look at me as you speak. This is family business that I'm no part of and we all know I have nothing to offer. I have never met your parents and it is only now I wonder why. Eventually the two of you concoct a story about Chloe being mugged on her way home from work. Only when you've agreed and memorised every detail do you turn to me and ask what I think. Without thinking, I speak the words that have been on my mind the whole time I have sat here listening to your white lie.

"It's a believable story but I think you need to be honest," I say, looking at Chloe even though you are the one who has asked my opinion. "Lies have a way of catching you out sooner or later."

Chloe says nothing but your stare falls heavily upon me so I look away and pull at my necklace. "You don't understand our parents," you say. "This is the best way." How can I argue with that when they are strangers to me?

I wait with Chloe while you call your parents from the kitchen. She is shaking even though the heating is on so I fetch my blanket and wrap it around her. I take the opportunity while you are out of the room to ask her what your parents are like and she shakes her head.

"Not easy to talk to. Or be around. Both of us chose universities as far away from home as possible, so I suppose that says it all. Mum's just so nosy. She has to know every little thing we do. She can't do that now, though, can she? It must eat her up that we live so far away. And Dad, well...he was just *so* strict. We could barely breathe in that house."

I listen to Chloe, convinced your parents can't be that bad if their only crime is being strict or wanting to know what their kids are up to. I start to feel uneasy that you have never introduced me to them, or even spoken much about them.

Chloe must sense my thoughts because she quickly reassures me. "It's no wonder Michael's never taken you to meet them, they'd probably interrogate you like a prisoner of war." She chuckles at her analogy and, despite what we're talking about, I'm glad to see her brighten up.

"What's funny?" You appear in the doorway, slipping your mobile into your pocket. Without waiting for an answer, you perch on the edge of the sofa between Chloe and me. "Not good news, I'm afraid, Chloe. Mum and Dad say you can stay there but they can't pick you up. Apparently they've been wine-tasting today and neither of them is up to the drive. But it's fine, you can stay here, can't you?"

Chloe looks distressed. "Can't you take me? It's not that late and it's Saturday tomorrow so you don't have to get up early–"

"No, sorry, I've got phone calls to make to all the parents I wasn't able to see tonight because...well, anyway, sorry, but I can't."

"I'll drive you," I blurt out, and you and Chloe both turn to stare at me.

You open your mouth to speak but Chloe beats you to it, thanking me profusely and leaning over you to hug me.

"You do know they live in Cambridge? That's at least a two-hour drive. And you'll get stuck in Friday night traffic." You stand up, nearly unbalancing Chloe.

"He's right," she says. "It's too far and I can't expect you—"

"Don't argue. We're leaving in ten minutes." I scoop up the mugs and leave you and Chloe as surprised as I am at my offer.

In the passenger seat, still cocooned in my blanket, Chloe falls asleep as soon as we're on the M11. All I'm left with is the radio and my growling stomach for company but I won't wake her, even though I had hoped to use this time alone to get to know her better. Being around Chloe when she is alcohol-free and in a kind mood is a rare opportunity. But like everything else I've tried to plan today, nothing will come of it. Several times I'm tempted to turn the radio up as loud as it can go – just for a second – to jolt her awake but when I turn to her she looks so peaceful and childlike that instead I just speed up to get her to Cambridge faster.

The sat nav guides me directly into the driveway of a large converted barn house in the middle of acres of fields. I know this was your childhood home but I have trouble imagining either of you living here. It's so far-removed from anywhere I've ever seen in London and doesn't seem to fit either you or Chloe. It's too dark to see much but I imagine plenty of horses and sheep also call this place home. It's only when I pull further up the cobbled drive and stop the car that Chloe begins to stir. "We're here," I tell her, and her eyes snap open.

She unbuckles her seatbelt and looks towards the house with a heavy sigh. "That was really quick. I can't believe we're here already." She unravels the blanket and folds it up before placing it on the back seat. "I really appreciate this, Olivia. Thank you. And sorry I wasn't much company."

Before I can reply, two circles of light beam into the car, dancing from side to side as they search out our faces.

"My parents," Chloe whispers, and I quickly open the door to greet them.

I don't know if I've ever imagined what your parents are like, but if I've ever had any expectations then the two figures standing by the car don't match them. Both of them tower above me, clutching their torches like weapons and wearing the same stern expressions. Like Chloe, your mother is thin and straight with no hint of a curve anywhere on her body. But your father is the complete contrast of you: heavily built with a beard covering too much of his face. I am immediately intimidated but hold out my hand and smile my brightest smile. Your mother takes my hand lightly and pulls away quickly. It's too late to offer your father a handshake because within seconds he opens Chloe's door and helps her out.

"You must be Chloe's friend?" he grunts at me over the car roof.

"I, er—"

"Thanks so much for bringing me, Olivia," Chloe interjects, her eyes widening when I turn to her. She ushers your father towards the house and I am left alone with your mother, who looks me up and down.

"So you live in London, do you?" she asks, raising her eyebrows.

For a moment I am tempted to tell her I'm your girlfriend and that we live together but the words fall away under her harsh glare. Instead I tell her I've lived there all my life.

She shakes her head slowly and turns away. "I don't know how anyone can live in that awful place," she mutters, as she heads back to the house. "I told her not to move there. I knew something like this would happen. I'm only surprised it's taken this long."

I don't know whether these words are meant for me or if she's just ranting to herself, but within seconds the lights ping off and I am left alone in unfamiliar darkness.

As I reverse out of the drive, Chloe appears on the front porch, wrapping her arms around herself. She offers a shy wave and I flash the headlights at her in response. She's been through enough today so I can't drive off and let her think I'm angry with her. And it is only now, in the brief moment I have met your parents, that I appreciate why both of you needed to leave this place. It takes me until I am back in the comforting bustle of London to relax a bit and erase the coldness of your parents from my mind.

"Don't worry about them," you say to me, when I finally collapse into bed. "They're just miserable."

You drape your legs over me, your body heat welcome under the icy cold duvet. "At least now you understand why I've never introduced you." I don't reply but it is still on my mind when a few moments later you kiss my neck and whisper that you want me.

You fall asleep quickly but all I can do is lie next to you, my eyes closed in a parody of slumber, while my mind searches for answers. I want to believe the only reason you haven't introduced me is because you were worried about what I would think of them, but that is too simple an explanation. Too convenient.

I am interrupted from worrying when my phone beeps and with blurry eyes I see I have a text message from Jonathan. My heart races as I click on the message and read the single word he has written. *Goodnight xx.* It is simple and harmless but loaded with meaning. I delete it and turn my phone to mute. And now, lying in the darkness, your parents are no longer on my mind.

CHAPTER TWENTY-ONE

Henny turns and stares at me. Perhaps she is looking for something, a clue or sign, to show her who I am. I wonder if she sees me as a challenge and this is why she has come here on her day off when there are a thousand better things she could be doing. If she's got children then why is she bothering with me? Doesn't she know how important and precious time spent with them is? Maybe she feels the need to break me, but if so, she is underestimating me. I stare back at her, but when only kindness shines in her eyes I have to look away. I prefer it when they are harsh; it is what I deserve.

"You need to talk if there's any hope of getting better," she tells me. "It doesn't matter what you say, just say something. Anything." She pulls down her t-shirt so the smooth strip of her stomach is covered.

A magpie swoops down and lands in front of us, pecking at something hidden in the grass. "Oops, that's one for sorrow," Henny says, giving the magpie a salute. "But then again, I think we can say sorrow's already paid this place a visit. Several times over." She sighs and we both watch the bird, shiny and elegant, as it forages in the grass.

I wonder how long she will keep waiting for me. Everyone has a breaking point and she must be a saint if she hasn't reached hers. I am hard work, which is why they have all given up on me.

"You're not the only one who's ever felt pain, Olivia," she says in her soft, sing-song voice. In my head I scream out: *But what pain could possibly be worse than this? Tell me that!* But I don't say a word. I sink my head into my hands and lean forward, rocking gently backwards and forwards to calm myself. To stop myself from smashing myself against the wall we sit against. The magpie launches itself upwards and glides away, off to spread its warning to someone else.

Time and people pass us by but we are both glued to the bench, lost in our own thoughts until finally, keeping my head in my hands, I bring myself to speak to Henny. "What do you know about pain?" I demand. "You have no idea. You swan in here and then go back home to your nice little life, leaving all of this behind you. D'you know what I'd give to be able to do that?"

I turn my head towards Henny but keep rocking. I want to see the expression on her face when she realises she has no response to what I've said. For a moment she looks shocked but I can't be sure if it's the words I've uttered or the fact I've spoken at all. Then she laughs. Not a witch's cackle but a resigned chuckle.

"What do I know about pain? Hmmm, I guess not much at all. Unless, of course, you count seeing your husband murdered right in front of you?"

The world freezes as I stop rocking and take in what Henny has just said. I search her face and miraculously there is still kindness in her eyes, even though she should hate me at this moment. "Wha...what happened?" I stutter, brimming with shame.

I don't want to hear Henny's story but once words are spoken they can never be forgotten. They leave scars that are a constant reminder of what should never have been heard.

Her voice is deeper as she speaks now and there is no melody to her tone as she recounts the tragic night her husband was murdered in Zimbabwe, shot down in front of her while their small children clung to her, fearful for their lives.

"He was a good man," she says. "All he wanted to do was stand up for people and fight for their right to have a decent life. His punishment was losing his life." Henny's voice is calm and steady, as if this is someone else's story she is telling and not her own. And when she's finished speaking I know without a doubt this woman knows what pain is.

"I'm sorry," Leon says.

Myrah, Sophie and I stare at him, our mouths gaping. I have spent days feeling uneasy about Jonathan's text and not paying much attention to anything else, so I am unable to digest the news Leon's just delivered. He lowers his head and, unable to face our reactions, stares at his shoes. I can't blame him. He knows how important this place is to all of us. Panic rises within me but I try to stifle it and focus on what Leon is telling us.

"I've been trying to keep the business afloat for a while now but with fewer advertisers and the hike in rent...well, I'm bleeding money." Sweat coats his forehead, even though it's chilly in the office, and my heart wrenches for him. After all, there are other jobs out there but for Leon this is his business, his life. "I don't want any of you to worry, though. I have lots of contacts and I'll be helping you all find work as soon as I can."

My panic subsides slightly because Leon is a man of his word but Sophie, finally digesting what his news means, storms off to her desk and begins tipping the contents of her drawers into her oversized handbag. Nobody rushes to comfort or reassure her. All of us are fearful of her sharp tongue.

"There's no need for anyone to rush off," Leon says, leaking more sweat than should be humanly possible. "Stay until the end of the day, won't you? All of you, that is." Over at her desk, Sophie shakes her head and I myself wonder if there's much point in prolonging the agony. But I won't leave Leon alone.

Over the next few hours the office is a different place as we shed its life. As I throw things I probably don't need into boxes, I mentally calculate all the things I have to worry about now. Ellie's happiness is top of the list. I've been hoping her wanting to live with Carl is a phase she'll grow out of so I still haven't addressed the issue properly. Even though she hasn't mentioned it lately, I know the topic will resurface.

I am still a shameful secret from your parents and even if they aren't the friendliest of people, I at least want them to know about us. It would be nice for Ellie to meet them too, especially now she no longer has any grandparents. I have tried a few times since meeting them to convince you to tell them about me but you remain resolute. They are to have no part in our life together. This is a puzzle to me, which you won't even try to explain, and I am desperate enough for answers to contemplate asking Chloe to help, even though she was complicit in hiding my identity.

Perhaps I shouldn't be too worried by Jonathan's text message but it has unsettled me. I am sure I have never given him the impression there can be anything between us and even if I had, it's over a year and a half since our date, so his sudden appearance back into my life makes no sense. No solution occurs to me so all I can do is wait to see what he says next and confront him then.

Despite all this, when I look at Leon, crumpled and forlorn as he piles books and magazines into a green plastic crate, I am grateful I can at least work through my issues. They are problems for which I can eventually find a solution. It won't be as simple for Leon to rebuild his life.

When it approaches six o'clock, Myrah declares she has to get home and hugs Leon tightly, almost sucking the air from him. "I'll keep in touch," she promises, and hugs me too. I want to tell her about Jonathan's text message; perhaps so she can reassure me again, but now is not the time. This place, our work, is the only tie that binds Myrah and me together; without it our friendship seems frail and unsustainable, so will I get another opportunity? I almost change my mind and follow her outside until I notice Leon has his head buried in his hands.

Left alone, Leon and I finish clearing up, communicating only with smiles and occasional arm squeezes. What is there to say? There are no words of comfort I can offer him and small talk is unthinkable right now. So we work steadily away, cleaning too much and putting off the dreaded moment when we turn the lights off and close the door.

When it's nearly eight o'clock, Leon tells me I should get home and won't accept my offer to stay with him until he leaves. "Go, Olivia. It's late and you've got someone waiting for you at home," he says grimly.

I don't hug him or make a big fuss because I need him to know this won't be the last time I see him. He is a loyal friend, someone I won't let disappear from my life. So, holding back a well of tears, I pat his arm and tell him I'll call him.

"Will you be all right?" he asks when I reach the door.

I turn back and smile. "I've got some savings that should last me till I find something else. I'll be okay. Please don't worry about me."

"It's my job to worry about you," he says, and as I leave him alone to say a private goodbye to his business, I know he means every word.

Outside, the cold hits me and the numbness I have felt since Leon delivered his news quickly evaporates. Suddenly I feel lost and small, as if the city is far too big for me and I no longer have a place here. I am frozen to the spot and can't seem to turn in the direction of Waterloo station, a short distance I normally navigate subconsciously. My phone beeps and I think I see Jonathan's name glaring at me from the screen until I open the message and realise it's from Chloe.

I'm so sorry about not telling the parents the other night. Will explain later. If there is any small thing that can make this day more tolerable, it is Chloe being nice. After her attack the other night, I have chosen to forgive her for what's gone before. Even if she did answer my phone and deliberately not let anyone know I was at work when Barbara was in hospital, I have to rise above this. There have been moments over the last couple of days when I've wondered if her vulnerability the other night was just an act, but perhaps what happened to her has genuinely changed her. I have to believe that because as long as you are in my life, she will be too. And now is my chance to find out about your parents, a topic which you have made taboo.

With my mood slightly lifted, I pay no attention to the figure looming in front of me until I hear my name called. Within seconds my stomach sinks as I realise Jonathan is barely two inches away from me, a misshapen smile plastered on his face as he reaches out for a hug. I instinctively take a step back and the smile crumbles away.

"Hi, what are you doing here?" I try to keep my voice upbeat and hide my annoyance.

"I came to see Myrah. Is she still in the office?" He glances behind him and shifts from one foot to the other.

I try to remember how Myrah knows Jonathan but can't recall the details. All I am sure of is that he's more a friend of her husband's than of Myrah's, so why would he come here to see her? Especially at this time. I must look doubtful because he quickly informs me he's been invited to their house for dinner and thought he'd travel back with Myrah.

"You could try her mobile," I suggest, stepping sideways to show him standing in the cold chatting is the last thing I want to do.

Jonathan nods. "Hmmmm. She's probably on the tube by now. Never mind." He looks at me as if he's waiting for me to offer another suggestion and thrusts his hands into his pockets. "It's freezing out here. How about a quick drink? I've got time before I need to be at Myrah's and there's a pub just across the road there." He points but I don't bother looking.

"No, sorry, I can't. I have to get home."

Jonathan doesn't say anything and his expression is blank.

"See you, then," I say, turning away without waiting for a reply. As I cross the road I feel his eyes drilling into me until I round the corner and sprint the short distance to Waterloo station. I don't dare to think about what's just happened until I'm on the train and a safe distance has passed between him and me. The man I just saw bears no resemblance to the Jonathan I had a drink with and I don't know which one is real. All I do know is that whatever he's doing is escalating and I need to do something about it.

I have so much on my mind that when I arrive home and find you packing clothes into a suitcase, my stomach lurches. I stare at the scene before me, open-mouthed and scared to ask what it means.

"The school trip," you say, smiling at my expression. "Did you forget?"

I still can't get my head around what I'm seeing and your words may as well be delivered in a foreign language. "What?"

"Olivia, I told you months ago about this. I got talked into going to the Lake District for the Year Nine trip. Remember? I even mentioned it earlier this week."

I hear your words but nothing you say sounds familiar. The only explanation is that I've been so wrapped up in worrying, I haven't acknowledged the things happening right in front of me. And if I've neglected you then I've probably been distant from Ellie too. I decide I will treat her to her favourite takeaway and make the time we have alone special. I offer to help you pack and scan the bathroom carefully to make sure I fill your wash bag with everything you'll need for the week. There is only one tube of toothpaste but I add it to the bag; I can worry about getting another one later.

Back in the bedroom, you finish packing and carefully place your wash bag between two neatly folded t-shirts. You seem relaxed about going away and I wonder if part of you is relieved to be having a break from Ellie and me. I haven't had a chance to tell you about losing my job but now it will have to wait. I can't let you go away for a week with my news hanging over you.

At the door, you kiss my cheek and I breathe in your scent. I am angry with myself for not knowing last night I wouldn't see you for a week and I pull you into me, trying to tempt you to stay a bit longer.

"I wish I had more time but the coach is leaving in fifteen minutes." You peel my hands away. "I'll text you when we get there." And then you are gone and I close the door, feeling sorry for myself until I think of Ellie waiting upstairs. Only my daughter can snap me out of my melancholy and, as if she's been summoned, she shouts from upstairs. "Mum, what's this?"

I look up to see her waving a pink, sparkly cardigan, too big to be hers and definitely not mine either.

I spring upstairs to get a closer look at the garment but I still don't recognise it. "It must be Chloe's. She was here a few days ago."

Ellie brings a sleeve to her nose and inhales. "Yuck, it stinks of her perfume," she declares, before throwing it on the floor. "Can we have a takeaway, Mum, please?" She makes an angel face at me, making it impossible to refuse. I pretend to consider her request for a moment but she knows I'm teasing and can't hide her smile.

"Go and get the menus," I say, scooping up Chloe's cardigan and folding it into a neat square.

We order a large pizza and I let Ellie choose the toppings. While we wait, hoping they will honour their forty-five-minute delivery promise, we sit at the table and Ellie studies a picture of Barbara from her wedding day. Carl must have given it to her because I have never seen this one before.

"Doesn't she look beautiful?" Ellie says, and I nod, choked up that she's no longer here. "I'm going to draw her now." She reaches for her pencil and I watch as she brings Barbara to life.

Ellie looks relaxed as she draws so I decide to risk asking what she thinks of you. Keira's words still ring in my ears but I need to hear it from my daughter's own mouth. "Do you like Michael?" I ask, trying to sound as casual as possible.

Ellie shrugs her shoulders. "I dunno. He's okay. Just a bit boring maybe." She guides her pencil carefully over the paper in light strokes. So Keira was right. Now this is another thing I need to talk to you about when you get home. I don't question Ellie further because in her few words she's told me all I need to know.

I pour us both some fresh orange juice and sit mesmerised, watching Ellie sketch. Minutes pass like this and I forget we've ordered pizza until the doorbell chimes, snapping me out of my daze. "You get the plates out, Ellie," I say, but she is also lost in her world and continues drawing.

When I open the door, my stomach rumbling, I am stunned to see Chloe standing there instead of someone holding out a pizza box. She smiles sheepishly and shoves a bottle of wine in my hand.

"This is for you," she says. "To say sorry for...you know...And thank you for driving me to Cambridge."

I wait for her to barge in like she normally does, but she stands in the doorway, shivering in a thin denim jacket and leggings. I tell her you're not in but she explains it's me she's come to see. "I know he's away. I thought we could use this time to...you know...clear the air, maybe?"

I invite her in, wondering if one large pizza will be enough for three people and feeling a bit annoyed that she chose this moment to turn up. Ellie, awoken from her trance, rushes out of the kitchen and almost skids to a stop when she sees Chloe follow me up the stairs. "I...er...."

"Ellie, Chloe's just going to join us for some pizza." I shoot her a warning look before she has a chance to protest.

Her face drops and her chin starts to tremble. She looks as if she's about to cry or scream or have a tantrum so I break one of my rules and tell her she can take her pizza to her room when it comes. Without a single word to Chloe, she nods and heads to her bedroom to wait.

Embarrassed, I apologise to Chloe. She has never been my favourite person but Ellie has been brought up better than this.

Chloe dismisses it. "Oh, don't worry about it, Olivia. Now, when's this pizza arriving? I'm starving!"

With you away, we sit on the floor and eat pizza straight from the box, washing it down with the wine Chloe has brought. I listen intently as she tells me about Adam and the day he beat her. She is convinced he's never done anything like that before and that he feels awful now. "That's why I won't go to the police. He's texted me a million times since that night and...well...it just wouldn't be right to press charges. I did dump him, after all, so he's bound to be upset."

Chloe's eyes plead with me to agree with her but I can't. She's forgiving a man she hardly knows for a heinous act he carried out simply because she didn't want to be with him anymore. But I keep quiet and let her justify her choice. It is just that, after all. *Her* decision. She doesn't ask my opinion because she knows what I think without my saying a word.

I bide my time but when it appears Chloe's unloaded everything she wants to about Adam and the attack, I ask her how it's been staying at her parents'. I feel guilty for changing the subject but now she is here I need to understand why she didn't tell them who I am. And why you won't either.

She lets out a long sigh and I wonder if she'll ever speak again. "It's been hell. Like you could never believe." She gulps wine and goes quiet once more.

I grow frustrated that she is stalling for time and feel awful for thinking this way, but I need to get information from her before she's had too much to drink. "They seemed okay," I lie. "And very worried about you."

Chloe looks away from me and eyes the bottle of wine on the floor between us. Her glass isn't yet empty but already she looks thirsty for more. I try to distract her by offering her the last slice of pizza but she wrinkles her nose and shakes her head. I can't blame her; the cheese has already started to congeal. But the question I want to ask lies between us like an open, bleeding wound. Sooner or later one of us will have to bring it up. After a moment, Chloe grabs the bottle and pours us both a glass but then says she needs the bathroom.

I go and check on Ellie and she is tucked up in bed, finishing her sketch of Barbara. "It's fantastic," I say, grabbing her empty plate from the floor. She smiles and carries on drawing. "What will you do with it when it's finished?"

She shrugs a reply and then, without looking up at me, says, "When is she going?"

When I get back to Chloe, she has nearly finished her glass of wine. "I think you got a text message," she says, nodding towards the coffee table.

I lean over to check it. "It's Michael. Telling me he's arrived safely."

"That's sweet. My brother can be caring sometimes, I suppose. Don't tell him I'm here, will you?" She pulls her knees up to her chin and smiles sadly.

I raise my eyebrows and she explains she just wants to give him some space and lay low for a while after all their arguing. As strange as it sounds, I understand what she means. There have been plenty of times when I've felt like that myself, with you.

"He's just that kind of person, isn't he?" I tell her. "When you push him too far it's best to just walk away."

After another half hour, I begin to admit defeat and give up on ever getting any information from Chloe. We talk

233

about everything but your parents and I wonder if she's doing it on purpose. But just when I am convinced this is the case she dispels my preconception. "I know what you want to ask, Olivia. And I'm so sorry I let my parents think you were just a friend of mine instead of Michael's girlfriend."

My heart races. "But why did you? Did he tell you not to tell them about me?" She studies her fingernails and bites into one. "It's Michael. He's such a private person and it wasn't my place to tell them what's going on in his life. He's the one who needs to do that. Plus there was so much going on, it just wasn't the right time." Chloe must notice what her words are doing to me because she takes my hand. "Don't get upset. I didn't tell them about Andrew until he proposed to me and we'd been together for over two years by then!"

I will never understand this, but losing both my parents years ago means I have no yard stick to measure what's normal and what isn't. I have to let this go, but first there is one more question I have to ask. "Did they know about Sarah?"

Chloe frowns. "Who?"

"Michael's ex? Sarah?"

She stares at me for a moment. "Oh," she says, swirling her glass around and taking a long gulp. "No...no, I don't think so."

There is a lot more I want to know but it's not fair for me to grill your sister when you are the one who should be filling in the gaps. Chloe stands up and announces she'll make us both coffee. As she reaches the hall she turns back to me. "You know, the past is the past, Olivia. Sometimes it's best to leave it there. You and Michael are happy together and that's all that matters. Who knows or doesn't know is irrelevant. Just focus on the two of you."

"Three of us," I correct her.

"Oh...yes, sorry. And Ellie, of course."

By the time we've finished our coffee, it's past midnight and I haven't even thought about where Chloe is staying or how she'll get there. She hasn't mentioned it but I decide it won't hurt if she stays here on the sofa tonight. Ellie won't be pleased when she wakes up but I can't turf Chloe out onto the street and there won't be any trains back to Cambridge until morning.

"Are you sure?" Her face lights up when I suggest it.

"One night's fine," I say, just so she knows it's not an extended invitation.

"Thanks, Olivia. I'll make breakfast in the morning. A full English. For you and Ellie." I don't tell her that Ellie probably won't eat it if she knows Chloe's made it.

I stand up and, for the first time this evening, spot Chloe's pink cardigan folded neatly on the arm of the sofa. "Thanks," she says, sliding her arms into it. "I'd forgotten I left this here."

When I hand Chloe some spare sheets for the sofa, she thanks me and wraps them around her on the floor. "D'you mind if I just watch TV for a bit? I don't think I can sleep at the moment. I'll keep the volume down."

Heading off to bed, I am more at peace than I have been for weeks. Chloe's icy facade melting fills me with hope that we might have a good relationship from now on. And maybe when Ellie sees that she's changed she will come around too. I can only hope. I am asleep almost before my head sinks into my pillow and oversleep for the first time in years.

The glare of the sun fighting through the curtains wakes me up and I am smiling even before I'm fully awake. I remember the previous evening and how things between Chloe and me feel different now, better and stronger. I'm in the mood for the huge cooked breakfast Chloe has promised. Perhaps if the three of us make it together, Ellie might be more likely to eat it. She loves helping me cook and spending time with Chloe could be just what's needed.

I pull on my dressing gown, feeling as light as air, and spot my mobile on the bedside table. Wondering if you've texted me again, I unlock it and the screen springs to life, showing me I have a text message. But when I see who the text is from and reluctantly open the message, I come crashing down with a thud. *Bitch. It's rude not to reply to people.* And suddenly I have no appetite.

CHAPTER TWENTY-TWO

By the end of the week Chloe is still here and neither of us have mentioned her leaving. She goes out most evenings – I don't ask where and she doesn't volunteer the information – but is always back early and never inebriated. Not that I can tell, at least. I don't know what her reasons are for wanting to stay so long, but mine are clear. She is a welcome distraction from worrying about Jonathan. With no work to keep me busy, I focus on getting to know her better. Our conversations are friendly and there no longer seems to be tension between us, even if we disagree on something. I begin to enjoy her company, perhaps because we both know Chloe will not be here when you arrive home. Her presence is no longer a burden to me and I can sense her going out of her way to do whatever she can around the flat to make things easier. She constantly dusts and cleans and cooks most evenings so I can spend extra time with Ellie, even though she rarely stays for dinner. But she doesn't need to do any of this. I enjoy her company and don't need anything more from her. I can only assume she is trying to make up for her past behaviour.

Unfortunately Ellie doesn't share my revised view of Chloe and stays out of her way as much as possible, shutting herself away in her bedroom after school until I have to coax her out for dinner. When I keep her company in her room she takes every opportunity to ask me, in a hushed voice, when Chloe will leave. Every day I tell her the same thing: that I'm sure she will leave before you get home. But she rolls her eyes at me as if I'm either mad or stupid to believe this.

No matter how much I ignore my phone, Jonathan's hate campaign continues and all week he bombards me with abusive text messages. There is no pattern to their arrival; they come day and night and his acerbic, hateful words are like splatters of poison. I don't reply to these texts because I don't want him to know I'm bothered by them.

I consider calling Myrah about it but it feels too awkward and I have no idea how to explain to her what's happening. As far as she knows, Jonathan is a respected dentist and family friend, so how could I hope to convince her otherwise? Although I have saved a couple of his texts, showing them to her would only make her believe something must have happened between us to cause his hatred.

Telling you is also out of the question, for the same reason. You would jump to conclusions and assume I have done something with Jonathan, a man I barely know and have never been attracted to, even when you and I weren't together. I try to imagine if this were happening to you instead; would I believe you were innocent? It does seem implausible that someone would act this way after one innocent drink. So I have to carry the burden alone, pushing it to the furthest part of my mind, where it stays until each new text message arrives.

But on the day you are due home, without any plan or intention, Chloe becomes the one person I confide in about Jonathan. Before her attack I would have done anything to prevent her finding out even the smallest detail about me, but the Chloe I have seen over the last few days is a different person, someone to whom I now feel able to open up.

It is Friday morning and I drop Ellie off at school, excited that you'll be home this evening. Even Ellie is glad you're coming home. "At least then Chloe will go," she says. Her comment surprises me, not because she wants Chloe gone but because she has picked up on the fact that you don't want Chloe around either. As far as I know, nothing has been said in front of Ellie – we are careful to keep adult talk quiet and confined to bed time – but somehow she has sensed the tension between the two of you.

When I get home, Chloe's bag is in the hallway, bulging more than I remember seeing it when she arrived last week. I find her at the kitchen table, toasting her hands against the heat of her coffee mug. She looks sad and I know without asking it's because she has to leave today.

"I've just boiled the kettle. D'you fancy one?" she asks, standing up before I've had a chance to answer.

"No, no, I'll get it." I motion for her to sit down. She's done enough around the flat since she turned up last week and I'm beginning to feel awkward. While I make coffee, Chloe tells me a friend of hers in Kilburn has offered to put her up for a few days until she sorts herself out. She doesn't reveal whether this friend is male or female and I don't ask; I already know the answer.

"What about all your things? Aren't they still at Adam's?" As I ask this, it dawns on me just how unsettled Chloe's life is. Sleeping on sofas and living out of bags is not the life a woman in her early thirties should be living. She's only a few years younger than me yet our lives couldn't be more different.

"My friend's going to take me to get them," she says, attempting a smile, and I wonder if this kind deed is out of altruism or whether Chloe will have to pay back the favour.

Shrugging the thought away, I take my coffee to the table and we sit companionably, neither of us mentioning any more about Chloe leaving. I spot her denim jacket draped over her chair and shiver just imagining how cold she'll be. "I'll be back in a sec," I tell her.

In my bedroom, I flick through my clothes until I find what I'm looking for. Hidden at the end of the wardrobe is a long woollen coat with a thick fur collar. My favourite item of clothing. It was a Christmas present from Carl a few years ago and still looks brand-new. It's too dressy for me to wear every day but it will keep Chloe warm until she gets her things back from Adam's.

Chloe is speechless when I hand her my coat but her face lights up and she wraps it around her, smiling gratefully. I tell her she's welcome to keep it as long as she needs but make sure she knows how much it means to me.

"Thank you so much, Olivia. I'll never forget how kind you've been to me."

Embarrassed by her compliment, I nod my head towards the window and we both stare out at the icy white sky. The tops of the bare trees sway in and out of view, shaken by the violent wind, and I am so mesmerised by the stark beauty of this winter day that I almost forget Chloe is here. Perhaps she is feeling the same because neither of us speak until my mobile beeps, permeating the silence and forcing us both to turn back to the table.

Chloe watches me, waiting for me to check my phone, but I don't move. There are plenty of reasons I could offer for ignoring it, but none come to me and before I can say anything at all, Chloe panics.

"Is that Michael? I hope he's not here yet!" She stands up and her mug nearly topples over.

She has got a point. After all, it can't be Jonathan every time so why shouldn't now be one of those times? I lunge for the phone, just in case Chloe gets any ideas about checking it for me, and stare at the screen, willing your name to appear before me. Thankfully it does. Your message is short but in it you tell me you're looking forward to getting home tonight.

"Yes, it is," I tell Chloe. "But don't panic, he won't be back till this evening."

But Chloe looks doubtful, as if she is convinced Michael will walk through the door any second and throw her out. She is so flustered that for a moment I push aside anything to do with Jonathan and ask her what's going on.

"I'm just not his favourite person at the moment. You know that."

I nod. "Well, he did invite you to stay instead of going to your parents', so maybe he's okay with you now?"

Chloe snorts. "I'd just been attacked, Olivia. He's not that heartless. But now my bruises are fading he won't want to see me here."

"It's no secret your relationship is strained. But what I don't understand is why?"

Chloe sits back down and takes a sip of coffee, wrinkling her face when she realises it's no longer warm. "I'm just a big disappointment to him. I mean, look at the difference between him and me. He's successful and in control while my life's just one big mistake after another. Michael sees me as a huge let-down and he's ashamed I'm his sister."

I shake my head and try to convince her that this isn't the case. I do this even though I don't know myself what the truth is. "He just worries about you, that's all. And we all make mistakes, Chloe. I've definitely made enough of them. But no one can judge you if you learn from them. And try to do things differently." I haven't intended to preach to her, but it must come out this way because she looks at me as if I've just said something that will set her free.

"I know you're right," she says, slowly nodding her head. "And I am trying to change things, believe me."

"I do," I tell her, patting her arm for reassurance.

"Anyway, now that's out in the open, are you going to explain why you didn't want to check your text message?"

For the next half hour I tell Chloe all about Jonathan, carefully emphasising that we only went for one drink and nothing physical ever happened. She assures me she believes me and is as flummoxed as I am about Jonathan's stalker-like behaviour.

"Whatever you do, don't call him to confront him or reply to anything he texts," Chloe says. "That would be the worst thing you could do. It would just encourage him to keep sending messages."

I hadn't thought of doing this – hearing Jonathan's voice would sicken me – but Chloe is right. It's not an option. We both agree that there is not much I can do except change my mobile number, but I refuse to do that. If I have to change anything in my life then he has won, he has controlled me.

"Give me his number," Chloe says suddenly.

"What? Why?"

"Do you trust me?"

I nod and Chloe seems relieved. If she had asked me the same question a week ago my answer would have been different and we both know it.

"Good, then, that's settled. Now, what's this Jonathan's number?"

All evidence of Chloe staying here has vanished by the time you get home. It's only eight o'clock but you are exhausted by the coach journey and no doubt even more by the busload of boisterous kids you've had to supervise all week. I kiss you and take in your scent. Being away from you has made me forget how you smell and taste, even the intricate details of your face which I can usually recall from memory. For a moment you are like a new person before me and I search you out with every part of me, hungry for the person I know to come back.

"I need a shower," you say, extricating yourself from my clasp. "And then I've got some news. Good news, I mean. At least, I hope you'll see it that way." You rush to the bathroom before I can interrogate you, leaving me standing in the hallway, confused and frustrated.

While you're showering I rustle up some food, assuming you won't have had dinner yet. All I can find that's edible in the cupboards are some eggs, tomatoes and potatoes, so something resembling a Spanish omelette will have to do. There's some bread that's just about in date so I toast several slices, drown them in butter and pile them on a plate. I find an old candle that's only half burned out so I light it and turn off the main kitchen light. It's not exactly a romantic dinner but it might help relax you after your trip.

You take longer than I expect and I begin to worry the food will be cold by the time we get to eat. But eventually you appear in the doorway in your dressing gown, your hair damp and ruffled. "Sorry," you say. "There didn't seem much point getting dressed again, it's nearly nine o'clock and I'm shattered." Then you notice the food on the table and wink at me. "This looks great."

We devour it as if it's the first meal we've eaten in weeks, and you begin to appear more energised. I can't put it off any longer so I tell you Leon's had to let us all go. I wait for a frown to appear on your face but instead you tell me it doesn't matter. "You'll easily find something else."

Confused by your reaction, I remember you have something to tell me too. "So what's your news? And please let it be better than mine."

A gigantic smile stretches across your face. "Well...how would you feel about moving?"

"Oh. Well, I...I suppose the flat's a bit small for the three of us, so it wouldn't hurt to have a look around."

You laugh and shake your head. "No, no. I mean to Spain."

I don't know what I'm expecting your announcement to be but it's not this. I am dumbstruck until it occurs to me this must be a joke. "Very funny," I say, taking a sip of water. "What's the punch line?"

You look offended and push your knife and fork together even though there is still omelette left on your plate. "Olivia, I'm serious. I want us to go. I know it sounds crazy but what have we got here? And now you've lost your job..."

"But I'll find another one —"

"I'm fed up of my school and Ellie's not exactly the happiest kid at the moment, is she?"

"But—"

"Listen, I've got it all figured out." Your voice fills with excitement. "Finn told me his company are transferring him to their Madrid office in a few weeks. They're renting him a three-bedroom flat and he can work there for as long as he wants. If he doesn't like it after three months and wants to come back to the UK then they're fine with that."

"But just because Finn—"

"Wait, listen! We were talking and I told him how fed up I've been lately, so he suggested we move out there too. We can stay with him until we find our own place and he's sure I'll easily find a teaching job there. This is a great opportunity to change our lives, Olivia. Come on, what do you think?"

I stare at you, feeling a whole mixture of emotions, none of which are anywhere close to what you want to hear. You are speaking as if moving to another country is like deciding which restaurant to pick for dinner. As well as this, I am disappointed. You have chosen to confide in Finn feelings that you should be able to share with me, so what does that say about our relationship?

"I don't know. If you're serious I need to think about this. I mean, what about work for me?"

"Well, we'd manage on my salary to start with. And you can look for freelance work. You don't need to be in London for that, do you? As long as you've got a computer."

This is all too much and I start to feel angry that you've sprung this on me so suddenly. I don't need to fire excuses at you because there is only one thing I need to consider. Something you seem to have overlooked. "And Ellie? She won't want to leave. How can I take her away from Carl?"

You pause for a moment, convincing me I am right to believe you haven't thought of Ellie in all this. "Look, I know there's a lot to think about. All I'm saying is please just consider the idea. Is that asking too much?"

I rise and begin clearing away the dinner plates while you continue to spurt reasons we should go. "I'll think about it," I say. "But it's not something that can be decided with one conversation, Michael. There's a lot to consider. And I'll need to speak to Ellie."

You rush round the table and hug me, whispering into my hair. "Thank you." I pull away from you and continue clearing up, ignoring the disappointment on your face. Pouring two glasses of wine, you tell me you're taking yours to bed.

"Don't be too long," you add. "I want to show you how much I've missed you."

CHAPTER TWENTY-THREE

Every day now I listen for signs of Henny passing my door. I have grown to recognise the clomp she makes as her shoes slap against the tiled floor, her sing-song voice and melodic whistling. But I have heard none of these things for a long time. It's hard to tell whether it's been days or weeks since I've seen her – I don't even know what month it is so I can't be expected to judge time accurately – but it's been long enough for me to worry.

Others come, carrying out their duties without a word or smile, hurriedly doing the bare minimum before they can rush to the safety of the corridor. But how can I blame them? Nobody wants to be in the presence of madness for too long. Perhaps they are afraid it's contagious, a disease that will seep into them as easily as oxygen enters their lungs.

But Henny isn't like the others. I am a human being to her, albeit just a shadow of one. So I am puzzled now why she hasn't come to check on me. Perhaps she has given up on me like the others have. I want to ask for her, grab one of the nameless robots who come in and beg them to bring her to me. But even if I try this, no sound will come from my throat. So I sit and stare as one food tray merges into the next, the nameless people tutting as they take away untouched meals.

Eventually Henny appears in front of me like an apparition, smiling warmly when I open my eyes. "Hello, lovey," she says. "Did you miss me?"

I want to nod and say yes. Maybe even shout at her for not being around, but I don't because she already knows. She perches on the side of the bed and fishes a bar of chocolate from her pocket. It is a Twix, my favourite, and my mouth starts to water as I remember how it tastes.

"Now then, are you going to eat this or will I have to munch it myself?" She waves it in front of me and I grab it from her, rip it open and crunch into the biscuit. Caramel sticks to the roof of my mouth but I devour the whole bar in less than a minute. Henny chuckles as she dusts the crumbs from my sheets. "Good," she says, and I once again earn a nod of approval.

"What the hell's this?" you shout, storming into the bathroom. I spit a mouthful of toothpaste into the sink and turn to see what the problem is. You wave a pink cloth in my face and I'm about to laugh until I realise it's Chloe's cardigan. "Tell me she hasn't been here," you say, lowering your voice.

"She left it here the night she was attacked," I say, turning back to the sink. This is not a lie; the cardigan was already here the night Chloe turned up. I'm sure I gave it back to her but that whole week is a blur now, a mixture of worrying about Jonathan, you, Chloe and Ellie, so I can't be certain of much.

I rinse my mouth and turn back to find you staring at me, unconvinced. "I'm sure she wasn't wearing this that night," you mumble.

"Turn around," I say, grabbing your arms and spinning you so you can't see me. "What am I wearing?"

"What? Jeans, of course." You try to look round but I whip behind the shower curtain and wrap it around me.

"I mean what top am I wearing?"

You sigh heavily, clearly in no mood to humour me. "It's black."

I unravel myself from the shower curtain and you spin back around. I pull my top out towards you and smile triumphantly. "Wrong. Purple."

"Who cares? What's the point of this?" You sound like one of your students.

Feeling proud of myself, I try to explain that if you can't even remember the top I'm wearing when you've just been talking to me, how can you know what Chloe was wearing weeks ago?

"I hope you're going to clean out the sink," you say, before slamming the door.

I chuckle to my mirrored self but it isn't long before this light moment passes and I remember the heavy cloud hanging over me. I need to speak to Chloe to find out what's happening with Jonathan, but it's difficult with you in the flat.

Once I'm dressed, I scribble a short shopping list and try to bribe you to go to the shop, promising to cook dinner again tonight. I hope you won't scrutinise the list or check the kitchen cupboards because the only thing we actually need is milk. You moan something about wanting a quiet day at home but eventually throw your coat on and trudge off to the shop.

I dial Chloe's number before you've closed the door and watch you from the window while I wait for her to answer. I'm just about to hang up when her voice, louder and chirpier than I've heard it lately, pierces my eardrum.

"Olivia! What's going on? Michael didn't find out I stayed, did he?"

I assure her that's not why I'm calling and waste no time asking about Jonathan. She doesn't say anything and I wait patiently, listening to the static coming through the line. Only when she begins speaking do I realise I am biting my nails, a habit I thought I'd waved goodbye to long ago.

"Jonathan. Hmmm...My plan was to talk to him and get him to back off but I haven't been able to get hold of him. I'm so sorry, Olivia. I keep calling his mobile but he never answers."

I try not to sound disappointed. After all, she doesn't have to do this for me. "Okay, well, I think I'll have to change my number. There don't seem many other options."

Chloe tells me not to do anything hasty and promises to keep trying Jonathan's mobile. "What are you doing tonight? Fancy a drink?" she asks, as I'm about to hang up.

"I'm sorry, I can't. I'm meeting my friend, Leon, tonight. He's my ex-boss and, well, I haven't seen him since the magazine folded." I think about asking Chloe to join us but don't know if it would be fair to Leon. They've never met before and I can't see them getting along, even if Chloe has mellowed over the last few weeks.

"Another time, then," she says, before hanging up. I put the phone back in its stand, hoping I haven't offended her.

Sitting on the bed, you watch as I pull clothes on and rip them off again, unsure what to wear tonight. I feel your stare on me and cover as much flesh as I can while swapping tops. Even though you've seen me more naked than this a thousand times, there is something different about being seen under the glare of a light bulb. Somehow it is more personal. It's not like you to sit around without a purpose but I don't dare to hope it's sex you want. There is no lust in your eyes, just the distant look I've come to recognise as a warning to let you be alone.

"Have you told anyone about Madrid?" you ask.

I join you on the bed, covering myself with my dressing gown. "No. I need to get my own head around it all first. It's a huge, life-changing thing you're asking so I need more time."

You nudge closer to me and drape your arm across my shoulder, pushing all your weight down as you sigh. "I know, I just really want this to happen and I'm disappointed you don't feel the same."

Suddenly I wonder if Chloe knows. She hasn't said anything but maybe she's waiting for me to bring it up. "Have you told anyone?"

"No. There's no point upsetting people when you haven't agreed yet. Which reminds me, please don't say anything to Chloe, will you? I can do without that hassle."

"I don't even talk to her," I say, the lie sticking in my throat. "And anyway, it's not my place to tell her, is it?"

Your arm begins to crush me so I wriggle out from under it and yank a strappy vest top over my head. I'm fed up of trying on clothes now so this one will have to do. At least it's got sparkles along the neckline so it feels a bit dressier than anything else I've tried this evening. "Just give me time and I promise I'll make a decision soon," I say, and you nod before going back to watching me, the same blank look on your face.

It is later than I want it to be when I say goodbye to Leon and jump on the night bus. He has been in good spirits tonight, and rather than dwelling on his loss, is planning a future which he intends to start with a well-earned holiday. It will be at least forty-five minutes before I'm in Putney so I clamber upstairs and sit at the front, watching the city roll past in a blur of darkness and bright flashes of light. I am surprisingly relaxed; partly because my phone has been silent all day but also because Leon is doing okay.

When I get home I find you on the sofa, sitting in darkness with the curtains still open. I wonder if you've had too much to drink but there are no bottles or glasses on the coffee table. Your arms are folded across your chest and you glare as I walk towards you. There is only one thing I can think of to explain your anger; you have discovered Chloe was here. My brain attempts to conjure up an excuse but it falls apart as soon as you speak.

"Who's Jonathan?"

I freeze. I have misheard you. There is no way you can know about Jonathan. But then I remember Chloe knows everything and now the only thing that makes sense is you finding out from her. I feel foolish for trusting her and vow to myself that will never happen again.

"What?" I ask, trying to buy myself more time even though I am certain now you know everything. I sit on the sofa opposite you and smooth out my jeans, forcing myself to look directly at you to confirm my innocence. "What's happened?"

You glare at me, already convinced I have done something wrong. "Just tell me, Olivia. I want to hear it from you." Your voice is calm and measured, your lines as rehearsed as if you are performing on a stage.

And now I have to make a split-second decision. I can lie and deny all knowledge of Jonathan but clearly you know something. And if you have spoken to Chloe it is pointless to deny knowing him. I should have told you from the beginning, especially as I have done nothing wrong. Perhaps then things would never have escalated this far. You would have helped me deal with Jonathan. Even though it's overdue, I tell you the truth now, hoping you will trust me and see through any lies Chloe might have spread. I search for clues in your expression as you listen but your face is poker-straight throughout.

"I just don't know what to believe, Olivia. He came here tonight. Looking for you."

Horror floods through me and I stiffen, unable to contemplate what you're saying. "What? What did he say?"

You shake your head. "Well, I didn't exactly want to have a conversation with him. He just asked for you."

I spring up and flop down next to you, trying to grab your hand. You pull away but, ignoring the humiliation, I continue to defend myself. I have the truth on my side so it shouldn't be too difficult to clear this up. "I promise you nothing is going on with him and it never has. I told you everything that happened; he's just a sick freak who won't leave me alone. And I promise you the only time I met up with him was when we'd split up. It was just a drink. Nothing more."

"Well, I hope he was good, Olivia. I hope it was worth it." Your voice is less assured as you say this and it gives me hope.

I beg and plead with you to believe me but I am wasting my breath. You say nothing, but sit with your arms folded, shaking your head as I speak. Eventually I give up and decide to give you some space. I can sleep in Ellie's room tonight, as she's with Carl, and see what happens in the morning. I'm sure when you've had time to think about this you'll realise I wouldn't lie to you. Jonathan's name alone fills me with dread and now he's crossed this line I don't know what he's capable of anymore. When it was just text messages I could convince myself that's all it would be, that it would peter out when he got bored and could see I wasn't responding. I could even pretend him turning up at work was just a coincidence and he was telling the truth about looking for Myrah. But now he has come here and intruded on my life, I can no longer ignore him.

At least I can still trust Chloe. If your relationship wasn't so bad right now, she might even be able to help me convince you Jonathan is lying. But you won't trust Chloe at the moment and getting her involved will only make things worse. Myrah is the only other person I can turn to now but it's too late to call her. First thing in the morning I will beg her to help me. It will mean telling her about you but I have little choice. If Jonathan is disturbed enough to turn up here then I don't even want to think about what else he is capable of.

Gathering up my nightshirt and dressing gown, I sit on Ellie's bed and bury my head in my hands. At least she is with Carl, safe and away from this mess. I hear you slamming cupboards in the kitchen and anger replaces my fear. You should be with me, comforting me and telling me we'll sort this out together, not vilifying me, sentencing me without a trial. Every time we take a step forward in our relationship we just seem to get hurled back to where we started. All the feelings of rejection I felt at the beginning of our relationship flood back but this time feel crueller than anything that came before. This time we are meant to be a team.

For some time I sit hunched over, too many thoughts swirling around my head and cramps shooting across my back. The rest of the flat is quiet and I wonder if you've gone to bed. Maybe when you wake up you'll see things more clearly and accept what I have told you. I remind myself of my plan to call Myrah. It may not be much but at least I will be taking some action. I've left this problem unresolved for too long.

I'm in the middle of searching for some spare sheets when you slip into Ellie's room. I don't hear a sound so scream when you're suddenly standing in front of me, demanding to know what I'm doing. I ignore the laugh that escapes you when I begin making up Ellie's bed. I'm too tired to continue our fight. All I want now is to sleep, even if it is in my daughter's single bed. But I can't ignore when you knock the sheets from my arms and force me to the floor, pinning my wrists against the carpet and jamming yourself in between my legs. My jeans are a barrier between us but if you try to take them off I will be able to wriggle out from under you. Smiling, I don't struggle but lie still, waiting to see what you will do next. You must be having the same thought as me because you press your body on top of me, flattening yourself against me so I can't move. And with no barrier you are free to do what you want, free to not care whether it's causing me pleasure or pain. I ignore the words spewing from your mouth, trying instead to focus lower down.

Afterwards, we lie sweating and hot, trying to slow our breathing so we can be human again. And finally you are quiet, too worn out to say anything more about what I am and what I've done. I close my eyes and wait for you to lift yourself off me, picturing in my mind where I can retrieve each item of clothing you've ripped from my body. But you don't move so neither do I.

When I wake up it is still dark and you have moved to my side, but still lie draped across me. You stare at me, your eyes wide like a hunted rabbit's, and I wonder if something has happened while I've been asleep.

"I'm sorry, I'm sorry," you say repeatedly. "Please tell me you'll still think about Madrid." I want to punch you and rip your skin with my nails for doing this, for always having to apologise. But as you lay your head on my stomach, I stroke your hair and know I will do what you ask because this is how we are.

CHAPTER TWENTY-FOUR

Sunday mornings no longer have the same urgency they did when I had a job. Apart from the times you persuade me to lie in, I am used to jumping up early to make the most of the few hours I have before the slog of Monday morning arrives. But now it's nearly ten o'clock and I can't summon any energy to lift myself up and welcome the day. It is difficult when I know the first thing I have to do is call Myrah.

This morning you have already been up for hours, making phone calls and surfing the internet. I don't need to ask what you're doing; arranging a new life for us in Spain is the only thing that could have got you up so early. Even though I can't hear the words you say, just mumbled sounds, I can tell you are excited. It doesn't seem to occur to you that I might refuse to go. And what would happen then?

You tone your excitement down when I make an appearance but I'm not sure whether this is to relieve the pressure on me or because you still don't believe I've told the truth about Jonathan. I questioned you about this last night when we traipsed to our own bedroom, shutting the door on Ellie's and what we did there, but you wouldn't discuss it. Nor would you talk about what had just happened. I'm relieved about that because there's no space in my head at the moment to think about you breaking your promise.

So now I don't move but pull the duvet up to my chin and pretend nothing is happening; that it's just a normal day and I don't have to make any uncomfortable phone calls or life-changing decisions. It is only when my stomach rumbles, reminding me I have a life outside our bed, that I fling my legs to the floor and brace myself for what lies ahead.

Myrah is surprised to hear from me and doesn't sound like the woman I've seen almost every day for years. I know we haven't shared many intimate details of our lives with each other, but I thought she would be pleased to hear from me. I ask her how she's been since I last saw her and she offers only a vague reply. She's now helping her husband at his dental practice until she finds something else. Myrah doesn't hide her frustration at our small talk, but at least she is too polite to ask why I'm calling out of the blue on a Sunday morning. She sighs and hesitates before speaking, making it impossible for me to mention Jonathan now. But when I remember how he turned up here and lied to you, I know I have to see this through.

I take a deep breath and blurt out what I've wanted to say since she picked up the phone. "I know it's asking a lot, Myrah, but is there any chance we could meet today? I need to speak to you about something but can't really do it on the phone. Face-to-face would be better."

She hesitates again and I am sure she must know what this is about. Last time I mentioned being worried about Jonathan contacting me she dismissed my concerns and defended him, assuring me he was just offering friendship. But even though I now have plenty of evidence to suggest otherwise, I can't be sure of Myrah's reaction.

"What's this about, Olivia?" she asks, her tone becoming even colder.

Now it is my turn to hesitate. "Please, Myrah. I just need a few minutes of your time. It's really important."

Myrah grunts. "Well, I'm guessing this is about Jonathan...I'll call you in the week to arrange when we can meet."

"I was hoping it could be today. Please, Myrah." As I say this I can't believe I have resorted to begging. I feel as if I'm talking to a stranger, not the woman who cared enough about me to fix me up on a blind date.

"Sorry, but I'm cooking a roast dinner today so I don't have the time to go anywhere."

"I'll come to you. It won't take long. You're in Kingston, aren't you? That's right near me, I can be there in half an hour."

This time the silence stretches longer than before, giving me a chance to form a back-up plan in case she says no. I can't force her to see me so I will have to talk to her on the phone after all. It's not ideal but I need to sort this problem out quickly. I have to stop Jonathan harassing me and convince you I've done nothing wrong.

Myrah finally speaks. "Okay, fine. But I won't have long."

Even though I have programmed Myrah's address into the sat nav, I still manage to get lost so it's nearer an hour and a half before I knock on her door. The house is a large, detached new build in pristine condition, exactly the kind of home I imagined Myrah to live in. When she lets me in, her face is stony and only softens when I apologise for being late and having to be here at all.

She leads me into the lounge, which is as tidy and clean as the outside of the house but cluttered with an array of personal items. Hardly any wall space is left unadorned with framed photos or paintings, and every table and shelf is crammed with scented candles and mementos from different countries. This is what is lacking in our home: a personal touch.

"Cup of tea?" Myrah asks, almost back to the friendly woman I used to work with.

I thank her and she leaves me alone in a room I have no right to be in. Ordinarily I wouldn't hesitate to inspect things more closely, but given the tension between us now I stay rooted to Myrah's comfortable fabric sofa and wait for her to come back.

The house is silent and I wonder where her husband and children are. Before today I had forgotten how many children she has but all around the room, three chubby, smiling faces announce their presence. It's Sunday so her husband shouldn't be at work and Myrah is cooking a big dinner so they must be here somewhere. It's possible she's told them to avoid me, just so she can get me out as quickly as possible.

It's not long before I start fretting about what to say to her. If Jonathan is such a firm family friend then I have to pick my words carefully. But how can I put a positive spin on his abusive text messages and stalking? I am so consumed with these thoughts that it takes me a while to realise Myrah still hasn't appeared with our tea. I can't remember the exact time I got here but am sure it's been at least twenty minutes. Panicking that she has forgotten I'm here, I head to the lounge door.

"Do you need any help?" I call, my voice drifting into the silence. I don't know where the kitchen is but I've spoken loudly enough for anyone downstairs to hear me.

After a few seconds, Myrah pops her head out from the door opposite. "Sorry about that. I had to answer the phone. It was for David but they kept me talking. We'll have to talk in the kitchen now as I need to get lunch started." She holds the door open for me and I head towards her, wondering how she could have taken a call when the phone didn't ring.

Like the rest of the house, the kitchen is cluttered but clean and Myrah busies herself boiling the kettle and preparing what she needs for lunch. She doesn't say anything, even once the kettle has boiled, so I offer to make the tea. Anything to defer the conversation we're about to have.

"So what's this about?" she asks when I place her mug in front of her. "Jonathan?" Mentioning his name brings back her frostiness and I want to shake her until she remembers the friendship we used to have.

Taking a deep breath, I tell Myrah everything. Not surprisingly, the hardest part is explaining about you and why I haven't mentioned our relationship before. I show her the text messages I've saved but Myrah's face remains emotionless and she carries on chopping vegetables and peeling potatoes until I finish talking.

"I have to be honest, Olivia, I don't really know what to say to all this. Jonathan's worked with David for years and, well, we know him really well. This all just seems so out of character. He's never done anything like this before."

I want to ask her how she could possibly know this and explain that sometimes people don't even know what their own spouses are up to or capable of. I'm tempted to cite Carl as an example of this because before his affair I have no doubt all his friends would have described him as a loyal and faithful husband. But I keep my mouth shut. At least Myrah is talking about this and not throwing me out of her house.

"Are you sure you've told me everything?" she continues, her forehead creasing into a frown. "Because...well, you didn't before."

I put my mug down. "Please believe me, I've told you everything and every word I've said is the truth."

Myrah clatters around in her cupboards, eventually pulling out a casserole dish from the back of one of them. "I do believe you, Olivia. I just don't know what you want me to do."

"Well, believing me is a start, so thank you for that. Now I just need to get Jonathan to stop. And I've got to convince Michael I'm telling the truth."

Myrah shakes her head. "But I still don't know what *I* can do. I hope you don't want me to confront Jonathan? I'm not saying I condone what he's doing, but he's my husband's friend and colleague so I can't stir up trouble."

Up until now I haven't really known how I expected Myrah to help. I just knew I needed to tell her. But now that she says she can't confront Jonathan that's exactly what I think she should do.

"Can you at least talk to David? See what he thinks?" I ask, grateful I can't see the desperation scribbled across my face.

Myrah tuts and shakes her head again. "I don't know, Olivia. I need to think about this. I won't do anything without talking to David first, but I can tell you already he won't want to get involved. Let's just leave it there and I'll call you if I think we can help."

I finish my tea and don't push Myrah any further, all my hope of a speedy resolution evaporating. "Where are David and the kids?" I ask, trying to end our conversation on a positive note.

"They're at the park. David always takes them on a Sunday while I cook lunch."

"Yes, it must be hard to cook with three little ones running around." I think of Ellie when I say this and feel sad that Myrah and I have never got all our children together.

"Well, I better get on now," she says, ushering me out of the kitchen. On the worktop her mug of tea remains untouched.

At the front door, Myrah puts her hand on my shoulder. "Have you tried talking to Jonathan? Perhaps that's all that's needed. A conversation between the two of you might clear the air."

There are several reasons why the thought of this terrifies me. How can a man who's said the things he's said be expected to have a civil conversation about his behaviour? But I don't say this to Myrah. "Maybe," I tell her, knowing it will never happen.

The sun burns into me as I head to my car, even though it's bitterly cold. I start the engine to get the heating going but don't drive off. Instead I sit for a while, listening to the whir of the radiator, feeling deflated. It was okay when I had a plan to deal with Jonathan, even it was only half-formed, but now I am at a complete standstill. Then I remember Chloe's offer of help and wonder if she's had any luck. Picking up my mobile, I scroll to her name but before I click on it a text message comes through. *Nice try.*

"Let's go. I've had enough here so let's just do it."

I have barely walked in the door before I announce my decision. Your face breaks into a wide smile and suddenly I know, despite Jonathan and everything else, that we'll be okay. You pull me towards you and squeeze me too tightly but I make no move to escape, grateful you're not still angry.

"But Ellie has to be okay with it too, okay?" I pull away and check you've understood how important this is to me.

"Of course. When will you tell her?"

"Carl's dropping her back about five so I'll do it tonight." Mentioning Carl's name reminds me that Ellie is not the only person I need to consult about our plans. Even if she is okay with it, I can't see Carl being happy for me to drag her to another country. My stomach tightens at the thought of telling him and bile rises to the back of my throat. There will be no way to soften the blow, no way to dress it up and put a positive spin on things. Carl will be losing Ellie in a way, no matter how much I try to convince him otherwise.

I look at you and feel sad at the unfairness of the situation. You seem to be the only person who is truly happy about this move. You are still smiling when you say, "Do you know you've just made my day? I've even been emailing some schools this afternoon."

I hate dampening your excitement but Carl and Ellie aren't the only problems. "What about Jonathan? He's not just going to stop harassing me, is he? And how can we move to Spain when you think I've cheated on you?"

You grab my hand and lead me to the top of the stairs, pulling me down so we're both sitting on the top step. "Look, I've been thinking about that and I'm sorry about how I reacted." You pause to gather your thoughts. "What I mean is, I believe you. I know last night I was angry but now I've had a chance to see things clearly, I don't believe anything's going on. I trust you, Olivia."

I should be relieved to hear your words, grateful for your trust in me, but instead I am furious. You could have said this last night or even this morning and saved me a humiliating conversation with Myrah, but now feels far too late. I'm about to explode but my anger sticks in my throat. We've fought too many times in our relationship and I don't want to start another battle. What's important is that you believe me, even if your faith in me has come too late.

"So will you help stop him harassing me? Talk to him, maybe?"

You smile proudly. "Even better. Let's get you a new mobile number."

The rest of the afternoon hurtles by, yet by five o'clock I can't recall doing a single thing since getting back from Myrah's. You left to meet a friend from work hours ago and by now I imagine you are ensconced in a booth in his local pub, telling him about Spain and losing count of the beers you both consume. I stand by the lounge window with the curtains open and only the hall light filtering in, waiting for Carl and Ellie to pull up outside. It feels as if I have been standing here all day, just waiting. I text Carl to ask him to come to the door, something he still never does, even though he has met you now and seems to like you. It goes through but I know he won't check his phone until he's stopped the car.

By five thirty there is still no sign of them, but instead of using the extra time to plan how I will broach the subject of Spain, I start to panic. On the rare occasions Carl has been late bringing Ellie back, he has always found a way to let me know where they are. It is a courtesy we have always extended to each other without ever arranging to do it. I'm sure we both know why we do this; we just can't bear to speak of it.

Finally, when I've resorted to sitting on the front door step even though it won't make them get here any quicker, Carl's silver Mondeo appears and I sigh with relief. On the inside, though, I dread the conversation we are about to have. Ellie springs from the back of the car and runs towards me, a puzzled frown on her face at the sight of me out here in the cold.

"I just couldn't wait to see you," I tell her, and she hugs me. She says she's needed the toilet since they left

Winchmore Hill so I usher her inside and tell her I'll be up in a minute.

I turn back to the car to see Carl waving his phone at me and beckoning me over. He rolls down the window and I am taken aback by how different he looks. His hair is shorter, almost shaved to his scalp, and it makes him look younger. I remember telling him years ago to cut it shorter but he always refused, proud of his ruffled locks. Either Keira is more persuasive than I am or Carl must care more about her opinion. I shake myself out of this train of thought; he is someone else's now.

"Sorry we're so late. We got to the end of the North Circ and then discovered Ellie had left her bag at home. It's got her school books in it, so we had to go back." Carl pauses to look at me and he must know exactly what I'm thinking. "I know I should have called but I just wanted to get here. Sorry, Olivia."

I let it go because Ellie is here safely and now I have to deliver news to Carl that will devastate him. As I look at him, a new man with a new outlook, my heart aches because if he were trying to take Ellie to live abroad my world would collapse.

"Anyway, what's going on? Why do you want me to come in?" The car engine is still running and Carl, oblivious to the destruction I'm about to wreak, makes no move to turn it off.

I lean in closer and the car radiator envelopes me with warmth. "I need to talk to you...it might be better if you come inside." His eyes flick to the dashboard clock. Keira is probably waiting for him, dinner perfectly timed so it's ready the second he gets back.

"Is this about Ellie? Because she really is much better, you know. She's been cheerful all weekend and hasn't even mentioned Mum, so–"

"No...it's not Ellie. Please, Carl, just come in for five minutes. Michael's not in so we'll be alone."

Carl drums his fingers on the steering wheel and looks at the clock again. It's nearly six thirty and I know he's thinking of Keira. "Can't you just talk to me here? Come on, get in, you're frozen. Where's your coat?"

All the while I've been out here waiting for them I haven't noticed the temperature, but now that Carl's said it, I shiver and give in to his request. I check Ellie's okay and tell her we're having a quick chat then climb in beside Carl. This is Keira's seat now and I am once again an intruder.

"So what's going on, Olivia?" Carl turns his body towards me and waits for me to explain but he keeps the engine running.

Folding my arms, I stare straight ahead. I don't want to see his expression once I've spoken. And then the words fall from my mouth yet I speak unconsciously, unaware of how it all sounds, just needing him to know.

"Is this a joke? Why are you saying this? What's going on?"

I say nothing but turn to him and see his face drop as he realises from my silence I'm serious. He slowly shakes his head. "No. No way. You can't just decide to move to another country. This is ludicrous!"

I reach for Carl's arm but he pulls away. "Does Ellie know about this? She didn't say anything..." He frowns as if trying to work out how this is possible.

"We haven't told her yet. I wanted to speak to you first. Look, now's probably not a good time to go through all the details so I'll call you in a couple of days."

Carl shakes his head again and I don't know what's gone through his mind in the last few seconds but when he speaks he is calmer. "There's nothing to talk about. I can't let this happen, Olivia. You know that, don't you?"

I watch as he drives away, relieved I've finally told him but convinced he will fight us. I didn't expect him to be happy about our plans but I imagined anger, not the calm certainty he showed me before leaving. I am numb heading back into the house, distancing myself from the situation because I am not the one who is desperate to move to Spain.

Inside, Ellie sits at the kitchen table with a new sketch pad in front of her. Carl must have bought it for her at the weekend because I've never seen this one before. And Ellie is saving all her pocket money so I know she hasn't spent any for a while.

"Are we having a roast?" she asks, reminding me I haven't even thought about dinner. Keira would never forget something so important.

"I'm sorry, Ellie, not today." I try to figure out what else we can have. I can't even remember going food-shopping this week so don't know what's in.

"That's okay," Ellie says. "I'm not really hungry. Can I just have cheese on toast, please?"

I smile at my daughter; she has unwittingly saved me from ordering yet another takeaway and now that she's mentioned cheese on toast there's nothing I'd rather have.

There is no pressure on me after dinner when I tell Ellie about our plan to move to Spain because without her agreement I will not go anywhere. I'm sure parenthood experts will tell me I am the adult and therefore the decision is ultimately mine, but nothing will make me drag my daughter away without her blessing. So, unlike earlier with Carl, we have a tension-free conversation about Spain. Before I mention moving there, I show Ellie pictures of Madrid on the internet.

"Wow!" she says. "There are so many things I could draw!"

I take her excitement as the opportunity to explain the plan, emphasising if she doesn't want to then we won't go. To my surprise she doesn't burst into tears or run from the room. Instead she checks Chloe isn't coming. Then, when I confirm this, she says, "Claudia at school says her family is moving to France in the summer. She says it's much nicer over there."

And at that moment I couldn't be any prouder of my daughter.

It's past midnight by the time you get home and as you lean in to kiss me the smell of beer is overwhelming.

"So? Did you speak to Carl and Ellie?" Even inebriated you are still excited about Spain, so telling you Carl's response is out of the question. Instead I relay how well Ellie has taken it and watch your smile expand as if we have won the lottery. You forget to ask what Carl thinks and we head to bed, you rattling off dates and things we need to do before we leave this summer.

CHAPTER TWENTY-FIVE

It is hot outside today; I can tell this even though I am on the inside, looking out of this goldfish bowl. Men are dressed in t-shirts, women in strappy tops or dresses, and their children run around in shorts, their knees stained with grass as they roll around in the sun. Today is family day and I don't want to be here, a witness to their joy. I want to scream at them; remind them where they are and that they have no right behaving as if they're on holiday while their relatives stare through them, oblivious to it all. I turn away from the window. I am not able to look down any longer.

"Here we go," Henny says, sliding a tray of tea and two vanilla cupcakes onto the shiny table. It's white like the chairs; a cliché from a 1950s movie that saddens me. It would have been simple for them to add a splash of colour to this place, but why would they bother when the effort would be wasted on us? We are as blank as the walls, furniture and everything else in here.

At least the tea is in mugs this time, but that's only because Henny fetched it. We are allowed these privileges when we're supervised. There is nobody else in the dining room this afternoon and I wonder if that's also Henny's doing. Does she have that much power in this place?

"We don't have too long," she says apologetically. "They'll be preparing for dinner soon. But at least we've got tea and cake and each other's company, right, lovey?" Her bright white teeth sparkle as she smiles and places a mug in front of me. I stare at my tea, as if it is an alien liquid, and try to decide whether or not I want it. I can't remember what tea tastes like. All I've had to quench my thirst since I've been here is vile, tasteless tap water. Henny looks at me expectantly and picks up a cupcake, crumbs flying in every direction as she sinks her teeth into the sponge. She doesn't tell me to try one or even coax me to have some tea because she has promised if I come here she won't force me to do anything I don't want to. I believe her now. She is not like the others.

"A lot of kids here today," Henny ventures, after she's demolished her cupcake. She wipes her lips with a napkin but a small speck of icing remains in the corner of her mouth. She reaches across the table for my hand and I let her take it, comforted by her warm, thick skin. "Are you okay with that?" she asks, and I am taken aback by her question. Lately I have known that it will only be a matter of time before she asks me something like this, but I wasn't expecting it so soon.

I take a deep breath and shrug because I don't know how to answer her. Children. Right outside. Their giggles and screeches floating up towards me despite the double-glazed windows. I feel weak and pull my hand away, sinking into the corner of my chair, as far back as possible, to stop myself from falling.

"It's okay, it's okay," Henny says, rushing over and kneeling on the floor beside my chair. I stare at the crumb in the corner of her mouth and banish from my mind all the things that try to crowd in. "We can go back to your room?" Henny says, but I shake my head and sit up straight. She will be disappointed if I give in now so I will force myself to sit here for a while, make her proud of me, let her know she is not wasting her time on me.

My hand shakes as I reach for my mug of tea and clasp the handle. The taste of the tea is strange but the warmth of it soothes me. Henny – back in her chair now – watches but doesn't patronise me by congratulating me on my small achievement. She picks up her own mug and I wait for her to speak. When she doesn't, I begin to worry she will say it's time to leave and I will be alone again. And for the first time since I've been here, that is not what I want. I need to talk to her, to keep her interested in me.

"Will you tell me about your children?" I ask, and her eyes widen in surprise. I don't look away from her so she'll know I'm serious. That I'm ready. But her expression is contemplative, small lines forming on her forehead.

"Okay," she says eventually, reaching for my hand. "But you know we can talk about anything. Anything at all. You decide."

Henny thinks I'm not ready and maybe she's right but I can't let her leave yet. And I do want to hear about her life, however painful it may be for me. I nod and she sits back and in her sweet voice starts to speak about her children. Her face glows as she talks and although I am listening, I don't hear a word she says. But I do notice that the cupcake crumb has fallen away.

True to your word, you buy me a new SIM card for my mobile and I no longer dread its beeping or vibrating. Unfortunately, Jonathan's tirade of texts is replaced by almost-daily messages from Carl, begging me to reconsider moving and at least talk things through with him. I don't ignore him deliberately, but we have so much to organise before the summer that every second is taken up by something to do with the move.

For the first few weeks after I break the news to Ellie, I carefully monitor her, checking for any signs that she's changed her mind or perhaps not realised the seriousness of a permanent move abroad. She often speaks about it and pumps you for more details almost daily. For a while I wonder if this will bring the two of you closer together. I still haven't broached the subject of you spending more time with Ellie so maybe this move is a blessing in disguise. But on the few occasions you try to do or talk about anything else with her, she shuts herself in her room again, clearly preferring her own company to yours.

Walking Ellie to school one morning, I mention Spain and ask her if she's sure about being away from Carl. It's a direct approach but I've got to be certain she knows all the consequences of us moving. I remind her it was not long ago she was begging me to let her live with Carl.

She bobs her head from side to side as she skips along beside me. "I do want to go, Mum, and I'm sorry about saying I want to live with Dad. I just hate Chloe. She's horrible."

We're approaching the school so I slow down to give us longer to talk. "I know you don't like her but she hasn't done anything to you, has she? You know you can tell me if she has and I'll sort it out."

"No...I just don't like her." Ellie chews her nail and looks at me anxiously. "I'm not in trouble, am I? Keira always says it's wrong to hate people but I can't help it, Mum."

I stop walking and turn to face Ellie, crouching down so I am looking up at her rather than towering over her. "You're not in any trouble, Pumpkin. All I ask is that you give her a chance. I haven't always gotten along with her myself but I really think she's changed now." Ellie doesn't look convinced but I won't push her; Chloe is the least of our worries. "Anyway, about Spain. Are you sure you're happy to move away from Dad? It means you won't get to see him as much."

"I've thought about that, Mum, and it will be okay because when I do see Dad it will be for longer, you know, the whole of school holidays, so I'll see him even more!"

Before I have a chance to tell Ellie how proud she makes me, the school bell chimes and swarms of latecomers swoop past us. I usher Ellie to the gate and watch her attach herself to a friend she's just seen and hurry inside, not turning around once to see if I'm still there. It's part of growing up, I tell myself. Her acceptance of the move and the way she's put a positive spin on it are all signs of a new, mature side to my daughter. It is a side I welcome, even though it makes me ache that she will end up needing me less as each year goes by.

As soon as Ellie disappears inside the building, I cross the road before any of the other mothers notice me and want to stop and chat. Normally I am rushing off to work, so if anyone does see me slinking away they will assume I'm running late and hopefully won't call out to me.

Walking back home, I think about what Ellie said about Chloe and am still puzzled that there is no concrete reason for her hatred. Even during the times when Chloe has been someone I wish I'd never had to meet, I can't say I've hated her. Pitied her and maybe even envied her for her carefree attitude and confidence, yes, but never hated. And now thinking about her reminds me I haven't spoken to her for a while and don't know what she's been doing or where she's been staying for the last few weeks. She was meant to get back to me about Jonathan but I've heard nothing from her. And you haven't mentioned her since you found her cardigan so I have to assume you are both still on bad terms. This is another puzzle to me, as you were there for her when she needed you after the attack. Chloe is another person we will be devastating by moving to Spain, but this time you will be the one breaking the news.

Before I reach the front door, I notice patches of white on the lawn and can't work out what it is. It's only when I lean down for a closer examination that I realise what I'm looking at are hundreds of shredded pieces of paper, scattered like giant confetti. I look around to see if any of the neighbours are nearby but, strangely, the street is quiet. I pick up a piece and it's blank on one side but the other has pencil lines dashed across it. Part of a sketch. A sketch that Ellie has done. I check more pieces and they're all parts of Ellie's drawings. The only thing that could explain this is if she's thrown out some she didn't like and the bin has been knocked over. But when I check it, the lid is firmly closed. I'm sure the lawn wasn't in this mess when we left for school this morning, but I was on autopilot, running late and wanting to talk to her about Spain, so I don't remember glancing around as we set off. I will ask her when I pick her up this afternoon, but for now all I can do is clear up the lawn before someone passes by and wonders what I'm doing.

It doesn't take me long to put the incident out of my mind. After all, Ellie is free to do what she likes with her sketches, so my thoughts flicker back to Chloe and why we haven't heard from her for so long. The air in the flat feels stale so I open the lounge window – even though it's cold for May – and hang my head outside, breathing in the damp freshness. I fish my mobile from my pocket and dial Chloe's number, trying to ignore the noises from the street and focus on the ring tone. Chloe answers within a couple of seconds and I feel a wave of guilt at not having contacted her before.

"Hi, Chloe? I'm so sorry I haven't called before now. Just wanted to check you're okay?"

There is a pause and something rustles in the background. "Sorry, who is this?" Chloe says brusquely.

For a moment I am stunned and wonder if I've dialled the wrong number. Chloe always knows who's calling. "It's Olivia."

There is another pause and then, when Chloe speaks, her voice is a huge contrast to the one I heard at the beginning of the phone call. "Olivia! Hi, I didn't recognise the number. Are you calling from someone else's phone?"

And then I remember. It's been so long since I've spoken to her that she knows nothing about my new mobile number. I fill her in and she listens quietly, only speaking once I've finished.

"So the Jonathan problem has been dealt with, at least. Sorry I couldn't help but he would never answer his phone when I tried. Probably wary of unknown numbers. Well, it sounds like Michael's being very understanding so that's good." The rustling starts again and I wonder what it is she's doing.

"How have you been?" I ask, not wanting to give Jonathan any more of my time.

Chloe tells me she's found a new flat in Fulham she can move into next week. Even though she describes it in detail, there is no hint of enthusiasm in her voice and I wonder if she's ready to live alone. Since she left Andrew she's always found someone's spare room or sofa to encroach on, so I doubt she's spent more than an evening on her own. Even if we did have the space to offer Chloe a roof over her head I'm still not sure I'd be able to cope with her permanently. Then it hits me. We won't be here for much longer so we couldn't help her even if we wanted to.

"Fulham's so close to us, we'll practically be neighbours," I tell her, trying to lighten her mood. But my guilt multiplies because I'm not being honest with her. You have told me you want to be the one to tell her about Spain, so I can't say anything, but I wonder if you'll find the right moment before it's too late. Or more likely, your intention is for us to sneak off without a word.

"Yes," she says without conviction. "It will be handy living so close." As she says this, I wonder whether you will share this sentiment.

Chloe falls silent and even though I'm the one who's called her, I struggle to think of what to talk about next. There are so many things I can't say to add to the things I won't say so that only leaves small talk. "How have you been?" I ask her, hoping she can't see my desperation.

She clears her throat and the gritty sound pierces my ear. "Well, I was a bit depressed this morning. I'm just not...you know, where I thought I'd be...I woke up alone and now I have to work late on today of all days. But Michael's cheered me up. I hoped he'd call me today and he didn't let me down, for once."

It takes me a moment to fully digest her words but once I have I'm still confused. "Michael called you?" I try to hide the surprise in my voice, to keep it casual.

Chloe huffs. "Well, of course he did. He might be an arse a lot of the time but he wouldn't ignore my birthday."

And now everything Chloe has said starts to make sense. I feel terrible that I didn't realise it was her birthday but it's too late to pretend otherwise. "I'm so sorry, Chloe. I've just had so much on my mind and completely forgot."

"Don't worry about it," she says, but it's also too late for that because I am.

"How about I take you for a birthday meal this evening?" I say, pleased with myself for finding something that can make things up to her. "I'm sure Michael won't mind staying with Ellie so we can have a girls' night out."

"Thanks, Olivia. That's really sweet of you but I already have plans tonight. Didn't Michael tell you? He's taking me out for birthday drinks. He mentioned the West End but to be honest, who cares as long as there's a good atmosphere and some alcohol?"

Now it is my turn to be silent. "Actually he probably did mention it but my brain's been like a sieve lately. It's all the Jonathan stress, probably, and not having a job. But I haven't spoken to him this morning and maybe he decided on the spur of the moment to do something nice for you." Although I say this to Chloe, I have no idea what could be true. "Well, anyway, I'm glad you've got plans tonight and you've sorted things out with Michael."

"Well, I'm not sure about that. But it's a start, isn't it?"

For the rest of the afternoon I wait for you to call or text and tell me your plans tonight. I try to find reasons you wouldn't invite me, but all I can come up with is you only decided to go for a drink with Chloe while talking to her this morning. And now, of course, it's too late for me to find a babysitter for Ellie so there's no way I can come. All that's been on your mind lately is our move to Spain so I can't be angry if you forget to mention things. Distracted by these thoughts, I put little effort into cleaning the flat, and even then I am late to pick Ellie up from school.

By four o'clock you've texted a few times but still haven't mentioned Chloe. It is only when I reply and ask what you want for dinner that you call and tell me your plan.

"I thought I'd better do something," you explain. "Especially as I'll have to tell her our news soon. Not tonight, though, of course. I'm not that heartless."

I'm glad you've said this. Chloe deserves to have a stress-free birthday and I know she'll be devastated when she finds out you're leaving. But I don't have a chance to say this because Ellie shouts out from her bedroom. It sounds like she's calling for me but her words are muffled and inaudible. I hang up and rush to her room, flinging the door open to find her wailing on the floor.

"It's lost, it's lost!" she cries, her arms flailing in all directions.

Joining her on the floor, I ask what she's talking about and she stares at me, exasperated, as if I should automatically know because I'm her mother.

"My pad! My sketch pad! Her voice is high-pitched and pierces my ears.

"What did you say?" I ask, praying I'm mistaken.

"M...my...sketchpad...It's gone...I've looked everywhere!"

Then I remember what I found on the lawn this morning and my insides turn to jelly. If Ellie didn't rip up her sketch pad then who did? You and I are the only other people in the flat and I know you wouldn't do something like this. There is no way it was an accident either; Ellie's drawings were torn deliberately. I pull her closer to me, wondering how I can explain all this. All around her are old sketch pads, bursting with pictures she's put all her time and effort into for years.

"It's my new one, Mum. The one with Grandma in it..." Her voice trails off and she erupts into heavy sobs.

Even though she's already in a state, and telling her about her sketch pad will make her feel worse, I can't put it off any longer. So, still hugging her and wiping her tears away with an already-soaked tissue, I tell her everything, including how I assumed she'd just thrown away some drawings she didn't like.

"Noooooooooo!" she shrieks, burying her head in her knees. I let her cry herself out and eventually she asks if she can see the torn pieces.

We go outside and check the dustbin together, confirming what I already suspected. Surprisingly, Ellie remains calm and it tugs at my heart to see her being so strong. "Who did this, Mum?" she asks.

"I don't know, Pumpkin, but we'll find out." I look up and down the street, a mute witness to this nasty act, but nothing is out of the ordinary. Goosebumps rise on my arms and I grab Ellie's hand and lead her back inside. She doesn't complain but looks sadly back at the dustbin.

Once we're inside, I double-lock the door and suggest we call you to see if you know anything. But when you answer the phone you are as shocked as we are.

"There's just no explanation for this," you say, clicking your pen. It's what you always do when you are deep in thought. "Unless..."

I don't like the sound of this. "Unless what?"

You take a deep breath. "Well, you're not going to like it."

"Michael, just tell me. There's not much you can say that's worse than what's already happened."

But I am wrong. There is something much worse.

"Well, if it's not you and it's not me then that just leaves Ellie. She must have done it. I don't know why. Perhaps she's trying to get our attention? Maybe this is a protest about Spain?"

Your words are a shock to me but I can't deny what you have said makes sense. Chloe is the only other person who comes to the flat, but we haven't seen her for months so it can't be anything to do with her. Even though I am now beginning to believe Ellie must have something to do with it, I can't help but defend her.

"But she's happy about Spain and she's been much better lately. Why would she do this now?" But you don't have any answers – neither of us do – and I feel even more frustrated by the end of our conversation because all I'm left with now is suspicion.

Hating every second of it, I question Ellie more about her sketch pad before she goes to bed. I am like a detective, covering the who, what, when, where and whys, but Ellie doesn't seem to mind. To her I am just being a caring mum, trying to determine what's happened so my daughter will feel better. She tells me she can't remember the last time she saw it and I'm surprised. Ellie is rarely parted from her sketch book. She also says she never takes it to school because she's scared she could lose it.

I study her face as she speaks, searching for any clues to suggest she's lying, but there are none. She looks directly at me and her eyes are still swollen from crying. I tuck her into bed and pull the duvet up to her chin. Somehow this futile act seems as though it should be comforting.

"I'll buy you a new sketch pad tomorrow," I tell her.

"Thanks, Mum," Ellie says, without a smile. "Then I can draw Grandma again."

Once Ellie is asleep, I borrow your laptop and order a CD that claims to have anyone speaking Spanish within weeks. I'm not convinced I can learn this quickly but buy it anyway, hoping to at least make a start on learning the language. I don't want to be someone who moves to another country and can't interact with its people. You will be able to scrape by because you studied Spanish at school, but I won't be joined to your hip. I refuse to shout English at people or only go to English-speaking places. I have no worries about Ellie; she has easily picked up French at school so it shouldn't be too difficult for her to master Spanish as well.

All of this takes my mind off her sketch pad and the more I think about Spain, the more appealing it is.

When the key turns in the front door, I freeze, panic setting in because it's only eight thirty p.m., so it can't be you. I think of the incident with Ellie's drawings and wonder if someone other than the two of us has a key. But before I can work out what to do, you are shouting up the stairs, announcing your presence in a voice that's loud enough to wake Ellie up.

I rush to the top of the stairs. "Ellie's asleep. Keep it down. What are you doing back so early?"

Striding up the stairs, two at a time, you don't answer but pull me into the kitchen. "Chloe knows. It was awful, Olivia. I didn't mean to tell her but it slipped out. And now I don't know where she is. She just stormed off." You fill a glass with tap water and gulp it down before taking off your coat and throwing it over a kitchen chair. Usually by now it would be hanging on the peg downstairs.

"Slow down and start from the beginning."

When you speak, your words come in slow motion, giving me time to picture Chloe's crumpled face as the news we're leaving sinks in. I clearly see the initial disbelief, the half-smile that appears as she's about to tell you off for messing around. And then the horror as she questions you further and sees the excitement you can't hold back even for a moment. Lastly will be the sadness as she comes to the conclusion that she can't be very important to you if you can leave her alone. I can even picture her after she's stormed out, her face soaked with tears because this shouldn't be happening on her birthday.

"I should call her," I say, when you finish telling me everything. "We have to see if she's okay." I don't wait for your approval and am already on my mobile and connected to hers when you start shaking your head.

"She won't answer," you tell me, refilling your glass of water.

And you are right. Her phone goes to voicemail and I hang up, frustrated and worried.

"She'll be fine," you say, grabbing your laptop from the kitchen table and leaving me alone with my concern.

Throughout the evening, I keep trying Chloe's mobile but she never answers. At first her phone rings and rings, taunting me with the hope she might pick up at any second, but the last few times I try it goes straight to voicemail. I try to tell myself this is because her battery has died, but when I text a couple of times they both show up on my phone as delivered so I know her phone is still on.

Eventually, worn out with worry, I head to bed, adding phoning Chloe to my list of things to do tomorrow after getting Ellie a new sketch pad. But when I'm tucked up in bed, the glow of my phone tempts me to try one last time and as I do, a text message comes through. It's not Chloe, though, and a number I don't recognise shows up instead of a name. Opening the text, I am stunned by the words staring back at me. *I love art. Such a shame when talent is wasted.*

CHAPTER TWENTY-SIX

"It's not a threat. You're overreacting."

I stare at you, unable to digest what you're saying. We've read the text out loud several times now, last night and this morning, and instead of the words becoming less sinister, they cement even more in my mind that this is a threat against Ellie. But now is not the time for a battle with you; I need you with me on this because apparently there is a real enemy to fight. Swallowing my anger, I try to be calm, rational. I will never convince you if you think I'm hysterical. "Okay, maybe on its own it doesn't seem much but remember Ellie's drawings? How can the two not be related?" I want to shake you and scream until you listen to me and realise this makes sense.

You shake your head and sigh. "But if the two things are completely separate then on its own the text doesn't really mean much, does it? You're not thinking logically."

I stand up too quickly and my mug slides across the kitchen table, tea sloshing over the rim. We both stare at the brown river spreading across the wood but I'm too angry to care about cleaning up the mess. "Don't patronise me! This is about my daughter and I can't take any chances. If you won't help me then I'm sure the police will." As soon as I say this, I wonder why I've never considered it before.

Grabbing a tea towel, you soak up the spilt tea and wipe the table. "That's ridiculous! They'll just laugh at you. And worse than that, you'll be wasting their time. They've got real crimes to solve, Olivia."

I don't realise I'm about to cry until it happens. Floods of tears I can't control, even though I ferociously rub my eyes with my sleeve. You look horrified and stop wiping the table. Within seconds you are wrapping me up, pulling me into your chest so my tears soak your crisp, white shirt.

"I'm sorry," you whisper into my hair. "I just don't think we should bother the police with this." You guide me back into a chair and suddenly I've had enough of being helpless. I need to be strong for Ellie and sort this out – whatever it is – before it gets any worse.

"Maybe I won't bother the police yet but I have to do *something*. What if this is just the beginning?"

You start wrapping your tie into a knot and I look at the clock. You should have left for work ten minutes ago. "All I'm saying is you need to be logical about this. First of all, if this is some kind of threat then who do you think is doing it?"

I have spent all night thinking about this but can't produce an answer that makes sense. After all his abusive text messages, the obvious suspect is Jonathan. But there is no way he could have got hold of my new mobile number. I haven't given it to anyone except you, Carl and Chloe, so there's no possibility he could have it. Carl is not even an option, so that just leaves Chloe. I tell you all this and for the second time this morning you look at me with horror.

"Now you're just desperate. Chloe would never do anything like this and for you to even think that..."

"I'm sorry," I say, meaning every word. Now I've said it out loud, it does seem ludicrous. I'm just thinking of everyone who has my new number."

"Well, it's obvious then, isn't it? The text is from someone you don't know and wasn't meant for you." You rush off, leaving me with this thought.

Once I'm alone, I'm no longer upset or scared. All I feel now is intense anger. Part of it is with you, for leaving me to deal with things on my own again. Part of it is with myself, for being weak and shedding tears when I should be holding things together for my daughter. The list goes on and on. Jonathan, Myrah, Carl and even Chloe all have equal shares in it.

After walking Ellie to school, I waste a couple of hours, half-heartedly cleaning while trying to decide what to do if going to the police isn't an option and you're not showing any willingness to help. I want to believe you're right and perhaps the business with Jonathan has made me paranoid and quick to overreact, but how can I be sure? And if the text is a threat against Ellie then I can't take any chances. Then it comes to me; not a solution but a diversion tactic that will buy me more time to sort everything out.

Feeling pleased with myself for at least getting this far, I call Myrah, knowing she won't have done anything about Jonathan. And I am right. She tells me, with no apology, that David says it's out of the question that Jonathan has done anything like this. And they won't discuss it with him now or in the future. Stunned into silence, I don't object or protest, but politely thank her and say goodbye.

With the phone tucked under my chin, I dial Chloe's number and make a strong black coffee while I wait to see if she'll answer. I can understand why she didn't answer last night, but this morning she has had time to think about things. She must have something to say to us, even if it's a plea to stay or answers to questions she must have, so when her voicemail kicks in I am unable to keep the panic from my voice.

"Chloe, please call me, we really need to talk. I'm worried about you. Just let us know you're okay." A dark sense of foreboding hangs over me as I end my message. I picture Chloe's face plastered across the news and your stony-faced parents as they read out a robotic plea for help finding their missing daughter.

But it's not long before I'm snapped out of my reverie. My mobile phone vibrates on the kitchen table and when I check the screen, Carl's name flashes at me. He is the only other person who will be just as worried as I am about the text message and Ellie's drawings being destroyed, but I'm not ready to talk to him yet. He'll be calling to try once again to persuade me not to take Ellie to Spain. Telling him what's happened won't convince him it's a good idea to leave; he will instead believe Ellie needs to be with him. That he is the only one who can protect her. So I ignore my ringing phone, and the voicemail beep that comes shortly after, and text Carl instead. I lie and tell him I'm busy but will call him later. None of this feels good. If I am right about Ellie being threatened then Carl needs to know. But I can't deal with that now.

Even as I search the internet, looking for just the right place – not too close to London but near enough to get back quickly in an emergency – my plan is only a half-formed blur. Luck is on my side, because when I check my diary, I realise it's half-term next week so I won't have to take Ellie out of school. Google has found me hundreds of hotels in Surrey but I don't have time to be picky. It's already late notice so most of them will probably be full up, but I start at the top and click on the first link. Within a second I am staring at a beautiful hotel, surrounded by bright green landscaped gardens. Even though I haven't checked the price, the Wotton House hotel in Dorking will do. It's easily the kind of place a family might go for a break away from the city. Nobody needs to know that the few days away has another purpose for me. I don't feel guilty about this; I need time to think about what to do before something worse happens. Somewhere Ellie will be safer than she might be here. As I book the room, I am weighed down by sadness. It shouldn't have to be like this. Home is the place that's supposed to be a safe haven, especially for a child. But now it is a place that's been violated for us.

"I'd really like to go with you but I just can't. It's too short notice and I've got a ton of marking to do. I'm sorry."

My appetite vanishes and I stare at the fish and chips on my plate. Ellie looks across the table at me, thoughtfully chewing a mouthful of chips. Both of you are waiting for me to say something. To give in or object. Either way, someone loses and our family dinner is ruined. It is meant to be a treat for Ellie, to take her mind off what's happened, but so far nothing is going to plan. Even the chips aren't right, drowning in vinegar and far too salty, and I push mine to the side of my plate, unable to stomach them. And now the relaxing break I'd planned for us is evaporating in front of me.

"Why didn't you check with me before you booked it?" you ask, incredulous at my stupidity.

"It was meant to be a surprise..." I don't need to say anymore; this is enough explanation.

"Can't we still go, Mum?" Ellie blurts out. We both turn to you and wait for you to finish your mouthful of fish.

"That's a great idea," you say, to Ellie more than to me. "You don't want me getting in the way, do you?"

Ellie nods her head vigorously then realises what she's done. "Sorry, I mean—"

You laugh and pat her arm. "It's okay, I know what you mean." Turning back to me, your expression becomes graver. "Seriously, Olivia, it will be great for you and Ellie to have some time together."

I nod and shovel some lukewarm fish into my mouth. Normally, spending quality time with Ellie on our own would be my top priority but this time I need you to be with us. Not only was I hoping to use the time away to convince you the text was a threat, but with you there I would feel a lot safer. But I can't tell you any of this. You already think I'm overreacting. So I change the subject and ask if you've heard from Chloe.

"No. I even called Andrew, just in case she's bothering him again, but he hasn't spoken to her for months. I'll give it till tomorrow and then I'll have to call my parents. I didn't want to worry them because...well, this is Chloe we're talking about. Disappearing is her speciality. Anyway, she's probably with them again. I'm sure her friend's despairing of her by now and has chucked her out."

"Mmm," I say, unconvinced. Something feels different this time.

I count the days, hours and minutes until Ellie and I can leave for the hotel in Surrey. But time drags its heels because I'm confined to the flat, fearful of what I might come back to if I leave. I only venture out to take Ellie to school and pick her up again and for the whole short walk there and back my stomach is in knots, my pace far too quick for Ellie to comfortably keep up with me. Every day she moans and asks why we're rushing but I can never tell the truth. Not just because it will scare her, but also because speaking it out loud makes me feel I am being paranoid, as if I am describing the plot of a lousy film.

Friday finally arrives and I rush Ellie home, this time allowing the pretence of excitement to be my excuse. When

287

she finds her small pink suitcase already packed she gives a shriek of delight and it becomes her turn to hurry us along.

In the car, leaving London behind us, I finally relax and join Ellie as she sings along to countless songs on the radio. I don't know many of the words and Ellie bounces around in the back seat in fits of giggles. The outside world doesn't exist until I look in the rear-view mirror and catch sight of Ellie's new sketch pad.

Ellie stops singing and frowns. "What's wrong, Mum? Why aren't you singing anymore?"

"I just don't like this one," I say, turning the radio over to another station.

We are both starving by the time we arrive at the hotel, and as we crunch along the path, dragging our suitcases behind us, I promise Ellie we can order room service as a treat.

"Wow," she says, taking in the façade of the hotel. "It's like a palace! I'm going to draw this later."

"Perhaps tomorrow," I say. "It will be dark by the time we've eaten."

There are no other guests around when we check in at reception, nor do we see anyone on the way up to our room, so it's not long before I question the wisdom of coming here. It's so quiet that it's easy to believe we are completely alone in this old mansion. But Ellie doesn't seem disturbed by this and quickly settles into our room, which is almost as large as our entire flat.

Ellie checks the menu and begs me to order us both burgers and fries. I try to remember what we've eaten this week and for a change can't recall having any junk food or takeaways so I agree, hoping even the burgers will be slightly healthy in this place.

While we wait for a knock on the door, Ellie settles onto her bed with her sketchpad and pencils. "I'm drawing you, Mum," she says, and my heart melts. "Dad gave me a photo I can keep."

"That's nice, "I say, distracted by the hotel leaflet advertising things to do nearby. Chessington World of Adventures is less than half an hour away and I contemplate taking Ellie there tomorrow. After all, we're here for four nights so I can't keep her cooped up in the hotel the whole time. And surely we'll be safe among hundreds of other people?

It is only later on, when Ellie has fallen asleep clutching her drawings, that I notice the photograph Carl has given her is one of our wedding pictures. It's not one of the professional ones, but whoever has taken it has frozen a moment in time that Carl and I can never have again. We're both smiling, thinking together we're infallible, unaware of the brevity of our union. Gullible. And as I stare at the photo, two strangers look back at me.

My plan to go to Chessington the next day is scuppered when Ellie wakes up in the night and vomits all over her bed. Her complexion is grey and she clutches her stomach, sinking into her pillow. It takes me a while to move her to the sofa so I can remove the dirty sheets, but when she finally settles there she drifts off to sleep again. I check her temperature and she's warm but not excessively, so I let it play out and coax her to drink water whenever her eyes open.

By morning she is still no better but at least has stopped throwing up. I haven't slept much but have drifted in and out of something resembling it, in between worrying about the text message only I seem to be taking seriously. After stewing it over all night, there is only one answer that makes any sense to me. Jonathan. If the man can send abusive messages and turn up at my home then surely it's not far-fetched to think he might threaten my daughter? And it's easy to find people's phone numbers. The internet makes anything possible.

All day I think about this as I sit on the floor by Ellie's freshly made bed, convinced I'm right one minute then talking myself out of it the next. My mobile vibrates on the carpet several times, silenced because I don't want to disturb Ellie. I let it go to voicemail but check the messages later. Every one of them is from Carl, anxious to know why I'm not answering his calls. I finally give in and call him back, accepting that I'll be lectured with a long list of reasons why Ellie shouldn't live in Spain. But this time it's his turn not to answer.

By seven o'clock I'm climbing the walls and the quaint room I loved yesterday has become a prison cell. I call you but there's no answer so I assume you're buried in a pile of marking. There's nothing on television to distract me and Ellie is fast asleep, finally looking peaceful and no longer clutching her stomach. All I can do is stew about what's happening. If I wasn't completely convinced about moving to Spain before, I am now.

At some point during the evening, I fall asleep on the sofa, this time more heavily, and am only awoken by my phone vibrating again next to my arm. It's Carl returning my call so I can't avoid him anymore. I accept the call and rush to the door, slipping outside the room to talk.

"Carl, I'm so sorry I haven't spoken to you for–"

"Don't worry about that. What room are you in?"

Still half asleep, I assume I've misheard him. "What?"

"What's your room number? I'm in reception."

"What? How?"

"I got worried I hadn't heard from you for so long and needed to talk to you about something so I went to your flat. Michael told me you were here. I couldn't even get hold of

Ellie. What's going on with her phone? Well, never mind, I'm coming up. What room are you in?"

I check on Ellie then wait for Carl outside the door. When he doesn't appear after five minutes, I wonder if I've dreamt the whole conversation. But when I check my mobile the call log proves I've spoken to him. Finally, the lift door pings open and Carl steps out, stroking his newly shaved head. It is strange to see him standing there when it should be you here with me, but I'm still pleased to see him.

"Well, this is strange, eh?" he says, giving me a brief hug. "How's Ellie? Michael said she's been ill?"

I nod. "Just a stomach bug. She's resting now so we'll have to be quiet." I begin to push the room door open but Carl pulls me back.

"Let's just talk out here, it will be easier. We can sit over there." He motions to a chintzy sofa in the corner of the hallway. It's close enough to allow us to see the room but we won't have to whisper and strain to hear each other. I hadn't noticed it before and am surprised Carl has in the few seconds he's been here.

"Michael's told me everything," Carl says, as soon as we sink into the faded cushions. "About Ellie's drawings and the text. I even know about that Jonathan guy. Why the hell haven't you told me about all this?" There is no anger in his voice, just concern, so I tell him everything again. I know he's heard most of it from you but I want to make sure he knows all the details. There is no way, once he's heard it all, he won't agree with me.

Carl listens without interrupting, even when I pause, waiting for him to add something or ask me to clarify things. It is only when I ask him what he thinks that he finally speaks. "I think you're right. We shouldn't ignore this. Ellie would never destroy her own drawings, especially the one of Mum. It's got to be this Jonathan guy. I wish you'd bloody told me about him before. I'll call the police tonight and see what they think. Making a phone call isn't wasting their time."

I nod gratefully and fight back tears. Finally someone is listening to me and taking this seriously. And even if it does turn out to be nothing, at least we're not taking any chances.

"Thanks," I manage to say. "And I'm sorry for not telling you all this before. It's just...we've got separate lives now and...I just needed to get through this with Michael's help. And you've got Keira now..."

"Olivia, Ellie will always be my concern, you know that. Don't shut me out. It doesn't matter if we're separated. I'm still her dad and I need to know things if they involve her." He shakes his head. "I never thought I'd have to say this to you." He must notice the expression on my face because as suddenly as it's started, Carl's lecture is over. There is nothing more he needs to say because he is right. By trying to bond as a family with you, I have ended up shutting him out.

Noticing Carl looks as tired as I feel, I offer to get us both some coffee from downstairs. We could both do with a caffeine boost and probably a break from our conversation too. I opt to take the stairs rather than the lift and as I disappear, Carl slips into the room to check on Ellie. I feel a surge of gratitude that he is here. As if in his presence nothing can harm us. I try to ignore the fact this is only a temporary visit and he'll soon be driving home, back to his life with Keira.

"Do you love her?" I ask, when we're once again ensconced on the sofa, cradling our coffee cups.

Carl turns to me, his eyebrows raised. "I...erm...why are you asking me this?" His cheeks flash pink; I am the last person he wants to discuss this with.

I don't know how he will answer, or whether he will at all, but it is something I suddenly need to know. It's not that I want him to say no, or for him to still love me, but I can't bear for there to be things he cannot tell me. I know that makes me a hypocrite – there is plenty I haven't told him about us – but it's too late to worry about that now. The question is out there, floating between us, and I can't take it back. "I know it's none of my business but it's something I just need to know."

Carl's cheeks return to their normal colour but he shuffles uncomfortably next to me. "Yes, I do," he says finally. My chest constricts and I feel as if I will suffocate, but I can't let him see this. I take a sip of coffee to distract myself but the liquid sticks in my throat and it is far too long before I can swallow. Carl doesn't notice anything. "But not the way I loved you," he says. "I messed up and I'll have to live with that, whatever I do. Whoever I'm with."

Now that he's said this, I wish I hadn't asked him. Things have been simpler now we've both moved on; we both love other people. Fearful I've opened a floodgate, I try to steer Carl somewhere more comfortable for both of us. "Keira's a wonderful woman," I say. "You're lucky to have her."

"Oh, I know she is. I love her to pieces. I didn't mean it the way it sounded. But...anyway, she's great and we're really happy. Something I never thought I could be after you left."

I look away and refrain from starting our usual argument about whose fault that is. Carl doesn't deserve that. He's a good man in spite of what he did.

In my silence, Carl continues. "I just meant with Keira it's a different kind of love, but still love, if that makes sense?"

And it does. It makes more sense than anything I've ever known because that's how I feel about you. Whatever love is, it can never be the same feeling with different people. It can never be one emotion that's easy to define, a glove that fits everyone no matter what size they are. I nod at Carl and his shoulders relax because he knows I understand.

We finish our coffee and Carl finally mentions the subject I've been dreading for weeks. "Well, I suppose there's nothing I can do to stop you leaving," he says with a sigh. "But actually, given what's been happening with this Jonathan, it may be the best thing for Ellie after all."

This is not the reaction I am expecting. "Really? You're okay with it?"

He shakes his head. "No, I'll never be okay with it. But I'll find a way to live with it. Anyway, I like Spain and Ellie will too. And Keira and I will visit as much as we can."

I want to question Carl, ask him why he's had a complete change of heart, but I don't want him to remember the reasons he was against it in the first place. Instead I thank him and assure him he'll see even more of Ellie than he does now because she can stay with him during school holidays.

It's nearly midnight when Carl stands up to leave. He pops his head round the room door to say goodnight to Ellie, but she's still sleeping so he doesn't go in. I walk him to the lift and while we're waiting he assures me he'll call the Putney police station in the morning. As I hug him goodbye, I remember there was something he wanted to tell me.

"Oh, don't worry, that can wait," he says, pressing the lift button again, even though it is already glowing orange.

"Well, you're here now so you may as well tell me, whatever it is," I insist.

He stares at the floor. "This isn't really the place—"

"Please, Carl. Otherwise I'll just be worrying all night." I tug at his arm like a petulant child.

"Okay, well...this isn't how I wanted to tell you but there's probably no right time or place..." He pauses, still refusing to look at me.

His hesitation makes me nervous and a list of scenarios fills my head. At the top is that he's going to ask for a divorce so he can marry Keira. I need to know now. Whatever it is, I need to hear it so I can deal with it. "Carl, just spit it out!"

"Okay. Well...Keira's pregnant. Three months gone. We're having a baby."

CHAPTER TWENTY-SEVEN

Today Henny and I are out walking. It's not even seven o'clock in the morning so the air is brisk, despite it being summer. We are alone out here in the gardens with only a scattering of birds and a chirpy grey squirrel, weaving its way through the bushes, for company. But I know without looking up at the grim, grey building behind me that there are eyes following us; stony-faced white ghosts wondering why Henny is wasting her time on me.

She grips my bony arm to keep me steady and I lean into her. I cannot do this alone; perhaps because I have not walked more than a few metres for too long now, or maybe because I'm mentally exhausted at the thought of moving forward, moving in any direction. It's safer to be still. It's probably a combination of both these things and because, for the moment at least, Henny is my rock.

I don't know how long we spend shuffling along but the air starts to warm up and I welcome the sun's comforting embrace. Henny's grip loosens. She must believe I can do this on my own while I am quite sure I can't. But I don't want to disappoint her, so, feeling like a child learning to find its feet, I edge away from her slightly and stand up straighter. It's not as bad as I think and Henny knows this because next to me she is smiling and nodding her head.

"Tell me about your girl," she says suddenly, an unexpected explosion that is too close.

"Wh...what?" I know exactly who she means but have to be sure.

Henny turns to me and looks straight at me, fixing me with her stare so I have no chance of cowering away. "Your girl. Ellie."

I conjure up images, bright colourful shapes that merge together to form Ellie's beautiful face. But there is nothing else. No body attached and no background to show me what she is doing. Just a smooth, pale face snatched out of context. I have to speak quickly, say anything at all before the image is replaced by something worse. "She...she loves drawing. She's really good at it..." This is all I can manage, but for now at least I have banished the images away before they can make a full appearance.

Henny stops walking and almost lets go of my arm completely before she composes herself again. "A wonderful gift," she says, her prolonged sigh drifting into the air

"Ellie is special," I say.

Nodding, Henny turns away and we continue our crawl around the garden.

"I'll have to bring her here," I continue. "She can draw the trees or those roses over there." Henny looks sceptical but smiles politely.

"Honestly, she can bring colour to her sketches, even though she only uses a pencil. I don't know how she does it but she can."

Henny tightens her grip on my arm. We have come full circle and now the only direction in front of us leads back to the heavy oak doors that squeak while they open and clang shut like the doors of a prison cell.

I count the days until we can leave. Escaping from London is now more important than ever, because how can I sit by and watch as Keira grows bigger and gives Ellie a brother or sister who has nothing to do with me? I put on an act for Ellie, of course, matching her excitement and speculating on baby names, but my insides are a furnace every time the subject comes up.

You seem uncharacteristically pleased when I tell you the news and I wonder if it's because now the bond between Carl and me has been weakened further. A separation can be reversed but a baby cannot. But I keep all these feelings to myself, letting them eat away at me and fill me with longing for the moment we can board the plane and leave this mess behind. I know Ellie will still need to come back to see Carl but I have no ties at all here now. Nothing to make me nostalgic, no regret niggling away at me.

I'm so consumed with these thoughts, and packing away things we won't need during the next seven weeks, that I am able to push aside the business with Ellie's drawings until Carl sends me an email updating me on his call to the police. Even though I should be grateful he's kept his word to help, I am baffled that he's chosen this means of communication for something so important. How can he be sure I bother checking my email? Keira isn't even showing yet but things are already changing between Carl and me.

In his email, Carl says he has given a statement to the police and they informed him they will keep all the details on record and that we must report anything else immediately. He doesn't have much faith they can do anything but says at least we've done what we can.

I don't mention any of this to you – and you don't know about Carl turning up at the hotel – because you will only say that you were right all along, that we're wasting police time. Instead I feel as if I am waiting for something else to happen. Something that will prove to you I'm not overreacting. I never pay attention when people say be careful what you wish for, but now I know it's true.

I am not alone the morning it happens. It is Saturday and I oversleep even though there is no reason I should be tired. I haven't worked for weeks and have barely exerted myself except to pack and clean the flat. But I awake late to hear you tapping the keys on your laptop, so engrossed in whatever website you're on that you don't notice me watching you.

Only when I reach across to you and slip my arm through yours do you acknowledge me. "I've found us the perfect place," you say. "It's so much nicer than here."

I strain to see the screen but the pictures are too small for me to tell if you're right. I have a feeling that to you, any apartment in Spain will be better than here. If it wasn't for everything that has happened lately I would object to what you've said, argue that your desire to go has skewed your perspective. I would miss this place because it's become home to me in a strange way, even though I still think of it as your flat. But things are different now and I'm as desperate as you to run away.

For some reason, thinking of this forces an image of Chloe into my mind. We still don't know where she is or how she is but your concern doesn't seem to have increased.

"Have you heard anything from Chloe?" I ask. I'd like to think you would have told me by now if you have, but keeping me up to date with things often slips your mind.

"No, but I called my parents. That was a mistake." You continue clicking keys and don't look away from the laptop screen.

"Oh? When? What did they say?" I ask, too eager for information.

"Can't remember. A few days ago. They said she's with them and to leave her alone and then they hung up on me. You see, this is why I don't bother with them."

Unhooking my arm from yours, I sit up straighter, intrigued that you're finally speaking about them. "Why did they do that?"

"Who knows? Anyway, what d'you think of this place?" You turn the laptop screen towards me and click on a photo to enlarge it. It is a bland, neutrally decorated apartment in the middle of the city. Nothing about it jumps out at me and it mirrors an infinite number of flats in London.

"It's okay," I say. "Not very Spanish but not bad."

But you are no longer listening. Instead you're back in your world of flat-hunting.

"Michael, why did they hang up on you?" I persist.

You click the laptop shut and sigh. "It's not important. Come here." As you pull me towards you, I attempt to relax and let you distract me, trying my best to shut everything out and focus on what we're doing.

Afterwards I fall asleep again and only wake up when you burst into the room, holding a large cardboard parcel. You're fully dressed now and study the parcel, flipping it over to check each side.

"Have you ordered something?" you ask. "What is it?"

I sit up and rub my eyes, as confused as you are about what it could be. "I haven't ordered anything. Are you sure it's for me?"

You wave the parcel in front of my face so I can see the label. "Only if your name's Olivia Taylor."

Grabbing the box from you, I give it a shake and hear something slide around inside. It's fairly light but I can't guess what it is.

"Are you going to open it then or just stare at the box all day?"

Intrigued, I rip the masking tape off and pull the flaps apart to find something carefully wrapped in tissue paper. I open it, my confusion growing by the second, and find a smart black knee-length dress. It is identical to one I already own.

"I thought you hated ordering clothes online," you say. "And don't you already have one like this?"

Suddenly I feel hot and throw the duvet off me. Rushing to the wardrobe I hurriedly flick through all my clothes, desperate to see that I'm wrong. But there is no black dress hanging up.

I delve around in the box but there are no papers and no company name or logo on the outside either.

"What's going on?" you say. "Did you order it or not?"

I sink to the bed and examine the dress. There is no doubt in my mind as I find the words to tell you what's going on. That this is my dress. The one I wore to Barbara's funeral. You stare at me in disbelief, at a loss for words. Before either of us can speak, my mobile beeps with a text message and when I check the screen, time freezes around me. *Nice dress. You'll need it again soon. By the way, how is Ellie?*

It is hours before you manage to calm me down and even then I am a mess. You have to call Carl for me and he assures me Ellie is fine and enjoying gardening with Keira. He tells you to take me to the police station immediately to show them the dress and text message. But we cannot go when I'm still not dressed and my legs are jelly, so you call them instead to get their advice. As I expect, they say they still can't do much without a direct threat but we need to go down there to make a statement. Now the urgency is lost and I sink back into the sofa, unable to stop myself shivering.

"It's him, Michael. I know it's him."

You put your arm around me to try and stop me shaking. "It looks that way. Sick fuck."

I need to call Myrah. She's my only link to Jonathan and she needs to know what he's done now. "Her husband is his *friend*. They have to help us." I explain to you.

"Not until you've calmed down a bit," you say, and I have to agree. Myrah already resents my accusations so I need to be level-headed and rational when I speak to her.

On our way back from the police station I call Myrah, expecting her to be distant again when she realises it's me. But this time her greeting is warm and friendly, catching me off guard so I stumble when I speak. I tell her what's happened and wait for the attack.

"Oh, Olivia, I'm sorry this is happening to you. I've had a lot of time to think about it all after your visit and I'm sorry for not being very helpful." She clears her throat and waits for me to speak. I don't want to hold a grudge but it's difficult to gush a "don't worry". "Anyway," Myrah continues, when I don't say anything, "even though Jonathan's a good friend of ours, I did start to wonder about it all. But when I finally decided to confront him he turned up here for dinner with a girlfriend! I couldn't believe it; he'd never mentioned her but it turns out they've been together for a few months. She's lovely. Very attractive. And they did seem really happy together, so you see, I just don't think it's him now. Especially this latest prank."

I ignore her description of the threat and thank her for telling me all this. I'm still not convinced of Jonathan's innocence but it does seem unlikely if he's got a girlfriend.

"Well, that could just be a cover up," you say, when I've repeated what Myrah has told me. But the look on your face shows me you're not convinced of your own words.

302

Later on I sit through dinner, shovelling tasteless food into my mouth. You try your best to draw me out of the fog I'm under, but to no avail. And then it hits me. There is only one solution and I can't believe it's only now I'm thinking of it.

"We need to leave now," I blurt out, causing you to drop your fork in your pile of spaghetti. "I mean in a few days. There's nothing to stop us and it won't be too bad taking Ellie out of school a few weeks early."

"Seven weeks early? And what about my notice? I can't leave before the end of term, it's impossible."

"You could just tell them you have to leave early for personal reasons. What does it matter? You're leaving anyway."

Picking your fork back up, you twist a strand of spaghetti around it but don't lift it to your mouth, choosing instead to keep twirling it. "I suppose I could. But why the rush? I thought I was the one desperate to leave."

I shake my head, frustrated you need it spelt out to you. "I'm not going to sit by while some sick fucker threatens my daughter. I know she's not yours but surely you feel the same way?"

What I've said must strike a chord because you slowly nod. "Of course. You're right. Let me speak to Finn and try and organise some flights."

And with those words you are finally my rock.

CHAPTER TWENTY-EIGHT

Henny has gone and she won't be coming back. I hear them whispering about her, saying her mother is ill and she has flown home to be with her. They add that she let herself get too attached and I presume they're talking about me. But they don't know her; they can't see that she's stronger than all of them and even if she has befriended me it won't do her any harm.

She has left me a letter and it feels foreign in my hand as I examine the fat envelope, turning it over and over before I dare to open it. When I finally rip it open, my heart races as if the words I am about to read will change my life. I know this is silly; I still have the ability to think. To rationalise. Despite what they think. But Henny has come to mean a lot to me so anything she writes is significant. Her writing is large and neat, each letter perfectly shaped, and I spend time admiring it before I read a word.

When I finish the letter, I read it again, then a third time. It's not that I don't understand what she's written; I just want to feel as if she's here, speaking the words to me in her singsong voice. In the letter, Henny tells me I will be okay, that humans are capable of surviving any atrocity if we just allow ourselves to heal. To grieve. In capital letters she tells me I must acknowledge the truth, accept things as they are now. But she makes no promises that this alone will heal me. These words coming from anyone else would enrage me, make me withdraw further into myself instead of pushing my way out, but coming from Henny they have meaning. Because *she knows*.

For the next few days I am swept along by a tornado, too busy to think about anything but getting us all out of here as quickly as possible. You manage to book us flights for the coming Sunday so we have less than a week to get everything sorted. I am determined there will be no reason for us to come back and I work through the night sorting out paperwork. There's not enough time to sell your flat so you agree to rent it out and leave the organising to a lettings management company. I pull Ellie out of school and ignore the disapproving looks from the head teacher when I go in to sign forms.

Things are almost going too well. Your head teacher agrees – although reluctantly – to let you go early and without even being asked, Carl says Ellie can stay with him until we leave. I don't hesitate to take him up on his offer. If there is one place Ellie will be safe it's with her father. The texts have stopped for now but I won't let myself relax until we are all cocooned on that plane.

In the chaos, I don't have time to give any thought to what we're leaving behind, including the people I care about, so when you suggest throwing a leaving party on Saturday, I instantly dismiss it. We already have too much going on so how can we plan something like that at the same time? Especially when we're leaving the next day.

"It won't take much planning," you insist. "We just call people up, get them over on Saturday night and have drinks and a bit of food. What's there to plan?" You make it sound so simple but I'm not fully convinced, even when you offer to make all the calls and buy everything we'll need. I still feel uneasy about partying when my daughter's been threatened. "Don't let him win," you say. "We've got to try and enjoy our last night in London. Who knows when we'll see our friends again?" And you are right. In just a few more hours we will be away from here and Ellie is safe with Carl for now.

By the day of the party, everything is sorted and I finally exhale, determined to try and enjoy the evening. While you're out stocking up on food and drink I walk around the flat, and as I stare at the bare walls and floors, I allow myself to finally believe we are leaving. It no longer feels like home here. You don't like the idea of tenants using your furniture so most of it has been put into storage, leaving the flat stark and lifeless. But at least in the lounge the sofas remain until Stephen can put them into storage for us after we leave. They will also be our beds tonight as the bedroom is stripped of everything but our suitcases. I'm glad Ellie is staying with Carl; she would hate it here now.

When you get back from the supermarket, I'm sitting cross-legged on the floor, listening to the radio churn out eighties music I haven't heard for years. It lifts my spirits so when you've dumped all the shopping bags in the kitchen, you find me grinning and tapping my fingers on my legs.

"Looks like the party's started already," you say, joining me on the floor. "I'm glad to see you smiling."

I nestle into you, burying my head in your armpit. "We will be happy, won't we, Michael? In Spain, I mean. We're not just running away, are we?"

You kiss the top of my head. "Yes, we probably are, but that doesn't mean it won't work out."

Once you say this, I feel a weight has been lifted from my shoulders. That we both finally feel the same way about our life together. Our future. But I still want all the loose ends tied up.

"What about your parents? And Chloe? Aren't you going to see them before we go?"

You shift away from me and stand up. "The thing is, they're all just upset I'm leaving so they won't talk to me at the moment. There's not much I can do about that, is there?" You stare at the carpet before disappearing back to the kitchen.

"Leon! You're here!" I grab his hand and lead him upstairs where the music is so loud it drowns out my words. I don't remember if you've told me you invited Leon but I've never been so pleased to see him.

"What?" he shouts in my ear and I hand him a can of Heineken. He takes a grateful sip and points to my half-empty glass of wine. "Looks like you're way ahead of me there!"

I hold my glass up and study its contents. I don't know how much I've had but I'm sure the party has only just started. "You better hurry up, then," I tell him with a wink. I haven't seen Leon for months now and he looks different. Slimmer perhaps, more groomed. But it's more than that. He looks happier. I lead him through the forest of people in the flat to the kitchen so we can talk without shouting in each other's ears.

"So I'll finally meet the man in your life," he says to me. "I hope it's all going well now?"

"Better than ever." But it is only at this moment that I dare to believe this. Even if we are running away, it's not from anything to do with *us*. And if nothing else, it will bring us closer together once we're away from anything that can threaten our happiness.

Leon takes a long sip of beer and sadness glazes his eyes. "Good, I'm glad to hear that. Just, you know, be strong."

I don't know what he means by this, but I'm not going to ask. I'm in too good a mood to let anything spoil it. Besides, Leon always looks out for me and he never speaks out of spite. I want to tell him everything that's been happening but something stops me. Leon worries about me when there's nothing at all going on so I can't let him stress about my mess. I also don't want to hear him say leaving for Spain in the midst of a crisis is a bad idea. So I keep quiet and tell myself I'm doing the right thing.

"So what's been happening with you?" I ask him, refilling my glass. "And don't leave anything out."

Faces swim before me, reminding me of the last party you had here. But this time it's different. People are here for both of us and I have nothing to fear, so I am fuelled with confidence as I mingle and do my best impression of a hostess. But I am out of my comfort zone with all this small talk and my legs are unsteady as I swerve between people, attempting to be graceful. I remember Chloe at your birthday party; how confident she was, gliding in and out of the crowd, ensuring nobody had an empty glass. I am as far from Chloe as it's possible to be and this thought makes me laugh as I wobble to the kitchen, determined to sober up a bit.

Once I'm there I sit alone with my coffee, alone in a flat full of people. But it's not for long. Before I've even taken a sip the door bursts open and Ellie runs in, followed by Carl and Keira. My eyes automatically drop to Keira's stomach, even though there is no way to tell she's pregnant yet.

"Mum!" Ellie calls, running towards me.

"Ellie wanted to surprise you," Carl explains. "But I've told her we're just here for an hour." I'm so excited to see her I forget she probably shouldn't be at an adult party.

"That's fine," I say, ruffling Ellie's hair.

"Hi, Olivia," Keira says and I plaster on a smile for her before Ellie drags her off to see her old room.

I offer Carl a beer but he declines, opting for water instead. For the first time since I've known him I can't think of anything to say. Everything has changed now and we're different people.

Carl clears his throat and already I know what he's about to say. "Look, I know this isn't the right time but you're leaving tomorrow and...well..."

"It's fine, Carl. It's probably about time we did it. We can't stay married now, with everything that's happening for both of us."

Carl breathes out heavily. "Thanks, Olivia. It will just tie things up for us, I suppose. And I was thinking of asking Keira—"

"That's great," I say, cutting him off before the words leave his mouth. "Look, do you mind if I just have a moment alone?"

When he's gone I stand up and fill a glass with water, gulping it down to distract myself from thinking about what Carl's just asked me. I don't know how long I've been in the kitchen but it must be long enough for people to wonder where I am.

"There you are," you say, making me jump so I almost drop my glass. "I hope that's not water? What are you doing in here?"

I look up at you and suddenly the thing I need most in the world is your comfort. "Will you just hold me?"

You don't ask why but pull a chair up to me and let me cling to you, smoothing my hair to soothe me as if I'm a child. "It's okay," you say. "Everything will be okay." And I believe this. I believe you.

Unexpectedly, Myrah turns up and even you are surprised to see her. "I didn't invite her," you whisper, and I cringe, hoping she hasn't heard you. Her husband is with her and he is not what I've imagined all these years. He's a small man and in her heels Myrah towers over him. I politely shake his hand but won't let myself forget he is Jonathan's friend. Once again I silently thank God we're leaving tomorrow.

"I know we've had our issues lately but I'm sorry you're leaving," Myrah says, as I hand her and David each a glass of wine. "Promise you'll keep in touch?"

"Definitely," I say, imagining a Christmas card friendship that will fizzle out within a couple of years.

David wanders off, confidently introducing himself to strangers, but Myrah doesn't follow him or even seem to notice him go. Instead she gushes about her new job and I am forced to listen, feigning excitement when I just want to let her know how much she has let me down.

Thankfully, Leon soon appears and whisks Myrah away, leaving me to find Ellie and spend some time with her before Carl announces they have to leave. He's probably squirming; after all, this isn't the best environment for a child or a pregnant woman, even if we've insisted people go outside to smoke.

I find Ellie and Keira in Ellie's room, both of them sitting cross-legged on the floor, each of them holding a fan of playing cards. I don't know where they've conjured up a deck of cards from because the room is completely empty.

"Mum!" Ellie squeaks. "Keira's teaching me card games. Come and play with us."

"Maybe later, Pumpkin." I need to find you because the wine is running low and one of us will have to venture out to buy more. It's still quite early so I don't expect many people to leave just yet.

"Okay," Ellie says, not showing any disappointment at all. But I don't mind because from tomorrow we'll have all the time in the world to play cards.

It takes me a while to find my coat and track you down to tell you I'm going to the shop. You hand me a wad of notes and in the background I hear someone telling you to get used to doing that once we're in Spain. I don't worry about this comment; you know I will pay my way.

I spring down the stairs, eager to get this wine expedition out of the way so I can be back here, enjoying the last hours of our goodbye to everyone. When I open our front door, it gives too easily and I shut it and try again before I realise someone has left it on the latch. Quickly pulling the latch down and checking that the door clicks behind me, I don't worry too much until I notice the main door is also unlocked. I think of Jonathan but there's no way he is inside; even though the flat is crammed with people, it would be impossible for him to go unnoticed with me, you and Myrah all there. And Ellie is safely in her room with Keira. But even though I dismiss my uneasiness as paranoia, I still walk briskly to the shop, almost breaking into a sprint on the way back, the wine bottles clanging together in the flimsy plastic bag I've been given.

Relieved to be able to offload the wine bottles, I shut both front doors tightly, checking they're not on the latch. The stairs are shrouded in darkness so I don't immediately see the figure standing at the top of them until I am halfway up. And even then I don't recognise who it is. The impossibly tiny frame should be a giveaway but Chloe is the last person I expect to see and the last person on my mind. Sensing someone behind her, she spins round and falls against the wall.

"Ahhhh....here she is!" Chloe's face cracks into a smile but it fades as quickly as it appears so I know she's not here to wish us well.

"Chloe, I'm glad you came," I say, trying my best to ignore her antipathy. "Would you like a drink?" I don't know why I've asked her when it's clear she's already had enough alcohol.

She stares at me, her eyes sharp daggers forcing me to look away. "A drink? A fucking drink? Is that what you think I want, Olivia?" She stands up straighter and peels herself off the wall, still not taking her eyes off me.

I check the hall and although there are a few bodies hovering around, nobody pays us any attention. "Chloe, I understand why you're upset...Just come in the kitchen with me and we can talk about it."

Chloe cackles. "Talk about it? I'm not supposed to *talk* about anything. I'm just a dirty little secret. But that's better than being a dirty whore, isn't it, Oli-vi-a?" She staggers back and once again the wall catches her fall.

I try to keep calm, even though I'm growing angry with Chloe for finding a way to ruin our last night here. "I think you're overreacting. Spain's not exactly the other side of the world, is it? And you can come and stay with us whenever you want to—"

"I don't give a fuck about Spain," Chloe shrieks. She reaches out her arms and shoves me backwards so now it is my turn to stagger. She continues screaming at me but her words are half-drowned out by the music and I'm too dazed to notice what she's saying.

Reeling from shock, I somehow manage to regain my composure and step out of her reach just as a crowd of bodies, drawn by Chloe's shouts, swarm around us. I assume her abuse will stop now we've got company but this doesn't seem to deter her. Bounding forward, she swipes out at me, her fist thundering into my face and knocking my head sideways. I don't know how she has so much power in her minuscule body but I feel as if I've been hit by a brick. The loud gasps from around us are quickly drowned out by Chloe, screaming like a banshee that she wishes I was dead.

Someone grabs her but she wriggles and squirms in their grasp and soon breaks out of the fragile hold. Too many people speak at once and I can't make out anything until your voice booms out. "What the hell are you doing, Chloe? Pull yourself together, you're making a fool of yourself."

Chloe turns to you, finally breaking the cold stare she's fixed on me since I got back from the shop, and aims her venom in your direction. "Oh, I hardly think *I'm* the fool, Michael," she says, glancing back towards me.

You freeze for a moment and stare back at her, both of you locked in a silent battle of wills. But neither of you speak. Voices rise and fall beside us as speculation and disbelief amalgamate into confusion. Somewhere behind me I hear Myrah but only catch the tail end of her sentence. "...that's her. Isn't it, David?" she says, but I don't have the energy to wonder what she's talking about.

"Come to the kitchen and we'll talk," you say to Chloe, but she shakes her head, her mane of curls flying around her.

"It's far too late for that," she says.

Without warning you grab her arms and drag her towards the kitchen. She kicks out at you and flails her arms but you don't release your grip. Someone stops the music and the voices hush along with it. People who didn't realise what was happening now flock to the hallway like gladiatorial spectators.

"Tell her!" Chloe bellows into the silence. "Tell her or I fucking will!"

You yank her harder and turn to me, sweat and fear coating your face. Turning back to Chloe, you scream at her to shut up, but this only makes her cackle again.

"Come on, Michael," she slurs. "You're not ashamed of love, are you?"

Suddenly your anger is directed at everyone in the hallway. "Get out!" you yell. "Everyone, just get out. Now!" But our guests are all statues, unable or unwilling to comprehend your instructions, until Leon starts to usher everyone out. I too am frozen, watching you and Chloe, half-believing this is a nightmare I'll wake up from.

"What's going on? What's she talking about?" I demand, pulling at your sleeve.

Chloe turns to me, her eyes wide with excitement. "Why don't you answer her, Michael?" she taunts, finally breaking free from your weakening grasp.

You lower your voice, even though most of our guests have gone now. "Just leave us alone, Chloe. Why can't you let me be happy?"

"Because you're not!" she screams.

Myrah brushes past me and pulls me towards her. "Olivia, what's Jonathan's girlfriend doing here?" she asks, nodding towards Chloe and my stomach hits the floor. Before I can answer, David leads her away. "Be careful," she says, turning back to find me staring after her.

When I turn back to you, you have given up trying to lead Chloe to the kitchen and instead are begging her to keep quiet. I don't know what hold she has over you, but fear like I have never known expands inside me, crushing my organs so that every breath I take feels like it will be my last.

Then Carl appears from the bathroom and asks what's going on. I can't explain but urge him to take Ellie home. Thankfully I don't need to say anymore. He rushes to Ellie's room, leading her out by the hand with Keira trailing behind them. All three faces are etched with confusion.

"I need the toilet," Ellie groans.

"When we get home," Carl says, as determined as I am to get Ellie out.

"No, Daddy, I need it now."

I grab Ellie's hand. "I'll take her," I say to Carl. "You and Keira get the car ready."

I watch them rush downstairs but when I turn back, still clutching Ellie's hand, Chloe is blocking my way. I stand in front of Ellie even though I realise by now Ellie has never been Chloe's real target.

"Tell her you don't want her, Michael," she says, even though she is not looking at you. That you don't love her. Tell her it's me!"

Your voice is commanding behind me. "You're wrong, Chloe. Leave Olivia out of this."

Chloe turns to you. "But she's not me, is she?"

"You're wrong. I keep telling you you're wrong. You're nothing to me now!" Your voice booms out and Chloe's face crumples.

"Michael?" My voice, my eyes, every part of me begs you to tell me this is a mistake. That Chloe is trying everything she can, even something as sick as what she is suggesting, to stop you leaving. But instead of denying it you sink to the floor in a heap, a broken man like the time I found you in the cupboard under the stairs. And now everything makes sense: our dysfunctional sex life, you needing to run away, all of it.

Behind me Ellie begins to cry and loses control of her bladder. Nobody but me notices the pool forming between her shoes. And I see it even though Chloe lunges towards me, her hands wrapping around my neck until I feel myself growing fainter. I don't know where you are at that moment and although I can't see her, I feel Ellie kicking at Chloe, gasping as her tiny feet batter into Chloe's legs. And even though I must be turning blue, I hear Ellie's tiny voice begging Chloe to get off me.

And then suddenly I can breathe again, hard choking breaths as I desperately gasp for air. Finally Chloe has let go. I don't know how long it takes for me to realise why. At first I assume you have finally stopped her attack but then I hear the violent smack as she swipes Ellie away from her. The thump, thump, thump as Ellie crashes down the stairs. The sickening crack as her head crashes against the door. I fly down the stairs but I am powerless to stop the sea of blood fanning out from under my silent, still daughter.

Too late, you are by my side, pulling me away, shouting at Chloe and yelling into your phone that there's been a terrible accident. At the top of the stairs, Chloe cries hysterically and I wonder how you will cope with this. How you will be able to stand by and see the woman you love in so much pain.

CHAPTER TWENTY-NINE

My hatred of you and Chloe doesn't stem from what you did, what you had together; it exists because you drew me into your world. Me, Ellie and Carl. Even Andrew. If only he could have expressed to me the thoughts haunting his mind.

Did anyone else know? Or even suspect? It would explain your parents' cold and unemotional behaviour and the distance you kept from them. What about Finn and Stephen? Is it possible you could all be such close friends with neither of them guessing? Perhaps we are all complicit and I am the worst offender because how could I not have known when I shared my life with you?

I have no sympathy for him but Jonathan must also be scarred by this. After all, he was just a pawn in a game of chess, manipulated and stripped of his humanity by Chloe. He didn't stand a chance once she'd answered his call on my mobile, and a seed was planted in her mind, just as I didn't stand a chance after meeting you in our hallway that autumn.

I know Henny would tell me I have to rebuild something resembling a life, something that will eventually blossom into a new one. But it is hard enough thinking of the next hour, let alone a future without my daughter.

A thin beam of sunlight shines across my face but I don't get up to reposition the blinds. It is progress, the nurses and doctors will say. A step in the right direction. So I let the sun bathe my skin and imagine Henny is here with me, humming a song, waiting patiently for me to take a small step.

My door creaks open and Carl stands in the corridor, anxiously looking in, probably not knowing what to expect. "Are you ready?" he asks, and I haul myself up in the bed and smooth out the sheets. I nod slowly and he frowns. He doesn't want to make a mistake, do something that can't be taken back. Too much of that has already happened and he wants me to get better, not worse. I nod again, to reassure him. To reassure myself.

"Okay," he says, and disappears outside again. When he returns he is holding her. A tiny pink bundle nestled into the crook of his arm. If it's possible to feel both love and pain at the same time then I feel it now. It is gut-wrenching and suffocating but I cradle Carl and Keira's baby, a beautiful doll smiling up at me. And as I take this momentous step, I begin to believe that maybe there are second, even third, chances to live again.

Message from Kathryn Croft

Thank you for choosing to read *Behind Closed Doors*. I really hope you enjoyed it and, if you did, I'd be grateful if you could leave a review on Amazon. I'd LOVE to hear what you thought, and it will help other readers discover me.

It would also mean a lot to me if you could tweet your thoughts or click 'like' on my Facebook page too. If you'd like to keep up-to-date with all my latest releases, just sign up at my website:

www.kathryncroft.com

Thank you!

Kathryn x